ADMIRAL'S OATH

BOOK ONE OF THE DAKOTAN CONFEDERACY

A **CASTLE FEDERATION** UNIVERSE NOVEL

ADMIRAL'S OATH

BOOK ONE OF THE DAKOTAN CONFEDERACY
A **CASTLE FEDERATION** UNIVERSE NOVEL

GLYNN STEWART

FAOLAN'S PEN
PUBLISHING
faolanspen.com

This edition published in 2022 by:

Faolan's Pen Publishing Inc.

22 King St. S, Suite 300

Waterloo, Ontario

N2J 1N8 Canada

ISBN-13: 978-1-989674-13-0 (print)

A record of this book is available from Library and Archives Canada.

Printed in the United States of America

1 2 3 4 5 6 7 8 9 10

First edition

First printing: January 2022

Illustration © 2022 Viko Menezes

Faolan's Pen Publishing logo is a trademark of Faolan's Pen Publishing Inc.

Read more books from Glynn Stewart at faolanspen.com

1

THE UNIVERSE COULD CHANGE in a thousand ways. A proud old indigenous nation could divide itself across the stars, guarding new worlds and old alike against the failures of mankind. A child of that nation could rise to some of the highest ranks of the military that guarded that nation and a thousand others.

But grandmothers didn't change, and Rear Admiral James Tecumseh of the Terran Commonwealth Navy grinned at his incorrigible ancestor as she waved a hand at him.

"Always the excuses with you, James," she told him. Nizhoni Tecumseh was an old woman, even by the standards of the twenty-eighth century. Her hair was thinning and pure white now, but her century and a half of life hadn't slowed down her mind or will.

"There are a thousand reasons I'd accept for this, you know," she said. "But you are in Dakota, child. There are as many Shawnee on

Dakota as there are here on Earth! And children of a thousand other Old Nations like ours.

"You could find a nice girl of our people, or a similar one as your father did."

James laughed and gestured around him. The dark-skinned Shawnee officer was currently sitting cross-legged in the meditation chamber attached to his office. Unlike his grandmother, his hair was still pitch-black, drawn back into a short braid that ended in the middle of his neck.

He was also in full uniform with black suit, tie, red sash—and the stars and sleeve stripes of his Admiral's rank. That uniform and insignia marked him as the senior officer aboard the carrier *Saratoga* and the commander of her two-ship battle group.

The uniform also helped cover the scarring where three of his limbs had been amputated and replaced with prosthetics. His *current* limbs were the best cybernetics available, but the original emergency procedure had left some permanent reminders.

"I am responsible for twelve thousand lives," he reminded his grandmother gently. "And under something of a cloud with my superiors still. I have no *time* for personal attachments, Grandmama. I love you, but you'll have to wait for great-grandchildren."

She sighed and waved a hand again.

"Like your father before you, so focused on the here and now," she said. A moment of deep sorrow crossed her face. "Of course, the future can sometimes disappear on us unexpectedly, can't it?"

James bowed his head in silence. His parents had died a long time before.

"There will be time," he promised her—and as if to prove his words a lie as he said them, an emergency alert suddenly pinged the neural implant that linked James Tecumseh to the massive starship around him.

"Strategic Omega alert," his chief of staff snapped over a silent communicator in his head. "Multiple core systems are under attack, including Sol and Tau Ceti!"

Those were two of the key star systems of the Terran Commonwealth, the interstellar nation James Tecumseh served—and one of them was both the home world of humanity *and* the system his grand-mother lived in.

"I have to go," he interrupted Nizhoni Tecumseh before she could say anything. "Duty calls. I..." He paused. He *shouldn't* tell her anything, but if an enemy force was in Sol, he couldn't *not*, either.

"Grandmama, I need you to get somewhere safe," he told her. "I can't say more, but you need to get to safety *now*."

Nizhoni had served in the Terran High Guard once, a long time before. She *knew* that tone, and her hologram straightened to look James directly in the eyes.

Every motion each of them made was being transmitted across almost a hundred light-years by use of quantum-entangled particles, making their conversation as clear as if they were in the same room, and she studied him carefully.

"Our family is named for a great hero," she told him calmly. "Walk your path, James Tecumseh. You will prove yourself worthy of your name, I promise.

"Go!"

———

TECUMSEH'S MEDITATION chamber was one of two attachments to his main office, but his office itself was connected to the main flag bridge by a single secured door. It was a matter of seconds for him to traverse from the space he used for resting and personal communications to his main battle station.

His flagship, the *Lexington*-class carrier *Saratoga* was the better part of a kilometer long, an elongated egg flattened at the front and back to open the carrier deck to space. Her scale was set by the Alcubierre-Stetson drive system that would propel her faster than light, and it left plenty of space for an Admiral's flag bridge.

That space was a thirty-meter horseshoe shape, with a large holo-graphic display extending out from the flat end, concealing the access to the Admiral's office. Rows of consoles and work stations filled the room, holding the support crew for Tecumseh's staff and the Admiral himself.

Saratoga was designed to act as a fleet flagship, but she was also twelve years old and five years out of date. Tecumseh commanded Task Group Dakota-One, a carrier group consisting of *Saratoga* and the battlecruiser *Booth*.

The battleship *Adamant*, clearly visible twenty thousand kilometers "above" *Saratoga* relative to Dakota, held Vice Admiral Gabriel Banks, the commanding officer of Sector Fleet Dakota and James Tecumseh's boss.

"Report," James ordered as he glanced past the status reports on *Booth* and *Adamant* to check on the strategic alert.

"Alliance forces have launched deep-penetration strikes across the Commonwealth," his chief of staff, Captain Arjun Ferreiro—addressed as "Commodore" aboard *Saratoga* to avoid confusion with the ship's commanding officer—told him.

The darkly tanned Mediterranean officer focused the main hologram on the strategic display, an astrographic map showing the extent of the Terran Commonwealth, the largest human nation ever known.

A hundred and five star systems with inhabited planets and over three hundred claimed systems without planets, the Commonwealth was a large green sphere in the heart of the display. Toward the galactic rim were the Rimward Marches—also known as the Alliance of Free Stars, a loose collection of almost seventy star systems that was defying an attempt to militarily annex them into the Commonwealth.

And, it seemed, doing so with style.

"Locations?" Tecumseh asked, watching as red icons began to sparkle across the green marking the Commonwealth's systems.

"Sol. Tau Ceti. Bastion. Beowulf. Sigma Draconis. Keid. Astral. Meridian. Muscovy." Ferreiro sighed, gesturing at the map. "Fifteen star systems, sir. I'm not sure what the connect—"

"It's the switchboard stations," Admiral Banks's voice interrupted, a hologram of the Sector Fleet commander appearing on the corner of the big display, the platinum-blond man looking more afraid than Tecumseh had ever seen them.

"Leviticus is also under attack," Banks told them. "My aide is trying to make contact with my wife aboard the switchboard station, but communications are clogged."

Leviticus was twenty-four light-years from Dakota. Not part of the Dakota Sector, the six-system administrative and military district that Sector Fleet Dakota—and both James Tecumseh and Gabriel Banks— was tasked to defend, but still their closest quantum entanglement switchboard—or q-com—station.

"Three of the switchboard stations have already gone down," Banks continued. "Tecumseh, I need you to make contact with the deployed units of Sector Fleet Dakota. This is a recall order. All ships are to return to Dakota *immediately*."

"Surely, this won't *work*," James asked.

"We have to assume it will," Banks replied grimly. "This is a Hail Mary, Rear Admiral. The Alliance has thrown everything they have at knocking out our communication network."

"What happens if they *succeed*?" Ferreiro asked.

"There are supposed to be fallbacks," Commander Rylie Prebensen said softly. Tecumseh's communications officer was a petite raven-haired woman from Tau Ceti, and like Admiral Banks, she looked scared.

"But we'd lose q-com communications with our fighters, our probes and the rest of the Commonwealth," Tecumseh said softly. "Correct?"

"The fallbacks are likely only enough for basic communication between systems and starships," Prebensen confirmed. "And...I doubt they came this far without at least *thinking* they knew about all of our backups."

James nodded grimly and met Banks's gaze.

"We'd lose our q-probes and our communications with our fighters at the minimum," he noted to the senior Admiral. "While in two simultaneous wars."

Here in Dakota, it didn't normally *feel* like the Commonwealth was at war. The Stellar League was a perpetually dysfunctional but large nation to clockward—clockwise around the galactic disk—of the Commonwealth, currently more unified than usual under a dictator determined to make Terra pay for what Tecumseh would freely admit were several centuries of economic exploitation.

"I'm trying to get in touch with my wife," Banks said quietly. "Can you recall the ships, Tecumseh?"

"Yes, sir," James confirmed with a crisp salute. "Nothing else we can do, I'm afraid."

Even Leviticus was almost ten days away. The faster than light Alcubierre-Stetson drive had to decelerate as much as it accelerated, which made longer-distance trips more efficient.

The good news was that meant the Alliance task forces couldn't reinforce each other. The *bad* news was that the first Alliance ships had entered Sol barely forty minutes earlier…and seven of the seventeen q-com switchboards had already gone dark.

So far, *Saratoga* had enough spare q-com blocks to keep her communications up, but James had mirrored Prebensen's primary console to his implants. No one else could see the virtual screen hanging in the air in front of him, but it gave him the metric he was worried about.

Combining *Saratoga* and *Booth*'s communications together, Dakota-One had lost thirty-five percent of their bandwidth already. And as he watched, the Beowulf station went dark…and his task force lost another six percent of their FTL communications ability.

———

THE MOST FORTIFIED q-com switchboard station in the Commonwealth was probably the Central Nexus, the first-and-largest station suspended in Earth orbit. At oh eight hundred and fifty-four hours on October tenth, the Alliance fighter strike landed…and James Tecumseh's bandwidth projection fell to zero.

"My god," he whispered. "Prebensen, can you confirm for me?"

"We have lost all q-com connections," she said. "Approximately sixty percent of our entangled-particle blocks are simply…no longer entangled. Their counterparts have been so badly disrupted that the entanglement effect has been lost.

"The remainder are simply spitting garbage data. They are loose particles that happen to be entangled with particles in our systems. There is likely no way to usefully retrieve the other side of those pairs, even if we were present in the systems with them."

"Which we are not," Tecumseh concluded. "Can you confirm which of our subordinates received my message?"

"*Mediterranean* in the Gothic System confirmed receipt," Prebensen told him. "Captain Werner did not confirm compliance, but if he received the message, I assume he'll be on his way.

"I believe that *Valiant*, in the Desdemona System, received the message, but we did not receive automatic or manual confirmation," she continued. "I...am not certain at all about whether *Arctic* received the message."

James nodded grimly, zooming in the main display with a thought. There was no point in considering the wider Commonwealth at the moment. Their entire universe had just shrunk to their area of responsibility.

The Dakota Sector was eleven star systems with six inhabited worlds—but it was also purely a civil and military administrative structure. There was no sector government. No one between the planetary governments—like the Dakota Confederacy itself—and the Star Chamber on Earth.

With no communications between the Sector and Sol, though...

He shook his head.

Arctic was in the Shogun System, the farthest clockward of the Sector's systems. That still put the strike cruiser thirty-odd light-years from the front of the war with the League, but it also made her the most vulnerable ship in Sector Fleet Dakota.

Fortunately, the totality of the nightmare didn't fall on James. After his last independent command had nearly ended in a court-martial, he'd managed to escape with his career intact—and somehow picked up a Rear Admiral's star along the way—but Central Command had decided to have someone else keep an eye on him.

This was Gabriel Banks's problem, and James reopened the link to *Adamant*'s flag deck.

"Admiral Banks, what are your orders?" he asked.

Only silence answered him, and an icy chill broke through his determined calm. Everyone around him was walking the line of panic. James *had* to be calm and collected, projecting a cool readiness as the galaxy collapsed around him.

But *he* needed his superior officer to give *him* orders...and he wasn't getting an active communication link.

"Commander Prebensen," he addressed his com officer. "Can you double-check the radio links to *Adamant*?"

"I've been coordinating with Commodore Mac Cléirich for the last five minutes," Prebensen confirmed. "We have an integrated three-way radio network between the Navy units and are working to incorporate Dakota Fortress Command."

That was good—that was the minimum James would have expected, but he was pleased that both Prebensen and Captain Sumiko Mac Cléirich, Banks's communication officer, had started on it without any prompting.

On the other hand, it also meant that his channel to Banks was working fine and the Admiral wasn't responding. That was...bad.

"Get me a link to Commodore Voclain," James ordered. Madona Voclain was Banks's chief of staff, his equivalent to Ferreiro and the third-ranked officer of the entire Sector Fleet Dakota.

It took a few seconds, longer than it should have, before the hawk-nosed blonde woman appeared on the screen, looking utterly shattered. Her uniform jacket was askew, her formal sash appeared to have been torn and she had the beginnings of a black eye.

"Admiral, apologies," she greeted him instantly. "We have a situation."

"Report," he ordered. "I was trying to reach Admiral Banks."

"That would be our situation, sir," Voclain admitted. "We managed to connect with Leviticus Communication Prime and get Madame Banks on the call...for about forty seconds before the station was blown to hell."

James swallowed hard, focusing on his calm. Whatever had happened, his people needed him now.

"And the Admiral?" he asked.

"Went into shock, sir," Voclain told him. "Dr. Piccoli is on his way, but he ordered me to disarm the Admiral before the medical teams arrived."

"He resisted." James said quietly. It wasn't a question.

"Violently, sir. He was not attempting to use his sidearm on *me*, though." She touched the bruise forming around her eye.

"He was attempting to use it on himself," the Rear Admiral guessed.

"Yes, sir. We have restrained Vice Admiral Banks. I was about to reach out to you... Dr. Piccoli will have no choice but to relieve Admiral Banks on medical grounds.

"That puts you in command of Sector Fleet Dakota, Rear Admiral Tecumseh."

2

Colonel Anthony Yamamoto stood straight-backed in the corner of the Captain's breakout room on the supercarrier *Krakatoa*. The rest of the carrier's senior staff was seated around the table, but Anthony had made a habit out of standing in meetings a long time before.

It helped keep him sharp—and it had long since ceased to be a *conscious* power play on the fighter pilot's part.

Right now, though, focusing on his posture was helping the tall and slim Japanese-looking officer remain collected in the face of the briefing Captain Young Volkov had just given her crew. Anthony's posture, like his completely clean-shaven jaw, was an intentional call-back to the ancestor every military officer thought of when they heard his name.

With his tanned skin, short-cropped black hair, and wide-set flat features, Anthony could pass for Admiral Isoroku Yamamoto, the architect of the twentieth century's Battle of Midway. Of course, his purple-lapelled black uniform and purple sash declared him an officer of the Terran Commonwealth Starfighter Corps.

"We have no communications?" he asked, his strong Scottish accent putting the lie to his appearance. While Anthony *spoke* Japanese, he'd grown up in Edinburgh, and it was that culture that had formed his voice and attitudes.

"Not faster than light," Young Volkov agreed, the Korean-Russian Alpha Centauri–born officer eyeing her Commander, Air Group, carefully. "Just this once, Anthony, can you sit the hell down?"

Everyone else in the room was silent as two of the carrier's three most senior officers stared at each other. While Volkov would use the title of *Captain* aboard the carrier, her actual *rank* was Commodore—which made her senior to Anthony.

Wordlessly, he stepped over to the table, turned a chair around and sat on it the wrong way.

"Do we have any confirmation on how this was allowed to happen?" he demanded once he was seated.

"Intelligence appears to have been completely blindsided," Volkov told him, turning her gaze to survey the rest of her senior officers. "That said, we need to get ahead of the rumor mill and do so *quickly*.

"Right now, every officer and spacer who saw what happened is still on duty, but I guarantee you that the stories are already beginning to spread. I look to each of you to brief your departments and get ahead of any doom-mongering."

"What doom-mongering? The Commonwealth is *fucked*."

"Never," Anthony snapped at *Krakatoa*'s executive officer. London-born Commander Patricia Jack was practically a neighbor to the CAG, but he generally found the woman *far* too pessimistic.

She might be English, but she'd apparently never heard of the British stiff upper lip.

"Our communications may be temporarily down, but we are the *Terran Commonwealth*," he said fiercely. "The oldest and greatest of human interstellar nations. We will no be stopped by an inconvenience like this. The Alliance will learn that."

"And that's the attitude we need to bring to our people," Volkov agreed. "We, as *Krakatoa*'s senior officers, must have full confidence that our Commonwealth will overcome this. And we must communicate that confidence to our subordinates."

"What about our mission?" Jack asked.

"We can't divert from Dakota at this point, anyway," Volkov replied. "We will arrive on schedule in forty-seven hours. What happens after that will be up to Admiral Banks."

The Captain shrugged and gave them a dark smile.

"I know the *plan* was for Sector Fleet Dakota to send two of their older ships Rimward, with us as their replacement, but I suspect that may change now. Nonetheless, *our* duty and direction do not change.

"We proceed to Dakota to join the Sector Fleet. For now, the primary focus of the officers in this room must be to maintain the morale of our crew."

Anthony's gaze was focused on Patricia Jack, and he suspected Volkov was watching the XO closely as well.

"Our own morale must be watched as well," he warned. "Our people aren't stupid, my friends. They will realize if we're feeding them a line of bullshit. Mean what you say. Say what you mean.

"Understand that we must have faith in the nation and the service we are sworn to. Only then can we communicate that faith to our spacers and hold together the morale of this crew."

Volkov chuckled.

"Colonel Yamamoto has it in one, people," she told them. "We will endure. The Commonwealth always has. I don't know how and I don't know what it will take.

"But I *do* know that *Krakatoa* and her crew *will* do their duty. Am I understood?"

———

THERE WERE dozens of exotic-matter-based mass manipulators woven through the decks of *Krakatoa*, providing her crew with full comfortable gravity throughout the entirety of the ship. Even the massive main flight deck, home to two hundred starfighters, had full gravity.

Unlike other sections of the ship, the flight deck's gravity could be readily adjusted downward to make handling the multi-thousand-ton parasite warships easier. The Katana fighters and Longbow bombers that made up Anthony Yamamoto's command were twenty and forty meters long, respectively, and the "lighter" starfighters still massed fifty-five hundred tons.

Starfighter was, after all, a relative term. They didn't require the massive Class One mass manipulators that fueled a starship's Alcubierre-Stetson drive—and made up half the cost of even a warship—but they were still complex and powerful spacecraft.

They were just more expendable than their motherships, a harsh reality Anthony Yamamoto had made his peace with long before. He burned the candles for his dead every Sunday, remembering the names of the over five hundred pilots, gunners and engineers who'd died under his command, and then he did his job.

Today that job brought him onto his flight deck, following his suspicion to find his people. Fighter crews were a specific breed in his experience, and worrisome rumors had one main result.

"CAG, what's the word?" his deck chief asked.

Senior Chief Petty Officer Thales Brahms was an olive-skinned man from the Krete System. He was also Anthony's senior noncommissioned officer...and definitely *not* on the duty schedule right now.

Anthony didn't even need to check his neural implant to know that. Like any starfighter pilot, he was in the top percentile for his ability to interface with the ubiquitous neural cybernetics, which made it hard to tell where organic memory ended and silicon memory began —but he knew the roster for every senior officer and NCO under his command.

"How many of our people are on the deck?" Anthony asked calmly.

"I'd say seventy percent of the officers and sixty percent of the enlisted," Brahms confirmed instantly. "Maybe ten percent of both are asleep—or pretending to be—and the rest are in the mess or the pilots' lounge."

"Pilots' lounge" was a misnomer, since it was open to all three roles in the starfighter and bomber crews, but the Terran Commonwealth

Starfighter Corps had pulled a *lot* of old traditions out of mothballs when it had been created.

"Ping 'em," Anthony ordered. "And get me a soapbox."

"Will an ammo crate do?" the Senior Chief replied.

"So long as it doesn't blow up while I'm standing on it."

ANTHONY WAITED until his implants confirmed his crews and support staff were all in the deck before mounting the crate. Between the crews of his two hundred fighters and bombers and the support staff necessary to keep those two hundred parasite warships in space, just over sixteen hundred members of *Krakatoa*'s six-thousand-strong crew reported to him.

Since the deck *was* their duty station, everyone who wasn't asleep was present—and from the numbers, very few of the Starfighter Corps personnel aboard *Krakatoa* were asleep.

The box Brahms had sourced contained replacement parts, not ammunition. The only *ammunition* on the flight deck were the Javelin missiles carried by both of his spacecraft and the massive Tsunami torpedoes that rivaled *Krakatoa*'s own heavy missiles for range and power.

"All right, everyone pay attention," Anthony barked, intentionally sharpening his brogue for a moment. It served the purpose, creating a rippling field of silence through the massive crowd.

Thanks to a combination of his implants and theirs, he could be certain every one of those fifteen hundred–plus souls could hear him, and he smiled grimly.

"Rumor is doing what rumor does," he continued once he had all of their eyes and ears. "I'm not going to grace *rumor* with challenge or explanation, but you all need to know what's going on."

Whatever noise had remained vanished now, and he could hear the slightest shuffle of his people's feet.

"At oh eight hundred hours ESMDT this morning, task forces of the Alliance of Free Stars hit fifteen solar systems of our Commonwealth in overwhelming force." He waited for that to sink in. "As of the last reports we had, they had either destroyed or successfully bypassed all defenses and starships in those systems.

"We *know*, with absolute certainty, that they engaged and destroyed their targets," Anthony said flatly. "That is because their targets, officers and spacers, were the q-com relay switchboards that linked together our Commonwealth.

"By oh nine hundred hours this morning, our entire quantum-entanglement network was gone. Here aboard *Krakatoa*, we now have no communication with the outside world. We have no choice but to complete our journey as scheduled and acquire what updates we can in the Dakota System.

"While I and the rest of *Krakatoa*'s command crew have the utmost faith in our Commonwealth's ability to recover from this defeat, the resilience of ships like *Krakatoa* and Commonwealth military personnel like yourselves will be critical to that recovery."

Anthony surveyed his people.

"We must make certain that every aspect of this fighter group is prepared to do whatever we are called upon to do. We serve the Commonwealth. I, for one, do not intend to fail her."

Inevitably, the crowd dissolved into an incoherent array of questions thrown at Anthony from every corner for several minutes. He waited out the chaos, allowing the assorted noncoms and more senior officers to calm their subordinates.

"Senior Chief Brahms, the most pertinent questions, please," he said crisply.

"Most of them want to know when they can contact their families again, sir," Brahms told him.

Anthony nodded firmly and looked at his people.

"We don't know," he admitted. "It will take some time for our Commonwealth to build new networks of communication, either by rebuilt switchboards or starship couriers. I can't give you a time frame on when we will have communications again.

"I can assure you that everyone else in the Commonwealth is in the same boat. Your partners, children, parents... They'll all know why you can't contact them. I won't pretend this is going to be easy. But the difficult is what we do, isn't it?"

He turned his attention back to Brahms, trusting the deck chief to have pulled together a useful aggregate of the questions thrown at the CAG.

"Next question."

3

Dakota System
11:00 October 10, 2737 ESMDT

THE HOLOGRAPHIC CONFERENCE FELT CROWDED. With no time to resolve James's sudden promotion to command of the Sector Fleet and the presence of two flag staffs, he'd simply looped *both* full staffs into the conference, and then added all three ship Captains into the system and Colonel Avedis Maeda, *Saratoga*'s CAG.

That meant there were fifteen people on the call including James himself. The conferencing software made the breakout meeting room attached to James's office holographically "grow" to contain them, but the back of his mind knew the room was barely big enough for the eight people physically present.

"We are in a state of catastrophe," James told his people, focusing on keeping his tone calm. "Without communication with the greater Commonwealth, we are thrown back on our own resources.

"Our *responsibilities*, on the other hand, have not changed," he continued. A map of the star systems of the Dakota Sector appeared in the middle of the virtually extended table. "We are responsible for the security and peace of the Dakota Sector.

"Dakota, Shogun, Gothic, Desdemona, Krete and Arroyo," James listed. "Six inhabited planets. Another five systems with registered outposts and mining operations. Eleven star systems with a total of sixteen *billion* human beings."

He let the weight of those numbers sink in.

"We have six starships," he told them quietly. "Except...in practice, we have *three*. We have no communications with *Valiant*, *Mediterranean* or *Arctic*. Fortunately, all data I have also shows that *Krakatoa* is on schedule and should arrive within the next few days."

"So, seven ships...or four," Voclain said flatly. She hadn't even taken the time to change into a new uniform after her struggle with Admiral Banks. "What do we do, sir?"

James Tecumseh had *very much* wanted to offload the key parts of that decision to Admiral Gabriel Banks, but that hadn't been the fate in store for him. There was no one to give him answers, no one to take charge.

"What we have to," he told them all. "This room contains over four *centuries* of accumulated military and strategic experience. We command more starships and starfighters than many star nations with six worlds. More than all of that, we represent the Terran Commonwealth. We represent her progress, her power, her resolve—and her virtues."

He waved a hand in the air.

"Democracy. Freedom. Justice. Unity. These are not merely words, my friends. They are our guiding pillars, and the worlds we are responsible for *know* that." He sighed. "We must be frank and admit that there are worlds that are less certain of the Commonwealth's allegiance to those pillars and that there are *reasons* for their uncertainty."

The Commonwealth's military and civilian leadership *knew*, with the certainty of fanatics, that all of humanity would be better off unified under one government linked together by the q-com networks. That certain knowledge had led to expansion at any cost, by any means.

The war with the Alliance of Free Stars had been part of that expansion, a part that might still cost the Commonwealth *everything*.

"None of the worlds in our area of responsibility feel that way, to my knowledge," James concluded, but his attention fell on two individuals.

Commander Thandeka Dubhain was a pitch-black woman from Alpha Centauri. Commodore Ove Bevan was a blond Welshman from Earth. They were James's and Banks's intelligence officers, respectively. Eventually, Bevan would likely end up in charge...but right now, James *trusted* Dubhain more.

"There is a reason *Valiant* was in Desdemona," Bevan said quietly. "They were considered our most likely problem child. There's a large anarchist political movement on Desdemona that has never quite tipped over into active resistance to Commonwealth membership.

"Given the current circumstances, we will need to keep a more careful eye on them."

"I will not engage in suppression operations against our people, Commodore," James said, his tone icier than it had been so far. "We have all seen the footage that the Alliance was distributing from their incursion into the Presley System.

"That *any* Commonwealth military personnel engaged in actions such as Admiral Roberts encountered there sickens me. We will not add to that tally of mistakes."

An Alliance fleet under their Vice Admiral Roberts had raided the Presley System to reduce logistics support for the fleet engaging them. They'd stayed, according to their reports at least, to help the locals throw out a Commonwealth Pacification Corps that had brutally suppressed local attempts at independence.

"That's propaganda, nothing more," Commodore Bevan replied.

"I've met Admiral Kyle Roberts," James said softly. He wouldn't draw much attention to that point—it was related to why he had been under a cloud with TCN command and very carefully assigned to serve under someone else, even as they gave him his first star.

"I trust the Admiral more than I trust many people in this conference," he continued. "So, if Kyle Roberts tells me that the footage from the Presley System is unedited, you'd better have some damn hard proof to say it's propaganda."

The conference was silent for a long pause.

"Do you have that proof, Commodore?" James finally asked.

Only silence answered him, and the Shawnee man snorted.

"It's irrelevant to the moment anyway, I suppose," he admitted. "We need to reopen communications across the Sector. Mac Cléirich, Prebensen."

The two communications officers met his gaze in turn.

"Prebensen, I want you to start hailing every Alcubierre-Stetson-capable ship in the Dakota System," James ordered. "All of them are on a hard stop, *now*. Nobody leaves until I authorize it.

"Any of them give you grief, tell them that it shouldn't be for more than forty-eight hours. If that isn't enough for any of them, you are authorized to send Marines in to secure the ships. We have *no* allowance for problems right now; am I clear?"

"Yes, sir," Prebensen said grimly, her eyes dark. "That shouldn't be necessary."

"Good. Thank you." He turned to Mac Cléirich. "Commodore Mac Cléirich, I need you to get in touch with the First Chief and the rest of the Confederacy government. I need to know that Dakota has our back and is prepared to support the Sector Fleet out of their own resources."

While Dakota itself was almost pristine, an entire planet settled and cared for by the principles of the Old Nations, the *star system* was heavily industrialized, with massive deep-space foundries and asteroid smelters sufficient to *rebuild* the Sector Fleet, let alone maintain her.

"We're also going to immediately activate Commonwealth Security Protocol Twenty-Six," James continued. "I'm taking direct command of all guardships and fortifications in the sector. For now, that's only going to be relevant here in Dakota, but it'll give us some flex to work with.

"So, I'll need you to coordinate with Dakota Security Command, Mac Cléirich." He grinned. "Whichever one of you two finishes your list first can start talking to the sector administration team."

There was no government that functioned at the sector level, but the Commonwealth's administration was divided up much like its military. Most federal-level bureaus and agencies would have a sector headquarters there on Dakota.

Those personnel and their knowledge and resources would be critical in the next few weeks.

"I'm aware there is no individual that all of those admin personnel report up to," he continued. "We'll need to get that sorted. Most likely, we'll temporarily run the Sector admin through the Dakota government. Their structure gives them the flex to help handle the rest of the systems."

Dakota, after all, had been colonized by a partnership of over *eleven hundred* aboriginal nations from across Earth and even now was run as a confederacy of nations rather than one unified government.

"For that reason, the highest immediate priority for *me* is to sit down with First Chief Chapulin," he noted. Quetzalli Chapulin was the current elected chair of the Confederacy's Assembly of Nations. "If we were *only* looking at the loss of communications, I'd expect to continue receiving our usual supports.

"Except that we also know that fifteen key star systems just had their defense forces reduced to rubble by our enemies," James continued. "We won't know the full consequences of that for weeks or months, but I imagine that a lot of resources, ships and supplies are going to be poured into those systems.

"For now, we will plan on needing to support Sector Fleet Dakota entirely out of this system's resources. To do that, we will need the full and *enthusiastic* buy-in of the planetary government."

He shook his head.

"It is going to be absolutely critical, everyone, that the worlds of the Dakota Sector understand that we are their friends and guardians. That perspective will save effort and time—and, in the end, lives. Both ours and those of the people we are sworn to protect.

"We speak for the Commonwealth, but these worlds *are* the Commonwealth," he reminded them all. "Remember that."

4

Dakota System
21:00 October 10, 2737 ESMDT

THERE WERE a thousand balls in the air, and James Tecumseh knew that none of them were settled yet. Barely twelve hours had passed since things had changed forever, and only the most basic of groundwork had been laid.

The biggest problem was the most fundamental: communication. Even *inside* the Dakota System, the speed of their communications had just been slashed. That morning, James had been able to communicate with the fortresses and fighter squadrons at Virginia, Dakota's single immense gas giant, instantaneously. Now a back-and-forth message would take eighteen hours.

From the lists his suddenly expanded staff had put together, they were probably going to miss at least one Alcubierre-Stetson-drive helium tanker leaving the system. Her captain might decide to wait and see what was going on—James likely would have in their place—

but they were scheduled to have been on their way at eighteen hundred hours.

His order to hold the freighter would only have arrived at twenty hundred hours, and he wasn't going to hear *back* until oh five hundred.

That was his new reality. James had no idea how long it would take to get enough entangled particles manufactured to rebuild even one switchboard station…but he doubted it was going to be *quick*.

"Sir, the First Chief is available now," Prebensen told him. "I suspect she has been as busy as you, but she's only three minutes late."

James chuckled.

"Connect us, Commander. What's the time lag?"

That was a question he'd rarely needed to ask in the past. But even from high orbit, the time gap would be noticeable now. *Saratoga* was orbiting just inside the radius of Missouri, Dakota's moon. That gave the carrier some shielding from unfriendly eyes but also kept her two hundred thousand kilometers from the planet she was guarding.

"Just over one point three seconds' round trip, sir."

"Thank you, Commander."

His office faded away as he linked into a virtual conference, straightening his shoulders and tugging the red sash of his uniform into place as the conference began. The meeting space might be virtual, but the image Chapulin would see would be a faithful replication of him.

The Nahuatl woman who appeared across from him gave him a slight bow, carefully adjusting her immense feathered headdress. The politician was delicately built, almost lost in the regalia of her role, but James had read Quetzalli Chapulin's military record when he'd arrived in Dakota.

Every feather, every bead, every scrap of color in the headdress Chapulin wore meant something specific. Some of those meanings were unique to her particular nation. Some were drawn from shared reconstructionist traditions spread across all of Dakota. Some, like the forest-green sash of a Terran Commonwealth Marine Corps officer woven through the headdress, were Commonwealth.

Chapulin had served sixteen years in the Corps, rising to Colonel and commanding a Marine strike regiment in the first war against the Alliance, twenty-odd years ago now. She'd seen as much combat as anyone in Tecumseh's command, and he knew better than to take her lightly.

"First Chief Chapulin," he greeted the woman. "I appreciate you making time for me. This has been a hell of a day for us all."

"I appreciate *you* making time for *me*, Admiral," Chapulin replied with a smile. "I understand that Admiral Banks is…unwell?"

"Unfortunately," James confirmed. "He is receiving the best medical care the Navy can provide, but our doctors had no choice but to relieve him of command on medical grounds. Until I am replaced or he recovers, I command Sector Fleet Dakota."

"I understand, Admiral," she said. "I've been out of uniform for a while, but I know how that goes. How can Dakota assist you?"

"There's a list," he said drily. "On the other hand, I also want to know how I can best assist Dakota and the Confederacy's government. I'm going to need to lean on you and the Assembly heavily until we have regular communication with Sol again."

"Right now, we're still finding out what pieces *broke*, let alone figuring out how to put things back together," Chapulin told him. "It will probably help some of our grumpier souls that you're Shawnee, though. Dakota joined the Commonwealth of our own accord, but that doesn't stop the muttering."

"Quiet mutters, I suppose," James said. "Quiet enough that my intel isn't worried."

"They're just mutters. But they'll get louder, depending on how the Sector Fleet handles these next few weeks."

She was poking for something. James wasn't sure *what*, but she was definitely testing him.

"Right now, I'm mostly going to be waiting on hulls," he told her. "We tried to recall our deployed units before the coms went down, but we're not sure we got through to all of them. We need communications, and today, that means starships."

And starships were not cheap. It took four Class One mass manipulators to create an Alcubierre warp field. Those took enough exotic matter, time, special equipment and specialist skills to manufacture that a *single* Class One manipulator cost approximately a fifth of a percent of Dakota's annual Gross System Product.

Dakota was a *rich* star system, rivaled by few in human space, and the average A-S freighter would cost almost a full percentage point of her entire GSP to build. There were twelve in the system, not including the tanker James figured had jumped before his hold order had reached it.

"The Dakota Confederacy only directly owns three starships," Chapulin noted. "None are currently in the Dakota System, though I trust their captains to return as quickly as they can."

"But there are fourteen registered here," James countered. "I'll be imposing on every starship captain I can find for the foreseeable future to carry our mail. I hope to make that service available to you as well, though, frankly, I can't see myself offering those captains a choice.

"We are too desperate to make contact with my subordinate commands and the rest of the Commonwealth."

"If you have ruffled feathers, I will talk to people here," she promised. "I agree with you on the need. What are...your next steps, Admiral?"

"We're not quite into waiting stages yet," he admitted. "I have a virtual meeting with the starship captains currently *in* Dakota in a bit over an hour. Hopefully by morning, my communications teams will have figured out a solution for sending secure messages to ships in other star systems when we never even had a *reason* to agree on a physical encryption cipher."

He sighed.

"I am responsible for the security of the entire Dakota Sector, First Chief," he told her. "I now have access to the budgets and resources of Admiral Banks, but truthfully, Commonwealth dollars won't do me much good if your people won't accept them."

"My people, Admiral?"

"The Dakota System is not only where my fleet is based, you are the only ones with sufficient manufacturing and refining capacity to provide parts, munitions and fuel for my fleet," he said. "I cannot rely on my normal logistical train, which means I must look to Dakota itself for those resources.

"I can and will pay for them, but any support your government can give me in establishing those contacts and contracts will be worth its weight in anything you care to name."

"I see," Chapulin agreed. "I have some thoughts and will connect with the members of the Assembly that work closely with the space industrial cooperatives. I should have some suggestions for you by end of day tomorrow?"

"That will more than suffice," he said gratefully. "Hopefully by then, I will have managed to make some sense of the Sector Administration Offices and worked out who to talk to there.

"I can't see any situation in the foreseeable future, First Chief, where we do not need to run a local semi-autonomous administration for the Dakota Sector. Since the offices for administering the federal agencies are already here…I hope to impose on your experience and personnel to pull that together."

"The people of the Dakota *Sector* do not really think of themselves as a group, Admiral," Chapulin warned. "Operating as a regional government… It may be harder than you think."

"I expect it to be almost impossible, to begin with," James told her. "But I am responsible for the safety of eleven star systems and six habitable planets. While feeding and organizing those systems isn't *officially* part of that responsibility, I cannot see any justification for *ignoring* that part of affairs, either.

"Once we have regular message routes, more detailed conversations will be had with all six planetary governments," he assured her. "I have no intention of imposing anything on anyone. But if the Commonwealth is to survive, each sector must pull together first."

"Fascinating." Chapulin's eyes sparkled as she smiled at him. "I and the Assembly of Nations will provide whatever assistance we can, I think. You are, after all, one of our own, Admiral—and it seems that I like the path you are planning to walk.

"So far, anyway."

Whatever test Chapulin had been putting James to, he appeared to have passed.

Hopefully, things stayed that way. He *needed* her if he was going to keep the systems he needed to protect safe!

5

Dakota System
0:30 October 11, 2737 ESMDT

"CAPTAINS, I apologize for the chaos and confusion," James told his guests. He stood in front of a virtual window showing the planet of Dakota, forcing himself to appear chipper and fully *on* as he faced another virtual communication conference.

This meeting was with the freighter captains he'd shortstopped from leaving the system, and was already looking to be more hostile than most of his calls in the last twenty hours. If he was *very* lucky, though, he'd be able to go to sleep after this one.

"There wasn't much confusion in the threat to *board and seize my ship,*" one of the captains snapped.

"That, Captain Kos, would have been unnecessary if you had simply followed the instructions you were given," James replied sharply. *Blackbird*'s captain had already been underway when they'd ordered her to hold position.

Elva Kos had objected and James's people had done exactly as he'd ordered. Kos, it seemed, was unimpressed.

"You have no authority to hold us like this," she barked.

"This is an emergency situation, and with the full support of the Dakota government, I have activated the appropriate emergency protocols," James replied gently. "I don't need your *cargo*, Captain Kos. I need your ship and her Alcubierre-Stetson drive."

He looked around the holograms watching him. Only ten people were actively on the call. The other three ships were in orbit of Virginia and would get a recording of this meeting—including the captain of *Festival Promise*, the tanker he'd expected to leave before his message had arrived.

The comparison between Elva Kos, who had almost forced him to board and seize her ship, and Ráðúlfr Radcliff, who had voluntarily held his ship's departure until he'd heard from Dakota and the Sector Fleet, did the woman no favors.

"As things currently stand, I expect to release the hold order at oh eight hundred hours," James told them all. "I *do* have the authority to impose it, Captains, but I have no intention of holding you longer than I have to.

"We needed time to sort out what the hell was going on and what messages I needed to send."

"How does that involve us?" Captain Helga Maradona asked. A tall dark-haired beauty, *Encarnación*'s Captain was a Krete native and one of the few captains on the call not already scheduled to leave inside forty-eight hours.

Merchant starships were expensive and uncommon—and that meant they were rarely at rest.

"If any of you read the small print of your merchant-officer licenses, the ones that came with your very fine hats, you'll find that you agreed to allow certain impositions by the Commonwealth in times of crisis," James reminded them.

The hats comment got him the chuckle he hoped for. All of the captains on the call wore identical high-peaked white hats, an old tradition of the Terran Merchant Marine. Those hats meant they'd all met the training and ethical standards imposed by that licensing body.

And that they were bound by the orders James was about to give.

"I have no intention of leaving any of you out a single *penny* for the services I need to require of you," he continued. "Captain Kos, I am aware that there are potential penalties built into your contract in particular for late payment."

She grunted, hopefully acknowledging the fact that James *had* reviewed the transcripts of her angry conversations with Commander Prebensen.

"My calculations say you will miss that window by a minimum of four hours if we release you on our current schedule," he conceded before she said anything. "If your recipient insists on enforcing those fees despite the current crisis, direct them to the Sector Fleet. The Commonwealth will cover those costs."

He traced his gaze across his audience.

"That goes for *all* of you," he told them. "Any costs you incur because of the hold order or because of my requirements will be borne by the Sector Fleet and, through us, the Commonwealth."

As the Acting Commanding Officer, Sector Fleet Dakota, James Tecumseh had access to a frankly staggering amount of money. If *that* ran out—entirely possible, as he was also responsible for a frankly staggering amount of expenses—he was quite certain that he could borrow from any and all local banks on the Commonwealth's credit to fund his operations.

Even if everything *truly* went to pieces, it would be a while before anyone stopped being willing to lend money to Sector Fleet Dakota.

"So, what do you need from us?" Kos asked grumpily, echoing Maradona's question.

"Your merchant licenses authorize me to require you to carry messages on the Commonwealth's behalf," he told them. "We're going to need to coordinate that on a scale that humanity has never needed before. That means, Captains, that you're going to be wearing a postal-worker's hat for the foreseeable future."

He smiled gently.

"We will have a basic package for each of you to carry to your existing destinations by oh eight hundred ESMDT," he told them. "Chunks of those packages will be encrypted, for local military commands, and others will be carried in the clear for general transmission.

"Among those packages will be instructions for relay and establishing relay *networks* as we go forward," he continued. "At least one of you is heading to each inhabited system in the Dakota Sector, which makes my life easier.

"Otherwise, I'd need to co-opt some of you for new destinations, and I *know* what hiring a merchant ship to fly empty costs."

Even Kos gave him a begrudging chuckle at that.

"I, frankly, have no idea what goes into building quantum-entangled particle pairs except that it requires zero gravity," James admitted. "But my people are telling me six months for the most basic replacement communications—and we were everybody *else's* backup, so getting entangled blocks from other nations may be more difficult than we'd like.

"For now, holding together the communications of the Commonwealth is going to fall on you and people like you," he told the merchant captains. "I have faith in the spacers of the Commonwealth to take up that burden and carry it forth."

None of them were *quite* willing to challenge that to his face.

"I appreciate the explanation," Kos finally said. "So, we wait until we get your package?"

"Exactly, Captain Kos," he confirmed. "Those of you with already-listed destinations will receive further communications from Commander Prebensen and Captain Mac Cléirich. Once you have received the data packages for transfer, you are released to continue on your original courses.

"Those of you who are planning on leaving after oh eight hundred hours will receive updated communications packages prior to your scheduled departures," James told them. "Any further questions?"

———

THE CONFERENCE FADED OUT, each hologram winking out one by one until only Captain Maradona remained, the Kretan captain looking mildly amused at being the only one left.

"Your Commodore told me you needed to talk to me once everyone else was gone," she noted drily. "Considering what my next cargo is supposed to be, I'm guessing that has something to do with it."

"It does," James confirmed. With a thought, he collapsed the virtual room. Now Captain Maradona's hologram hung in his office as he took a seat in his chair and studied her.

She laughed and followed suit, each of them sitting in their respective offices. There was about a three-quarter-second delay in each part of their conversation. Not enough to really slow things down, but enough that the distance between the ships was clear.

"Exotic-matter coils and other components and materials for the munitions factories at Leviticus," Maradona listed. "There were other items too; even the TCN doesn't often fill a fifty-million-cubic-meter freighter."

"But your primary haulage contract was with the Commonwealth Navy," James pointed out. "My information suggests that the Leviticus armaments facilities are gone. It seems quite unlikely that the Alliance of Free Stars took out the defense fleet and the q-com switchboard but left the munitions plants and refit yards intact.

"So, I've already stopped that shipment," he told her. "There *is* a missile manufacturing plant here in Dakota that we're upgrading to manufacture the latest missiles. Those materials will be used to manufacture munitions here in Dakota, which means that your next haulage contract is effectively canceled."

"There are terms and allowances in the contract for that," Maradona said. "I'm sure I could find another cargo in short order, but I somehow suspect I'm not on a direct call with a Navy Rear Admiral because you think I'm pretty."

James snorted. Captain Maradona was quite attractive, but she was also correct. He wasn't adding on to his oh-dark-thirty meeting because a freighter captain was cute.

"You're correct," he said. "We're converting your contract. You're scheduled to be done off-loading by oh eight hundred, correct?"

"Around there," she confirmed. "I can probably wake some people up on both *Encarnación* and the transshipment stations if we need to start loading cargo sooner."

"I need you empty by oh eight hundred," James told her. "But there's no cargo. You'll be paid for full haulage, but you're flying empty."

She whistled softly.

"I can't complain about what that's going to do to my bottom line, but that begs some huge questions, Admiral," she said.

"Sol, Captain Maradona," he said, answering the first and most obvious question. "Twenty days each way. Hauling empty, you should be able to sustain Tier Two acceleration and cut a full day of sublight time out on each end."

Though that would eat the extra margin Maradona was anticipating for running without cargo. The combination of mass manipulators, artificial gravity fields and antimatter engines allowed for extraordinarily efficient accelerations, but there were clear plateaus in the calculation.

At Tier One, a starship accelerated at roughly fifty to seventy gravities, depending on the setup, and consumed an astonishingly small amount of fuel to move tens of millions of tons of mass. Very few civilian ships would voluntarily exceed Tier One acceleration.

There was then a near-asymptotic spike in fuel consumption until the calculation plateaued again around two hundred gravities, Tier Two acceleration. Fuel consumption at Tier Two was roughly one hundred times that of Tier One. Tier Three and Tier Four followed similar patterns—Tier Three, used by starfighters, was around five hundred gravities, versus Tier Four's thousand-plus, as used by missiles.

"That's going to use a chunk of fuel, but a full haulage contract will cover it," Maradona told him, confirming his thoughts. "I'm carrying messages and data?"

"Exactly," he told her. "Not quite the same package as everyone else, but similar. We need to report in and establish a coms link with Sol. My team will update the contract to cover a return trip here as well. I *need* to know that I will have heard from the Commonwealth government in forty or so days.

"If you manage to find a cargo you can load in Sol in under twelve hours, I'm not going to mind, but I definitely prioritize a swift return and am prepared to pay for it."

Maradona studied him silently.

"A standard full haulage contract each way is already generous enough, Admiral," she told him. "Get me your package as soon as you can, and I'll be back in forty-one days. You have my word."

James bowed his head in silent thanks. Running empty both ways, she'd still come out ahead, but they both knew she could have asked for more money and he'd have given it.

Helga Maradona clearly understood just how bad things could get.

6

Dakota System
9:00 October 12, 2737 ESMDT

"CAP UP, CAP UP!"

The bellowed command was completely unnecessary, but Anthony Yamamoto wasn't one to argue with tradition.

The Scottish-Japanese officer stood straight-backed in the center of *Krakatoa*'s primary flight-control center, watching the screens and virtual displays around him as two dozen mixed Navy and Starfighter Corps personnel ran through the process of updating scanners immediately after emergence from Alcubierre-Stetson drive.

Their primary task right now was getting the carrier space patrol—acronymed as *CAP* by tradition dating back to wet-navy carriers—off the decks and into the void around the big carrier.

"Upper launch paths are clear," a Petty Officer declared. "Second and Third Squadrons are clear to launch."

"Port launch paths are clear," a second officer reported. "Fourth Squadron is clear to launch."

"Starboard launch paths are clear. First is clear to launch."

"Lower launch paths are clear. Fifth Squadron is clear to launch."

Five of Anthony's twenty squadrons could be launched at once, through a total of fifty launch tubes mounted along the sides of the carrier. In a combat environment, the rest of his fighters would be prepped on the decks, ready to be loaded into the launch tubes like oversized missiles.

Krakatoa could put her entire two-hundred-starfighter group into space in sixty seconds. Right now, though, that *probably* wasn't needed. But, to be fair, normally Anthony would be putting up a five-*fighter* Carrier Space Patrol.

"Launch Group *Krakatoa*-Alpha," he ordered calmly.

Fifty Katana starfighters blasted into space before he'd even finished speaking. No one involved had truly been waiting for his order. Every part of this evolution had been planned in advance—including Anthony's decision to deploy a five-*squadron* CAP to make sure the carrier was safe.

They had been unable to make contact with anyone in Dakota in advance, after all. Normally, they'd know what to expect when they returned to unwarped space. Today, they knew nothing.

"Yamamoto, we have the squadrons on the screen," Captain Volkov declared over the ship's internal network. At least half of all the work of running the ship took place in the virtual environment that linked together every officer's and spacer's neural implants.

"Lieutenant Colonel Ó Cochláin has his orders," Anthony replied. "Fighters will assume defensive formations and accompany *Krakatoa* into the system."

Helvius Ó Cochláin commanded Starfighter Group *Krakatoa*-Alpha. He was Anthony's most senior subordinate—and his most trusted. When Anthony flew in combat himself, he flew with *Krakatoa*-Alpha and with Lieutenant Colonel Ó Cochláin on his wing.

"So far, everything looks green, but it will still be several minutes before we hear anything from Admiral Banks," Volkov warned. "Any concerns around maintaining the CAP, Colonel?"

"None," Anthony said firmly. "My people launched with full supplies and munitions. I'd rather not leave them out there for more than a four-hour patrol, but I suspect I'll be launching everyone *else* if we need that!"

They'd emerged four light-minutes from Dakota. It would take three hours and twenty minutes for the carrier to make orbit, and if Anthony still needed a fifty-fighter CAP in orbit of Dakota, things had gone *very* wrong.

"Agreed," Volkov told him. "Integrating your people's eyes into the sensor network, but I'm already missing q-probes."

Those q-com-equipped robotic spacecraft would have been fired ahead of the carrier at a thousand gravities, rapidly expanding their real-time visibility sphere. Without the q-probes...they didn't *have* a real-time visibility sphere.

"Sector Fleet Dakota is still here, as are the system defenses," the Captain continued after a moment. "I expected that we were being excessively paranoid, but I'm glad to be proven right."

"You haven't been proven right yet, sir," Anthony sent on a private channel. "*My* biggest fear isn't that something happened to Sector Fleet Dakota… It's that Sector Fleet Dakota has gone rogue."

That was Anthony's biggest fear across the board. There were twelve Sector Fleets and two March Fleets across the Commonwealth, and without any control from Central Command, *any* of those fleets could set their commanding officer up as a warlord in their region. If Banks was heading in that direction, the biggest danger in the Dakota System *was* Sector Fleet Dakota.

In which case, *Krakatoa* and her flight groups would have to convince Vice Admiral Banks of the error of his ways.

———

"Looks like we've received standard challenges from orbital control," Brahms told Anthony, the deck chief clearly watching far more than his own station as the carrier accelerated toward their destination. "Nothing out of the ordinary, except for the lightspeed time delay."

"We are expected," Anthony murmured. "And they can assume we're friendly, since they know who we are. It's going to be visits in the future that are going to get...more complicated."

"No one is going to have a damn clue who to expect," Brahms agreed.

Anthony was still standing in the center of Flight Control, letting the organized chaos swirl around him. His implant let him keep on top of everything going on, including a running link watching the telemetry summaries from his squadron leaders.

He might *look* like he was standing still, but he had his mental finger on the pulse of the entire carrier. His people knew it too. They were used to his style and they knew that if they had a question, he'd be immediately available to answer it.

Open-door policies were only required if an officer spent any time at all in their office.

"Any word from Vice Admiral Banks?" he asked Brahms. He could ask the bridge as well, but the quiet side-networks of NCOs were often faster for that kind of information.

"Nothing yet. Sector Fleet Dakota is being silent."

"Colonel, I need to loop you into a call," Volkov's voice interrupted. "Well, a playback. We just received a recorded message from the Acting Commanding Officer, Sector Fleet Dakota. Pull up a window."

They'd only been working together for two months, but Volkov already knew how her CAG operated. A virtual window appeared in Anthony's vision as he mentally swept most of his other feeds into subconscious processing and focused his attention.

Krakatoa had been under construction in Sol when then-Commodore James Tecumseh had returned from his spectacularly mixed mission into the stars on the far side of the Alliance of Free Stars. Anthony had already been assigned as her CAG, since he'd been on medical leave to regenerate an arm lost in action against the Alliance.

Like every military officer in the system, he knew Tecumseh's face and story. He wasn't quite sure *how* he felt about a task force commander who'd lost one of their Commonwealth's most advanced cruisers to pirates, then made common cause with the local Alliance commander to destroy the ship.

From the fact that Command had promoted the man to Rear Admiral and then stuck him as the second-ranked officer in a *very* quiet area, the TCN wasn't any more sure as a body than Anthony was. But if he was Acting Commanding Officer...

"Captain Volkov, this is Rear Admiral James Tecumseh," the dark-haired officer introduced himself. "Unfortunately, Vice Admiral Banks is on an indefinite leave from duty and I have been required to assume command of Sector Fleet Dakota.

"We're still in the process of establishing communications with the Sector and with the Commonwealth government in Sol, but we believe we have things stable for the moment. I'm damn glad to see *Krakatoa*, though.

"We have no idea what's going to happen now, and every hull available gives us another fire we can potentially put out at the same time. You and your senior officers are invited aboard *Saratoga* for a working dinner once you're in orbit.

"Let my staff know what you need in terms of supplies and fuel. I have no expectation of needing to deploy *Krakatoa* in the near future, but I want to make sure all of our ships are ready to go as needed."

There was an awkward moment as the Admiral finished his message several seconds before the recording stopped. No one was used to sending recorded messages yet, Anthony judged.

That would change. Probably just in time for them to get reliable FTL coms again, in his experience.

"What do you think, people?" Volkov asked.

Anthony checked and confirmed that Commander Jack was also on the very short list Volkov was talking to. It was just the three of them who'd watched Tecumseh's message.

"He's saying the right things in the right ways," Anthony said. "Everything looks right. I believe we may actually be okay."

"We were being too paranoid from the beginning," Jack added. "Dakota is secure space. There's nothing to really be afraid of here."

"Both Colonel Yamamoto and I were as much concerned about Sector Fleet Dakota having gone rogue as we were about some kind of second-wave attacks from the Alliance," Volkov told her.

They'd *had* this conversation, Anthony knew. But Jack thought they were being paranoid.

"You were right, Commander," he admitted. "But better paranoid and wrong then naïve and dead. *Krakatoa* would only have a chance against the ships in Dakota orbit if we kept the carrier herself well out of range."

Ignoring the system defenses, *Krakatoa* had two hundred fighters to the Rear Admiral Tecumseh's hundred and eighty—and the difference was *all* bombers. Anthony's people had a good chance of taking down a last-generation battleship, battlecruiser and carrier.

If they could keep the battleship and cruiser from landing positron-lance hits on *Krakatoa*. The whole reason for starfighters, after all, was that modern battle was a matter of eggshells armed with jackhammers.

"And now, Captain?" Jack asked, her tone careful.

"We will proceed to Dakota orbit and plan for the three of us to attend dinner on *Saratoga*," Volkov said firmly. "But Colonel Yamamoto will keep the full five-squadron CAP up until we are in the security radius of the Sector Fleet's carrier space patrol."

"Understood," Anthony confirmed. "I'll make contact with *Saratoga*'s CAG as we get closer as well. The original plan was for me to become Sector Fleet Dakota's senior CAG, but that was because *Saratoga* was supposed to leave."

"And Rear Admiral Tecumseh was planned to move his flag aboard *Krakatoa*," Volkov said. "What the plan becomes now, I suppose, we will establish over dinner."

7

Dakota System
19:30 October 12, 2737 ESMDT

TWO DAYS INTO THE CRISIS, James knew that his hopes of anything resembling a regular sleep cycle were a waste of mental energy. He was grabbing an hour here and there as best as he could and then leaving it to his implants to wash the sleep toxins out of his system.

It wasn't a sustainable plan for the long term, but he was frankly surprised by just *how many* minor problems and crises suddenly required immediate attention when no one could call Earth for further information or to pass the decision up-chain.

The civil administration of the Sector had accepted him as the senior Commonwealth official in the system, which was a big-enough problem. There were *nineteen* agencies with offices on Dakota, and none of them wanted to accept the director of another office as a local administrative head.

All of them wanted to report to James…and James didn't think that civilian agencies should be reporting to a Rear Admiral. That fight was still incomplete, though he already knew his solution. He just needed to get the bureaucrats to stop arguing and panicking long enough for him to suggest the plan.

That hadn't happened yet. He was *looking forward* to a dinner with just military officers.

"Everything is in order, sir," Chief Steward Sallie Leeuwenhoek told him. The pale redheaded Petty Officer had been assigned to him along with the star, and she seemed to take most of his quiet introspection in stride.

"Thank you, Chief," he told her. "I don't know how I'd have survived these last few days without you."

"You'd have been eating whatever crap the officers' mess could put on a tray and send up to your office," she said cheerfully. "And then panicking when you tried to host a working dinner party." She chuckled. "Do you care what the menu is?"

"Does it account for everyone's allergies and dietary restrictions?" James asked.

"Of course." Leeuwenhoek sounded offended at the idea that she *wouldn't* have pulled that information from everyone's files and made sure of it. "Captain Bardakçı would be more complicated if this wasn't his ship and we didn't already have several cooks used to prepping halal. Otherwise, the only major allergy is Colonel Yamamoto's to peanuts. We're fine."

"Then I don't care what the menu is," James said drily. "So long as we can feed all nine of us, I'm happy."

"And if I wanted to brag?" Leeuwenhoek asked with another chuckle.

"We'd be out of time," he told her. "Gulshan is here."

The door to his dining room slid open a moment later, admitting the broad-shouldered form of Commodore Gulshan Bardakçı, *Saratoga*'s commanding officer. Walking a polite one step behind the captain of the ship they were on was Commodore Young Volkov, a slimly built woman who looked almost too young for her red-sashed dress uniform.

Barely behind them were the two executive officers. Despite coming from different star systems and with ancestors hailing from different ends of Europe, Commander Patricia Jack and Captain Harkaitz Zyma shared an athletically tall build and shoulder-length black hair.

They didn't necessarily look *related*—Jack had a far smaller nose than the impressive hook of the Alpha Centauri–born Zyma—but their coloring was closely matched.

The last pair couldn't have resembled each other less, though. Colonels Avedis Maeda and Anthony Yamamoto were both from Japanese families and that was where the resemblance ended. Maeda was a good twenty centimeters shorter than Yamamoto with far darker skin—compared to Yamamoto, who was tall with light skin and was recognizably related to his famous ancestor.

James hoped that he looked less like his *own* famous forebear than Yamamoto did. Tecumseh, after all, was generally a more positive role model to the Shawnee than Isoroku Yamamoto was to the Japanese, and James wasn't sure he lived up to that weight.

"Welcome and thank you all for coming," James greeted them. "Commodores Ferreiro and Voclain will be joining us in a moment."

The only people in the room who *weren't* going to be causing rank confusion, he reflected, were James himself and the two Starfighter Corps Colonels. The two starship captains in the room were both actually Commodores, but only Bardakçı could be addressed as *Captain* aboard *Saratoga*. That meant that Saratoga's executive officer and one of James's two chiefs of staff would both be *called* Commodore but held the *rank* of Captain.

He thanked whatever deities were listening for neural implants to keep track of it all, and then nodded to the two chiefs of staff as they came in. At some point, he'd sit down with the staff and sort out a proper org chart.

Right now, though, he was basically running his staff for Task Group Dakota-One and the staff for Sector Fleet Dakota at the same time. The confusion was inevitable, but they had no time to do anything else.

"All right, this is everyone," he confirmed. "I believe the introductions have mostly been made and most of us are known to each other by reputation already. We've got a lot of work to get through, but the stewards have put some effort into the meal, so I figure we should spend *some* time enjoying it before I start picking all of your brains."

He smiled. "And, of course, for those of us with Sector Fleet Dakota, this is the first chance we've had to sit down for a meal in two days. It's been…interesting."

———

IN JAMES'S EXPERIENCE, no admiral's staff had ever delivered a less-than-brilliant meal for the admiral's working meetings. His staff was not the exception to the rule, and it was easy to avoid talking shop while they worked through Chief Leeuwenhoek's arrangements.

When the dishes were cleared away and the Chief's minions had delivered coffees and teas around the room, James surveyed the senior officers of his two carriers.

"Commodore Volkov, I presume you and your staff have been brought up to speed on what we know?" he asked.

"Yes, but that doesn't seem to be much," Volkov replied. "With no confirmation of the status of the March Fleets…the status of the Commonwealth itself is in question. We don't know how bad our losses or the Alliance's were in this strike."

"We have to assume, at least as a worst-case starting point, that every fleet the Alliance engaged has been destroyed," Voclain said grimly. "The fate of the March Fleets is more in question. Walkingstick and Amandine both had powerful forces, but without communication, they are at risk of the Alliance or the League concentrating forces for a fight our people might lose."

"Walkingstick is probably safe," Yamamoto said in the Scottish brogue so incongruous in the man. "I can't imagine the Alliance had much *left* after sending the ships they needed for this insanity."

"Insanity or not, it worked," James noted grimly. "We won't have any news from Earth for at least eighteen days—and we should be prepared to not hear anything until Captain Maradona and *Encarnación* return. That will be thirty-nine days, people, until we are certain we will know the position of the leadership of the Commonwealth on our response to this."

"There's only one acceptable response," Maeda snapped. *Saratoga*'s CAG looked like he'd eaten a lemon, fury twisting his face unpleasantly. "We buy off the League and hammer this entire so-called *Alliance* into space dust."

The dining room was silent and James sighed.

"Based on the intelligence reports I have read, Dictator Periklos is unlikely to be buyable for the foreseeable future," he told the Colonel. "We find ourselves trapped between two enemies and, frankly, we almost certainly just lost our entire strategic margin.

"On top of that, it will be at least a year, potentially more, before we have any level of strategic communication, let alone operational or tactical," he continued. "Were we to attempt to continue to prosecute the wars we're currently fighting, I suspect the Commonwealth would not survive."

"You can't mean..." Maeda trailed off.

"In the Star Chamber's place, I would sue for peace with both the League and the Alliance," James said quietly. "Thankfully, that isn't the decision of anyone in this room. The only immediate decision before me is whether to send *Saratoga* forward to join Marshal Walkingstick's Rimward March Fleet."

Marshal James Walkingstick was a Cherokee-descended North American. He was not, so far as James Tecumseh knew, part of the Cherokee nation on Earth, but he did adopt at least some surface elements of the culture.

It had been something the two men had bonded over when they'd served together. Walkingstick had been something of a mentor for James once, though fate had long since marched on *that* point. Central Command might have decided that James Tecumseh keeping his lost flagship out of both pirate and Alliance hands outweighed his being ambushed by his own executive officer to lose the ship in the first place...but Marshal Walkingstick had been far less forgiving.

"Captain Bardakçı," James continued, gesturing to *Saratoga*'s commander. "Your thoughts? It's your ship and escort we're discussing here."

Bardakçı leaned into his hands on the table for a moment.

"I'm not sure, sir," he admitted. "And I guess it comes down to whether you're right that the Star Chamber will sue for peace. If we're continuing the war, Marshal Walkingstick will need every ship and every fighter he can get.

"But if we negotiate a peace, we are likely better served keeping *Saratoga* here to assist in local security. Having the ability to, for example, put a starship in every system of the Dakota Sector could be hugely valuable."

"Agreed," James said. "And that is what weighs on me, people. Marshal Walkingstick has, what, eighty capital ships at his command? Marshal Amandine has fifty. We have *seven*, once we have reestablished contact with the rest of Sector Fleet Dakota.

"Dakota had fewer capital ships than many other sector fleets, but we weren't responsible for the security of a q-com switchboard. Based off the sensor data we have, we can reasonably assume that any sector fleet with a switchboard has lost half its strength—and that Home Fleet has been *destroyed*."

The room was silent until Yamamoto finally spoke.

"We can't send any ships to the Marches, sir," *Krakatoa*'s CAG said. "Not without more data. We're more likely to be needed at Meridian, or even Leviticus, than at Niagara, sir."

"That is my own conclusion as well," James admitted, nodding to the younger officer. "But I am prepared to admit that I may have missed something. If anyone has a different perspective to offer, I am willing to listen—but understand that the decision is mine."

"We don't have enough information to start changing our orders," Maeda argued after a moment. "Without further data, shouldn't we continue on with the original movement orders?"

"We have enough information, I think, to realize that we cannot risk binding ourselves to orders and deployments decided prior to this catastrophe," the Admiral replied. "I need more than 'those were our orders' to give up *half* of the capital ships I have immediately to hand."

Maeda spread his hands. "I don't like it," he admitted. "But that was the only real argument I had."

"We keep everyone, then," James decided aloud. "For the moment, my intention is to consolidate the Sector Fleet and sector administration here in Dakota. The situation is going to require some level of regional governance, but that will need to be agreed to by the assorted planetary governments.

"All of them have been *invited* to send representatives here." He shook his head. "All of this is temporary, but it's going to be a pain. Until we have updated orders from Earth, all we can really do is keep the lights on and everyone saluting the same damn flag."

"And what happens if someone decides they don't want to be Commonwealth anymore, sir?" Volkov asked slowly.

"That's a bridge we'll cross when we come to it, Commodore," James admitted. "And it's a damn spiky one. Depending on how that decision gets made...we may have to let them go.

"The Commonwealth is meant to be the defender of democracy and justice. I will not use its flag as a club to crush either of those virtues."

8

Dakota System
16:00 October 15, 2737 ESMDT

ANTHONY YAMAMOTO WAS RELIEVED to be getting back into a starfighter again, no matter how boring the mission profile was looking. For three days, he'd been buried in the chaos and datawork of taking over as Sector Fleet CAG. He was senior to Maeda by just over two years in grade, which put him in charge.

He walked the exterior of his Katana. The craft was a seventh-generation interceptor, taking the shape of a twenty-meter-long egg. His flight engineer walked the exterior with him, checking each of the four missile launchers in turn.

As they reached the emitter for the positron lance, Anthony's implant chirped silently with an incoming message. The Admiral was comming him.

"Yamamoto," he answered crisply, gesturing for Şenol Badem to complete the task. Badem was a more-than-competent engineer, with visible additional circuitry implanted along the side of their face and shaven skull.

And if they were an artificially intersex cyborg who near-literally worshipped at the altar of the singularity, well, Anthony was a Scotsman who could pass for a long-dead Japanese Admiral. He wasn't one to say much about anything.

"Colonel, I have good news and bad news for you," Tecumseh said with his usual annoyingly calm voice. "Both are the same news."

"That's never promising," Anthony replied. "I'm about to take the CAP out, sir. What's going on?"

"The Dakota Confederacy government has signed off on a more-complete implementation of Security Protocol Twenty-Six than I was hoping for," the Admiral told him. "We now have complete command of the entire Confederacy Security Force. That gives you another hundred Katanas and two hundred Scimitars."

Anthony paused to consider that. He was surprised that the local security force had *any* Katanas—the fighters were less than a year old, though they'd seen a level of mass production unusual even for the Commonwealth.

Part of the reason for that, however, had been the recognition that their predecessor, the Scimitar, had been a painfully inferior sixth-generation starfighter. The Alliance of Free Stars' assorted seventh-generation fighters would have walked all over a *decent* sixth-generation combatant, but the Scimitar's fundamental design flaws had left the Commonwealth's pilots at a disadvantage that had taken two-to-one numerical odds to offset.

Pilots like one Anthony Yamamoto.

"The birds are good news, the admin is bad news," Anthony agreed. "I assume they have their own bases and no carriers?"

"Exactly. I'll want you to think about ways we can bring them with us if needed," the Admiral told him. "It'll give you something to consider as you fly in-system patrol. I'm told that can be boring."

"Right now, sir, I was looking *forward* to boring," Anthony admitted. "So, thanks for the headache."

"Believe me, Colonel, you don't have one-tenth the headaches I do," Tecumseh said. "Fly safe."

Anthony accepted the instruction with a chuckle of amusement and turned to Badem. He trusted the flight engineer to do their job, but a Katana's main lance put out a beam of antimatter equivalent to a sixty-kiloton nuclear bomb every second.

He was more than happy to double-check everyone's work on that gun!

———

EVEN WITH EVERY mass manipulator on a fifty-five-hundred-ton starfighter set to create gravity fields offsetting acceleration, being fired from a carrier's launch tubes felt like being stepped on by a giant.

The sensation was quick and it was an old friend to Anthony Yamamoto, the crushing sense of pressure a firm reminder that his sphere of responsibility had just shrunk from hundreds of starfighters to mere dozens.

"This is Charlie-Three squadron, reporting in," a voice said in his mental ear. "All fighters confirmed present and accounted for.

"This is Bravo-Four squadron, reporting in," a second voice added. "All fighters confirmed present and accounted for."

Anthony sank deeper into the network of his neural implant, doing the neural equivalent of nodding comfortably to his own fighter's two crewmembers—Badem and the even-younger gunner, Navin Strøm. After a fraction of a second, he *was* his starfighter—and linked into the twenty other Katana starfighters forming up around him.

"Maldonado, Alexandersson," he greeted the squadron commanders flying with him today. "You have the flight routes?"

"Fast and far, sir," Major Kyveli Maldonado told him, the Alpha Centauri officer leading *Krakatoa*-Charlie-Three sounding almost bored. "Accelerate up to ten percent of lightspeed, head out ten light-minutes, do an arc of the system as we decel to zero relative to Dakota, head back."

The Carrier Space Patrol wouldn't normally be spread that far out, but Anthony and Tecumseh were improvising. The CAP normally stuck close to the carriers—and Anthony had left a third squadron, one of *Saratoga*'s, to provide close cover—with q-com-equipped drones scattered out across a fifteen-light-minute sphere.

"Deployment is by flight," Major Ikechukwu Alexandersson continued on from where Maldonado had finished. "We'll get decent sensor coverage across about eighty percent of the ten-light-minute sphere."

He paused.

"I'm not sure what the value of this is, sir," he admitted. "Even with only lightspeed links from the drones, they're still just as able to provide this sensor coverage as we are. Hell, we *have* a fifteen-light-minute sphere of drones."

And unlike a normal deployment, there were only a handful of smaller spheres layered inside that outer perimeter. Since nothing could provide real-time data to the fleet, the need to layer drones to expand the real-time view was gone.

"The point isn't to put sensors on the perimeter, Majors," Anthony told them. "The point is to put *brains* on the perimeter. AI is good, but someone has to make the judgment call on whether something is a threat—and there are a lot of things that can cause a lot of trouble given fifteen minutes before the Sector Fleet can assess them.

"Whereas if we're only *five* light-minutes away, we can decide and act to intervene."

There was a long pause as the Majors processed that.

"Two Katanas can't do much," Alexandersson said slowly. "But they can do...something."

Anthony wasn't sure he agreed with "can't do much." A single Katana carried four launchers with three one-gigaton antimatter warheads apiece, plus the sixty-kiloton-per-second positron lance. With Tier Three acceleration, they could maneuver at five hundred gravities and had a total available delta-v of just over seventy percent of lightspeed.

They might be parasite warships, dependent on their carriers to move them between star systems, but it was only in comparison to true Alcubierre-Stetson-drive warships that they were anything resembling *incapable*.

"We can do a lot," he told the Majors. "Divide your squadrons by flight, Majors. Alexandersson, I'm with your E flight."

Once he got down into the two-ship minimum deployment unit, the naming scheme became ridiculous. But Anthony knew that *Krakatoa*-Bravo-Four-E flight had the least experienced pilots out of the ten flights he was about to scatter across the Dakota System.

And since Anthony Yamamoto was quite certain he was the *most* experienced pilot in the entire Sector Fleet Dakota, he would back them up himself.

"Understood. Transferring them to your network," Alexandersson replied.

An entire conversation flashed by in seconds between the Major and the six junior officers he was assigning to the Fleet CAG. Anthony *could* eavesdrop, but he didn't need to. He knew, more or less, what the Major was telling them.

"E flight," Anthony addressed his new wings. "Form on my wing and stand by to go to full thrust on my command."

───────

AT THE TEN-LIGHT-MINUTE MARK, Anthony and his companions swung their vectors sideways and back toward the carrier. It would take them the same hundred and forty minutes it had taken them to get out there to decelerate to zero relative to *Krakatoa* and the planet the fleet orbited.

When all was said and done, the patrols would be in space for almost ten hours before they returned to *Krakatoa*, which was longer than Anthony preferred to have his people deployed for. There were bunks, toilets, and even a kitchenette in the small habitation section between the cockpit and the engineering center, but the fighters weren't designed for long-term operation.

The Dakota System was about as busy as he was expecting. There was *nothing* in his section of the arc, though there was quite a bit of sublight traffic in several other areas. Alcubierre-Stetson ships might be expensive, but sublight freighters didn't require Class One mass manipulators.

Anthony's rough estimate was that there were roughly a *trillion* cubic meters or so of in-system freighters. Most of the tankers, transports and passenger ships he could see were far smaller than interstellar ships, coming in at maybe ten million cubic meters and five million tons or so apiece, but there were *thousands* of them.

He'd seen more in-system industry in Sol. *Maybe* Tau Ceti or Alpha Centauri. But the Dakota System was one of the most heavily industrialized systems he'd ever seen, for all that the planet had almost no manufacturing at all.

"Cherenkov flare," Strøm suddenly reported, the gunner picking up the sensor signature of an interstellar emergence before Anthony did.

"Got it," Anthony confirmed. "On the line from Shogun, it looks like."

The reason they were in an empty part of the massively busy system was because this was where many of the civilian FTL routes would emerge, usually around the ten-to-twelve-light-minute mark.

"Range is one light-minute, eleven and a half from Dakota," Strøm continued. "I make her a forty-million-cubic-meter hull."

Anthony nodded. That was a newer ship, the same generation of Stetson stabilizers as, say, *Saratoga*. Modern warships would be around sixty-five, with brand-new ships hovering around eighty—but civilian ships were usually a generation behind military ones, so only the newest freighters would be over fifty million cubic meters.

"She's moving," he noted after a moment. "I make it forty-five gravities; energy signatures make it twenty to twenty-five million tons."

"That's heavy," Strøm said. "I know freighters can run pretty full, but that's twice *Saratoga*'s mass on the same cubage. What's she hauling?"

"Could be any one of a dozen things," Anthony pointed out. "But still…that's strange. And she's not scheduled, either. She'd have left Shogun on the sixth, before this mess started, and we don't have her on the list."

They were expecting *Mediterranean* from the Gothic System inside the next twenty-four hours, but Anthony estimated the strike cruiser would show up on the next round of patrols. Plus, she'd be coming in on a different angle.

There were two ships expected from Shogun, having left on the eighth and ninth respectively, and Anthony knew everyone was hoping for *Arctic* to have left on the tenth, but none of those ships were due for two more days.

"E flight, stay on my wing," he ordered his wing fighters, considering the situation as he plugged in an intercept course. He had ten times the freighter's acceleration—assuming that she *was* a freighter and that was all the acceleration she had.

"We're moving to intercept our guest and check in on them," he continued, keeping his worries silent for now. "They'll have lost coms halfway here and are probably feeling pretty shaky. Let's give them a safe welcome."

New vector calculations played across the virtual screen in front of him—and new orders flashed out.

"Bravo-B flight, Bravo-C Flight, Charlie-E Flight," he reeled off, triggering an automatic record-and-transmit for those six fighters. "I'm sending you new courses to converge on the new contact. All signs point to friendly, but she's unexpected, so let's check in."

A vector from Shogun, after all, was *also* a vector from the Meridian Sector—and the Stellar League beyond it.

His own vector said he'd rendezvous with the freighter in fifteen minutes but would be flashing past at almost six percent of lightspeed still.

"What do we do, sir?" Strøm asked.

"Spin up our defensive systems," Anthony ordered. "Just the antimissile suite for now, but keep a finger on the electronic countermeasures. Something isn't right here."

"Understood."

New icons flickered up around Anthony as he lifted himself out of his deep communion with the fighter's computers. Information that he would have just *known* at the deeper level now needed to be displayed, but this level made it easier to open up a communication channel.

"Unidentified freighter, this is CAP-One out of Dakota," he told the ship. There was no point in giving them *all* of the information, after all.

"You're not on our schedule, and the world has grown rather scary of late. Please identify yourself and report your cargo and recipients."

Two minutes of lightspeed lag. Anthony let the recording wing its way across the void and focused on bringing his fighter closer to the ship.

"Visual confirmation on the contact," Strøm told him. "*Sanderson*-class freighter. Thirty-nine-point-six million cubic meters, standard loaded mass fifteen megatons."

Standard didn't mean *maximum*, of course. But the standard existed for a reason, and the higher mass that Anthony was picking up meant that the freighter was burning almost twice as much fuel as they normally would. At Tier One acceleration, that was still ridiculously efficient to haul twenty-plus million tons around, but something still didn't sit right.

The stranger's response to his hail came after about three minutes, which seemed reasonable for a recorded message that had a two-minute round trip, and Anthony played it immediately.

A broad-shouldered blonde woman with the standard high-peaked white hat of the Terran Merchant Marine sat in the center of the *Sanderson*-class's semi-circular bridge. She was heavyset for a spacer, but her dark blue eyes were bright and focused as she stared at the camera.

"Dakota Patrol, this is Captain Kristel Kahler of the freighter *Storm-light*," she told him, blinking oddly. "We are en route from the Shogun System, carrying a mixed cargo of unrefined fissile material, transuranics and sublight spacecraft. I am transmitting my manifest."

That all sounded normal enough, except that the woman was changing the pattern of her blinking. Anthony had only been paying attention because it seemed odd...but now there was *definitely* a pattern to it.

"I'm not sure why we are unscheduled, everything should have been sent out before we left Shogun, but it may have been delayed and then lost when the coms went down." She paused. "Do you know what's going on, Dakota Patrol? Our q-coms went dark five days ago, and we've heard nothing from anyone since."

The people who'd been in FTL were going to have the strangest experience in all of this, Anthony knew. Anyone in a star system would have other people to talk to, to confirm that it wasn't just them. They'd know within hours, as a worst-case scenario, that the entire communications network was down.

A ship in FTL without q-coms was dark. No one could communicate with them to let them know what had happened. All they could do was continue on their voyage, hoping that their destination would still be there.

The message had ended with that information, and Anthony grimaced.

"How do we gently tell them it's the apocalypse?" Strøm asked.

"I have the distinct feeling that Captain Kahler may actually have a more immediate concern than the breakdown of interstellar communications, Lieutenant," Anthony admitted, replaying the message. He'd turned the sound off this time and was focusing on the woman's eyes.

Three swift blinks. Three longer blinks. Three short blinks. Pause. Three short blinks. Three long blinks. Three quick ones.

She'd got the sequence out three times in total during her message, probably silently praying all along that whoever got the message understood Morse code. Military officers *should*, but how many would have noticed a merchant captain blinking?

S. O. S.

Save our souls. The standard distress signal for almost a millennium. Captain Kahler was in trouble—and the trouble *had* to be on her ship. Trouble that was trying to sneak past a Commonwealth fighter patrol without being caught.

Suddenly, Anthony Yamamoto was very aware that he had a twenty-minute communication loop with his superior officers.

9

"CAPTAIN KAHLER, the situation across our Commonwealth is unfortunately quite dire," Anthony said into the camera, wracking his brain for options to divert the freighter away from Dakota. "A surprise attack by our enemies has taken out the entire quantum-entanglement communication network. Sector Fleet Dakota is maintaining a high security level in case there is a follow-up strike."

And *there* was his answer. He didn't know what was wrong aboard *Stormlight*, but the *last* thing he was going to do was let the ship get anywhere near Dakota.

"Given that security level, we are diverting all interstellar craft into holding patterns until we have a chance for a more-detailed inspection. I will have a course for you momentarily," Anthony promised, gesturing for Strøm to rig up *something* to give them.

"Several of my fighters will escort you into the holding pattern, and you will need to stand by for a Marine boarding party," he continued.

He was…oh, ninety percent sure that Admiral Tecumseh would back his play here.

Strøm dropped the course into his feed, and he glanced it over for half a second before sending it on. It would put the freighter five light-minutes from Dakota and the Sector Fleet. Charlie-E flight would be able to rendezvous with them with matched velocity, but the other wings—including Bravo-E and Anthony—would pass by at high relative velocity.

"Your course is attached. I expect you to follow it exactly," he said ominously. "Diversion from the assigned course will be regarded as a potential threat to Dakota. No offense, Captain, but it's not like your cargo needs to be delivered today."

He closed the camera and hit Transmit. He flipped his attention to an entirely new message, this one to *Saratoga.*

"SFD-Actual, this is SFD-CAG," he said swiftly, tagging that he was transmitting to Rear Admiral Tecumseh. "We have a new civilian ship in-system that is not on the schedule. The Captain is attempting to communicate that they are in distress, which I suspect means she has been boarded by hostiles.

"I have ordered her to divert to a holding pattern, claiming this is our current policy, and will require a Marine boarding team to meet her there."

He also needed the people in Dakota orbit not to have sent any messages to *Stormlight* that would undermine his story, but that was down to planning and luck. The plan had been for the fighters to handle initial contact, but bad luck could easily see some overeager civilian space traffic controller try to be helpful.

"Sir, we're radio silent for seventy seconds and she is not adjusting course," Strøm warned him. "What do you think is going on?"

"I'm not sure," Anthony admitted. His best guess was *someone* from the Stellar League, but that left a range of options from the low end of the League's condottieri mercenaries up to the personal elite special operatives of Dictator Periklos, the League's ruler.

The League was normally a chaotic mix of only nominally connected single-system states that used mercenary fleets to play out a formalized form of war to resolve their differences. Some of those condottieri were elite carrier groups, easily able to go up against their own weight in Commonwealth forces. Others were little better than pirates.

Dictator Periklos had been a condottieri Admiral until he turned his fleet on his employers and waged a war of conquest that had seen the whole League fall to him in under a year. Anthony didn't know enough about the League to know if that structure was going to survive long—but it *had* survived over a year of active warfare with the Commonwealth.

Shaking his head, Anthony adjusted the wing's course, bringing them in more tightly to a matched velocity. They were a *long* way from any useful range of the freighter—but there was no way *Stormlight* could evade his fighters, either.

"Bravo-B flight, Bravo-C Flight, Charlie-E Flight," he repeated, once again pinging those six fighters. "Redesignate CAP-One, activate linked tactical channel. Maintain intercept courses on *Stormlight* and begin forwarding full telemetry to my fighter."

He turned his attention to his gunner.

"Strøm, I need you to integrate everything we get," he told the junior officer. "I figure we've got a decent chance of someone making a run for it, and I want to see them go."

Hiding a ship under thrust was almost impossible. Hiding a ship with her engines dark at almost a full light-minute would be a lot easier—but with nine different sensor angles, they *should* be able to watch anyone try to sneak away.

"What about *Stormlight*?"

Anthony studied the vectors. His vector was at an angle to the freighter, but he was still closing with her at almost five percent of lightspeed. Decelerating to try to match course was a weird mess, but they still had almost ten minutes until missile range, let alone any kind of intercept.

"We've got lots of time to talk them down, I suppose," he said drily. "Keep an eye on everything."

He brought up the camera again.

"Captain Kahler, this is Dakota CAP-One," he reiterated. "You should have received a course by now for a holding zone several light-minutes from Dakota orbit. If you do not adjust course for that holding zone within five minutes, I will have no choice but to assume you represent a threat to the planet and fire to disable your vessel."

He suspected that even Kahler would know that he *couldn't* hit her at this range. Even with the velocity in play, his missiles only had a range of two and a half million kilometers. If he'd brought bombers, their torpedoes would have had the range—but Anthony wouldn't have trusted their AI to manage *disabling* a starship after a fifteen-million-kilometer flight.

They'd need to get a *lot* closer to disable *Stormlight*, and Anthony wasn't sure that was going to be healthy.

————

THEY WERE within seconds of Anthony's five-minute timeline when *Stormlight* finally changed course, vectoring toward the location she'd been given. A message from Captain Kahler arrived a few seconds later, the heavyset blonde's gaze now strangely unfocused.

Anthony didn't like the look of that. He was no doctor, but it appeared that Kahler was now stoned out of her mind on *something*, and that didn't jive at all with his initial impression of the merchant captain.

"Dakota Patrol, we are complying," she told him. Listening for it, Anthony could pick out the slur in her voice. Something seriously screwy was going on aboard *Stormlight*. "Apologies for the delay; we are having unexpected…" She trailed off, staring blankly into space for several seconds.

"Unexpected computer problems," she picked up again after the pause. "We had to…replace a data…relay."

The slurring was getting worse, and Anthony smiled coldly as he realized what she was doing. He suspected that she'd been injected with one of the modern versions of truth serums, a drug that would render the captain cooperative to her instructions.

But she had *enough* self-awareness to actively play into the side effects of the drug, drawing attention to them for anyone paying attention.

With the game she'd played with blinking earlier, Anthony was *definitely* paying attention.

"Anything else in her message?" he asked.

"I'm not seeing anything," Strøm told him. "Standard recorded protocols. She's on the course now, but…"

"But?" Anthony prodded.

"Wait one sec. I'm integrating data from the rest of CAP-One," the young gunner told him. "Something is… Got them!"

"Lieutenant?"

"Contact, multiple contacts," Strøm reported crisply. "Flagging to the network now. I have twelve contacts deployed using *Stormlight*'s base velocity. They are drifting along her original course, en route to Dakota."

"And right past us," Anthony said grimly as the icons for the new ships appeared on his screen. "What have we got, Strøm?"

"Unsure, but it looks like a modified Hoplite. Not, confirm, *not* a Xenophon," Strøm noted. "Not a Spartan, either."

The Hoplite was the League's sixth-generation fighter, one of the better examples of the generation due to being one of the *last* examples of the generation. The Xenophon, the League's brand-new seventh-generation fighter, was arguably a *superior* fighter to the Katana, but its edge was far slimmer than the Hoplite's had been over the Scimitar.

The Spartan, on the other hand, was a direct copy of the Commonwealth's Longbow—like every *other* first-generation bomber. That design landing in the hands of New Athens Armaments had been the biggest intelligence coup of the generation—or counterintelligence *disaster*, from the Commonwealth's perspective—and NAA had happily sold the design to everyone.

Hoplites, though… Those were fighters Anthony would take when outnumbered two-to-one. Except he was outnumbered *four* to one and flying with *Krakatoa*'s two most inexperienced flight crews on his wings.

Unfortunately, there was only one way rookie crews became veteran crews.

10

"CAP-ONE, THIS IS ACTUAL," Anthony addressed his impromptu formation. "Hostile fighters have deployed on a ballistic course for Dakota. They're probably at least as concerned about not being found by the Marines when *Stormlight* is boarded, but they're going to pass right by my wing."

None of the other formations from CAP-One were in position to help against the Stellar League Navy fighters, either.

"All wings are to maintain course to intercept *Stormlight* and give no indication that we have detected the fighters," he continued. "All evidence suggests SLN forces. I'll pass that on to the Marines, but they're a long way out from boarding."

Assuming that the Marines launched as soon as they received his message—and that each of the four capital ships in Dakota orbit had an assault shuttle on standby with a platoon aboard—they would take just over two hours to make a zero-velocity/zero-distance rendezvous with *Stormlight*.

The stealth fighters would reach missile range of Anthony's wing in less than ten minutes. Three minutes after that, they would pass him at about a hundred thousand kilometers. According to his warbook, that was inside lance range for a Katana versus a Hoplite—but well *outside* lance for a Hoplite firing on his people.

The League fighters had weaker lances and weaker electromagnetic deflectors than his fighters. The math was in his favor in a lance-range engagement. The problem was that twelve Hoplites had thirty-six missiles to his three Katanas' twelve and the League weapon was comparable.

"Charlie-E wing," he addressed his wing fighters. "Close up your position to five hundred klicks at one hundred by zero degrees. Make certain your defensive lasers are ready and stand by your ECM for my orders."

That would put his bird at the point of the spear, able to engage missiles targeted at his subordinates. It put *his* fighter at risk, but all he sensed in the onboard network was firm agreement from his own crew.

"They won't fire at maximum range," Strøm said. "They'll try to open up the distance if they can and hope to evade detection— Yeah, there they go. Cold-gas thrusters."

Expensive and a pain to maintain, cold-gas thrusters could combine with the same mass manipulators that enabled the fighter's main engines to provide a reasonable degree of thrust without being detected. They weren't invisible, but they at least weren't adding to the starfighter's heat signature.

"They've got a hundred-gravity side vector now," the gunner continued. "Assuming they maintain it until, say, five million kilometers...they'll add another sixty-five thousand klicks to our separation. They'll pass outside our lance range. But they can't think we're *that* blind."

"They're hoping we're local militia and that they can sneak past us," Anthony guessed. "I doubt they have a good opinion of our local system commands—though they'd know that even the locals would put their best in their Katanas."

Time. Time was everything. Without q-coms, the Sector Fleet would only be getting the update on his plan and the diversion of *Stormlight* now. Whatever happened with the starfighters would go down in the next fifteen minutes—and then whoever was aboard *Stormlight* would have plenty of time to work out what they were going to do about intercepting starfighters and Terran Commonwealth Marine Corps shuttles.

"Dial them in by passive," Anthony ordered. "Load in a missile for each fighter but prepare for rapid salvo."

He was relying on Strøm to manage all the launchers of the three fighters, but none of the other crews objected. Three on twelve weren't odds *anyone* wanted to play games during.

"Five minutes to missile range," Strøm reported. "They've cut all thrust. Closest approach will now be one hundred and sixty thousand kilometers."

"Fire at five hundred thousand kilometers," Anthony ordered. "Or in response to their shot. No games. These are League fighters and we are at war."

The *problem* was that time and distance weren't interplaying the same way for their enemy. Everything the starfighters saw would be relayed instantly to their companions on *Stormlight*. There was no way this op *didn't* have a League q-com, after all.

The moment Anthony Yamamoto opened fire, they'd know they'd been made. He was *reasonably* sure it had been supposed to be a sneak scout mission, one that he'd short-circuited the moment he'd ordered them into a holding pattern.

But the flip side of that was that the League knew everything *Stormlight* had seen. The range was too high for them to get much, but they'd probably picked out *Krakatoa*. The League had already garnered more intelligence from this op than Anthony preferred.

"Missile range," Strøm murmured. "No activity. Two minutes to designated range."

The fighter's cockpit was silent now. Badem wasn't physically present in the space with Anthony and Strøm, as their station was in a separate engineering control center. The pilot could still feel the engineer's tension as they babied electronic-warfare systems held at one step below ready.

The Hoplites remained silent, hurtling toward Dakota on a ballistic course Anthony could never let them complete. Even twelve unexpected fighters could devastate the orbital defenses if they got into missile range without being seen. That wasn't going to happen today; he wasn't going to give them the chance.

"Range is one million kilometers," Strøm reported. "No activity."

Even if the three Commonwealth fighters *hadn't* detected the Hoplites earlier, they would have picked them up by now. Every second the Hoplites closed now without firing was either desperation or arrogance—and given the reputation of the ex-condottieri who made up the SLN's elite force, both seemed just as likely.

"Thirty seconds to five hundred kay."

"Stand by all combat systems," Anthony ordered. There was *no way* the League fighters were expecting to whip past him at under two hundred thousand kilometers without being detected. That meant they had to be waiting for the moment of *obvious* detection when his people blasted them with active sensors.

"Can we launch without active scanners?" he murmured to Strøm.

"Yes, sir. We lose a bit of accuracy, but not much. Not with missiles at this range."

The missiles were smart enough to go their standard two-and-a-half-minute flight time without further guidance. They could handle a thirty-second flight with slightly less accuracy.

"Bring the sensors up *after* firing the first salvo," he ordered. "It may just buy us a few seconds."

The neural network made that change in plans a matter of a moment's thought—and then the Hoplites hit Anthony's designated line in space.

"Firing," Strøm said calmly. Twelve new icons flashed into existence on Anthony's display as the Javelin missiles blazed into space.

"Maneuvering," Anthony warned, yanking the fighter into a tight spiral "upward" from his original course. He'd been maintaining basic evasive maneuvers in his designated zone before, enough to throw off any long-range capital-ship fire but not enough for a close-range fighter engagement.

Plus, this one actually changed his vector. He was no longer decelerating toward *Stormlight* and was building a new vector perpendicular to that course. One that cut into the extra range the Hoplites had created to keep him out of lance range.

He didn't think he could bring them to range of that beam weapon, but he *did* think he could make them worry—and if they worried, they were focusing on his fighter and its onboard antimatter cannon. Not the missiles already flying at them.

"Enemy ECM live, enemy missiles launching," Badem reported from Engineering. "Eighteen seconds. Slow off the mark."

Too slow. The Commonwealth missiles only had a thirty-two-second flight time, and the Hoplites hadn't activated their electronic defenses for eighteen seconds. Anthony's Javelins already had their targets locked in—and the League missiles were launching into the teeth of his jamming.

"Enemy is evading; lasers are engaging our missiles," Strøm reported.

"Enemy missiles at twenty seconds; our lasers are engaging," Badem added a moment later.

Each of the three people on the fighter had a job. It was Strøm's job to make sure their missiles hit home and killed the enemy. Badem was tasked with managing their electronic-warfare suite and their own antimissile lasers.

Both were helping the inexperienced crews of the other two fighters, running a wing-wide network that linked all three fighters' missiles and lasers together.

Anthony's focus was both wider and narrower. His main focus was on the maneuvers of his own fighter, adding an extra layer of complexity to the enemy missiles' targeting solutions, but he was *also* watching the maneuvers of the other two fighters and guiding the entire formation's course closer to the enemy, even as he was paying attention to the geometry of the entire battlespace, as *Stormlight* headed toward her currently planned rendezvous with the Marines.

"Impact, impact, impact," Strøm chanted. "Seven targets down. Second salvo in the launchers, re-allocating, firing."

Seven kills with twelve missiles was *amazing*—but they weren't going to get that lucky again. On the other hand, there were only five League fighters left and Strøm's second salvo was in space before the League salvo reached them.

"Enemy salvo is on us," Badem reported grimly. "We're clear, we're clear—eleven leakers, trying to cover!"

Anthony flipped his fighter in space as soon as their second set of missiles were away, burning back toward his wing fighters for a precious few seconds to give Badem more time to engage the missiles chasing his inexperienced escorts.

It wasn't enough. Both fighters took direct hits, coming apart under the force of antimatter explosions large enough to gut capital ships.

But...

"Pods on the screens," Anthony reported, for his crew's benefit more than his. "I have both emergency pods on the scopes."

"And we have fifteen missiles headed *right* at us," Badem said grimly.

"Cover the escape pods," Anthony ordered. "Strøm? Kill. Those. Fighters."

With twelve missiles on five fighters, the odds were good that they'd get at least one kill. The problem was that all five enemy planes had fired on him and he didn't have two more fighters' worth of defenses now.

Anthony threw the fighter into full evasive maneuvers, dropping his wider focus as everything came down to the critical task of surviving the next thirty seconds.

"Impact, impact, impact," Strøm declared. "Three targets down, two remaining."

The missiles came crashing in toward the Katana, and Anthony considered the whole situation—and then flipped the entire fighter two hundred degrees in space, wildly accelerating on a completely new vector seconds before the remaining weapons would hit.

He held his breath, knowing that if the maneuver failed, he would never exhale...and then breathed out as the missiles flashed past him.

"Last salvo outbound," Strøm said. "Two targets left. They are maneuvering to open the range at maximum thrust."

"So are we," Anthony replied, looking at the six missiles chasing his fighter craft. "Pass their courses to Sector Fleet and the rest of CAP-One. They aren't going to sneak away tonight."

The missile clash between his three fighters and the Hoplites had been unavoidable, but the vectors weren't right for him to force a lance engagement with the remaining League fighters. Their last three missiles might get one of the Hoplites. They might not.

Either way, there'd be multiple *squadrons* waiting for the fighters if they got close to Dakota now—and they no longer had missiles. They did, unfortunately, still have sensors and q-coms, but Anthony couldn't do anything about that now.

"Track the escape pods, ours and theirs," he ordered. "Make sure *Krakatoa* and *Saratoga* search-and-rescue get the vectors. We'll pick up everyone we can."

"Sir...look at *Stormlight*," Strøm told him. "The hell?"

Anthony had expected the captured freighter to turn and run once the fighters were taken down. The only question in his mind was whether they'd attempt to rendezvous with the survivors of their fighter wing.

Instead, she'd just gone entirely dark. Not just her engines had shut down but her running lights, her power plants...*everything*. The answer to just *what* had happened was in space around them, as a growing halo of electrons and positrons created a brilliant light show around the freighter.

The CAG waited for a half-impatient, half-nervous few seconds as Badem took down their pursuing missiles with practiced skill, then pinged the engineer.

"Lieutenant, what's the boot-from-cold time for a *Sanderson*-class freighter if her Captain just ordered an emergency purge of the zero-point cells?"

"Three hours, maybe more," Badem replied instantly. They then processed the question and examined the data. "Remind me, sir, to buy Captain Kahler a drink."

"You're assuming she's still alive," Anthony said grimly. "Because she just *fucked* the League intelligence op here, and those guys aren't known for polite surrenders."

11

Dakota System
04:00 October 16, 2737 ESMDT

"STORMLIGHT, ARRIVING."

Four Marines in full powered combat armor led the way off the assault shuttle, a defensive screen against a nonexistent threat. A full honor guard of their comrades was waiting, snapping to perfect attention and saluting the limping woman who walked off the shuttle second.

Captain Kristel Kahler was accompanied by a TCMC medtech with their attention entirely focused on their charge, with several large emergency-treatment casts locked around her limbs as she boarded James Tecumseh's flagship.

James and his flag captain were waiting at the end of the honor guard, and both joined the Marines in saluting the woman. From the reports, she'd been beaten within an inch of her life by the League special forces operator who'd *thought* he'd had her under control—right up until the moment she'd scrammed every power-generation system on her freighter and left the ship on a ballistic course the Marines had had no problem intercepting.

"Welcome aboard *Saratoga*, Captain Kahler," James told her, offering the fair-colored merchant his hand. "I'm Rear Admiral James Tecumseh, CO, Sector Fleet Dakota. You've had a hell of a week and I hate to add to it, but we need to debrief you before we lock you in sickbay for a week."

"I wasn't expecting the honor guard," she replied. "I *was* expecting the debrief. My people?"

"We're shipping your injured down to the surface, to the Tall Tree Healing Camp," James assured her. "They don't necessarily have *better* equipment than my people do, but they definitely have *more* of it—and more doctors."

"…'Healing camp,' Admiral?" she asked carefully.

"Welcome to Dakota, Captain," James said with a chuckle. "They do things their way, but trust me: Tall Tree is the best-equipped hospital in the sector. Your people will be fine. There were no…new fatalities during the boarding."

"Seventeen of my people died when those bastards took my ship in the first place," she said with a sigh. "And I know your Marines lost people. I'm sorry, Admiral."

"I will pass that on to Major Amundsen," he told her. Major Emmerich Amundsen was the commander of the company that had boarded *Stormlight* and taken her away from the special forces unit that had taken her over. "It always hurts to lose our people, Captain, but we recognize the cause we serve."

"Captain Kahler should sit down as soon as possible," the medic interrupted before anyone could say anything else. That was a prerogative James was more than willing to allow the man. "She is not in as good shape as she is pretending to be."

James hadn't been under the impression that Captain Kahler was pretending to be in particularly good shape at *all*, so that was a meaningful warning. He gestured for Captain Bardakçı to lead the way to the designated meeting room.

———

THE MEDIC HELPED Kahler into a seat, visibly pausing to check the civilian's readings through her neural implant, then stepped back to stand against the unadorned wall of the standard military meeting room.

A steward poured coffee and James took a seat. Commander Dubhain stepped in from the other door, bringing the number of officers in the room to three.

"Commodore Bevan is coordinating the prisoners with the Marines," she murmured to James. "He figured you'd be all right with that. So did I," she added.

James nodded silently. Admiral Banks had given his staff a surprising amount of leeway to run their areas of responsibility. So far, James hadn't had any choice but to allow the Sector Fleet staff to run things as they wanted.

They'd move everyone aboard *Krakatoa* shortly. Then things would end up more the way he preferred, but for now… Well, this was a logical split between his two staff intelligence officers.

"It'll do," he told Dubhain. "Grab a seat and a coffee."

He turned to their guest.

"Do you need anything more, Captain Kahler?" he asked. "*Saratoga*'s steward staff can get you just about anything."

"Three days' sleep and seventeen dead friends back," Kahler said bitterly. "I don't think your crew can do either of those before this meeting."

"No, sadly," he conceded.

There was a momentary pause, then James shrugged.

"As I believe you've realized, the entire Commonwealth q-com network is down," he told her. "Our enemies in the Rimward Marches sucker-punched us. The consequences have barely begun to shake themselves out, but for now, Sector Fleet Dakota has zero communication with Central Command.

"Any security risk created by your…unwanted passengers is going to end up being my responsibility."

"I understand," she said quietly. "What do you need to know from me?"

"If you can give us a rundown of the events that led to you being in

Dakota, I'd appreciate that," James told her. "With the network down, I can't definitely say where you were supposed to be, after all."

She nodded.

"Despite what I told your people when we arrived, we didn't come from Shogun," she told him. "Our last port of call was the Lulu System, on the far side of the Meridian Sector. Forty light-years from here."

Lulu, according to the files James pulled as she spoke, was regarded as part of the "front line" with the Stellar League. There were no warships positioned in the system at his last report, but there had been significant reinforcements to the in-system defenses.

"We were delivering in-system mining ships built in Tau Ceti and picking up raw ore for shipment to the refineries at Meridian," Kahler told them. "Half our cargo was standard sublight clippers meant for Meridian as well.

"Unfortunately, it turned out that our 'raw ore' came with some surprises," she continued. "Including a Stellar League spy ship and a squadron of stealth fighters. We'd barely brought up the A-S drive before I had commandos in my bridge and engineering sections."

She shook her head.

"They had us sublight and redirecting within twenty-four hours. I guess they already knew everything they wanted to about Meridian, because they brought us here. Given how completely *we* missed them hiding in the cargo, they've probably taken that ship through Meridian a couple of times."

"That's something we'll probably want to let Admiral Washington know," James said. "Make a note for when we send a data package to him," he instructed Dubhain.

Vice Admiral Pontius Washington commanded Sector Fleet Meridian, though given that the Meridian Sector edged onto the Clockward Marches territory of Marshal Amandine, he'd seen most of his ships stripped away for the war against the League.

"There's not much else to say," Kahler admitted. "It was probably the most unpleasant two weeks of my life, and it *started* with them killing a fifth of my crew when we tried to resist. You saw the results of our attempts to be clever. They worked in the end."

"They did," James agreed. "Dubhain, did we manage to take the spy ship intact?"

"We did," the intelligence officer confirmed. "They purged her books and burned any physical files, and she's sublight only. Not much use to us, but we do have her."

"Just the hardware gives us insight," James replied. "Thank you, Captain Kahler. Your 'attempts to be clever' prevented the League from getting perfect insight into the strength of Sector Fleet Dakota in a time period when I have no ability to request reinforcements or do anything complicated.

"The Commonwealth is in your debt. We'll see your ship repaired and your people treated before we send you on your way," he promised.

After the last week, he'd take the wins he could get—and this could have been a *lot* worse!

12

Dakota System
14:00 October 20, 2737 ESMDT

DESCENDING into the city of Tááła'í'tsin, James could see what had led the Navajo crew of the first explorer ship to decide that *this* world, of all the ones they and the rest of the survey ships had visited, was sacred and should be a new home for many of the ancient Nations of Earth.

At some point, the volcano above the valley where Tááła'í'tsin— One Tree or Lonely Tree—now sat had erupted. The northern side of the volcano had been hit with pyroclast and lava, but the southern side had *merely* seen an absolutely immense rock and mudslide.

A single Dakotan greatwood tree of what had to have been a good-sized forest had survived. When the survey ship had visited in the late twenty-third century, that tree had stood alone in a field of devastation —and stood almost six hundred meters tall.

Forests of Dakotan greatwood across the planet were carefully managed and nurtured by Dakota's new people, but the Lone Tree of

Táála'í'tsin was the single tallest known specimen, now towering just over a kilometer high and almost a hundred and fifty meters around the base.

In the rubble beneath the shadow of that tree, the Confederacy had built their first settlement, a sprawling low-slung city intermingled with smaller trees, bushes and farms. At the very southern end was the only part of the city that looked "modern" to James's Earth-trained eye, a spaceport large enough to handle significant sublight ships, built on the site of the first landing.

Interfaced with the shuttle taking him down to the surface, he could see the parts of Táála'í'tsin that were *not* obvious through the spacecraft's sensors. It was just as energy-dense as any modern city in the Commonwealth, drawing vast quantities of electricity from a geothermal plant that also served the dual purpose of reducing the likelihood that Grandfather Mountain would blow his top again.

The city might look different on the surface, but it was a fascinating hybrid of hyper-modern technology and incredibly ancient cultures and values, cultures preserved against destruction by a mix of fluke and sheer bloody stubbornness.

For every culture represented in the Dakota Confederacy, after all, there was an aboriginal nation that had died under the boots of its conquerors. James tried not to think too hard about the comparison between *that* and the missions he had taken on as an officer of the Terran Commonwealth Navy.

"First Chief Chapulin's people have confirmed there is transport waiting at the spaceport," his pilot told him. "They're asking if you need additional security?"

James glanced around his shuttle. He had two staff officers with him: Mac Cléirich, the Sector Fleet's chief of staff; and Dubhain, *his* intelligence officer—but he also had six Marines, and he hadn't been given any choice about them.

The Terran Commonwealth Marine Corps was attached to its Navy responsibilities, but the level of protectiveness they were giving *him* still bothered him at times. He was going to have to pin Colonel Sarah Vroomen down on that at some point.

For now, though, it meant that he had six heavily armed nurse-maids and did *not* need more.

"The offer from the First Chief's office is appreciated, but the TCMC appears to have it in hand," he said calmly. "Let them know we'll be fine, and I look forward to meeting the Chief in person."

If he'd been in command of the Sector Fleet for the entire five months he'd been in Dakota, not having met the head of the planetary government would have been a major faux pas—but as a subordinate flag officer, it hadn't been urgent and there'd always been *something* going on before he'd suddenly ended up as the Sector Fleet Commander.

Now he was in command and there was no one else to interface with the civilians for him. He'd managed to get the number of Commonwealth Sector Directors he needed to talk to down to five… but even they were going to wait until *after* he'd met the First Chief.

It was her planet he had a fleet in orbit of, after all.

———

THE TWO LOW-SLUNG cars that met them at the landing pad were even quieter than most electric vehicles James was used to. The entire city of Táálá'í'tsin was quieter than he was used to, once the echoes of the shuttle's engines faded away.

A young woman with long red hair with feathers braided through it was waiting next to the safety barrier to lead them to the vehicles, with several more people scattered around the vehicles and through the spaceport.

There *were* customs and security checkpoints, but the Navy officers' companions easily ushered them past the neatly uniformed personnel there. James may have declined a security detail, but he could tell that the team scattered through the spaceport wore both the traditional hairstyles of Navajo warriors—*and* extremely modern body armor under their severely cut civilian suits.

Their guide's suit was of the latest style from Terra, but she was also wearing body armor and a shoulder holster.

"I am Abey Todacheeney," the redheaded official introduced herself. "I am First Chief Chapulin's personal secretary."

"And the security detail?" James murmured as they reached the cars.

"Assembly Watch," Todacheeney said crisply. "Security personnel that report to the Confederacy's Assembly of Nations. They're responsible for the security of all of the Chiefs, including the First Chiefs."

And if having the personal security of the Chiefs of the various nations reporting to the planetary assembly wasn't explicitly part of the subtle power balance structure of the Confederacy, James would eat his sash.

"Of course," he agreed. "We shouldn't keep the First Chief waiting."

———

QUETZALLI CHAPULIN WAS a pale-skinned woman for the Nahuatl Nation, though much of that was from a life spent in space and power armor. Like most Marines and ex-Marines James had known, she had a distinct set of permanent indents at the top of her cheekbones, where power-armor helmets pressed on the face to secure them in place.

In person, she was even *more* drowned under the regalia of her role and station, the headdress clearly having been carefully structured to link on to her waist to avoid dragging on the ground.

Still, she offered James Tecumseh a delicately boned hand and gestured him to a seat at a clearly hand-carved table. The First Chief's house was surprisingly small, but everything in the two rooms James had seen had been handmade, from the furniture to the wall hangings whose delicate patterns spoke to a part of his soul he rarely heard.

Todacheeney took a seat at Chapulin's right hand, the two locals facing James and his pair of staff officers across the table like they were expecting a negotiation.

"Welcome to the surface of Dakota, Admiral, Captain, Commander," Chapulin told them. "Captain Mac Cléirich and my staff had dealt with each other quite a bit before this crisis, but we've all become quite familiar with each other's recorded faces over the last ten days."

"I would apologize for not meeting you in person sooner," James agreed, "but given the last ten days, I believe you'll understand."

"It's been interesting," the First Chief said. "I understand your people ended up dealing with a League spy ship?"

"We did," he confirmed. "We didn't learn anything particularly surprising from the prisoners we managed to take, though. The League has been running a series of covert scouting operations across the entire front. Captain Kahler is braver than most of the captains they've captured, and it ended poorly for *this* scout crew."

"So, there are other ships serving the same purpose?" Todacheeney asked, the Nahuatl secretary looking disturbed at the thought.

"At least three," Dubhain confirmed quietly. "Their operational information security is solid, though, so we don't know *what* ships. We've included that information in the next set of data packages to go out, but we haven't even had a full round-trip communication with Gothic yet."

James now knew what had been going on in the Gothic system on October tenth when everything had come apart, as *Mediterranean* had arrived three days earlier. They'd seen at least one ship from post–network collapse from four of the Sector's six systems, but Shogun and Desdemona were ten days away.

He *should* have seen *Valiant* and *Arctic* by now if they'd received the recall order via q-com. Their absence now meant he didn't expect to see them until the end of the month.

"We have no communication from Sol, of course," Chapulin said calmly. "One ship arrived from Sol yesterday, but she left in September."

"And that is going to be our situation for a while," James told her. "The manufacture of entangled particles is entirely outside my realm of expertise, but I'm told it will be months before we have any."

"I don't know anything about it either," the First Chief agreed. "Ms. Todacheeney, on the other hand, has dual degrees in interstellar commerce and interstellar network engineering. Could you fill the Admiral and his staff in on what you briefed the core council about?"

The redheaded secretary nodded and smiled thinly.

"Bluntly, Admiral, you may be underestimating how long it will take," she warned. "Manufacturing communication-grade entangled particles requires zero gravity and some very complicated equipment.

"The *entirety* of the Commonwealth's coms-grade entangled-particle production took place on our switchboard stations," she continued. "That was part of why the switchboard stations were in space—combined with the fact that there is a clear degradation risk for entangled particles in a gravity well."

"I know we keep the ones aboard our ships in zero gravity," James murmured. "I hadn't realized that was that important."

"Increases the expected lifetime of the particle pair about fifteen-fold," Todacheeney confirmed. "Hence the inherent vulnerability of the switchboard stations. No one really thought of them as military targets, though. In hindsight, that was a failure of imagination on the TCN's part."

James coughed but didn't argue. She wasn't wrong, after all.

"But we not only need to rebuild the *switchboard* network, we need to rebuild the manufacturing facilities for entangled pairs in the first place," the secretary concluded. "And then the particle blocks need to be taken to their destinations.

"Even assuming that Terra has entangled-particle production online in, say, six months, it will be a minimum of a month before they could get enough entangled particles here for even a handful of megabits' worth of bandwidth."

"Which wouldn't handle video calls, let alone tactical telemetry or the amount of information normally flowing through the network," James assessed. "And even that is assuming they didn't focus their entangled blocks on systems closer to home."

"Exactly."

"The answer is a homegrown solution," Chapulin told him. "The Confederacy possesses the technology and knowledge necessary to assemble our own entangled-particle production facility and switchboards. We have traditionally used the overall Commonwealth network because it was cheaper and easier."

The Commonwealth network of q-com switchboard stations had only expanded when the Star Chamber or the Navy had put money behind building new stations. Otherwise, economies of scale had always led to the expansion of the individual stations.

A sovereign single-system nation might absorb those costs to control their own communications, but the Commonwealth was one nation, one entity. Sharing a communication network had made sense and saved vast amounts of money.

"That assessment has changed," James said.

"Exactly," the First Chief agreed. "The Assembly has put together an investigation team to talk to our industrial and scientific groups. My preference, always, is to assemble a cooperative venture of several of our operating groups and support it fiscally from the Assembly.

"Assistance from the TCN would be appreciated, of course."

"Chief Chapulin, we would be delighted to provide any technical or monetary assistance the Sector Fleet has access to," he told her cheerfully. "Of course, the price is that *we* will need access to a significant portion of the entangled-particle blocks as they come available, for both strategic and tactical communication."

He shook his head.

"Our engagement with the stealth fighters from that spy ship drove home to my team and myself just how dependent much of our doctrine and operational policy is on faster-than-light communications," he admitted. "Our first priority must be to reestablish coms with Sol and the rest of the Dakota Sector, but the ability to have near-real-time views of most of a star system cannot be undervalued."

"Even from a political and economic perspective, we would like to be able to talk to Virginia," Chapulin said. "And that's just in *this* star system!"

There was something in her tone that James couldn't recognize. Was there something about Virginia he didn't know? He wasn't going to admit ignorance in this meeting, but he resolved to look into it.

"Give it another two weeks or so and we should have a solid network of freighters acting as postal couriers to keep the Sector interlinked," James said. "I think a twenty-day turnaround is probably the longest anyone would tolerate for civil or military communications on a regular basis, which means we're basically going to be running the Commonwealth government for the Dakota Sector from here."

Ten days to Shogun or Desdemona, ten days back. The other three systems were closer, but those two set the limits of the sector. Some Commonwealth sectors would have shorter time loops—Meridian, for example, would have their longest loop at fifteen days—but none would be much longer.

"Do we have any idea how that is going to work?" Todacheeney asked.

"That's my *next* meeting," James said with a chuckle. "The problem is that the sectors are purely administrative structures. The federal agencies all have central sector offices here in Dakota, but they report back to Sol.

"There was never a central sector authority. Now we need to create one, and that's going to take some time and require buy-in from the sector's planetary governments like the Confederacy."

He shrugged.

"And everyone seems to regard the TCN as the 'first among equals' of federal Commonwealth organizations, so all of the regional office heads want to talk to *me*."

"That, I suspect, makes you the effective regional governor until we sort out something more long-term," Chapulin pointed out, her tone sharp.

"That's been my conclusion as well," James admitted. "Which means I'm going to be doing everything I can to sort out that 'something more long-term!' No soldier should be giving civilians orders on that scale!"

Chapulin grunted in what sounded like relief.

"That's fair," she said. "We both have more meetings today, Admiral. Should we get to the discussion of just what Sector Fleet Dakota is going to need in terms of immediate logistics?"

13

Dakota System
12:00 October 31, 2737 ESMDT

"CONTACT on the Shogun approach line. Multiple A-S emergences."

"Understood," Anthony Yamamoto said, pulling the data into his own feed from his wing pilot's report. "I make it three?"

"I have the same," Navin Strøm reported. "I also make the timing right, sir."

"Do we have an IFF?" Anthony asked. His fighter was once again on the extended patrol as flights of two fighters moved around the perimeter of the system. With *Mediterranean* in the system, he was up to five full squadrons running those patrols, a bit more than a seventh of his total fighter strength.

He *also* had two more squadrons of fighters flying top cover for two ready squadrons of bombers—and five squadrons of Dakota Confederacy fighters flying high guard over the planet itself.

"No IFF yet, sir," Strøm replied. "I'm resolving as three contacts. One thirty-million-cubic-meter, two forty-million-cubic-meter."

They were *expecting* a forty-million-cubic-meter freighter, sent from Dakota on October eleventh, plus a thirty-million-cubic-meter strike cruiser. The *Ocean*-class strike cruisers were, in Anthony's opinion, a classic case of "jack of all trades, master of none" *and* small for their age.

Like the *Assassin*-class battlecruisers, they'd been born of an era of *economizing* on the part of the TCN—before someone had finally pointed out that building starships smaller than the largest you could saved you almost nothing. The A-S drive was so much of the cost of a starship that making a smaller ship barely made any difference at all.

But the *Ocean*s fielded sixty starfighters and a dozen missile launchers and were FTL-capable starships. Anthony mostly cared about the first number, especially since Sector Fleet Dakota's *Ocean*s carried two squadrons of bombers apiece.

"Can we validate that we're looking at *Arctic*?" he asked. "Our lives are easier if one of those freighters is *Blackbird*, much as Captain Kos wanted to cause trouble for us before!"

"One of *Saratoga*'s flights is closer," Strøm told him. "Should we relay?"

Anthony checked which of the officers was in command and silently grimaced. He didn't know Major Aina Romão, *Saratoga*'s Bravo-Two Squadron CO, at all. On the other hand, better a Major in position to make the first contact than one of the more junior pilots.

"Let Major Romão know I need IFF confirmation ASAP," he told his gunner. "I suspect she'll already have it by the time she gets our message, but that's the game, isn't it?"

He was just over three light-minutes from the emergence point of the three Alcubierre-Stetson-drive starships. Romão and her flight were only forty light-seconds from the emergence—and just over two and a half light-minutes from Anthony. She'd have time for multiple full back-and-forth messages with the new ships before his request for identification reached her.

"Message on its wa— *Contact*. Multiple contacts at forty-six light-seconds!"

Anthony was on the scanners before Strøm finished reporting. This was only two contacts, but they weren't on any of the routes he was expecting, and there was an ugly spike of radiation from one of them.

"Do you see what I see, Baden?" he asked.

"One of the ships has a partial exterior Stetson failure," the engineer confirmed. "Looks like the internal fields held, but they knew they had a problem and they diverted their course to make sure nothing was in the danger zone."

"Which, of course, put them on top of us," Anthony muttered.

An Alcubierre drive swept up a lot of particles and energy as it warped space. The amount of energy trapped in the warp field was, quite literally, cataclysmic. It was only the Stetson stabilization fields that made the drive useful. The interior fields protected the starship itself from that energy warp—but the *exterior* fields prevented that energy warp being unleashed in a wavefront of destruction that could take out a planet.

Given some of humanity's darker proclivities, Anthony was quietly grateful that you needed both for either to work—and that some of the other fail-safes were so inbuilt to the drives that no one really knew how to *remove* them now.

"Equivalent to a three-hundred-teraton energy release," Strøm said grimly. "Angle is well away from anything—planets, ships, patrols."

"Good," Anthony replied. "Please tell me that wasn't *Valiant* or *Arctic*."

As he scanned the data, it looked like both of the new contacts were the right size to be the *Resolute*-class battleship.

"IFF coming in from *Valiant*," the gunner reported a second later. "Captain Mašek's people are *also* sending a request for emergency assistance for *Garnet Hopeful*. Fifty-million-cubic-meter freighter, assuming that all fifty million of her is *left* after that."

"We'll see," Anthony replied. "I'm setting a course to take the flight out to help. I think all we can do is tow *Garnet Hopeful* to meet the rescue craft the Admiral will send, but that may save her an hour or two."

It was turning into a busy day—busy enough that he almost missed Major Romão's message.

"CAG, this is Romão," she greeted him swiftly. "Confirming that our Shogun-origin friend is *Arctic*. Her companions are *Blackbird*, under Captain Kos—as expected—and *Faerie Fire,* a TCN collier from the Clockward March Fleet.

"*Fire* is carrying dispatches from Marshal Amandine."

So, Sector Fleet Dakota was assembled at last—but if the Marshal of the Clockward Marches had orders for them, that might not last!

14

Dakota System
20:00 October 31, 2737 ESMDT

"MY DISPATCHES ARE for Admiral Banks, sir, but I understand that you're the Acting Commanding Officer of Sector Fleet Dakota," Captain Valli Ivov's recorded image told James. "We won't be stopping for long, but I will remain in-system to receive any dispatches you have for Sol.

"I stopped at Meridian on the way, so they are fully updated as well," she continued. "From here, I'm making a straight run to Sol, where I expect to deliver my dispatches and hopefully pick up a new load of missiles and other supplies for the Clockward Fleet."

According to the information James was reviewing as he watched Ivov's recorded message, the reason *Faerie Fire* had been selected was that the collier was basically down to bare walls. Commander Ivov— given the usual courtesy promotion to Captain while she commanded the logistics ship—had been responsible for supplying the Clockward

Marches Fleet through the debacle that had been the punitive expedition into the New Edmonton System of the League.

The collier had carried missiles, spare parts, even entire crated spare fighters and bombers. Thirty million cubic meters of supplies in total, expended over the course of a six-month battle that had ended in ignominious retreat.

If Captain Ivov felt perturbed by that failure, it didn't show in her fair coloring. She was clearly far more worried about the network collapse—which made sense. So was James at this point.

"Full details of Marshal Amandine's agreements and plans are in the dispatches for Admiral Banks," Ivov told him. "The summary, though, is that we had access to captured League q-coms when the network collapsed.

"While they aren't linked to anything we can use to talk to *Sol*, the Marshal was able to use them to talk to Periklos. She is suing for peace under her own authority and has arranged a peace conference."

James nodded to himself. He was alone in his office on *Saratoga*, though his chiefs of staff would be reviewing the dispatches as well. His office was almost as bare-walled as *Faerie Fire* at the moment, with most of his personal effects being moved over to *Krakatoa*.

He'd officially transfer his flag at midnight. *Faerie Fire*'s timing was inconvenient, but that was life. It had taken them over two weeks to find the *time* to move and consolidate James and his staff.

"If the timing worked as it was planned on the thirteenth, Marshal Amandine is meeting with Star Admiral Peppi Borgogni tomorrow," Ivov continued. "It will take some time for news to percolate from that meeting. I *am* supposed to advise you—well, Banks, but I guess you now—that there is a cease-fire in place."

He shook his head and chuckled. In theory, he supposed Yamamoto opening fire on the stealth fighters without warning them was potentially a violation of the cease-fire. On the other hand, he was *quite certain* that sneaking starfighters and spy ships into a system over forty light-years from the farthest Clockward Commonwealth systems *was* a violation of the cease-fire.

"Hopefully, Walkingstick has been as wise," Ivov said grimly, a statement that was well above the authority of a junior O-five commanding a logistics ship. "If we can shut down our wars, I think we'll have a chance to get all of this sorted out."

She saluted crisply.

"As I said, all details are in Marshal Amandine's dispatches, sir," she repeated. "I will remain in the Dakota System for one hour to receive any dispatches you have for Terra, then *Faerie Fire* will be on her way."

The message ended and James leaned forward onto the desk. That was standard-issue and wouldn't be moving to *Krakatoa*. There was an identical newer desk waiting for him on the heavy carrier.

He *could* shortstop Captain Ivov's ship, commandeering her to act as a logistics support ship for Sector Fleet Dakota. It wouldn't even be particularly hard to justify, as he was slowly building a regular communications loop with all of the systems he needed to talk to, including Sol, and he *didn't* have a proper military logistics collier.

If *Fire*'s mission had been even slightly different, he might have been tempted. But Sol needed to know that Amandine was negotiating peace. It would hopefully be as much of a relief for them as it was for *him*.

He'd received no updates from Sol since the network collapse. Captain Maradona's *Encarnación* would only have arrived in Sol that day. Even if a ship had been sent from Sol the day the network collapsed, they would have only arrived just then—and the last data *he* had said that Sol had been heavily beset by Alliance ships on the tenth.

No, *Faerie Fire* needed to complete her mission. Both halves, even, though he doubted Captain Ivov would find many supplies in Sol right now.

Activating his recorder, he assembled his best commanding and sympathetic smile.

"Captain Ivov, I appreciate the summary of your dispatches," he told the young woman. "I'll have my staff forward our latest set of dispatches for Sol to you along with this message. I do want to confirm, however, if you have any dispatches from Admiral Ferrara in the Meridian System?"

———

JAMES REVIEWED the reports on his new arrivals aboard the shuttle. The work never really stopped, and *Garnet Hopeful*'s spectacular entrance had certainly drawn everyone's attention.

Thankfully, it appeared that the ship's interior Stetson field had remained fully stable throughout. While the exterior field failure had been spectacular, the captain's adjustment of her course at the last minute, combined with the standard fail-safe measures, had prevented any damage to anyone else.

Dakota's shipyards would be easily able to handle *Garnet*'s repairs. Her captain's last minute maneuver had been impressive—but James was actually *more* impressed by *Valiant*'s command crew. Identifying that another ship *existed* outside your own Alcubierre bubble was hard enough. Realizing that said ship was maneuvering differently from expected was even more difficult.

To identify *Garnet Hopeful*'s maneuver and then *match it perfectly* without any ability to talk to *Garnet* was the work of absolute virtuosos, and James's report on the incident already reflected that. If *Garnet* had emerged in greater distress than she had, those officers' reaction would have saved lives.

As it was, those officers weren't going to be collecting any medals for it, but they *had* earned the distinct attention and respect of the Sector Fleet's acting commander.

They hopefully wouldn't need those skills, with seven capital ships assembled in Dakota orbit, but even as everything appeared to be going *right*, part of James found him just waiting for the other shoe to drop. Something was going to go wrong.

The Alliance of Free Stars didn't appear to have followed up their sucker punch with a death blow. Not *yet*, anyway. Unless the Star Chamber was destroyed, though, James was certain the Commonwealth was going to sue for peace with the Alliance.

His nation had lost the war, and yet James couldn't quite bring himself to regret it. For all of the blood and treasure the Commonwealth regularly poured out in pursuit of unity, he himself was more focused on his nation's *first* three principles—the principles of freedom, democracy and justice he was all too aware were often sacrificed in that pursuit.

And sometimes the price was just too damned high.

"Sir?" The copilot stepped back into the passenger compartment, reminding James that he was completely alone on this shuttle. His staff was taking the *originally* scheduled shuttle over to *Krakatoa*.

"We're on final approach to *Adamant*, and Captain Zubizarreta is asking if she needs to lay in a shore party," the very junior officer told James, his voice unsteady.

He wasn't surprised at the poor man's discomfort. No junior-grade Lieutenant wanted to get caught between a Rear Admiral and a Commodore, and James hadn't announced this trip in advance.

"No. Let Captain Zubizarreta know that I'll be visiting sickbay and then heading on to *Krakatoa*," he told the young man. "I can make some time for her, but I'm coming aboard to meet with Admiral Banks."

His conversation with Captain Ivov had reminded him of a duty he should have discharged weeks earlier.

15

Dakota System
23:00 October 31, 2737 ESMDT

"I'LL NEED you to surrender your sidearm, Admiral."

James paused at the doctor's words, taken aback for a moment—not least because he didn't always consciously remember that he was *wearing* a sidearm. The five-millimeter caseless automatic was as much a part of the uniform as a weapon, as far as he was concerned.

So much so that he chuckled as he unclipped the holster.

"It isn't loaded, Doctor," he admitted. Even holstered, though, he checked the safety before handing the weapon over. "But he's that bad?"

Tihomir Piccoli was an older military surgeon with starkly salt-and-pepper hair and visible dark liver spots on his face. He didn't answer James's question initially, standing back to survey the Admiral from head to toe.

"Full suicide watch," he finally confirmed. "I assume I can trust you to keep your belt on, Admiral?"

"Of course," James said. The inherent silliness of the request was offset by just how serious the situation had to be for that to even be a *thought*. "*That* bad?"

"I can't give him any cutlery at all, Admiral. He tried to choke himself to death on a spoon, for stars' sake." Piccoli shook his head grimly. "I've seen a lot of broken men and women in my time, Admiral. We *can* help him back from the edge, but he isn't just staring into the abyss at this point.

"In terms of keeping him safe, we'd be better off keeping him fully sedated. That won't help him heal, though, and he's no danger to anyone else so far."

"I see. Thank you, Doctor," James said. "I feel like I should have been here sooner."

"Frankly, Admiral Tecumseh? It doesn't matter," Piccoli told him. "You're irrelevant to him. We all are. He lost his entire family three weeks ago. Nothing else matters to him yet."

"How long until it does?" James asked.

"I don't know. Months. Maybe years. I'm just counting out the days before I'm required to medically retire him," Piccoli admitted. "If he's still completely mentally compromised after eight weeks, I have to Article Fifty-Six him and transfer him to a civilian facility. TCN remains responsible for his care as long as he's alive, but he'll no longer be a serving officer."

"In some ways, that would make my life easier," James admitted. "But I'll be damned if I'd wish that on him."

"He needs the best care in the galaxy, and he will *get* it," Piccoli stated. "Whether it's aboard *Adamant* or in Táála'í'tsin or sent home to Leviticus, he will get the care he needs. That's part of the deal the TCN gives our people—whatever injuries they acquire in the service, they get taken care of."

"I know," James agreed quietly. "May I go in?"

"Be careful," the doctor ordered. "He hasn't been a threat to anyone else so far but… Well, he's only seen nurses and myself since the tenth. He may react poorly to you. We are watching."

"Thank you."

VICE ADMIRAL GABRIEL BANKS looked worse than James had ever seen him.

To be fair, they'd only worked together for six months, and James had never truly seen the other man distressed. Still, in everything he *had* seen, Banks had been perfectly turned out. His uniforms had been impeccable, his platinum-blond hair shining, the works.

Now Banks wore plain scrubs and sat on a mattress on the floor of the sickbay room. Other than the mattress, the room was completely empty, though between implants and audio commands, Banks would be able to access any entertainment he wanted.

According to James's implants, the other man wasn't accessing anything. He was just sitting there, slowly yanking tufts of his hair out, staring at them, then tossing them on the ground.

"Hi, James," he said before the junior Admiral could speak. "Surprised you got here so quickly."

"So quickly?" James asked. "I was about to apologize for taking so long."

He was worried for a moment that the other man had lost his sense of time.

"Don't worry, James; my sense of time is fine," Banks told him. His voice wasn't calm so much as...toneless. "I am also aware of how much work you inherited from me."

There was a long pause, then Banks made a noise that could have been called a chuckle. If James was being generous about the toneless sound, anyway.

"I don't much *care*," Banks admitted. "That's a *this world* problem, and this world has no real appeal left to me except for ways out. I don't know what you want from me, James, but you're not getting it."

"I don't know if I want anything from you," James said. "I owed it to you to be here, to make sure you were okay."

"'Okay,' he says." Banks laughed dully. "Leave a gun behind, James Tecumseh, and I might be okay again. But I don't think you have it in you to do what I need to be 'okay.'"

The sheer calm with which Banks spoke of ending his own life sent chills down James's spine.

"I *won't* do that," he told the other man. "Not can't. Won't. They can fix this, you know. You need time to heal."

"I never realized just how arrogant it was that our doctors assume they know what's best for us," Banks replied. "My family is in the next world. All I want to do is join them. But they won't let me and neither will you.

"And if you're not going to help me leave this bullshit behind, I have nothing to say to you, James. Go. Deal with the petty concerns of a world that no longer matters to me."

There was no fire or conviction in Gabriel Banks's voice. Just the flat monotony of a man to whom *everything* was meaningless now.

Somehow, that made James even more certain that the man meant it.

————

"I BELIEVED YOU," James told Piccoli as the door slid shut behind him. "I just didn't...understand."

"I don't think it's possible to understand the state of a man like Banks until you've seen it," the doctor replied. "And there was a chance that you, as a fellow Admiral and the man he dumped *everything* on, could get through to him.

"I figured it was worth the attempt."

"I don't think I changed his mind about anything," James said quietly. "That was...eerie."

"Give him time, Admiral Tecumseh," Piccoli said. "We've helped people come back from worse, but yes. This is a *very* bad case. My oaths say I will heal what can be healed—and my knowledge says he can be healed."

The doctor shook his head.

"Sometimes, though, I wonder if it would be better to let him go. That's not *allowed*, thankfully, which makes the decision easier." He smiled thinly.

"I appreciate that you came, Admiral Tecumseh, even if Admiral

Banks shows no gratitude," he told James. "The Admiral is as much a wounded soldier as an amputee. We need to care for our wounded."

James smiled and sharply tapped his left arm with his right hand at a specific angle. Under most circumstances, there was no way for anyone other than him to tell that his arms were prosthetics. That angle and impact, though, brought *just* enough of a metal-on-metal thud through for it to be obvious to a doctor.

"I know," he told Piccoli. "But the work remains. I need to finish transferring to *Krakatoa*, but…this was the best chance I was going to get."

"The work does remain," the doctor agreed. "Mine is to heal Admiral Banks. Yours is to heal the Commonwealth."

"*Protect* the Commonwealth," James corrected with a laugh. "*Healing* it is for wiser souls than I. It is not a soldier's job to *fix* their country. Only to hold it together so smarter people can."

"That too, Admiral, is part of surgery."

16

Dakota System
00:05 November 1, 2737 ESMDT

THE FORMAL TRANSITION of the Admiral's flag took place at midnight, the transition between October and November. Thanks to James's detour to *Adamant* and a confusion over routing prioritization between the shuttle he was on and the shuttle he was *actually* on, that formal transition took place with James and his entire staff *both* stuck in space as the flight directors tried to correct for the error...and ended up keeping everyone in space longer.

Still, James made it down onto *Krakatoa*'s flight deck only a few minutes later than planned. The implant networks were already set up to acknowledge him, and he was being fed information on the entire seven-ship strength of Sector Fleet Dakota, plus the orbital platforms of Dakota's security forces.

That transfer of information flow was more important than the ceremony, but there was still a small crowd waiting for him as he debarked from the shuttle. A double file of Marines formed an aisle to where Captain/Commodore Young Volkov stood at the head of *Krakatoa*'s senior officers.

She was flanked by her XO and her CAG. James had been working with Colonel Yamamoto as Fleet CAG for two weeks now, but he didn't know Commander Jack at all. The other officers were all unknown to him, though his implant filled in the names and ranks of the senior officers as he approached.

The surprise extra, though, dressed in a slim-fitted black suit with traditional feathers in her hair, was Abey Todacheeney. Unlike the officers, she didn't even try to salute. She just waited respectfully as James walked between the honor guard and returned Captain Volkov's salute.

"Welcome aboard *Krakatoa*, Rear Admiral Tecumseh," Volkov greeted him formally. "All systems record your flag transferred. My crew and I are honored to host Sector Fleet Dakota Command."

The original plan, after all, had been for *Krakatoa* to take *Saratoga*'s place at the center of the Fleet's main nodal force. Which cruiser or battleship would have accompanied the heavy carrier hadn't been decided yet, but while she would have *Tecumseh*'s flagship, she wouldn't have been Sector Fleet Dakota's flagship.

"I look forward to getting settled in with your crew," James told her. "These are certainly interesting times, but I have every expectation that *Krakatoa*'s officers, pilots and spacers will rise to the challenge before us."

"We will do our best," Volkov confirmed. "May I present my officers, sir?"

"Normally, I'd introduce mine, but they are delayed and... Well, frankly, you know them all already," James allowed with a smile. A lot of his people had been splitting their time between *Krakatoa* and *Saratoga* of late.

The rest had been splitting their time between *Krakatoa* and *Adamant*. James still had a full double set of staff officers—and, given the chaos he was dealing with, he was in no rush to change that!

The formalities with Volkov's officers took a few minutes, until they reached Todacheeney at the end of the line. She beamed at James, looking like the proverbial Cheshire cat.

"I believe you know Ms. Todacheeney," Captain Volkov told James. James shook the Navajo woman's hand and returned her smile.

"I do, though I wonder just what brings her aboard my new flagship," he admitted.

"I've been coordinating a surprise with Chief Leeuwenhoek and Captain Volkov," Todacheeney replied. "And the First Chief wanted someone here who could send her a video of your face when we spring it on you."

"Generally, most people find surprising Admirals to be a bad idea," James warned carefully.

"It seemed harmless enough to me," Volkov told him. "Trust us, sir, when we say that *Krakatoa*'s crew and your steward had only your best interests in mind.

"And that said, I believe that Ms. Todacheeney and I should escort you to your office."

James knew when he'd been trapped and nodded. Just what had the Dakotans got up to while he wasn't looking?

––––––––

JAMES BEGAN to suspect just what had been done when he saw that the nameplate on his door had been adorned with a recreation of an art piece he recognized as originally by Gibson Byrd, one of the famed artists of the Shawnee people.

When the door slid open, his suspicions were confirmed. James had been a military officer his entire adult life and had his last flagship stolen out from underneath him by a treacherous ally. He generally kept his offices relatively unadorned, mostly sticking to the standard-issue Terran Commonwealth Navy furniture.

It appeared that First Chief Chapulin had decided that was insufficient. The desk in the middle of the room was hand-carved wood with a distinct wave pattern burned into the top and covered in varnish. The desk responded to his implants in the same way the Navy-issue furniture would have, so the artist or artists had concealed modern technology in the traditional carving.

Hangings done in the Shawnee ktapif oowe style decorated the walls. Not all of them, of course—one wall was a fully operational screen, easily accessed from his implants and currently showing a stylized rotating globe of Dakota—but most.

The corners still held the traditional flags of the Commonwealth and the Commonwealth Navy, but even those cloths hung from hand-carved poles marked with similar water patterns to the desk.

"Stars," he whispered.

"Everything was made by Shawnee artisans on Dakota," Todacheeney told him. "First Chief Chapulin reached out to Chief Methoataske. She sends her regards to you, specifically, and also helped us source the right items and craftspeople."

"Shawnee on Earth and Shawnee on Dakota have diverged a bit, but not enough to rob this of one drop of meaning," James said in a choked voice, struggling with emotion as he stepped up to the desk and ran his fingers over the surface.

There had been plenty of furniture like this in the small town he'd grown up in, but none of it in his adult life. Everything about what they'd done to his office brought back memories of his childhood, and he realized he was actually crying.

"As I said, sir, we had only your best interests in mind," Volkov told him. "Your Chief Leeuwenhoek will be here in a moment, and I'll leave you two to her."

"We'll have work to do in the morning," James warned. What the Dakotans had done—what his Shawnee cousins had done!—was heartwarming, but it didn't change his job.

"Oh, I know, sir," Volkov agreed. "I believe Commodore Voclain has you scheduled for a big fun meeting over your new table of organization for eight hundred hours sharp."

That process was never going to go smoothly, and James wasn't entirely happy that he'd had to accept Voclain as his chief of staff as the senior member of the two teams, but that was the job.

"I hope what we have done may make your tasks a bit easier, Admiral," Todacheeney told him. "You...have not seen all of it yet, after all."

———

AFTER THE OFFICE, James was less surprised at the degree to which First Chief Chapulin's staff had, with the full cooperation of his steward, completely redone the Admiral's quarters on *Krakatoa*. He *was*, however, still stunned by the sheer *scale* of the Admiral's quarters.

His living room slash reception area was the size of the entire Captain's quarters on his last command—and *that* had been a modern *Saint*-class battleship! There was an attached private mess easily able to handle his doubled staff-officer contingent—or the normal staff contingent *plus* all of *Krakatoa*'s senior officers.

And the entirety of both rooms had been redone by the Shawnee artisans Chapulin had recruited. Someone had clearly given an interior designer the full specifications—probably even a three-dimensional model—of the quarters, and that designer had run with it.

None of it was overwhelming. James's previous lack of personal belongings had clearly been taken as a sign of austere tastes rather than having lost everything with his first flagship. They weren't *entirely* wrong on that front, though, and the careful selection of hand-made furniture and wall hangings felt just right.

"I am in awe," he told Todacheeney. "How did you sneak this past me?"

That question was addressed more at Chief Leeuwenhoek, his personal steward, who currently looked entirely unconcerned about the Admiral's potential wrath.

"You weren't on *Krakatoa*," Leeuwenhoek pointed out. "I had a blank check with *Krakatoa*'s steward staff to do whatever I needed to prep things for you, and the Captain brought Ms. Todacheeney's suggestion to me directly. So, I knew I had *her* approval."

James chuckled and took a seat, testing the comfort of the couches. As expected, they were about perfect.

"Thank you," he told both women. "Chief, I think I can manage to find the bedroom on my own. Any surprises I should be aware of?"

"Ms. Todacheeney and her artists have at least one piece in every room," Leeuwenhoek told him. "But I don't think there will be too many shocks."

"'Every room,'" James echoed. "How big *are* these quarters?"

"You have a second office, a private seating area, your sleeping quarters and personal bath, and a semi-private sauna and hot tub space."

"I think I may be at risk of becoming spoiled," he admitted.

"He has a *hot tub*?" Todacheeney asked. "I should have brought a swimsuit!"

"Another time, perhaps," the Chief suggested. "If you don't need me, sir, I'll take off for the night?"

"I'll need breakfast at oh seven thirty, before Voclain's meeting," James warned. "So yes, go rest, Chief. You need it as much as the rest of us."

The Chief saluted and bowed herself out, leaving James alone with the First Chief's secretary.

"This can't have been cheap," he said, still in awe as he looked around.

"Chief Leeuwenhoek gave us her entire budget for redecorating this space, which was generous," Todacheeney noted. "The First Chief's office pitched in a bit extra to help out our local artists and show support for you.

"Forgive us our cynicism, Admiral, but we have every reason to want you emotionally attached to Dakota!"

"That's fair," he conceded. "I suspect you will find this wasn't necessary for that." He waved around him. "Duty would be enough to keep you all very safe."

He sighed and yawned.

"And on that note, duty also requires that I get my own rest. I hope the Chief put you up for quarters?"

"Of course," Todacheeney said quickly. Too quickly. James realized something might have just flown *right* over his head...but if it had, that was probably safer for today.

"Then I bid you good night, Ms. Todacheeney," he told her.

17

Dakota System
08:00 November 1, 2737 ESMDT

ANTHONY YAMAMOTO HAD NEVER ATTENDED a fleet staff meeting for his new formation in person before. With Rear Admiral Tecumseh based off of *Saratoga*, the Fleet CAG had hologrammed into each meeting previously.

Now the oversized combined staff plus him had taken over a meeting room near the flag deck. Eleven officers were scattered through the space, waiting for the Admiral to arrive.

Anthony had met all of them virtually and about a third in person. Still, it was an awkward transition to seeing them all in person, and he took up his usual post of looming next to one of the doors.

It took him a moment to realize that Commander Dubhain had mirrored his position right next to him. He turned a level gaze on the Black intelligence officer, and she grinned at him.

"Put on all the show you want, Colonel," she whispered. "Some of us see *right* through you."

He didn't have time to respond before the door slid open and Admiral Tecumseh walked through.

"At ease," Tecumseh ordered as they all snapped to attention. "Take your seats, people."

Anthony followed his usual stance of standing behind his chair as everyone else sat, leaving him eventually as the only one standing as Tecumseh turned a long, calm look on him.

The Admiral didn't seem bothered by his standing. Just...amused?

"I hope *Krakatoa* has found everyone comfortable places," Tecumseh finally said. "I know Colonel Yamamoto is clearly comfortable here. Is there something I don't know about the chairs, Colonel?"

"No, sir," Anthony said crisply. "I just prefer to stand."

"As you wish," the Admiral allowed. He picked up a cup of coffee and took a long sip before continuing.

Anthony knew *he* still had problems doing that with every eye in the room on him. The Admiral seemed completely unperturbed by the attention.

"Officers, it's been twenty-two days since the world ended," Tecumseh continued, putting his coffee down. "We've relocated here to *Krakatoa* and, for the first time, have the combined staff of both Sector Fleet Dakota and what was Task Group Dakota-One in one place.

"I've spent my spare moments over the last three weeks considering how we were going to handle this," he admitted. "While, frankly, I am more comfortable with my existing staff, we cannot justify giving up the resources of the combined staff and Commodore Voclain, and the rest of you from the Fleet staff are both senior and know more about the total Sector Fleet situation."

That was probably more honesty than the Sector Fleet staff officers really *wanted*, Anthony knew. No one wanted to be told that your boss would rather have put you under the command of a junior he knew better than you.

"We're also in the position of having consolidated all of Sector Fleet Dakota's ships in one place," Tecumseh said. "For an extended period, one of the options I was considering was re-establishing Task Group Dakota-One under one of our Commodores."

Splitting off the lighter carrier and one of the other capital ships made some logical sense, Anthony supposed, but it also struck him as risky.

"Colonel Yamamoto."

Anthony jerked as the Admiral called on him, managing *not* to flush in embarrassment at his visible surprise.

"Yes, sir?" he asked carefully.

"This may perhaps be unfair," Tecumseh said calmly, "but are you aware of the generally accepted strategic mistake made by Admiral Isoroku Yamamoto and the Imperial Japanese Navy between the Battles of Pearl Harbor and Midway?"

Anthony paused, thinking carefully. He'd studied all three of his famous ancestors—two more Yamamotos in his direct line had served with historical distinction in space fleets over the intervening eight centuries, after all—but Isoroku was still the most known. Especially to carrier officers.

"He divided Kidō Butai, sir," Anthony said, carefully accentuating his Scots burr. "By splitting his carrier force, he allowed the USA to disable or destroy several carriers prior to Midway, evening the odds for the decisive encounter with Admiral Nimitz's task forces."

"Exactly," Tecumseh replied. "Thank you."

The Admiral turned to everyone else.

"For those of you who, like me, are not carrier officers and perhaps have not studied the Pacific War in the detail an officer like Colonel Yamamoto has," he said, "at the start of the Pacific War component of World War Two in the twentieth century, Kidō Butai was the IJN's First Air Fleet and represented the single largest, most technologically advanced and operationally capable carrier force in the world.

"But the commanders of Kidō Butai allowed themselves to be talked into sending a single division of carriers to support another operation, resulting in that division being disabled as a combat component of the First Air Fleet."

Tecumseh smiled thinly.

"There were, in the judgment of history, two types of targets available to the IJN: targets worthy of the full power of Kidō Butai and targets not worth deploying the carriers at all," he noted. "We are in a similar position.

"Either we will face a threat that justifies the full deployment of Sector Fleet Dakota, or there will be no reason to deploy the Sector Fleet," Tecumseh said. "I do not expect to see multiple threats against the Dakota Sector, and therefore I intend to respond to any potential threat with the full strength of this Sector Fleet."

He shrugged.

"Since that means I don't have anything else to do with you, Madona, I'm afraid you're stuck as my chief of staff," he told Commodore Voclain. "A full table of organization is being transferred to all of your implants, but the basic structure is that Dakota-One's staff officers are now the Sector Fleet staff's senior deputies.

"I expect you all to work in a collaborative manner, though I also expect Dakota-One's former officers to refrain from telling tales out of school unless there is a real problem," he concluded.

"And Vice Admiral Banks?" Commodore Bevan asked.

Anthony had been wondering the same thing. Running with a temporarily combined staff was one thing, but the organization tables he'd just received—and instantly processed, fighter-pilot-implant bandwidths were useful for that—were a very permanent change.

"It is not my place to break the confidences of the Admiral's medical condition," Tecumseh said quietly. "But my discussions with Dr. Piccoli are such that we have no expectation of his return to duty in a timely fashion."

Tecumseh lied like a tapestry: badly and clearly put to the wrong use. "Not in a timely fashion" meant *never*. Anthony could read that out of the man. Calm as the new Sector Fleet commander was, he was more honest than was probably healthy for his new job.

And Anthony doubted he was the only officer in the room who read the true meaning of Tecumseh's words. If anything, he guessed he understood the *least* amount of what the Admiral had just said.

He only knew that Rear Admiral James Tecumseh had written his superior off. The rest of the staff, unlike Anthony, clearly knew more about just what had seen Vice Admiral Banks medically relieved of duty.

18

Dakota System
10:00 November 6, 2737 ESMDT

ONE OF THE requests included in the dispatches that James had sent to every world in the Dakota Sector had been for each planetary government to send a representative to Dakota to discuss the setup of an interim sector-level governance.

Every key federal-level department of the Commonwealth government, from Inter-System Trade to Infrastructure to the Terran Commonwealth Navy itself, was represented on Dakota. But they were purely administrative centers, their authority and instructions delegated from Earth.

The Commonwealth's structure, at a fundamental ideological level, allowed for no barriers or friction between the planetary governments and the central government on Earth. The reality of a forty-day communication loop *created* that friction.

It wasn't James Tecumseh's responsibility to slice through the Gordian knot of conflicting bureaucracy, ideology and reality. Whether he liked it or not, however, he had the *effective* authority to say "send me people to sort this out" and have it obeyed.

Thankfully, none of the planetary governments had argued. Given that both Shogun and Desdemona had an almost-twenty-day round trip for communications now, any argument would have taken a *very* long time.

As it was, most of the representatives had arrived several days after the return of the freighters carrying his messages, riding on different ships. The Dakota Sector was rich enough that there was enough traffic to make that possible, which was part of the logic behind using the civilian transports as postal couriers in the first place.

The Desdemonan representative had arrived the night before, and James now found himself with the unenviable task of playing master of ceremonies to half a dozen high-powered politicians.

"Hold still," Abey Todacheeney told him cheerfully, adjusting the red sash of his formal uniform carefully. Her fingers lingered on his shoulder for a few seconds after she seemed to accept the cloth's position.

"Are you ready, Admiral? You seem a bit uncomfortable with this."

"I didn't make it to flag officer by completely ignoring politics, Miz Todacheeney," James told her. "But there is a large gap between playing nice with the occasional senator and knowing what to say when hauled before a senate committee, and finding the right words to convince the leaders of six star systems that we need to technically *violate the Constitution* to maintain continuity of government and preserve the Commonwealth!"

"Please, Admiral, call me Abey," she requested. "Everyone here knows that something has to change, at least temporarily, to keep the people we're responsible for taken care of and safe. You just need to point them all in the right direction."

"Then I must insist you call me James," he replied. First-name basis with the First Chief's secretary was safe enough, he figured. They were going to be working together for a long time.

"And I know," he conceded. "We're all on much the same page, I think, but I am a military officer. It's beaten into us, quite early on, that the Commonwealth military answers to our civilian government. We can give advice if asked, but we are ultimately and always responsible to the elected representatives of the people of the Commonwealth."

Todacheeney chuckled, but there was a nervous tone to it.

"How many Sector Fleet commanders do you think are going to fail in that charge?" she asked.

"Too many," James sighed. He didn't like to think about it, but he could see that taking direct control of the administration he was midwifing could make his life—and a lot of other people's lives!—easier in the short-term.

"One would be too many, though," he continued. "And I cannot speak to the integrities and failures thereof of officers I have never met. I can only speak to my *own* integrity. I am not perfect—but I *will not* be a warlord."

"Then, James, you need to walk into that room and tell *them* that," she told him. "Because even some of those politicians will argue that you taking control as a military governor is a reasonable option. Some will think it's just a decent short-term option—but others will see a chance to hitch their fates to yours and play kingmaker."

"I hope that none of our leaders are that desperate or that lost," he murmured. "But if they are, I will convince them otherwise. It is my job to *protect* the Dakota Sector, not rule it."

He snorted.

"I wouldn't even know where to *begin* with ruling it!"

———

NONE of the other five planets of the Dakota Sector had been able to spare their heads of government, which gave First Chief Chapulin an unquestioned precedence among the leaders present at James's conference.

That put her right in the center of the audience, her regalia helping her take up just as much space as the representative from Shogun to her left, who appeared to be a sumo wrestler.

A quick check of James's implant confirmed that Sanada Chō, currently minister without portfolio, had been the Shogun planetary sumo wrestling champion three years running before he'd become the Minister of Sports and Entertainment several years earlier.

Shogun's Prime Minister had clearly changed his role to send him there. While Sanada might officially have no portfolio, that was because it was impolitic for a Commonwealth member world to have a Minister for Foreign Affairs.

That piece of trivia carried James across the stage and to the lectern in the center, emblazoned with the spiral galaxy of the Terran Commonwealth.

"Ministers, secretaries, directors, First Chief Chapulin," he greeted them all. There were at least two hundred assorted dignitaries, negotiators and other team members in the room behind their leaders, but the front row was the people with plenipotentiary authority for their planets and the directors of the Commonwealth federal offices on Dakota.

Or whatever they were calling it. Like Sanada's "minister without portfolio" title, the worlds of the Dakota Sector would dance around the fact that these people had the power to commit their planets. As member systems of the Commonwealth, they weren't supposed to *have* interstellar politics.

But the world had changed, and James spread his hands.

"I am Rear Admiral James Tecumseh, Acting Commanding Officer of Sector Fleet Dakota for the Terran Commonwealth Navy," he told them. "In that role, I technically report to TCN Central Command on Ceres in the Sol System."

He let that sink in.

"As the Commonwealth has traditionally been structured, I actually have quite limited authority of my own," he continued. "I am expected to validate many of my decisions with Central Command. In exchange, of course, I also expect to have access to the analysis departments and other resources of Central Command to help me make those decisions."

He gestured towards the bureaucrats at one side of the hall.

"The directors present from our federal departments are in a similar boat," he reminded everyone. "Their authority and resources were all structured around the assumption that they could speak to their head office in Sol on a moment's notice.

"The entire structure of the Commonwealth is based around organizations like the Navy and the assorted federal departments being organized top-down from Sol. Director Haines, for example"—he gestured to a Hispanic woman in the front row—"is responsible for Commonwealth infrastructure spending and maintenance in the entire Dakota Sector, but she reports to a senior director on Mars.

"That official reports to a deputy secretary, who reports to the Secretary of Infrastructure, who reports to the Star Chamber of the Commonwealth," James laid out. "It is only through your planetary senators on Earth that you have any chain of command over Director Haines. That sequence of communication and authority *works*...when we have instantaneous communication with Sol and effectively no bandwidth limitations."

He wasn't telling anyone anything they didn't know, but it was necessary to lay out the groundwork. The Commonwealth Constitution didn't *quite* forbid the existence of a middle level of government. There was at least one multi-star-system semi-autonomous zone that had been absorbed into the Commonwealth as a unit, after all.

The Constitution *did*, though, mandate that Senators spoke directly for individual planets and that the Star Chamber could only pass legislation that affected *either* the entire Commonwealth or the individual planets thereof.

"Right now, Arroyo has a thirty-nine-day communication loop with Sol," James concluded, gesturing to the faded Black woman sent to speak for that system. "Dakota has a forty-day loop. Shogun is at forty-five.

"Inside the Dakota Sector, the longest loop is just under twenty days. That is, in my opinion, reasonable to operate a government with. A forty-day loop is long enough to render any short-term responsibility of a central government impossible. A delegation of power and responsibility to a more local mid-tier government is absolutely essential.

"Some of that was already inevitable because those communication loops were always our travel times," he noted. "And that, representatives, is why Sector Fleet Dakota and the Dakota Sector federal offices exist."

His audience was being surprisingly quiet. He'd expected to be challenged at least once so far—and he realized grimly that everything he'd said so far could be read as building up to him declaring a military dictatorship.

"It is by similar logic," he said, "that I have concentrated Sector Fleet Dakota here in Dakota and activated Commonwealth Security Protocol Twenty-Six in all of your systems. While I don't expect to be drawing on your system defense forces for more than fighter crews and perhaps munitions, we needed an unquestionable local authority.

"As the military commander responsible for the Dakota Sector, protecting your star systems from potential threats is my problem," he told them. "That put me in a position to be in contact with all of you and suggest that this conference be gathered and an interim sector government be established."

James could *hear* the inhalations across the room as everyone waited for him to drop the other shoe.

"It is most definitely *not* my responsibility to decide what form that interim government should take or, indeed, to even be involved in it," he told them all. "*That*, representatives, is up to you.

"Democracy. Freedom. Justice. Unity," he reiterated. "The ideals of our Commonwealth. We are in a dark time and our unity is threatened, but as a soldier of the Commonwealth, it is my duty to uphold all four pillars of our society, not merely our unity.

"I look to you to sort this out and to be as patient as you can. There is a great deal of work to do to put together even the most temporary of governance structures—and that, my friends, is the task I lay upon *you*."

————

JAMES WASN'T CONVINCED that he was needed for the next part of the conference, but a seat had been put aside for him next to Abey Todacheeney and it would be impolitic for him to abandon the representatives of the six star systems he was responsible for.

"Everyone gets ten minutes to make their pitch," Todacheeney told him by implant coms as Sanada Chō took careful steps up onto the stage.

The Shogun Minister was absolutely immense, but James knew enough about the type of build the man had cultivated to expect the delicate grace he moved with. There was an absolutely ridiculous amount of muscle concealed under the bulk the ex-sumo wrestler carried.

"First, I must thank the esteemed Tecumseh for his foresight in calling this meeting," Sanada began after his introduction. "I do not believe it would have occurred to most of our governments to attempt to restructure our systems and sector until we started to have problems —yet the simple fact that none of us have had a round-trip communication with Sol in almost thirty days tells us the problems to come."

He shook his head.

"Speaking for Shogun and Prime Minister Huỳnh, our analysis suggests that it will be some time before our communications are restored to the level necessary for a return to the status quo ante. We must not only make short-term plans for the next few months but medium-term plans for the next two to three *years*—understanding that those medium-term structures may prove difficult or impossible to dismantle when the time comes.

"As the good Admiral-san did, I must point to the founding principles that underly our Constitution and our nation: Democracy. Freedom. Justice. Unity." The big man raised his hands, palms upward. "We must stand for all of our principles—more so, perhaps, in a crisis than ever."

The rest of his speech was similar. As the first speaker after James himself, Sanada was long on *principles* and short on detailed suggestions—beyond a very clear position that any unelected government could only be a caretaker and should last no more than a few months.

The Arroyo representative was the next speaker, the mixed-race woman clearly nodding respectfully to Sanada as she stepped up to the lectern.

"I am Patience Abiodun," she introduced herself calmly. "First

Minister to Governor Noyabrina Hoxha."

"Hoxha is the head of government on Arroyo," Todacheeney updated James. *"Abiodun is his senior subordinate, though. They couldn't have sent anyone more senior without sending Hoxha himself."*

James's implant databases had told him that much, but he appreciated Todacheeney's updates. There were subtleties that no information database could convey, subtleties that the First Chief's secretary probably knew.

Among those subtleties, he was starting to realize, was just how much power was involved in being the "secretary" to the First Chief of the Dakota Confederacy.

"Both Rear Admiral Tecumseh and Minister Sanada have spoken in depth to the principles of our Commonwealth," Abiodun said. "I wish to neither undermine nor undervalue those principles, my fellow representatives, but I find I must be the voice of pragmatism here.

"This is a time of chaos. We have seen before us today an Admiral who is determined not to abuse the position he finds himself in, but we all know that not all of our Commonwealth's Admirals are quite as principled as Admiral Tecumseh.

"We will face warlordism around our systems. A resurgence of piracy, as the Navy can no longer respond instantly to a call for help. We are not, my fellows, as far from the war with the Stellar League as we would like.

"A strong central executive is required to defend our systems," Abiodun concluded. "And while my friend Sanada and Admiral Tecumseh have ignored it, there is a structure in place under our Constitution for exactly such a power structure.

"While clearly there is more discussion to be had, I feel it is within the power of our governments to declare Rear Admiral James Tecumseh Marshal of the Dakota Sector, with all of the power and responsibilities of that role."

James shivered. He couldn't help himself. He'd served directly under Marshal James Walkingstick, the man charged with defeating the Alliance of Free Stars and bringing the Rimward Marches into the Commonwealth. The amount of authority Walkingstick had in any successfully conquered system was insane.

A Marshal was a complete dictator, only limited by the geography of the area of their command, who answered to the Star Chamber of the Interstellar Congress of the Terran Commonwealth—and *only* the Star Chamber. Given the communication loop, that declaration would make James Tecumseh the absolute ruler of about sixteen billion humans.

It would make him the military dictator of the Dakota Sector, and he was absolutely *certain* it was the wrong solution.

———

FOUR MORE REPRESENTATIVES, one for each system, got up to speak in turn. Chapulin spoke last and, thankfully, joined a majority of the representatives in arguing against using the Marshal role to stand in for an elected Sector government.

When Chapulin took her seat, James rose again. He wasn't on the schedule, but Director Haines saw him stand and stopped her own approach to the stage.

He met the bureaucrat's gaze and she nodded, gesturing for him to precede her.

James stepped up to the lectern again and surveyed the gathered leadership.

"Thank you, Director Haines, for giving me a chance to speak again," he told the Commonwealth official, then very specifically met Patience Abiodun's gaze.

"I feel that I *must* speak to the option that was raised by several of the prior speakers," he continued softly. "It would be a failure in my duty to you and to your constituents to remain silent."

He hadn't prepared this part, so he paused and swallowed as he mustered his thoughts.

"I understand the temptation for a strong central authority," he finally said. "And I agree with Ms. Abiodun that the role of Marshal is the only existing structure we have for a regional authority. But...to risk a fallacy of slippery slopes, that role places too much power and too much temptation for one person in this circumstance.

"It is a position created for military conquest," he reminded them.

"We can debate the ethics and flaws of its very existence, but we must understand what it exists for. It was not created to govern but to *control*."

He took a moment to breathe and think before continuing.

"Even laying aside that the role is not intended to act as long-term governance, we must also remember that it is a *military* role. I do not feel that we should voluntarily surrender the concept of civilian control of the Commonwealth's armed forces in the absence of the most dire need.

"We have time, people," he reminded them. "Time to build a better solution. Were there an invasion fleet on our doorstep, and all the systems of the Dakota Sector needed to turn their resources to our common defense in a desperate struggle for our survival, I would *listen* to the argument.

"But there is no such invasion and no such struggle. To quote a man in a similar position, a man with many flaws that are often forgotten for the service he gave, 'If nominated, I will not run. If elected, I will not serve.'"

There'd been quiet conversation throughout the room when he'd stepped up to the lectern, but the space was silent again as he looked over them. Most of the reps in the front row looked thoughtful at worst. Abiodun, interestingly, was all but grinning at him.

Someone, it seemed, had intentionally set up a straw man for him to knock down.

"There is one last piece to this I must say," he said quietly as he realized there was a way he could make *absolutely* sure the path of dictatorship ended here. "A statement, a decision that takes upon myself certain authority I arguably do not have.

"I will not surrender authority over Sector Fleet Dakota to a regional government I regard as illegitimate," he told them, keeping his voice level and calm as he laid down his ultimatum. "I will not permit either a military or civil dictatorship over your people.

"As the commander of Sector Fleet Dakota, I am tasked to protect this sector's people from all enemies, external and internal. I will defend their freedoms and their rights to the death. I look to the members of this conference to do the same."

19

Dakota System
14:00 November 6, 2737 ESMDT

THE DAKOTA SECTOR governance conference broke late for lunch, which was the first point at which James saw it as being politic to leave. He'd dropped several bombshells, but the discussions had turned in the appropriate direction afterward.

"So, Admiral, think you made your point?" Todacheeney asked him as they stepped out into the brilliant sun of Tááła'í'tsin's afternoon. The city's daylight hours didn't quite align with the standardized time based on Earth's old systems—if nothing else, Dakota had a twenty-two-hour-and-forty-three-minute day—but it was close enough right now.

"I hope so," James said. "We do not serve our citizens if we break the ideals that we promised them we'd keep. Your representatives speak for elected governments. I can only hope we come to an acceptable agreement."

"Are you the final arbiter of 'acceptable,' then?" she murmured, gesturing for him to follow her toward a park bench.

Most of Táála'í'tsin was divided by small rows and plots of greenery, and the conference center was no different. Todacheeney's indicated spot was shaded by several smaller versions of the Dakotan greatwood that towered over the entire city and tucked against a set of pale pink rose bushes.

"No. The people of the sector are the final arbiter of 'acceptable,'" James told her as he took a seat next to her, breathing in the scent of the roses. "The Star Chamber, Congress, will probably weigh in sooner. I... am just setting ground rules."

"*No dictators* seems like a pretty basic rule. I like it," she told him, sitting close enough on the bench that her leg touched his. "It also works quite powerfully, coming from the man most of us would default to *making* dictator."

"Banks might have taken you up on it, if his family had lived," James murmured. "I might be doing him a disservice, but I think he could have justified it to himself. I can't."

"It may still be necessary," Todacheeney warned. "We're assuming we're safe, but if the sectors around us descend into chaos and their sector fleets turned to banditry and conquest..."

"I cannot see enough officers of the TCN falling far enough for us to reach that level of desperation," he told her. "I have *some* faith in my fellow Admirals. I fear some will fail in the face in temptation, but I think most will rise to the occasion.

"As will our civilian counterparts." He gestured back toward the conference center. "As everyone is doing in there. I don't think my push was as needed as I feared. This conference will produce something useful, something that may end up providing enough value that you choose to keep it when we get things fixed up."

"The world is certainly changing," Todacheeney allowed. "After today, Chapulin will mostly be out of the conference and leaving it to me. I do have this afternoon somewhat free, though."

"'Secretary,' huh?" James said with a chuckle. "You'll speak for her at something of this much importance?"

"Not all titles mean what they sound like on the surface," the redheaded woman next to him admitted. "I'm more of a deputy or chief aide than secretary, but we're used to it."

He chuckled.

"Up with 'Acting Commanding Officer,' I suppose," he said. "I should probably get back to my shuttle if I'm not needed here anymore. An Admiral's work is never done."

"Already?" she asked. James wasn't sure, but it felt like her leg was suddenly even *more* pressed against him. "Surely, you can take some time? For, say, lunch at least?"

"We've got a joint exercise going on with the Sector Fleet starfighters and the Confederacy wings," James told her. "I probably shouldn't have spent as much time down here as I did, but making sure the conference got off on the right foot was important."

"Your loss, I suppose," she said with a chuckle. "Someday, James, you're going to have to relax."

"Not soon," he told her. "Not while we all have work to do!"

"I'll call you a car," she promised. "It'll take a few minutes; you may as well sit and enjoy the roses."

Suddenly, she was on her feet, looking down at him. "I'll let them know where to find you."

As she walked away, James realized that he was, quite likely, an idiot.

But he hadn't been lying about the work, either.

20

Dakota System
18:00 November 9, 2737 ESMDT

"Sɪʀ, we have a new contact in the system, freighter coming from counter-clockward," Ferreiro reported.

James looked up from the report he was reading—a summary of the day's meetings and main discussions at the governance conference, intended to bring him up to speed before his now-nightly call with Todacheeney to discuss her analysis.

"We have two ships a day at this point, Arjun," he pointed out. Ferreiro was no longer his chief of staff, but he still held a special place in James's trust. He and Dubhain, James's old intelligence officer, still had an access most staff-officer deputies would kill for.

"And when was the last one on direct line from Sol, Admiral?" Ferreiro asked.

The files in James's mental vision all closed simultaneously, and he leaned forward to study the main holographic display.

"We haven't had one yet," James said. "And two were scheduled that are missing."

"There's a flight of Dakotan Scimitars heading in to confirm ID and course," the staff officer replied. "But the course is right. She'd have left on the twentieth, ten days after network collapse."

"So, before they heard anything from us," James concluded aloud. "But even if she isn't carrying any official dispatches, they'll actually have news from Sol. Once we've confirmed her identity, inform her Captain that I'll need to speak with them as soon as they make orbit.

"I need to know what happened in Sol after the switchboards went down."

There were scenarios, after all, that would result in everything he and the governance conference were doing being *completely* irrelevant.

———

THE FREIGHTER *VERDANT Fields* settled into orbit two hours later—six days after she'd been originally scheduled to arrive—with the four old Scimitar fighters flying close escort. One of James's assault shuttles rendezvoused with her before she even finished decelerating, bringing the Captain and executive officer over to *Krakatoa*.

"*Verdant Fields*, arriving," the PA system crackled as the shuttle touched down. Two older men stepped off the spacecraft, both giving James a credible salute as he greeted them.

"Welcome to the Dakota System and aboard *Krakatoa*, gentlemen," James told him. "I apologize for being quite so demanding, but as you can imagine, we've had no news for almost a month."

"We were expecting it, Admiral," the captain said. "I'm Aniket Kauffmann, and this is my executive officer and husband Reindert Kauffmann. We own *Verdant Fields* together."

"We're glad to see you. My steward has put on a meal, so that you aren't entirely put out by your trip over," James told them. "Walk with me, gentlemen?"

It wasn't really a question, and both of *Fields'* officers fell in beside him. From the way they walked, Aniket Kauffmann was ex-military and his husband was...trying to show the same respect.

"I hope you have dispatches from someone in Sol?" James suggested gently.

"Some, but not as many as you might like," Captain Kauffmann said grimly. "TCN Central Command is *gone*, Admiral. What dispatches I have were directed to an Admiral Banks?"

"Admiral Banks is injured and in recuperation," James replied. "I'm the acting commander of Sector Fleet Dakota, so I'll be responsible for your dispatches."

Gone. Central Command was gone? That was...all too possible, given that one of the switchboard stations had been in orbit around Ceres, and even the most fortified ground installations couldn't stand off an antimatter warhead.

"I also have dispatches for the Dakota government and federal offices, plus news agencies, plus..."

"I understand, Captain," James said, waving the door open. "Without the q-com, we're asking merchant captains to act as couriers between star systems in a way the Commonwealth, well, has never done before."

The earliest and crudest q-coms, after all, had been developed at the same time as the first functional Alcubierre-Stetson drives. Humanity had *never* operated without instantaneous communication across the stars...until humanity had taken it from one of its own nations.

That, James suspected, was a price of hubris—not that he could say that out loud to his people, let alone to the two merchant officers.

"Captain Volkov will be joining us in a moment," James told them. "Don't worry; we won't start interrogating you until she's here."

"I understand," Aniket Kauffmann confirmed. "You need to know what happened, and while *Verdant Fields* wasn't there on the tenth, we arrived two days later. We know what happened and we know how things were when we left."

"You're six days late. What happened?" James asked.

"We were delivering commercial fusion-power cores," Reindert Kauffmann said, rotating a glass of water. "Picking up exotic-matter coils for Dakota from the Saturn growth fields. But..."

"The Alliance still had the system occupied when we arrived," *Fields'* Captain said grimly.

"Occupied?" Volkov asked in shock, pausing in the door. "*Sol?*"

"Sol," Aniket Kauffmann confirmed. "They didn't try to hold on to the system and never landed troops anywhere, but for about two and a half days, the Alliance controlled Sol space. I'm not sure of the details, but my understanding is that they had three task forces and one got stuck in hard with Terra Fortress Command, forcing the rest of their ships to pull them out.

"None of Fortress Command's stations survived."

James grimaced. That was tens of thousands—*hundreds* of thousands, most likely—of people wearing his uniform who were dead. People who had likely figured they had one of the safest jobs in the Commonwealth's military, too, guarding the skies of the homeworld.

"Sit down, Captain Volkov," he told the Korean-Russian officer. "For now, it's just the four of us. But we're going to have a lot of questions, and this is going to be an unpleasant conversation for us all, I expect."

"It will be what it will be," the older Kauffmann told them quietly. "Reindert and I knew from the moment we arrived in Sol that wherever we went next, we'd have to answer a lot of questions."

"I'm guessing you have at least something of a prepared spiel, then," James said. "Run through that for us, and then we'll see what questions Captain Volkov and I have.

"I'll probably have to hand you over to the rest of my staff as well, but I wanted to make sure *I* knew what was going on as cleanly as possible," he warned them. "But I promise: you'll be paid for your time and efforts. There's nothing more I can do, but I certainly cannot do less."

"I appreciate that," Aniket Kauffmann replied. He paused, taking a sip of water and watching as Chief Steward Sallie Leeuwenhoek delivered the first of several plates of food. All of it was designed to be finger food, easily and quickly eaten—to make for simpler presentations.

Leeuwenhoek seemed to think of *everything*.

The merchant captain exhaled a long sigh, looking down at the food, then looked back up at James.

"We lost network along with everyone else on the tenth," he began. "No one did a very good job of getting what was happening onto the civilian merchant networks before they ceased to exist, so we had only the vaguest idea of what we were walking into."

He paused.

"We never got a good look at what was left of the Alliance fleet," he noted. "Some of the ships I saw were definitely no longer combat-capable, but they all left under their own power in the end.

"Mars Fortress Command held. One of the reasons we were delayed was that we got commandeered to relocate fortresses from Mars to Earth. There was also a request from the Star Chamber to hang on while they sorted out what the hell they were doing."

Kauffmann shook his head.

"You don't argue when you have requests signed by the Speaker of the Interstellar Congress show up in your inbox," he noted drily. "I assume there's more classified information in the dispatches we're transferring over, but I saw a lot myself.

"The Alliance left on the thirteenth. From what I can tell, pretty much the entirety of the mobile fleet units of the Alpha Centauri Security Force showed up the next day. Eight ships." He paused, then sighed. "Like I said, not sure what the Alliance *had* in Sol, but I suspect the ACSF didn't have enough ships to take them."

James also knew what Captain Kauffmann did not—that the *entire* ACSF deployment of the Commonwealth Navy was a glorified reserve unit of obsolete ships. They *might* have had modern fighters—maybe—but they would have been carrying them on ships that made *Saratoga* look brand-new.

They would have probably needed two-to-one odds to take on whatever the Alliance had brought to attack the heart of the Commonwealth, and he agreed with Kauffmann. They almost certainly hadn't had them.

"We left Sol on the twentieth," the captain concluded. "By then, there was a new Home Fleet of about twenty ships. Seemed...sparse to me, especially with the fortresses at Earth and Ceres gone. But they found some dedicated courier ships and sent them out, too.

"No one was telling *merchant captains* about what those ships were doing, but one headed rimward and one headed clockward, and they had senatorial delegations aboard. Commonwealth's suing for peace on all fronts, is my guess."

There were probably more details in the dispatches on that, but it was what James was expecting.

"How are we supposed to fight two wars when we can't even talk to each other?" he said grimly. "We sent a ship back to Sol on the eleventh, so you passed each other in warped space along the way.

"Is there anything you think is critical to tell us?" he asked.

"We got our cargo of exotic-matter coils to deliver to Dakota, but my contact warned me there wouldn't be any more. Anything like that made in Sol is going to stay in Sol for a while," Kauffmann said quietly. "The Alliance let them evacuate first, so I don't think the casualties were bad, but they took out the Lagrange yards. Gone shortly after we got there. I don't know how many ships were under construction, but that still feels...bad."

"It is," James said shortly. He wasn't going to elaborate to a civilian —but forty percent of the Commonwealth's warship construction was in Sol. *Another* thirty percent had been in systems that had held switchboard stations.

If the Lagrange Yards in Sol were gone, then the Commonwealth had almost certainly lost seventy percent of their warship-construction capacity. That had been part of James's worst-case scenario.

A scenario that sounded more and more plausible with each piece of information he learned.

21

Dakota System
11:00 November 10, 2737 ESMDT

"E<small>VERY ONE OF</small> you needs to sit down and chill," Anthony Yamamoto snapped into the chaotic hubbub of *Krakatoa*'s main flight briefing room. At least half of his flight-crew personnel were in the space, arguing and shouting as they downloaded and reviewed the dispatches from Sol.

"But...Sol, sir!" someone shouted out of the conversation.

"*Atten-hut!*" Anthony bellowed, practice and implants combining to cut through the noise like a knife. It slowly quieted, but he waited for full silence before he stepped up onto the stage and surveyed them all.

"Are you officers of the Terran Commonwealth Starfighter Corps or upset children?" he snapped as they finally listened. "We all knew Sol was under attack. We *knew* the switchboard stations had fallen and that the battle had likely been lost."

Anthony sympathized with them more than he wanted to admit.

There were no official casualty lists, not yet, but his younger brother, *Sean* Yamamoto, had been first officer on a High Guard corvette. From everything he'd seen, that meant Sean had died defending the Central Nexus, the Commonwealth's primary q-com station.

"Many of us have friends and family in Sol," he conceded. "And many of those friends and family wear the same uniform we do and rode fire in defense of the homeworld. *We do not know their fates.* No casualty lists have been issued. When *Verdant Fields* left Sol, we'd only held control of the system again for seven days.

"In the face of catastrophic defeat, that is not enough time for the full consequences to be known."

Anthony stared down his officers. There was a tone to their conversation he had to head off, much as he sympathized with it.

"But defeat is part of war. We don't have to like it, but there was no treachery or betrayal in the Alliance's operation. It was war, an attack on legitimate military targets. The Star Chamber is suing for peace, and *we*, as sworn officers of the Commonwealth, must accept that."

He very carefully did *not* pay attention to the details of the hubbub that answered him—especially when he definitely picked out the word *treason* in there.

"Chill," he ordered. "I will not hear accusations leveled at the civilian government we are sworn to serve."

In that, at least, he was *definitely* not going to follow his famous ancestor's example.

"It is the duty of our Senators to make the assessment of whether the Commonwealth prosecuting this war will be worth it," he continued. "The attack on our communications network renders us almost incapable of prosecuting a major war, let alone two.

"The Congress will make their decisions and *we* will obey them. That is our duty. This war is over. We lost."

That was verbally ripping the bandage off, he knew, but he *had* to do it. The last thing he could afford was to have *Krakatoa*'s fighter crews thinking that the *Star Chamber* were traitors. Anthony hated that they were suing for peace, that the attack that had almost certainly killed his brother was going to achieve its goal.

But he had sworn an oath to serve the Commonwealth, and he

couldn't see any way that continuing the war would serve the Commonwealth.

"We have to be calm," he told his people. "To think rationally. We will receive casualty lists and further updates over the next few days. We expect the ship the Admiral sent to Sol for updates to return on the twentieth—*Encarnación* will almost certainly have the details that *Verdant Fields* did not.

"So, be patient, be calm," he reiterated. "Be officers of the TCSC. Our focus must be on the duty before us: the protection and stability of the Dakota Sector."

———

THE STAFF MEETING that afternoon was very quiet. Anthony wasn't feeling much better than anyone else as he stood behind his chair, one hand on the back of the seat as he looked around at the other officers of Sector Fleet Dakota.

Finally, he sighed and looked over to meet the Admiral's gaze.

"Anyone else going to address the elephant in the room?" he asked. "I don't know about anyone else's people, but morale on the flight decks is trash. *My* morale is trash," he admitted. "I have…had… *Fuck*."

No one interrupted him as he swallowed down a spike of anger and grief.

"My brother Sean was first officer on the High Guard corvette *SKD-One-One-Five*," he finally ground out. "From the dispatches, none of the High Guard ships over Earth survived."

"Thirty-two percent of Sector Fleet Dakota's personnel have first- or second-degree family in Sol," Voclain said calmly. "Twenty-seven percent of our people have family in one armed forces branch or another positioned in Sol."

"Morale is pretty beat up across the fleet," Wardell Carey said grimly. The fair-haired Alpha Centauri–born operations officer looked tired. "I'm in touch with the admin teams on all of the ships. No one is quite sure how to handle this. The folks who didn't lose people in Sol…most of them probably lost people at the other q-com stations, though we only really know details about Sol and Leviticus so far."

"We need to keep a handle on it," Tecumseh told them all. "I have family in Sol myself; I understand where our people are coming from, but we cannot let morale in the Sector Fleet get tied up with something none of us can influence."

The Admiral shook his head.

"We'll get more answers in the next few weeks," he promised. "We should be hearing from Marshal Amandine on the status of her negotiations around the same time our own courier to Sol returns. By the end of the month, we'll have a far-clearer idea of what's going on in the wider Commonwealth.

"But right now, we know that the Star Chamber sent delegations to negotiate ends to both the wars we're in. We need to make sure our people *accept* that, angry as they are. Peace is better for now."

"For now, sir?" Voclain said quietly.

"I generally feel that peace is better overall," Tecumseh replied drily. "But I doubt that the Commonwealth has it in us to be this humbled and *not* retaliate in the future. That's not a promise we can sell our people on."

"We need to distract them," Anthony noted. "I've been carrying out virtual exercises with the flight crews, but I wonder if we might all be served well by some real space exercises with the entire fleet."

He knew *he* could use getting into a fighter and flinging virtual missiles around. If he could wear his people down into better-trained exhaustion...

"We honestly need the chance to exercise without q-coms," Voclain agreed. "Our entire combat doctrine is built around real-time communications and the use of q-probes to give us near-real-time sensor views.

"We *all* need to learn to adapt to that."

Tecumseh nodded.

"It's a good idea, Colonel, Commodore," he agreed. "Set it up." He smiled thinly. "Assume that I'll be running the OpForce. I have some...*thoughts* on handling the lack of instant communications."

22

THE *ALBERTO DA Giussano*-class carrier was in serious trouble. She was a big, modern ship with over sixty anti-fighter positron lances, but her fighters had been lured out of position, and now Anthony Yamamoto's bombers were sweeping in like the hand of death itself.

James was in command of the carrier and her escorts, and smiled as the starfighters took his bait. This was going to be a hopefully effective object lesson about seeing what you wanted to see for his Fleet CAG.

Currently, the role of the carrier was being played in real space by an electronic-warfare drone half the size of the bombers lancing toward her. Her appearance on everyone's screens was a virtual representation, assembled by the computers from the data being sent by the drone.

It was reasonable, James knew, to accept that the data in the computers was correct. But there were also key flaws in the information they had, intentional fragmentation to show the truth of what James was *actually* doing to his people.

Adamant and *Valiant* were barely half a million kilometers behind the starfighters, the battleships maneuvering in real space like the fighters. The cruisers were covering the two carriers, and the entirety of Sector Fleet Dakota was currently under Commodore Voclain's command.

But everyone's focus was on the starfighters as Yamamoto launched his bomber strike like the consummately skilled professional he was. Virtual torpedoes flashed into existence across the board...about five seconds before the computers ruled that the pair of *Venice*-class battle-cruisers were too close to evade detection, even with their engines off-line.

A hundred and twenty virtual fighters blazed into space from the Stellar League warships a moment later, half of them bombers. It was too many bombers—but the shortage of bombers in the carrier's wing had gone unnoticed before.

Now the League battlecruisers and their accompanying bombers launched their own torpedoes and missiles into the teeth of Sector Fleet Dakota's carriers. At the same time, the carrier that Yamamoto was hitting with everything he had flared with Cherenkov radiation as she punched her A-S drive and vanished from the display at a hundred and thirty thousand gravities.

She'd abandoned her fighters to do so, but the condottieri and ex-condottieri officers of the Stellar League were *very* aware of what their key assets were. In a real battle, the *Alberto da Giussano* would return to reclaim her surviving starfighters in an hour or so.

By then, the battle would be over—and at the speed James's battle-cruisers were closing with the carrier fleet, both of the cruisers were almost certain to make it out as well.

His opposing force was outnumbered seven to three—but he was about to wipe out Sector Fleet Dakota's carriers in exchange for no capital-ship losses of his own.

———

"You, sir, are one sneaky bastard."

James returned Voclain's commentary with an airy salute.

"That is the job of the opposing-force commander," he pointed out, looking around at his staff. "Would anyone care to offer justifications before I lay out exactly what you missed?"

"No, I'm pretty sure we just made the Battle of Midway look like a well-thought-out exercise on the Japanese part," Yamamoto griped. "Up there with the Centauri Defense Force assuming the Kaber pirate fleet *had* to be a civilian convoy because they'd never seen A-S warships before."

"I don't believe we are talking quite that deep a level of incompetence," James demurred. "And to give credit where credit is due, every maneuver and strike carried out during the exercise was carried out perfectly. Keeping the cruisers back with the carriers *would* have neutralized my trick."

"If we'd detected the ballistic cruisers at any point *before* they were practically in lance range," Voclain said grimly. "That was us forgetting we didn't have the q-probe sphere up."

"Agreed," James told her. "Which brings up part of why we need *a* probe shield, even if it's transmitting at lightspeed. A shell of drones at half a light-minute would easily have detected the two cruisers and rendered the whole sneak attack a failure."

He shrugged.

"That said, you had enough information as it was." Mental commands brought up the sensor records of the entire exercise. Seven ships and five hundred fighters had been in space, though their entire opposing force had been represented by drones for safety's sake.

Even with all of the precautions they took, there was still a very real chance of casualties in an exercise like this. The complete lack thereof was a feather in James's people's caps, so far as he was concerned. He'd raise that once he was finished pointing out their failures.

"First off, you had no solid enemy strength provided as part of the scenario," he began. "I ran through the flag-deck recording transcripts afterward—you all leapt pretty quickly to the theory of a spoiler raid with a single carrier.

"Your maneuvers to intercept and neutralize the carrier and her fighters were superb," he continued. "My plan actually didn't call for the carrier fighters to do more than drag their coats for you until the cruisers launched, but you used the fighters and hull-number advantage to pin me down quite handily.

"But you focused in on the carrier immediately and didn't even validate her mass and cubage versus the A-S Cherenkov flare," he pointed out. "That information was in the pre-mission sensor files you were given and would have allowed you to ID that there were at least two more ships in play. Assuming there was nothing critical in the historical sensor data you had was actually the first mistake.

"The second, of course, was focusing on the carrier and letting me lure you into exactly the spot I wanted you to be," he continued. "The third was not having enough drones out to pick up the cruisers incoming—but the fourth was not doing a wide-enough sweep with active scanners around the ships anyway.

"Active scanner beams should have picked up the cruisers at at least five million kilometers instead of the three million the thermal passives detected them at." He shrugged. "A closer inspection of the carrier might also have told you that her Stetson stabilizers were up— that was why she hadn't fired any positron lances or lasers of her own.

"While having her Class One mass manipulators online wasn't a blatant clue that she was ready to jump to FTL, the presence of active Stetson fields should have been a clue."

He tapped the image of the horseshoe-tipped League carrier with a finger.

"Remember that League condottieri regard their capital ships as almost un-riskable," he reminded them. "That the carrier had come in as close as she had was a hint that they were being clever—but she was still far enough out to initiate an A-S field."

"Which none of us considered," Voclain said grimly. "And light-speed lag means we actually would have been *more* hooped against a real League force. The carrier would have jumped the moment the cruisers fired, and neither of our two force components would have been able to communicate."

"I couldn't think of a way to duplicate that," James agreed. "Not in a real-space engagement. That's something we need to remember while we're doing these maneuvers: our *actual* enemies are probably going to have real-time coms and sensors in a way we no longer do.

"We can only compensate for that difference so much." He waved the initial sensor data away and turned to smile at his people.

"That said, folks, we carried out a seven-capital-ship and five-hundred-starfighter exercise with no major accidents or equipment failures," he told them. "Your actual operations, inside your assumptions, were carried out with skill and competence.

"Our subordinates, including the fighter crews and the crews of the starships, performed *impeccably*."

"But the command staff did not," Voclain said levelly. "*I* did not."

That was a very large check mark in the good column for one Commodore Madona Voclain, in James's opinion. Not only had she recognized where the actual shortcoming was, she'd stepped forward and taken responsibility for it.

It had been a broader set of errors than just Voclain, but James had put her in command.

"Yes. So, tomorrow, the lot of us"—he waved around the room—"plus the ship captains, are going to do some intensive pure virtual exercises to see if we can sort this out.

"Then we're going to split the fleet in two and do this again with a full-scale force-on-force exercise," he continued. "You get *Krakatoa*, Madona. *I'm* going to take *Saratoga*—and the battleships!"

He grinned.

"You'll have the most modern ship *and* four ships to my three," he told her. "I suspect the betting in the lower decks is going to be...*interesting*."

23

Dakota System
09:00 November 20, 2737 ESMDT

SARATOGA WAS BURNING. That was mostly metaphorical—ships in space generally only burned for very short periods of time as oxygen and other atmosphere vented from the ship—and even what wasn't metaphorical was entirely virtual.

James had tried something clever, concealing the arrival of his three ships in the shadow of the gas giant Virginia. Voclain had happily maneuvered her ships in a manner that suggested she'd fallen for his trick—and she and Yamamoto had turned his ballistic stealth trick against him.

Two hundred starfighters, including every one of the bombers not aboard *Saratoga*, had hidden in the light of Dakota's star. It wasn't a trick that would have covered them forever, but they'd sneaked to the edge of torpedo range—and James had only held thirty starfighters back to defend his carrier.

The old *Lexington*-class ship was now gone, ruled a wreck by the senior umpire—Captain Ferreiro. Most of the bombers and fighters were still intact and were now swinging around to catch *Adamant* and *Valiant* between Voclain's main fleet and her fighters.

After six days of both virtual and real-space exercises, the honors were *very* definitely in James's favor versus Voclain, Yamamoto and Volkov. His chief of staff and his flag captain had traded back and forth the "privilege" of commanding against the Sector Fleet commander, and Yamamoto had served as an all-too-capable deputy for them both.

He was content to give them this win and was, honestly, looking forward to getting back to his quarters on *Krakatoa*. Giving his subordinates the more-powerful ship also helped cover for when he *did* muck up, allowing him to pretend he was still the best.

"Sir."

He looked up as Harkaitz Zyma stepped into the flag deck. The carrier's XO didn't have a role there—most of Zyma's job right now was to be the person watching the real world while everyone else lived in a mix of virtual and real space.

"Yes, Commodore?"

"We have an Alcubierre contact on the line from Sol, sir," Zyma told him. "We have confirmed her identity beacon: it's Captain Maradona, sir. *Encarnación* is back, and she's transmitting a Star Chamber critical-courier beacon."

"Understood," James said crisply. "We're out of the rest of this exercise anyway, but if you can tell Mac Cléirich to pass the orders to stand down?"

"We'll pull everyone back to Dakota to see what the news from Terra is." He chuckled. "I should also check in on the governance conference. After ten days, I hope they've decided *something*."

"They are politicians, sir," Zyma noted.

"This is true," James conceded. "But they do have *some* sense of urgency, one hopes."

———

Encarnación downloaded a set of dispatches to *Saratoga* at James's request. Another copy was clearly flagged to go to *Krakatoa*, and from the directory structures James saw in his dispatches, there were more messages headed to the government of Dakota.

A lot of them. From the number of different messages, videos and updates that were tagged for James's attention alone, the Star Chamber and whoever was acting as Central Command had been *busy* since *Verdant Fields* had left the Solar System.

One message immediately popped to the top of the list, however. Flagged for James's eyes only and maximum priority.

He stepped into his old office, activating a privacy seal as he settled into the chair and had a momentary twinge, missing the far-more-comfortable, handmade seat he now had aboard *Krakatoa*.

Still, it served the purpose, and he activated the message. A hologram of an unfamiliar sallow-faced Admiral appeared in front of him, the four stars of a full Fleet Admiral pinned to her collar.

"Rear Admiral Tecumseh, I am Fleet Admiral Uria Oliver," she greeted him. "Until twenty days ago, as I record this message, I was the commanding officer of Mars Fortress Command. Now the fortunes of war and fate have made me the acting chief of staff of Central Command."

She paused.

"I'm recording a lot of these messages, Admiral Tecumseh, trying to give updates, authorizations and orders to sector fleet commanders where I, frankly, have no idea what's happened in their area of operations since October tenth.

"I don't know *much* more about what's happened in Dakota, frankly, but you're one of the few who made an effort to make contact. The news you sent wasn't what I may have wanted to hear, but you sent it nonetheless."

Oliver paused again, clearly considering what to say.

"It will have been over a month since Vice Admiral Banks was medically relieved of duty when you receive this message, but the assessment our doctors give me is that he is unlikely to have returned to fit status," she noted. "So, I don't see much choice. Yours was one of several dozen names submitted to the Star Chamber for emergency promotion this morning.

"Congratulations. You're a Vice Admiral. If Banks has returned to duty, he obviously remains senior to you."

It was pretty clear to James that Oliver didn't think that was likely. To his eyes, she was clearly riding the edge of a breakdown herself.

"Insignia and assorted formal paperwork will be on *Encarnación*," Oliver told him. "She's been loaded with... Well, as much logistical support as we could spare. It's not as much as we'd like, but it does include a full database of all TCN design schematics.

"You have *full* authority to contract with local Dakota manufacturers and shipyards to produce any and all matériel you judge necessary, up to and including the production of new warships. You may draw on the credit of the Commonwealth without limitation to achieve that production."

James grimaced. A blank check like that meant they weren't going to be sending him anything else.

"I've also been made aware that you were not cleared for Project Hustle," she continued. "Which, to be fair, neither was I prior to taking on this role. There are, Admiral, a number of shipyards where the TCN was constructing warships without any official announcement.

"One of those shipyards is in Dakota. The records here are...fragmentary, with the loss of the Ceres facility to an orbital strike." She sighed. "The worst part is, reviewing the battle records, I don't think the Alliance even *meant* to blow up Central Command. The missile that hit them was aimed for one of the *Ambrosia* battleships and got confused by ECM.

"While we are recalling the March Fleets, the truth is, Admiral, that we are in dire straits for hulls and new construction," Oliver admitted. "The protection of the Virginia shipyards is now one of your highest priorities, Admiral Tecumseh. Those ships may be the future of the Commonwealth.

"More information is included in the data packets you've been sent, but the truth is that the Commonwealth is going to be in rough shape for the foreseeable future," Oliver told him. "I've only heard from seven of the Sector Fleets. Geography and timelines mean I couldn't have heard from six of them, but that's still three sector defense fleets

—responsible for eighteen star systems and numbering sixteen capital ships—that have not reported in to Sol.

"You will need to act far more independently than any Commonwealth Admiral ever has. My understanding is that Congress is encouraging the member systems to assemble temporary sector-level governance structures.

"You are encouraged to assist and enable those efforts as best as you can, but you are specifically ordered *not* to place your fleet under their command. You answer to Sol, Vice Admiral Tecumseh. You will work with the civil governments of the Dakota Sector and you will protect those systems and their people, but I remind you that your first loyalty, your first duty, is to the Commonwealth."

She exhaled a long sigh and shook her head again.

"Good luck, Admiral. And if you find you have any of that luck to spare, feel free to send it my way!"

The message paused, and James touched the insignia of his rank. He hadn't even been a *Rear* Admiral for a year. Part of him had expected Central Command to stuff a handily available senior Admiral on *Encarnación* and send them out to relieve him.

Except...Mars Fortress Command was a Vice Admiral's command. If Uria Oliver had been the head of MFC, she'd been a *senior* Vice Admiral but still only a Vice Admiral. She'd been bumped to take over command of the entire Commonwealth military.

And James thought *he'd* been given a bad hand!

————

THE INSIGNIA and everything that came with them met James aboard *Krakatoa*. Captain Helga Maradona was waiting as he stepped off the shuttle, the tall Hispanic captain doing her civilian best at a salute after James traded formalities with his crew.

Volkov and Voclain were both present on the deck and appeared around the freighter captain as if by magic. Neither the flag captain nor the chief of staff really needed to be on the flight deck for the Admiral's return, but they'd been warned.

"There's probably some giant formality you Navy types prefer for this," Maradona said quietly. "My shuttle is stuffed full of molecular circuitry data drives stamped with the logos of the Navy, Centauri Interstellar and Dynamics International Armaments. I don't know what they contain, but I can guess."

"You're most likely correct," James agreed. "These aren't normal times, Captain Maradona. Which means we may as well jump past all the formalities and ritual we 'Navy types' would normally prefer."

There was a *purpose* to those formalities and ritual, and James would make sure to arrange *something* for later. Right now, though, they needed to move forward.

"Right. Here." She held out a black velvet jeweler's box.

Before James could take it, Voclain had. She opened it and passed part of its contents to Captain Volkov.

Both women were Commodores, his two most senior subordinates, and they were clearly taking it on themselves to make sure there was some ritual to all of this.

"We may not have the time for grand affairs and gatherings," Commodore Voclain told him, "but someone still has to stand witness."

James was vaguely aware that more people were filtering into the flight deck. A lot of the fighter crews clearly hadn't left—and everybody had registered that the training had been cut short for the day. The arrival of a shuttle from the ship arriving from Terra and the return of the Admiral were drawing a crowd.

Voclain and Volkov stepped up to face James, one on either side of him.

"Your insignia, please, Rear Admiral Tecumseh," Voclain said calmly.

Slowly, carefully, James removed the stars from his sleeves and collar and the boards from his uniform jacket. He passed them to Voclain hesitantly. He *knew* what she was doing, but to stand there on his flagship's flight deck without any rank insignia at all felt *wrong*.

"Captain Volkov."

"Commodore Voclain."

That was all the two women said before they stepped forward and each took one of James's arms. New shoulder boards clipped on to the uniform jacket, exactly as both pieces of clothing were designed for. New stars clipped onto his cuffs, and then Voclain leaned in to pin the paired stars to the side of his collar.

"Thank you for your patience, *Vice* Admiral Tecumseh," the Commodore told him.

"Company, attention!" a voice bellowed across the flight deck. James looked up to meet the eyes of *Krakatoa*'s deck chief, Thales Brahms, as they called the assembled random collection of officers and enlisted to proper form.

Blinking back sudden emotion, James found himself returning several hundred salutes as calmly as he could. The standard ritual might not have been possible...but his people had made their own to make sure they marked the moment.

And to James Tecumseh, that was probably worth even more.

24

Dakota System
19:00 November 20, 2737 ESMDT

ANTHONY YAMAMOTO's Admiral had picked up another star, and half the fighter crews were celebrating by getting moderately drunk in Tecumseh's honor. The other half, Anthony suspected, were going over the details of the last week of exercises to try to find places they could improve.

Anthony *himself*, though, was going through the inventory of what they'd received from Earth. Starfighters. Bombers. Fighter missiles. Torpedoes. Capital missiles. Spare mass manipulators. Spare zero-point cells.

The absolute numbers *looked* good—they now had enough spare Katanas to reequip the entire Dakota defense force and mothball the Scimitars, for example—except that Anthony knew he wasn't getting any *more*. Of anything.

He had enough replacement fighters for a moderately intense campaign, but he didn't have replacement pilots. Any significant battle would see his fighter wings pulling replacement hands from the system defense forces or even recruiting from the local population.

There was no structure in place for them to do the latter, but Anthony Yamamoto was entirely aware of why starfighters existed.

An A-S warship cost approximately ten trillion Commonwealth dollars. A starfighter cost about a quarter-billion. If Anthony's *entire command*, all five hundred–plus starfighters, were sacrificed to save a single cruiser, the Commonwealth would come out ahead in terms of both dollars and lives.

Starfighters existed to die so that starships didn't.

Replacement fighters and crews were always high on any CAG's mind. The TCSF graduated seventy-two thousand new flight-crew personnel every year. Between the fleet and the Commonwealth defense forces—as opposed to the system defense forces—the Starfighter Corps fielded two hundred thousand starfighters.

Only point nine percent of the population had the level of neural-implant bandwidth necessary to fly a starfighter. That still meant that the Commonwealth had *billions* of potential pilots, but they still needed training and practice and fighters to fly.

If things didn't change quickly, Anthony could see himself running out of pilots well before he started running out of starfighters—especially since he *also* now had the manifest of the data files and schematics supplied aboard *Encarnación*.

His plan to review that manifest and start listing out the resources he needed for munition and starfighter production carried him easily five steps into his office before he realized the lights hadn't turned on at his mental command.

Someone was in his office. His *secured* office, attached to the *secured* flight deck, aboard the *flagship of Sector Fleet Dakota*.

Unfortunately, while Anthony Yamamoto was a decent shot with the standard light sidearm, he didn't have any true instincts with it. He was still struggling with the holster when the door to his office closed and locked behind him and his office lights came up dimly.

"Don't worry about the gun, Colonel Yamamoto," the woman sitting on his desk told him. She lifted what looked like a small crossbow and gestured at his head with it. "If I wanted you dead, you'd be dead. I wouldn't even have set off the ship's scanners, though that gun will. Please don't shoot at me."

"You shouldn't be in here," he told her calmly, studying her. The dim light made it hard to be sure, but she was definitely on the smaller side. She looked delicately built and he would probably have found her attractive under better lighting and different circumstances.

"I *should* be anywhere I feel is necessary to protect the security and integrity of the Terran Commonwealth," she replied. "I work for CISS, Colonel."

Anthony stopped trying to draw his gun and sighed. If she was telling the truth, she hadn't been exaggerating about being able to kill him. The Commonwealth Internal Security Service—the acronym was pronounced "kiss"—fell into a particularly ugly subset of Commonwealth organizations.

Like the Pacification Corps, it was their job to head off secessionist activity on Commonwealth worlds and keep the Commonwealth together. *Unlike* the Pacification Corps, CISS at least officially existed, even if they were rarely acknowledged and even more rarely seen.

But everyone had heard rumors of a particularly outspoken friend of a friend—usually of some political or economic influence—who'd been in an "unfortunate accident." And those rumors always spoke of assassins and a shadowy hand in the darkness of the Commonwealth.

"I'm *reasonably* sure I'm no threat to the integrity of the Commonwealth," Anthony finally brogued at the woman. "And you have the advantage of me."

"Call me Reynolds," the CISS agent told him. "No, Colonel, you're no threat to the Commonwealth. I'm in *your* office for two reasons: one, that by every psychoanalysis metric we have available, you are the standout measure for loyalty to the Commonwealth among Admiral Tecumseh's senior staff."

"And two?" Anthony asked calmly.

"I knew your brother," Reynolds said calmly. "And he was, without a doubt, one of the Commonwealth's most solid and loyal supporters. That means I think I can trust you to put the interests of the Commonwealth above such niggling concerns as the *chain of command*."

"'Was,'" Anthony echoed quietly. "I hadn't seen a final casualty list yet."

"It's in *Encarnación*'s dispatches," Reynolds told him. "*SKD-One-One-Five* rode to the defense of the Central Nexus against an Alliance fighter strike. She was lost with all hands. I'm sorry, Colonel. I... thought you would have checked by now."

Anthony swallowed hard, then stepped past the woman to stand behind his desk chair and lean on it for hopefully concealed support.

"What do you need from me?" he whispered.

"An ear in the Admiral's most private meetings and updates on his plans," Reynolds told him. "Whether we like it or not, the Commonwealth has had no choice but to put near-complete authority over Sector Fleet Dakota in the hands of Vice Admiral Tecumseh.

"None of our usual controls and oversight measures are in place, but the Vice Admiral's record is far from spotless with regards to *loyalty*, Colonel," she said flatly. "In Barsoom, he stood aside while *Avalon*'s fighters took down not only *Triumphant*—whose crew was as guilty of war crimes as the Alliance claimed—but also *Saint Augustine*.

"Ten thousand Commonwealth spacers died that day and James Tecumseh did *nothing*."

"The situation was not clear-cut," Anthony protested, halfheartedly. "And the same dealing with the pirates and *Poseidon*."

"The man lost one of our most modern battlecruisers to pirates."

"To *mutiny*," Anthony corrected. "I don't necessarily disagree with you, Agent Reynolds, but the mutiny does change the situation."

"And then he allied with our enemies to bring that ship down," Reynolds pointed out. "As you say, the situations were not clear or simple. If they had been, Tecumseh wouldn't have two stars, let alone three."

She shook her head.

"He'd probably have been cashiered, if not executed, if the same events had occurred with different contexts," she told Anthony. "And now the Commonwealth has to rely on him to protect and secure six star systems.

"So, here I am." She spread her hands. "I need to know what he's thinking, what he's doing. You will be my eyes and ears in his meetings, Colonel Yamamoto."

"And what happens if he is starting to turn?" Anthony asked softly.

"KISS principle," she told him, and her smile at the double acronym was unsettling. *"Keep It Simple, Stupid.* I kill him and you make sure Voclain knows the risks."

"And if he is all that he appears to be, determined to uphold the Commonwealth as he has claimed?"

"Then Vice Admiral Tecumseh will never even know I was in this system."

25

Dakota System
09:00 November 21, 2737 ESMDT

"PROJECT HUSTLE?"

First Chief Chapulin studied James carefully for several seconds after he dropped the name. The call only had the two of them on it and was as encrypted and secure as Mac Cléirich could make it. Nobody was eavesdropping on the conversation between the leader of Dakota and the Admiral in charge of the sector's defense.

"I'm told I wasn't cleared for it," James said. "And my staff don't seem to know anything about it now that I *am* cleared for it. That tells me, First Chief, that the people who *do* know about it are civilian—and that means you would know about it."

Chapulin sighed.

"The question, Admiral, is whether the word of a military bureaucrat a hundred light-years away is enough to open that door for you," she told him. "Fleet Admiral Oliver is unknown to me. She wasn't on the cleared list for Project Hustle."

"But she is now the chairperson of the Joint Chiefs, First Chief," James said quietly. "The decision is hers."

"The decision is *mine*, Admiral, due to the realities of the situation," she replied bluntly. "Project Hustle has become not merely an ace but a joker in the deck, a wild card that changes a great deal. Keeping it secret protects Dakota."

"I cannot guarantee that Admiral Oliver will not tell others about it, whatever it is," James said. "While I'm sure at least some details are buried in my dispatches from Sol, I wanted to see what you had to say about it."

"The current state of the governance conference is a series of delegated meetings between analysts and lawyers, hashing out the details of our short-term agreement," she noted calmly. "I can take three days. Can you, Admiral?"

"Three days?" James asked slowly.

"It is best shown, I think," she said. "I have a sublight yacht that can make the trip in about a day each way. You'll need some time for inspections, I presume, but we should be able to make the whole tour in under three days."

"There is still a lot going on, First Chief," James replied.

"Barring the arrival of an enemy fleet, which I think we both know is unlikely to happen just yet, do you really have anything that will be hurt by waiting a day for an answer, Admiral?" she asked. "You need to know what Hustle is. It will, I suspect, impact your long-term plans quite a bit."

"All right."

———

"THREE DAYS, SIR?" Voclain asked when he filled her in. "Just what is the First Chief showing you?"

"Something at Virginia, I'm guessing," James replied. "A lot of things can be hidden at a gas giant, and that's about a day away if she has a yacht with Tier Three acceleration."

The chief of staff sighed and gestured an image into the air between them.

"*T̂hatȟáŋka Íyotake*," she pointed out. "Built on the chassis of an in-system gunboat designed by the Alpha Centauri Defense Force. I suspect the Dakotans ordered her to give them a chance to examine the gunboat's abilities.

"One hundred thirty meters, five hundred gravities of acceleration. She can keep pace with a starfighter but has no offensive weapons."

"The flip side of that, I presume, is that our fighters can keep pace with her?" James asked. "Check with Yamamoto on whether we can rig up something with the delta-v to fly escort out to Virginia."

"I think we might need to rig up fuel tanks if they're accelerating the whole way, but it should be doable," Voclain agreed. "But that's taking you well out of the loop, sir."

"As Chief Chapulin pointed out, we're now in a state where a twenty-four-hour cycle on communications shouldn't be a major problem," he told her. "And, honestly, I'm curious just what this project that everyone thinks is so important *is*."

"Shipyards?" Voclain suggested.

"Almost certainly. Which is interesting in itself," James said. "If even *you* weren't briefed on them, that strikes me as unusual."

"Extremely," she agreed. "So, I guess I see her point in wanting you to see them yourself. If they're TCN, we're going to end up absorbing them into the Sector Fleet anyway."

"Keep an eye on everything and keep me in the loop," James ordered. "We're basically in a holding pattern ourselves, but the governance conference has at least some conclusions. I imagine nothing will be locked in until Chapulin gets back, but she seems to think she has three days."

"As long as everyone is still Commonwealth, we don't care much, do we?" Voclain asked.

"I also object to dictators, even ones that pay lip service to Sol," he said. "Right now, the conference looks to be allocating caretaker powers to the assorted representatives as a joint council, with details of the longer-term sector-wide administration to be established over the next couple of months."

At this point, James suspected that the semi-permanent Dakota Sector government was going to look much like the temporary one, except directly elected in most cases. Six coequal elected councillors with a self-selected chairperson met his requirements for *not a dictatorship*, especially when a lot of decisions would still need to be run by both Sol and the system governments.

"Still feels a bit odd to be helping set up a regional government," his chief of staff admitted. "Feels like the first step toward secession— the Albany Congress that became the Continental Congress wasn't a revolutionary entity, after all."

"No, it wasn't," James admitted. "And, from a risk perspective, allowing that mid-level identity to take shape *is* a risk. But having every decision on inter-system arguments being resolved by someone on the other end of a forty day communication loop is an even bigger one.

"We'll keep an eye on those risk factors, but so far, the governance conference is very aware that they are setting up a *regional* government, one with strictly limited powers until we get some kind of grant from Sol.

"That's the best we can hope for and still manage to keep the sector functioning."

Voclain nodded.

"Ever wonder whether we're doing better or worse than the other sectors, sir?" she asked. "It seems like we're still falling into a hub-and-spoke coms model, even with that forty-day loop to Sol."

James stopped mid-step and swallowed a series of curses.

"We need to change that," he told her. "Damn. None of us thought of that, did we?"

She paused, then chuckled bitterly.

"Even having just *said* that, I wasn't thinking about it as a problem we can solve," she admitted. "I'll talk to Mac Cléirich and we'll see about contracting some people. We've already taken over half the facilities capable of building munitions.

"If Dakota can't ship out what it usually would, it should make people happier if we hire the ships to do something else."

26

Dakota System
13:00 November 21, 2737 ESMDT

KATANAS WEREN'T DESIGNED with enough endurance to accelerate for twenty-four hours. They had life support and every other type of supply required to operate for several weeks, but their fuel capacity was insufficient to keep up with a specially designed intra-system fast transport.

As James had guessed, however, *Krakatoa* had fuel tanks that could be substituted for missiles on a one-to-one basis to extend the space-craft's range. The four Katanas flying escort around *Ťhatȟáŋka Íyotake* only carried four missiles instead of the normal twelve, but they had the endurance and acceleration to keep up with the yacht.

Ťhatȟáŋka Íyotake herself was impressive. She had the sleek lines and armored hull of her original purpose as a gunship, but she'd been painted in a complex pattern of geometric shapes that reached back to the paintings of the nineteenth-century Hunkpapa Lakota.

Studying her on approach, James realized that the description of the yacht as "lacking offensive weaponry" was very carefully phrased. His practiced eye could pick out the blisters of the ship's antimissile laser turrets and similar short-range defenses—including both ventral and dorsal light positron lances, intended to engage starfighters.

Her more combative sisters would carry megaton-per-second heavy weapons, but *Tȟatȟáŋka Íyotake* could make a nasty mess of anyone who decided to tangle with her.

If James had been setting her up himself, he'd probably have included the deck space for at least a few fighters. The shuttle bay his transport settled into, however, was sadly lacking in the parasite warships. There was space for the three shuttles of the yacht's complement and *just* enough extra for the military assault shuttle carrying James.

First Chief Chapulin and Abey Todacheeney were waiting as James exited behind a trio of Marines. A dozen Assembly Watch troopers were scattered around the bay as well, maintaining a careful eye on the planetary leader.

"Welcome aboard *Tȟatȟáŋka Íyotake*," Chapulin greeted him with a handshake. "It's a long-enough flight that we've had quarters put aside for you and your escort, and Captain Húŋkešni has made arrangements to provide you with a secure communication link to *Krakatoa*."

"I appreciate it," James said. "Everything should be in order for the next few days."

In truth, it almost looked like the trip out to Virginia would be something of a break for him.

"I'd offer the tour of *Tȟatȟáŋka Íyotake*, but truthfully I don't know if there's much to see outside the 'hotel' part," Chapulin noted. "I know the way to the garden and the staterooms. More than that, I would need to impose on the good captain."

"For now, I'll take the tour of the hotel, then," James said. "If someone can tell the Sergeant here where to store my bags and set his troops up?"

"Of course. Abey?"

———

CHAPULIN AND JAMES ended up in the garden with surprising speed. The First Chief had carefully removed her headdress and other regalia, leaving her in a surprisingly plain-looking gray suit as she took a seat on a stone bench.

The garden was a small hemispherical space with artificial grow lights above it. James could pick out the places where the ship's air was cycled through the small zone of living plants to add a freshness no artificial means had ever been able to match.

A warship could recycle its air practically indefinitely, but only one warship James had ever set foot on had smelled like this. Every other warship he'd served on—and most standard civilian ships, at that—had the distinctly ozone-like odor of air cleaned and recycled forever.

He'd long grown used to the smell of warship, which had made visiting a Castle Federation warship years earlier a strange experience. The Castle Federation were the first among equals of the Alliance, providing almost half of the war-fleets that had held off the Commonwealth—and every one of their warships had a large atrium tucked away at its heart, serving as the morale and life-support center of the starship.

Tȟatȟáŋka Íyotake's garden wasn't on the same scale as a Federation atrium, but it served a similar purpose on the far-smaller ship. Even as Chapulin took a seat on the bench, he knelt on the carefully managed clover and ran his fingers through the plants and the dirt underneath.

"We're underway," he said aloud. It wasn't a question—even without checking his implant, he could feel the distinct, barely perceptible vibrations of a properly tuned set of engines and mass manipulators. If they were *more* than minor tremors, that would be a sign of serious problems—but completely smoothing engines based around firing beams of positrons into focused hydrogen jets was almost impossible.

He took a moment to check his implant and confirm that the two flights of Katanas were in formation. He wasn't worried—Anthony Yamamoto would have had to *try* to find four incompetent crews among the Sector Fleet—but verification was good.

"So," he said to Chapulin, his hands still buried in the dirt as his implant queried computers around him. "Where exactly *are* we headed? You've been surprisingly mysterious about all of this."

"With reason," she said. "We're headed to Virginia, but I wasn't exactly concealing that. There's a shipyard anchored on the outermost moon, over a dozen light-seconds from the rest of the infrastructure and activity.

"Virginia has enough traffic to conceal anything that was brought in, and the belts and Dakota's industry suffice to provide anything needed." She shrugged. "It's not a huge complex like the TCN yards in Tau Ceti or Sol, but when the Navy offered to fund doubling our A-S starship construction ability, my predecessor didn't turn them down."

"There are, what, eight full-size yards at Dakota's Lagrange points?" James asked softly.

"Two are newer than Project Hustle," Chapulin said drily. "There's only six yards at Virginia-Eleven. Base Łá'ts'áadah was started ten years ago." She chuckled. "You've encountered its products before."

"I have?" James said in surprise.

"*Saint Anthony* was built here," she told him. "We ran through a trio of *Saint*-class battleships at an intentionally slow speed. The ships were officially built in Sol, though. That was the whole *thing* about Hustle."

"An entire concealed shipyard?" James asked. "That feels paranoid, even for us."

"And right now, it may just save the sector." She sighed. "That's why I didn't tell you about it, James. At first, I assumed you knew, and then, well...None of the ships are close to done, and if things go strange enough, those ships might have served to protect Dakota from the Commonwealth."

"That's always a phrasing we should be careful with, isn't it?" he said, cleaning the dirt off his hands as he took in the North American native plant life around him. "My loyalty is to the Commonwealth, to the ideals and principles it serves."

"Mine is to Dakota, Admiral," the First Chief warned him. "Right now, between you and the messages I have from the Star Chamber, I'm less worried than I was. But you and I...we know the words of the colonizer, don't we?"

That phrasing sent a chill down James's spine. Aboard a ship named for a general who had almost successfully fought off the US Army in the nineteenth century, surrounded by plants that could easily have grown at Little Big Horn, those words had weight.

"Dakota joined the Commonwealth willingly," Chapulin said. "But we always understood the monster we bedded down with. Dakota is a disproportionately low contributor of Naval and Marine recruits to the Commonwealth. The Commonwealth's drive to unity always rang too harshly of *manifest destiny* to my ears, even while I served and fought for it."

"I'm no unification fanatic, Chief," James promised. "I serve in the Navy and follow my orders, but I'm not one of those who see resisting unification as a crime worthy of punishment in itself."

"Do you think we'd be having this conversation if I thought you were, Admiral Tecumseh?" Chapulin asked. "No, I have taken your measure, I think. So long as you and I and the council we're building speak for the Commonwealth in the Dakota Sector, I think my people are safe.

"But that thought, that *faith*, Admiral Tecumseh, is fragile and rests on far too fragmented a foundation. I fear for the future. I fear for what the Commonwealth may become."

James was still kneeling on the ground. Technically, some of what Chapulin was saying to him was probably treason—but he was *Shawnee*. Like anyone born to Earth's Old Nations, he had struggled with the balance between the Commonwealth's dream of a unified mankind and the blood-washed stories of the colonization of the Americas and Africa.

"So do I," he admitted. "I... I *know*, Chief Chapulin, that at least one Sector Admiral is going to try to turn warlord out of all of this. I know it won't be me—but even as we speak, somewhere in the worlds of the Commonwealth, the wheels are turning that will unleash the guns of the Commonwealth Navy upon itself.

"I fear how we will react to that. I fear how anger over what the Alliance did will shape our people and our military over the next few decades, too."

He shook his head.

"All I can do is guard one sector—and shield the souls of the officers and spacers who follow me from as much of that sickness as I can."

"I appreciate that, James," Chapulin told him. "But I have to ask... Is there a line that you won't see crossed? An act, a command, that will see *you* turn the Sector Fleet against Sol?"

He exhaled a heavy sigh, his gaze focusing in on a particular wild rose in the bunch.

"I don't know," he admitted. "And *that*, Chief Chapulin, is more honest than I can afford to be in *any* context."

"I understand," she said. "And thank you."

27

"BREAK" or not, James spent over four hours tucked away in the secure coms room that *Tȟatȟáŋka Íyotake*'s crew had set up for him. He was confident in Voclain's ability to handle the Sector Fleet for a few days, but he wasn't going to cut the woman entirely loose of support until he had to.

After eight hours, the yacht was still several hours short of making turnover and beginning to decelerate toward Base Łá'ts'áadah—"Base Eleven," translated from the Navajo name.

He now knew the basics of what he was heading out to look at, though Chapulin appeared to want to surprise him with the details. One of the complicating factors that Chapulin *hadn't* raised was that there was presumably a TCN contingent at the base who had reported to Admiral Banks.

With James's predecessor's sudden relief, they likely had no idea who they were even supposed to report to. Without FTL-capable shipping, *he'd* have reported in to the new Sector Fleet commander, but whoever was in charge at Base Łá'ts'áadah had chosen to stay dark.

That was going to be an interesting conversation.

Almost as interesting as the one he realized was imminent when he stepped into his stateroom to find the lights set to dim and soft music playing. Several ship-safe candles lit up on the small dining room table as the door slid shut behind him—*ship-safe* defined as "smokeless and will go out if knocked over," in this case.

Abey Todacheeney was sitting at the table, wearing a low-cut black dress. The lighting reflected off the highlights in her hair and the folds of the dress, managing to accentuate her curves even more than the dress already did.

"Ms. Todacheeney," he greeted her. "Am I in the wrong stateroom?"

"You are not *that* obtuse, James," she told him. "But if you somehow *are*, this is a seduction and you're invited."

She did *not* need the dim lighting to make herself look attractive, James had to admit. He sighed, leaning against the chair across from her and carefully studying the spread on the table instead of the cleavage of the personal aide to the most powerful woman in the Sector.

It was a relatively light-looking meal—teriyaki salmon or local equivalent on a vegetable risotto, he'd guess—that was located somewhere in the center of his personal preferences. He wasn't surprised Todacheeney had picked up that much from his people over the last few weeks.

"I'm flattered," he said carefully, "but I'm sixteen years older than you, Abey. *And* you're one of the senior politicians I'm working with. And…"

"Last time I checked, your rules were only about *chain of command*," she told him, rising to pour him a glass of wine to go with the fish and revealing that the dress didn't come anywhere near her knees.

James sighed and permitted himself at least one moment of near-staring. It was pretty clear that she *wanted* him to look, after all.

She smirked at him and handed him the glass of wine.

"If you were *uninterested*, I'd take that," she told him with a smile.

"But while I don't have access to your military records, my impression is that you do like women and you are attracted to *me*."

He chuckled and took a sip of the wine. As expected, it was a delightful blend, with just the right edge of crisp dryness to it.

"You are an extremely attractive woman, yes," he managed to get out with only a small cough. "And one who appears to have co-opted my own staff against me."

"Just Chief Sallie," Abey told him with a chuckle. "James...I'm not going to *push* this. If you want me to leave, say so, and this never happened. But I *do*, as it happens, find you attractive."

Her grin widened for a moment.

"I will be honest enough to admit that I originally planned to seduce you when I expected you to take over as military governor," she said. "I figured that even in our worst case, you seemed like a decent-enough sort that I could help protect Dakota from your bed."

James winced. That was a...painful concept.

"And *that* reaction, plus the screaming and running you did at the very *idea* of military government, meant I kept thinking about it," she purred. She'd moved around the table at some point, he realized absently, and was now well within reach.

Her free hand brushed over his cheek, and he shivered at the touch. He was barely conscious of leaning into her hand, and her fingers cupped his cheek.

James was intellectually aware of just how touch-starved his career was. Nobody *touched* the Vice Admiral. Even as *just* a starship commander, it would never have been appropriate for anyone to do more than give the CO a perfunctory handshake.

He breathed out wordlessly, realizing that Abey was even closer, still touching his face. He put his wineglass down on the table as he covered her fingers with his own.

"I'm not... I'm..." He swallowed his words as he stumbled over them, then sighed. "I'm career military and career Commonwealth, Abey," he warned her. "Whatever happens, that won't change."

"With the current mess, you look to be posted to Dakota for a while," she said. Her wineglass joined his on the table and her fingers laced into his other hand. "So, James, I'd say that unless you aren't interested in *me*, I'm not seeing any real objection to at least seeing what happens tonight."

Even James wasn't sure which of them stepped into the embrace first, her body molding against his like he was built to fit her, and he could only sigh as his whole body relaxed ever so-slightly into her touch.

"Okay," he whispered, his fingers finding her chin and gently turning her face to his. "Let's see what happens."

Then he kissed her.

28

Dakota System – Virginia Planetary System
14:00 November 22, 2737 ESMDT

JAMES JOINED Chapulin and Todacheeney in an observation deck as *Tȟatȟáŋka Íyotake* made her final approach to the military shipyard at Virginia-XI.

Base Łá'ts'áadah was clearly dependent on its distance from everything to avoid attention. Brilliantly lit-up building slips two kilometers long hung in high orbits around the tiny planetoid. The support stations were darker in the visible spectrum but visible enough in the twilight outer regions of a star system.

The stations held James's attention first.

"Four *Zion*-class battle platforms," he observed calmly. "That's two hundred fighters and a bit over six thousand people. Who runs them?"

"Navy," Chapulin said instantly. "They're your people, I suppose, but Commodore Krejči only reported to Banks. I'm not clear on the exact specifications or chain of command, but Izem Krejči is responsible for the security of Base Łá'ts'áadah.

"The construction facility itself is operated by a subsidiary of Centauri Interstellar, but that's a licensed-operator arrangement, and the yards, structures and, well, everything are owned by the Commonwealth directly," the First Chief said.

"They were receiving most of their communications through the main refineries in close Virginia orbit," Todacheeney told James.

She was all business now that they were back at work, with no sign on her face that she'd spent most of the previous night in James's stateroom. That was for the best—whatever that became, it wouldn't work if they let it impact their day-to-day tasks.

"I'm still surprised not to have heard from the Commodore," James admitted. "That's a conversation I'll have to have with him."

"That is Navy business," Chapulin demurred. "But if I may, Admiral, I'd like to direct your attention to what we truly came out here to see."

Now they were close enough that the observation-deck windows were able to zoom in on the six construction slips. The two Dakotan women had set it up in advance, and as Chapulin gestured, James turned to watch all six under-construction ships expand to fill the view.

It took a moment to establish scale. The yard slips were larger than he was used to, but the work craft jetting around the ships were of a standard style and construction.

Even by the standards of Alcubierre-Stetson warships, the ships were *immense*. He only recognized two of them, kilometer-and-a-half-long ovoids three hundred–plus meters wide and three hundred meters tall. Those were *Ambrosia*-class battleships, the long-awaited equals in size and mass to the Castle Federation supercarriers that had again and again overrun Commonwealth ships in one-on-one clashes.

The middle two ships were the same flattened cigar as *Krakatoa*. Shorter than the *Ambrosia*s, they maintained the same three-hundred-meter-plus width and height their full length. They were stubbier in appearance, but he could see where the framework of the carriers' flight decks was being installed.

The last two were narrower and longer than the battleships, sleeker builds that made the space for hangar bays though not full flight decks. Battlecruisers, multi-purpose ships built to carry every kind of fight on their own.

"My gods," James whispered. "They're huge."

He'd never actually seen any of the new eighty-million-cubic-meter ships himself. He'd commanded a sixty-four-million-cubic-meter *Saint*-class battleship—and *Krakatoa* was only a few hundred thousand cubic meters smaller—but these ships were almost a third again bigger than the last generation of warships.

"Like I said, we built one round of *Saints* to test everything, then we laid these keels," Chapulin told him. "You'll want to talk to Krejči about a bunch of details. I don't know much, but I know these were part of the second wave of the new ships, and my understanding is that we're not up to the speed and efficiency of the well-established naval yards."

James studied the ships. The main keel and bracing structures were complete, but none of the ships even had their armament installed or more than a third of their outer hulls. One of the *Da Vinci*–class battle-cruisers was the furthest along, but even that looked like it would be another year.

"I see why Central Command put protecting these yards as one of my highest priorities," he told Chapulin. He gestured at the closest battlecruiser. "Those are *Da Vinci*–class battlecruisers...except that *Leonardo Da Vinci* was destroyed in her slip in Alpha Centauri on October tenth.

"I don't know what we call a class of ships when the intended name-ship of the class is wrecked before launch," he admitted. "*Ambrosia* was at least built, though the Alliance took her to pieces at Ceres..."

He sighed.

"I'm not entirely sure, but I suspect that the Project Hustle yards— and I don't know where the other two are—represent at least three-quarters of the remaining warships under construction in the Commonwealth," he told his companions quietly. "And there aren't many systems where they could have *put* those yards that would be capable of producing every component of an A-S starship."

"We were not scheduled to produce the main positron lances," Chapulin told him. "But..."

"You have the ability," James finished for her. It wasn't a question. He was intimately familiar with Dakota's industrial plant now. The Dakotans may have kept far more industry in space than most systems, but they'd also been driven to avoid being vulnerable with a fury only the descendants of the conquered could match.

He'd been surprised at the numbers. Concealed in Dakota's three asteroid belts were mining and refining operations to rival any star system in the Commonwealth short of Sol itself. Tau Ceti and Alpha Centauri had likely exceeded Dakota's industry...*before* the Alliance's attack.

Now? James suspected there were *no* military shipyards left larger than Base Łá'ts'áadah, and only Sol was more heavily industrialized than Dakota.

"Project Hustle may have given Dakota the power to save the Commonwealth," he told Chapulin quietly. "I can see why you wanted to be sure you could trust me."

"And what does this change, Vice Admiral?" the First Chief of Dakota asked.

"Nothing," he replied. "Nothing at all. It tells me that in two years or so, I can not only secure the Dakota Sector but look to help the wider Commonwealth...but it doesn't change anything for now."

From her question, even now Quetzalli Chapulin had wondered if the sight of *that* fleet would tempt him toward warlordism. Still, no one in the room seemed surprised that James Tecumseh remained untempted.

Dakota, it seemed, had only one temptation to offer him—and even Abey Todacheeney wasn't likely to convince James he needed to be a king.

29

Dakota System – Virginia Planetary System
15:00 November 22, 2737 ESMDT

"SECTOR FLEET DAKOTA, ARRIVING!"

The standard bosun's pipe trilled across the flight deck of the *Zion* battle station as James exited the shuttle. His Marine escort traded the normal salutes and ritual with the honor guard waiting for him, and then he walked along the path laid out for him to meet the man in charge of Base Łá'ts'áadah's defenders.

Izem Krejči was a squat Black man nearly as broad as he was tall, with immensely muscled shoulders that threatened to tear out of his uniform shipsuit as he crisply saluted James.

"Vice Admiral Tecumseh, welcome aboard *Zion-K-Seven-Nine-Nine-D*," he greeted James. "And welcome to Base Łá'ts'áadah."

"Thank you, Commodore," James replied. He mentally noted that there were no *other* officers present. Just the Marine honor guard. Krejči clearly expected to be called onto the carpet and have a strip torn off him, and had declined to invite an audience to the event.

"I have to admit, I was surprised to discover that someone had concealed a major Commonwealth Navy construction facility inside the system I became responsible for and no one told me," he said, his tone intentionally mild. "But that is a conversation for you and I to have later, Commodore.

"I'm impressed with the scale of the facility and the work you've been doing here. Would you care to give me a tour and a briefing?"

The Commodore's failure to report in to his new boss when his superior had been relieved had earned him at least *some* recrimination, but James saw no reason to dress him down in public.

"Of course, sir!" Krejči responded. "Walk with me?"

James hadn't brought any subordinates either, though his Marines fell in behind him with the calm of long practice. Theoretically, a Vice Admiral didn't need an escort on a TCN base. In practice...his people were starting to regard anything that wasn't Sector Fleet Dakota as terra incognita.

And he couldn't bring himself to argue, either. He had enough suspicions of the other officers of the Navy to be paranoid.

"*K-Seven-Nine-Nine-D* is your basic Zion platform, as are the other three stationed around Base Łá'ts'áadah," Krejči told him, gesturing around the hangar deck. "We have two hangar decks, this one hosting two squadrons of Katanas and our shuttle complement, the other one hosting two squadrons of Katanas and a squadron of Longbows."

"I'm surprised to see a defensive installation with Longbows," James admitted. "We only just received them in the Sector Fleet before...well, everything."

Krejči nodded grimly.

"The Project Hustle facilities have the same security priority as the primary Navy shipyards," he said. "We actually received our Longbows six months ago, before the Sector Fleet. Admiral Banks was aware of them, but..."

"But he wasn't cleared to share that information with the rest of the Sector Fleet; I understand," James conceded. Presumably, Banks had written up plans to integrate those fighters into a defense of the Dakota System, at least.

"Is Base Łá'ts'áadah capable of manufacturing starfighters?" he asked after a moment.

"No," Krejči said instantly. "While we are a fully functional ship-yard, we lack many of the ancillary operations that are present at, say, the Sol or Tau Ceti operations."

"Were present," James corrected quietly. "I take it you haven't received the full classified military dispatches, since you weren't looped into my communication chain."

Krejči paused.

"No, sir," he admitted. "We only got the civilian updates via the refinery."

"We'll correct that," James told him. "Among other things."

His new subordinate winced but nodded.

"How bad, sir?" he almost whispered.

"Bad," James said. "This facility now represents at least a fifth of the Commonwealth's remaining warship-construction capacity. Possibly more. Show me *everything*."

––––––

THE NEXT STOP Krejči took James to wasn't a standard part of the Zion station. It didn't *look* improvised, but James was familiar enough with the layout of the prefabricated battle platform to be able to identify where a section of administrative offices had been cleared away to connect to a similarly opened-up chunk of living quarters and one of the main sensor-processing clusters.

That cluster now fed a massive array of two- and three-dimensional displays, acting as a combined traffic control, shipyard observation and defense command center. Pride of place in the operations center was a set of six holograms, at one-to-one-thousand scale, of the warships under construction.

All of those holograms were over a meter long, and the holographic tank they rested in looked like it could be adjusted to give a one-to-one-hundred scale view of any individual ship.

"*BC-Three-Seventy-Two* and *Three-Seventy-Three, BB-Four-Twelve* and *Four-Thirteen, SCV-One-Fifty-Eight* and *SCV-One-Fifty-Nine*," Krejči reeled off, indicating each of the six ships in turn. "There are names allocated for them all, but those are still subject to change."

"Given *Leonardo Da Vinci*'s fate, I have some sympathy for the idea that naming an unlaunched ship is bad luck," James replied. "What's the status on their construction?"

Krejči gestured a white-haired older woman over. She was close to James in height, though her skin was closer to Krejči's shadowed shades than his.

"This is Ekundayo Gardinier," Krejči introduced her. "She's one of the operational managers Centauri Interstellar has out here. They like to keep at least one of their middle-managers in our ops center to keep an eye on everything."

"We have much the same information on our stations in the Łá't-s'áadah Yard itself," Gardinier noted as she nodded to James. "It is, however, valuable for us to know what the Navy thinks is going on with their order."

"I understand, Ms. Gardinier," James agreed. "Vice Admiral Tecumseh, Commanding Officer, Sector Fleet Dakota."

"You're the man with the actual data on what the hell's going on, are you?" she asked.

"As much as anyone, I'm afraid. I take it you haven't received any updates from Centauri Interstellar HQ?" he asked.

"Not a bloody peep, and I know there's been ships from both Sol and Alpha Centauri come through," Gardinier confirmed. "We're worried. Friends, family, colleagues."

"I know Centauri fell and was retaken," James said quietly. "I'm not sure what happened to CI HQ, but I can't see the Alliance attacking a planetside facility.

"On the other hand, I know the military yards in Alpha Centauri were destroyed. I suspect they don't know what's going on anywhere, either."

"The one time I *want* headquarters to stick their nose in things," Gardinier grouched. "The least they can do is tell us they're still alive!"

"We've got the beginnings of a regular route to Sol, though it's frustratingly slow," James told her. "You can probably send a message to someone there to relay to Centauri."

"Maybe. Depends on what you say, actually," the shipbuilder noted. "We're subject to military secrecy here, and the Commodore has been erring on the side of listening and not talking."

"And the Commodore is not wrong," James said. "Keeping Base Łá'ts'áadah secret may be even more critically important than we think. Probably our best option is to relay your messages through Sector Fleet Dakota.

"I'm pretty sure my coms team can hide a message to get relayed to CI HQ," he promised.

"I'd appreciate that, Admiral. Now, apologies for distracting everybody, but what did you and the Commodore need?" she asked.

"Admiral Tecumseh was asking what the construction status of our future toys over there was," Krejči told her.

"Ah, figured," Gardinier said. "If the situation is as bad as it sounds for shipyards, of course that's what you want to know. With me."

James and Krejči followed the older woman over to the big central display.

"*BC-Three-Seventy-Two* is your Christmas present for 'thirty-eight," she told them bluntly, gesturing at the first of the *Da Vinci* cruisers. "The work crew on that one has earned themselves a hell of a bonus and they're almost three months ahead of schedule.

"*SCV-One-Fifty-Nine*, on the other hand, is going to be your Christmas present for 'thirty-nine, because we received a cracked damn fusion reactor liner that managed to pass inspection and blew a quarter-million tons of keel and structure to vapor when we tried to test-boot it. Rebuilding that took us months and put her almost nine months *behind* schedule."

She shrugged and James shared her grimace. The worst part to that, he suspected, was that the fusion reactors on a modern warship were a distinctly *secondary* power source. They'd lost a third of their build time to a mistake with a power reactor, and it hadn't even been the primary reactor!

"The other four will trickle in between those two. Target date was the end of March 'thirty-nine, but a lot of that depends on whether we get the parts we need," she concluded. "We've got enough positron lances on hand to finish up *Three-Seventy-Two*, but that's *supposed* to be the first four main guns for all six ships."

"What about mass manipulators?" James asked.

"We've got one installed on each ship already with the second on hand," she told him. "Deliveries were supposed to come from Tau Ceti, though. So, similar boat to the lances. We can guarantee *Three-Seventy-Two* if we use the parts meant for the other ships, but…"

"All right. Do you have people in this system with the expertise to help set up the right kind of production for both the manipulators and the lances?"

Gardinier was silent for several seconds.

"Dakota probably has the industry and the tools to build the tools, I guess," she said slowly. "But all of those designs are classified as void."

"We have the designs, schematics, CAM templates, everything," James explained. "If you need positron lances and Class One mass manipulators, we'll build them. But any help you can give Dakota as we set it all up will be worth its weight in anything you care to name."

"I'll check with the Director and the other managers," she promised. "I think we can do quite a bit, if you've already got the CAM templates and such."

"That's what I was hoping to hear, Ms. Gardinier," he said. "Dakota doesn't have a native armaments industry…but I was already planning on building starfighter and missile factories. And since I just found out that I apparently have a military-grade shipyard available, we can damn well make the parts you need to finish those ships!"

EVENTUALLY, the tour ended in a small office with a one-way window overlooking the operations center. It was a surprisingly quiet office, given that there were roughly a hundred people in the room James was looking out at, handling all of the administrative trivia of a military command of six thousand people attached to a shipyard with ten times that many workers.

"All right, Commodore," he told Krejči. "Lay it out."

"Sir?" the junior officer asked.

"We both know that I'm furious with you and why," James said calmly. "Furious" was certainly an exaggeration, but he most definitely should *not* have learned about the shipyard from First Chief Chapulin.

"All of that comes down to, really, one decision. So, before I leave you bloody and flayed on your office floor, please explain to me what insane troll-like logic resulted in the commanding officer of six thousand Commonwealth officers and spacers declining to report in to their new commander?"

The office was silent. James was still studying the six holograms in the center of the operations center, leaving Krejči to fumble through his own thoughts and words.

"At first, we were simply in shock," Krejči finally said. "I don't want to make excuses for that, but I know you know what I mean. I don't think anyone in the Commonwealth—and especially in the Navy—wouldn't. Everything just...came apart.

"Given the level of confidentiality on my communications with Admiral Banks, I didn't even know he'd been relieved for four days," he admitted. "And then... Well, medical relief often isn't permanent, and my orders around the secrecy of this facility are...drastic."

"But you had to eventually realize that Banks was out of commission and nobody else in the Sector Fleet knew about your command," James said quietly. "And yet you remained silent."

"Technically, I'm not authorized to read anyone in on Project Hustle," Krejči pointed out. "Explicitly. I have *zero* permissions to brief people on what we do here. Even though you'd inherited Banks's command and technically I reported to you, you weren't cleared for the existence of the Base.

"And without the ability to check in with Command for permission to brief you, I was stuck between a bureaucratic and a military hard place."

"But you *knew* what the right answer was," James said. "A lot of our regulations and orders became obsolete at oh nine hundred hours on October tenth, Commodore. Risking the security of this shipyard by following those orders was a *terrible* idea."

"I... I believed that the defenses of the base would suffice to stand off any likely risk until I knew more about what was going on," Krejči told him. "And…"

The Commodore trailed off and James finally turned to look at the squat man. Krejči was leaning on his desk, looking like he'd just sucked on a lemon.

"And *what*, Commodore?" James asked softly.

There was a long silence, and Krejči stared at the one-way window behind James.

"And a longer time ago than I care to think about, a very junior, very green Ensign Krejči got his ass hauled out of the fire by one Colonel Quetzalli Chapulin," Krejči admitted. "So, when she asked me to hesitate a bit longer while she got a feel for you, I went along."

The office was silent, and James sighed.

"That woman, Commodore, is going to get us all executed for treason *by accident*," he observed. "Consider that strip ripped, Krejči. You *should* have talked to me, but the entire Commonwealth is in the middle of the goddamned interstellar apocalypse, so that excuses a few sins."

"I'm…not sure I would phrase it that way, sir," Krejči said. "But thank you."

"Don't thank me yet, Commodore. We have a lot of work to do. Practicalities and logistics of the *shipyard* rest with the Centauri Interstellar people and whatever the new armament cooperative we're assembling here in Dakota ends up calling itself.

"Practicalities and logistics of *defending* that shipyard, however, rest on you and me. So, let's go over everything you haven't already told me and find the gaps where the Sector Fleet can provide some metaphorical duct tape."

30

Dakota System
03:30 November 23, 2737 ESMDT

IF THE ADMIRAL kept coming up with starfighters to add to Anthony Yamamoto's command responsibility, Anthony was starting to think he needed a raise. Or at least a brevet promotion. He wasn't even the only Starfighter Corps Colonel in Dakota, just the most senior one.

With the additional two hundred starfighters from the shipyard rolled into his command—plus his mostly theoretical authority over the militia starfighters outside the Dakota System itself—Anthony was up to somewhere around three *thousand* fighters and ten thousand flight crew under his command.

He was responsible for all of the Corps support personnel as well, along with their militia equivalents in Dakota. The Sector Fleet had taken control of all of the sector's defense forces, so Anthony also had authority over the local fighter-support crews.

That brought the headcount currently under the Starfighter Corps or seconded to it up to about fifty thousand people. That wasn't a Colonel's command, but Anthony and his people were making do.

Potentially, they were into one of the rare situations where the Corps actually called someone an *Admiral*, but Anthony would settle for *Wing Colonel*. That would at least make him unquestionably senior to his subordinates.

Of course, that promotion would require him to promote a CAG for *Krakatoa* and stick Anthony behind a desk. An O-7 Fleet CAG was a flag officer, reporting to the fleet commander, and had no business in a starfighter outside of full-deck launches from every carrier in the fleet.

That meant the patrol Anthony was flying today, with three other fighters arrayed around his Katana, was probably one of the last times he'd be able to justify putting himself on CAP. It helped him think, but the Fleet CAG really had no business being five light-minutes from the fleet.

"It's all quiet out here," Şenol Badem told him. The engineer was in the cockpit for once, the fighter's gunner currently asleep. The shaven-headed cyborg was watching Anthony, the CAG noted absently.

Badem did a lot of that, though. He figured it had something to do with their far-more-pervasive implants or something. The AIS engineer seemed to be watching Anthony most of the time they were around, but the Colonel figured he was misestimating things.

"Quiet is good," Anthony told them. "We don't have any scheduled arrivals, though that doesn't mean as much as it once did." He shook his head. "I can live without any more freighters arriving with failing Stetson fields."

The engineer nodded, running paired fingers down their cheek thoughtfully.

"They did a good job keeping that under control," they said. "I'm not sure I could have done it, though I'm out of practice with Stetson systems."

Anthony nodded, his implant feed flipping through status reports as he listened to his engineer. The Katana was humming along happily at five hundred gravities.

"Admiral is on the scopes," he noted aloud. "Still a few light-hours out, but he's on his way home and that yacht is *very* visible."

A five-thousand-ton fighter accelerating at five hundred gravities was a brilliant beacon of light and energy. Manipulating the mass of both the reaction exhaust and the starfighter itself reduced the amount of waste energy dramatically, but it was still a high-powered anti-matter rocket.

A half-million-ton yacht accelerating at the same speed had the equivalent of a *hundred* of said rockets. *Ťhatháŋka Íyotake* was almost as visible to Anthony's scanners as Dakota's *star.*

"Contact," Badem suddenly snapped, and Anthony's attention jerked back to closer affairs. "Cherenkov flare at forty-eight light-seconds."

"I have them," he confirmed, pulling in the data. Over sixty million cubic meters, but the initial engine energy signatures were all over the place. "Wake up Strøm and get to your post," he ordered. "That's no freighter—and someone has shot the *shit* out of whoever it is!"

———

THE STRANGER WAS A *HERCULES*-CLASS BATTLECRUISER, a sixty-four-million-cubic-meter behemoth and one of the Commonwealth's most modern warships.

She'd made her Alcubierre emergence without issue, but that appeared to be the *only* thing the big ship was doing without problems as Anthony redirected his patrol flights toward the cruiser. She was limping toward *Dakota* orbit at barely thirty gravities—and even at that thrust, her engines were clearly struggling.

The ones that were *left*, anyway. The *Hercules* had clearly taken an antimatter-warhead hit directly above her engines and at least one lance pass from a wing of starfighters.

"She's lucky to still be intact," Anthony observed as the sensor data continued to flow in. "Are we reading any coms at all?"

"Nothing, sir," Strøm reported, going over his own data.

"Depending on how quickly she punched into A-S after taking those hits, she might have lost most of her external antennae," Badem warned. "She'd have minimal sensors or communications if that was the case. And given that I'm seeing active, if slow, atmosphere leakage…"

"Wonderful," Anthony muttered. "Patrol flight, close up formation. It *looks* like our friend is in trouble, but this could be a trap, too."

He considered the situation for a moment more, then tapped another command.

"*Krakatoa*, this is Yamamoto," he said crisply. "Contact appears to be friendly but badly damaged. Indulge my paranoia. I want two bomber squadrons in space and headed my way with a four-squadron escort. Get the rest of the flight group prepped and in the tubes.

"If things go sideways, I want to be able to take the big guy down before she gets anywhere near Dakota."

Anthony issued more commands to his ship's system, spinning his own zero-point cells up to maximum and beginning the process of charging his positron capacitors. A badly damaged ally probably wasn't a threat—except that there shouldn't *be* anybody near enough to show up with this damage.

"Strøm, do we have an ID yet?" he asked.

"No beacon, no IFF," his gunner replied. "She'll have internal short-range radios that'll work within a couple of light-seconds, but if Badem's right on the external transceivers, they won't be able to say anything we'll pick up until then."

"A *Hercules* should have some internal receivers," the engineer noted precisely. "She can likely receive *our* transmissions; she just can't reply."

"That's good to know," Anthony said. "Thanks."

He reoriented his own communication systems and fired them up again.

"Unidentified battlecruiser, this is Sector Fleet Dakota CAP-Six," he said crisply. "We are thirty-six light-seconds away and closing on your forty-five by sixty-three. ETA to zero-zero intercept is forty minutes.

"We are standing by to provide emergency support and can relay to Sector Fleet Dakota. Please identify yourselves and the nature of your emergency."

Unless the people over on the cruiser were doing something *really* clever, the power signatures told him that they probably couldn't energize the zero-point-cells for their main positron lances. They almost certainly *could* spin up the anti-fighter lances, but that was why Anthony was hailing them.

They were probably friendly and they were definitely in trouble—which meant he *really* didn't want them to shoot him.

———

AROUND TWO LIGHT-SECONDS, they were close enough for Strøm to pick out specific details.

"First guesses were about right," the gunner said calmly. "Looks like she took an antimatter warhead just above the engines, blew most of her sublight thrusters to pieces and beat the rest around pretty hard. I'd say she was more of a secondary target for whatever fighter pass slashed her up, but she's got at least two dozen minor hits along the hull—and those are just the ones that breached the armor."

Anthony nodded, but he picked out another detail that made him nervous.

"*BC-Three-Twelve*," he read off the hull number. "Name is illegible, but the system says that's *Ajax*. Third-tranche *Hercules*, launched in 'thirty-five, assigned to the Clockward Fleet under Marshal Amandine."

That silenced his crew.

"Didn't Amandine have, like, fifty warships?" Strøm asked.

"Give or take," Anthony agreed. "So, no, I have no idea why one of them just showed up in Dakota having been on the wrong end of a fighter strike.

"But I can guess, and I don't like the guesses I'm making," he continued. "If we haven't heard from them by the time we make rendezvous, I'm taking us into the hangar deck. Rest of the flight will fly overwatch."

"Shouldn't someone *other* than the Fleet CAG make the dangerous, stupid boarding attempt?" Badem asked from Engineering.

"Maybe, but I'm the one who's here," Anthony said grimly. "So, let's hope they find a—"

"Incoming transmission," Strøm interrupted. "It's weak... Hell, if I'm reading this right, it's coming from someone's *implants*."

Anthony was already grabbing the transmission from the system. Audio-only; he read the side data the same way Strøm did. The message was coming from someone like Badem, with heavy additional augmentation allowing them to boost their own implant radio to a level that wouldn't be safe for most people.

"CAP-Six, this is Lieutenant Commander Tebogo Abram," a disrupted voice told Anthony. "I...appear to be the acting Captain of *Ajax*. My ship is badly damaged and we require any repair assistance Sector Fleet Dakota can provide.

"We are barely capable of Tier One acceleration. We're having problems tracking the remaining atmosphere leaks, and our repair-drone network has critical gaps in both transmission and units."

Abram paused, their voice trailing off in a choked breath that spoke of desperation to Anthony.

"I also have critical dispatches and information for Sector Fleet Dakota Command and hopefully to relay to Sol," they half-whispered. "The Clockward Fleet is gone. I... I have every reason to believe Marshal Amandine is either dead or a prisoner of the Stellar League."

Anthony swallowed a curse.

It appeared Dictator Periklos had rejected the Commonwealth's appeal for peace.

31

Dakota System
10:00 November 24, 2737 ESMDT

Lieutenant Commander Tebogo Abram looked absolutely shattered to James. Like most members of the transhuman movement, they were androgynously built with visible silver circuitry swirling around their skull. Whatever depilatory treatment the Black cyborg normally used had run out, however, and there was stiff, dark hair growing around the circuits.

They still managed a passable salute as their shuttle delivered them onto *Krakatoa*'s flight deck, which James returned crisply.

His own trip to *Krakatoa* looked to have been much less stressful than Abram's. He'd only returned aboard the carrier a few minutes before *Ajax*'s officer—but *he'd* transferred over from a luxury yacht he'd shared with Abey Todacheeney.

He'd been working most of the trip, one way or another, but it had still managed to be one of the most relaxing three-day periods he'd had in the last couple of years. Let alone since October tenth.

"At ease, Lieutenant Commander," he told Abram. "I'm not going to ask you to report from your feet."

Chief Leeuwenhoek had swept through and seized all of James's travel gear, but she'd taken a moment to tell him that his office breakout room was prepared for the meeting.

"I am going to have to debrief you with my staff, though," he warned. "I have the suspicion your dispatches and messages are going to change a lot of things."

"I'm afraid so, sir," Abram replied. "I have a data package to hand-deliver to Admiral Banks, Commanding Officer Sector Fleet Dakota."

"Unfortunately, Admiral Banks is on indefinite medical leave and has been formally and fully relieved of command of Sector Fleet Dakota," James told them. "I am now in command here. Are you able to deliver that package to me?"

"I..." Abram trailed off, then snorted. "Yes, sir," they confirmed. "I'm not arguing with stars, sir!"

"That's probably wise, Commander," James agreed, then held out his hand.

The young-looking cyborg laid a single black datachip, roughly the size of James's thumbnail, in the Admiral's palm.

"I also have verbal messages, updates and the full datastream from *Ajax*, of course," he told James.

"We'll run through it all with my staff once we've got you off your feet," James replied. "Walk with me, Abram."

———

A WAITING steward got Abram off their feet and put a large cup of coffee in the officer's hand while James's staff filed in.

James traded a calm nod with Voclain—*Ajax*'s arrival was the only real concern that had come up in the last few days, but the chief of staff had handled everything with skill and aplomb. Of course, while James had reduced his core staff down to six including the Fleet CAG, he still had a double set of staff officers and analysts supporting them.

Sector Fleet Dakota might have been the largest force James

Tecumseh had ever commanded, but he couldn't complain about his personnel resources.

Once everyone—except, as usual, Anthony Yamamoto—was seated, James turned his attention to the Lieutenant Commander at the end of the table. Abram was the youngest person in the room by half a decade or more, he judged, but they were still the centerpiece of this briefing.

"All right, Commander," he told them. "I haven't had a chance to review the data package, so you may as well lay out everything for everyone."

"Okay." Abram took a steadying breath and a swallow of coffee. "Amandine was worried about a counterattack after we fell back from New Edmonton. She'd split the fleet into three sections to keep the League guessing as to where the weight of our forces was.

"Task Force One was attached to Persephone's fixed defenses. Task Forces Two and Three were patrolling the system. Two and Three each had twelve ships, One had twenty-two, I think?"

They shook their head.

"I was the senior ATO," they admitted. The assistant tactical officer. Their battle station hadn't been on the bridge *or* the combat information center...which was probably why they were still alive. "I wasn't fully in the loop on fleet deployments, but we were with Task Force Two under Vice Admiral Rutherford.

"Amandine left on the twenty-second for her peace talks. Supposedly, we were under a cease-fire, but everyone kept up the watch and the patrol. Damn good thing, too."

"What happened?" Bevan asked, the Intelligence officer leaning in toward the younger officer.

"Peace talks were supposed to be on the first," Abram said. "Amandine took two ships with her; we were expecting to hear some kind of update on the tenth." They sighed and took another swallow of their coffee.

"Instead, at oh eight hundred hours on the tenth, Task Force Three got jumped," they said grimly. "Thirty capital ships on twelve—and they must have had q-probes in close, because they came out of warped space *inside* heavy-lance range."

James concealed a wince. Assuming any battleships and cruisers at all, that would have been a massacre—and one that had evened the odds between the League force and the Clockward Fleet at a single master stroke. Amandine's plan to keep her enemies guessing had played right into their hands.

When only one side of a battle had FTL intelligence, trying to force guessing games and win by being clever was dangerous.

"Their main fleet then moved on Persephone," Abram continued dully. "Admiral Rutherford maneuvered to try to intercept, but they threw most of their fighters at us. We couldn't stand off that many starfighters and were forced to withdraw.

"*Ajax* was our biggest ship and took the brunt of the damage. Bridge and CIC were both taken out, lost most of our sublight engines, but the A-S drive was intact, so Admiral Rutherford decided to use us as a courier."

The young Commander took another steadying breath.

"They'd kept their bombers back," he said slowly. "Managed a perfect turnover to hit the ships before they could return fire with anything except missiles. Cruisers followed up… They hammered Task Force One into debris."

"What about Persephone's defenses?" James asked. "There should have been a dozen *Zion*s there."

"We'd stripped them of fighters to restock the fleet," Abram admitted. "And the League seemed to know that. They took out Task Force One, then bombarded the forts from long range.

"Admiral Rutherford's messages for Sector Fleet Dakota are on the chip, but my understanding was that he was withdrawing from Persephone and falling back on Meridian," Abram said quietly.

"And the status of his task force?" James followed up. Admiral Washington's Sector Fleet Meridian was understrength, but he doubted that the League had taken Persephone cleanly. There should have been enough left between Rutherford's force and the Meridian fleet to make the League hesitate.

"After sending *Ajax* here, he was down to nine ships," the junior officer confirmed. "We lost *Saint Benedict* and *Hornet* in the same strike that crippled *Ajax*."

"We'll want to review the sensor data, but what was your impression of the losses suffered by the League?" Voclain asked. The chief of staff sounded tired.

James understood. This whole mess was bad. If the Stellar League wasn't prepared to accept peace, the only way to *make* them accept peace was to punch them in the nose. Hard. And if the League had attacked on November tenth, the November-first peace conference had almost certainly been a trap.

Most likely, Marshal Amandine was dead.

"They still had twenty-six hulls at the end," Abram said. "My own analysis suggests all of them were damaged to one degree or another and they were short on fighters and bombers, but they only lost four ships."

"Typical League tactical doctrine, then," Bevan noted grimly. "Protect the capital ships at all costs. The SLN may not be condottieri anymore, but they used to be and they haven't lost the habits."

"We're not far short of that doctrine ourselves when it comes to fighters," James pointed out. "Thank you, Commander Abram. There's a Marine outside the door waiting for you; he'll escort you to the medbay, where our doctor will examine you."

He raised a hand before the youth could say anything.

"Humor me, Commander." He smiled thinly. "And pick up some new insignia," he instructed. "You just lost the *Lieutenant* part of your rank, understood?"

"Yes, sir," Abram confirmed. "What about *Ajax*, sir?"

"For now, you'll remain CO," James decided instantly. "We'll have the local shipyards do a survey to give us a timeline and a cost, but we'll repair her. We'll need her."

In a different time, *Ajax* might have been too badly damaged to be worth doing more than salvaging her Class One mass manipulators. Today…while repairing and refitting her might end up costing the same as building a new ship with her mass manipulators, James figured his people could use seeing the ship added to their ranks.

And if using the existing hull saved even a few percent of the cost, that might make more of a difference than he wanted to think about right now.

ONCE ABRAM HAD BEEN HUSTLED AWAY to get checked over, James turned his attention back to his staff.

"It's been an interesting couple of days," he observed wryly. "We now know that Dakota possesses a major military shipyard that, thankfully, most people *don't* know exists. On the other hand, we're looking at over a year for even a single ship.

"*Ajax* is going to be a more-immediate increase to our strength, and I expect her to take at least six months to repair," he continued. "The loss of the Clockward Fleet, however, is…"

"Bad," Bevan concluded. "Included in that, remember, is that the senate sent a delegation to negotiate with Periklos. He is unlikely to treat them any more positively than he did Marshal Amandine."

James nodded.

"I have to agree with Commander Abram," he said. "Amandine is likely dead. The best-case scenario is that they captured her at the supposed talks but the ships she took with her escaped. The most likely scenario, though…"

"Is that they fired on her ships with lances at close range and obliterated her entire escort," Voclain finished for him. "Where does this leave us, sir?"

"We are tasked to protect the Commonwealth," James reminded everyone. "Not just Dakota Sector. So far, the other sectors around us have been quiet and calm. Much the same as Dakota has been.

"I'm going to need to talk to the representatives of the planetary governments," he continued. "And see what Admiral Rutherford's messages contain, but I strongly suspect we will shortly be deploying Sector Fleet Dakota.

"I need all of you to dig into your departments and talk to all of our ships," he told them. "If there is *any* reason we can't warp space inside forty-eight hours, I need to know about it. If there's any shortfalls or lacks that we can make up inside forty-eight hours with assistance from the Dakotans, let's do it.

"We have access to the full credit of the Commonwealth Navy. Spend what we have to," he ordered. "Persephone has fallen to the

Stellar League. That's just under three billion people now under the heel of a man who *calls* himself a dictator. We cannot expect that things will go smoothly for them—and we owe them protection."

"Our area of operations is the Dakota Sector," Voclain said. It didn't sound like she was arguing with him. Just raising a point.

"And our duty is to the Commonwealth," James said. "If I am confident in the security of the systems we are responsible for and I am aware of a desperate need for assistance one sector over, I will not twiddle my thumbs while fleets burn and worlds fall. We will need to rendezvous with Admirals Rutherford and Washington, but combined we should be able to drive the League out of our space."

Unless the system representatives told him their defenses were far weaker than he thought they were, he was confident in their security for a few weeks to a month or two on their own. He couldn't keep Sector Fleet Dakota away for more than six, maybe seven weeks—but Meridian and back was twenty-three days.

Persephone and back was only twenty-six. Even stopping at Meridian to join up with Sector Fleet Meridian and Admiral Rutherford's survivors, he could reach Persephone, liberate the system and be back to Dakota before the Star Chamber could even get a message back to him with orders.

"We cannot wait on Sol and Congress, my friends," he told his people. "If the League has refused peace, we must do all within our power to protect the worlds of the Commonwealth—and remind the League why they fear the TCN."

32

Dakota System
12:00 November 24, 2737 ESMDT

IT WAS a relief for James Tecumseh to sit down in the chair in his own office and breathe the air of his own space. The air aboard *Krakatoa* had the distinct taste of warship, since only the smallest of hydroponic air-filtration vegetable gardens existed on Commonwealth ships, but it was still his home.

He put the datachip from Vice Admiral Rutherford on the hand-carved desk and studied it in silence for several seconds. While it was quiet in his office, his flagship was buzzing with activity around him. He had set into motion a series of events that would take his fleet to Meridian—and to war.

James could guess the contents of the message from Rutherford. He certainly knew what *he'd* have sent out—though he wondered why Rutherford had sent *Ajax* to Dakota. There were three other sector capitals roughly equally distant or even closer.

Though, he supposed most of those were like Meridian: stripped to three or four ships at most to build up the Clockward Fleet, with Amandine partially tasked with their security.

A mental wave of his hand activated the reader concealed in the desk, and a hologram appeared in front of his desk. Vice Admiral Hans Rutherford looked out of place among even the more-martial Shawnee tapestries around James's office—broad-shouldered with a chiseled chin and carefully shaped muscles, he looked like he'd stepped out of a recruiting poster.

"This message is for Vice Admiral Gabriel Banks," Rutherford said crisply. "Primary encryption is K-C-Five-Nine-D-D-Three-Six-K-K-Five-Seven."

James didn't even have to *tell* his computer to apply that encryption key to the rest of the message, and the hologram continued speaking after a barely noticeable pause.

"Gabriel, it's Hans, and we are in serious trouble," the rigid-spined Vice Admiral said grimly. "The League played Amandine like a fiddle. Persephone has fallen and I'm taking my task force back to Meridian."

"As the senior officer of Clockward Fleet, I'll be taking control of Sector Fleet Meridian to reinforce my numbers, but we're still going to be understrength and undergunned versus Star Admiral Borgogni. I have only estimates of what his effective losses are, but right now, I think I'm looking at twelve versus twenty, minimum."

Rutherford spread his hands. It was clear from his body language and choice of words that he'd known Banks, likely better than James had.

"I need backup, old friend," he told a man who would never see his message. "I know you're set up to only really kick Tecumseh and his carrier group my way, but I need more than that. I need Sector Fleet Dakota—every ship you can spare, if you can't bring them all."

"I need any spare fighters you have, too," Rutherford admitted. "I think I can partially refill my decks when I get to Meridian, but the League burned my fighter wings pretty hard. *Ajax*'s flight group is already gone as I'm sending the kid your way."

The Admiral shook his head.

"Abram is in over their head, but I'm betting they can manage a wreck with an A-S drive long enough to get to you. I'm depending on it, in fact. If all I have is Sector Fleet Meridian and what's left of my task force, Star Admiral Borgogni is going to be giving Dictator Periklos the entire Meridian Sector as a late Christmas present.

"And I have other plans for Meridian."

That was…not a comfortable phrasing, to James's ears, but Rutherford didn't elaborate. The big Terran sighed and shook his head.

"We haven't had an update from Dakota yet, but I know about Leviticus," Rutherford said quietly. "I'm switching to our personal key. Hold on one."

The hologram fuzzed out and James checked. Whatever the personal key Rutherford and Banks had shared was, it hadn't been included in the files he'd inherited from the other Admiral.

On the other hand, it wasn't like James needed to see the part of the video where Rutherford tried to be sympathetic to Banks over the death of his wife. He'd seen what he needed to—he knew where he needed to take his fleet and what he needed to do.

But while he was under strict orders *not* to regard the interim Dakota Sector government as in his chain of command, he also wasn't going to leave the sector without talking to them.

"Flight deck, this is Tecumseh," he said aloud, connecting with the department with a thought. "I need a shuttle prepped for an ASAP run to the surface. Can you have her ready by the time I make the bay?"

It didn't look like he was even going to get a single night in his own bed before he went off to war. At least he was bringing his bed with him!

33

Dakota System
18:00 November 24, 2737 ESMDT

THE DAKOTA SECTOR governance conference had solidified the interim structure enough that James was, at least, only meeting with six people. There were another dozen people in the conference room, aides and support staff including Abey Todacheeney, but they weren't the decision-makers.

The tables were arranged into a horseshoe facing the presentation floor James calmly stepped onto. Sanada Chō was directly across from him, the ex-sumo wrestler requiring a special chair but *also* sitting in the central position.

Shogun's minister without portfolio appeared to have been selected as the chair of the provisional council. Quetzalli Chapulin sat to his right, the governor of the planet they all stood on having an inevitable special status.

Closest to James were Patience Abiodun to his left, wearing a conservatively cut purple suit as she watched him like a hungry hawk, and Chandler Leon, the Desdemonan representative, to his right.

The table was rounded out by Dayo Spitz, a tall and fair-skinned man with heavyset features who served as Gothic's Minister of Trade, and Hjalmar Rakes, a large blond-bearded man who was Krete's Deputy Prime Minister.

"I appreciate you all making the time to meet with me," James told them. "I understand that things are still very much in flux here in the Dakota Sector, but from the looks of the room, you have some idea of what we're doing next on the civilian side."

Sanada grinned, a brilliant expression that didn't soften the ex-wrestler's hard-lined face but still warmed the entire room.

"The exact details are being hammered out, Tecumseh-san," he conceded. "But the rough plan is that what you see before you is the Provisional Transitional Dakota Sector Council. We are assembling a proposal to send to Sol for Congress's approval as to the powers to be delegated, but we are in a position to at least coordinate a combined front of our planetary governments."

"One of the details we're still hammering out is the timeline to the first election," Chapulin noted. "We've agreed that it cannot be more than one year, but I can't help but feel that sooner is better."

From the way she glanced at Abiodun, this had been a running discussion.

"It is simply not practical to assemble the infrastructure and organization to hold a multi-system election for representatives on no notice, Madame First Chief," Abiodun countered. "But that *is* a discussion we have agreed to delegate to technical specialists—and irrelevant to what the Admiral wants to speak to us about."

Everyone seemed to concede that point, proceeding to focus their attention on James. The sensation of being a small animal inspected by multiple varieties of predator was hard to avoid.

He gestured, bringing up a hologram of Dakota and its orbitals. A moment later, it zoomed in on *Ajax*.

"I hope that most of you have been advised of the arrival of the TCN cruiser *Ajax* in-system this morning," he told them. "If you haven't been, let me know. We will need to make sure there is a communication channel between this provisional council and its elected successors and the military command of Sector Fleet Dakota."

James looked around. Of the six councillors, no one looked entirely surprised by learning of *Ajax*'s arrival. It also didn't look like anyone had enough information to guess why he was talking to them, which was how it should be.

He wasn't going to take the actions he was planning without *talking* to the local civilian government, but Central Command had made it clear that he didn't *report* to the new local government. That meant that his classified dispatches shouldn't be passed on to them without his knowing.

"*Ajax* was assigned to the Clockward Fleet under Marshal Amandine," James continued after a moment. "She and what is left of her crew were present for the defeat of that fleet at the hands of the Stellar League Navy."

He could have dropped a pin in the room and heard it. Councillors and aides were stunned.

"As of the network collapse last month, Marshal Amandine was commanding fifty capital ships," he noted. "She took two of them to a peace conference with Star Admiral Borgogni. We can only assume those ships are destroyed and Marshal Amandine is dead.

"Of the ships left in the Persephone System, *Ajax* is here…and nine capital ships fell back on Meridian under the command of Vice Admiral Rutherford. The rest were destroyed by the SLN."

If anything, the silence was sharper now. At least some of the civilians seemed to be holding their breath.

"From the estimates I've seen of the SLN's losses, this may well be the most one-sided defeat ever inflicted on the Commonwealth Navy," he said quietly. "My understanding is that Rutherford and Washington between them muster thirteen capital ships."

Thanks to Commander Abram, he knew which nine ships Rutherford had taken to Meridian—and he'd already known the makeup of Sector Fleet Meridian. None of those thirteen ships were modern warships.

A new image appeared in front of him. It was an eight-hundred-meter-long oval, flattened at either end where the flight deck accesses were.

"This, councillors, is the TCN strike carrier *Hancock*," James told them. "She is a *Lexington*-class carrier, built in twenty-seven-twenty-nine. Forty million cubic meters, twelve million tons…and the most advanced and powerful warship under either Admiral Rutherford or Admiral Washington.

"They have thirteen ships but only a total of approximately three hundred and seventy million cubic meters of hulls and seven hundred and fifty starfighters," he continued. "For comparison, with *seven* hulls, Sector Fleet Dakota musters two hundred and eighty million cubic meters and five hundred starfighters."

He gestured a comparative hologram of *Krakatoa* next to *Hancock*. His new flagship was half again the size of Sector Fleet Meridian's heaviest warship.

"Vice Admiral Rutherford has requested that I reinforce his position," James said quietly. "By the time any communication with Sol could be completed, Meridian could very easily have been overrun by superior League forces.

"I cannot permit that to happen. I *will not* permit that to happen," he reiterated. "I am sworn to the defense not only of this Sector but of the entire Commonwealth. There are six star systems and fourteen billion people in the Meridian Sector—and one of those star systems has already been occupied by Dictator Periklos's forces."

He let that sink in for a moment, the comparison hologram of the two carriers hanging in the air. Then he pinched them into nothingness and faced the Council.

"How much of your force are you intending to take?" Abiodun finally asked.

"There are two types of operations available in a crisis situation like this, Minister Abiodun," James told her. "Those that justify the deployment of the entirety of Sector Fleet Dakota and those that cannot justify risking any of our FTL-capable units.

"This is the former. I will be taking all seven of my Alcubierre-Stetson-capable warships to Meridian at ten hundred hours standard on November twenty-sixth."

"You intend to leave Dakota Sector defenseless?" Spitz demanded, the Gothic representative looking distressed. "The Stellar League is not the only potential threat, Admiral Tecumseh."

"I am aware of that, Minister Spitz," James agreed. "However, I have no reason to believe the Sector Fleets around Dakota are likely to engage in grand piratical attacks at this time.

"I do not expect to have the fleet away for more than six weeks," he continued. "There are no systems in the Sector that do not muster at least three hundred starfighters in their own defense.

"I do not intend to draw on that starfighter strength at this time, though we may need to in future if we take losses," he warned. "That is part of the purpose of Security Protocol Twenty-Six, after all."

"A fleet could already be on their way to assault any of our systems," Spitz replied. "We have no intelligence, no communications, no data on which to base our decisions."

"That won't change quickly, Minister," James told him. "But the defensive arrays emplaced in the Dakota Sector are powerful enough to stand off four or five capital ships on their own. It would take an entire sector fleet to threaten any of your star systems.

"The real threat on the board at the moment is that the Stellar League has refused the Commonwealth's efforts to negotiate a peace," he continued. "In our weakness, Dictator Periklos sees an opportunity to seize systems and resources he would never be able to threaten in other times.

"To preserve not merely the security of the Meridian Sector but the security of the Dakota Sector and indeed the entire Clockward frontier of the Commonwealth, Periklos and his ex-mercenary Admirals must be taught the price of attacking our systems.

"The Commonwealth is weak now," James admitted softly. "We are divided and we are afraid. We cannot let that fear divide us further. If the Meridian Sector and Admirals Rutherford and Washington stand alone, Meridian will fall. Six star systems of the Commonwealth will join the Stellar League in being ruled by a former mercenary determined to build a personal empire."

He looked around the room and spread his hands.

"You do not have the authority to stop me," he noted. "But I would far rather engage in this mission with your approval and assistance. Even without the communications we are used to, the Commonwealth must stand together or we will be overrun piece by piece."

James had no idea how he would deal with the inevitable push for secession from some Commonwealth worlds. So far, his efforts and the governance conference seemed to have kept the Dakota Sector content —and the situation in the Meridian Sector was thankfully black-and-white.

"The Vice Admiral is correct," Chapulin said quietly. "I was never a naval officer, but I *was* a Marine. I am familiar with pirate thugs and mercenaries. Periklos is of the smarter end of the breed, calmer and gentler on first appearance, but he is still a warlord who has bound sixty-six systems together at the point of a sword.

"If Admiral Tecumseh beats his forces back now, we buy the Commonwealth time to establish courier-based communications and begin manufacturing or purchasing new entangled particles. But if we let him take Meridian, they will only be the *first* sector to fall."

James nodded gratefully to Dakota's leader.

"Look around this room," Patience Abiodun told her compatriots, her tone quiet. "Three white men. Two of the Old Nations of America. One from Africa. One from Japan.

"Four of the seven of us are from nations that felt the boots of European conquerors and would-be conquerors. We *know* what it means to be *weak.*"

That was probably unfair to Leon, Rakes and Spitz, James knew. But Abiodun's point stood.

"If we stand with Meridian, we combine our strength with theirs and convince the wolves at the door of the Commonwealth's strength," she said. "If we let Meridian fall, we do not merely *show* weakness. We *become* weak. If we lack the will to fight for ourselves, men like Periklos will not give us a second chance.

"I move that this Council unanimously approve Vice Admiral Tecumseh's operation and deploy whatever resources we can command to support this operation."

Sanada had remained silent for most of the conversation, but he shifted forward now and ran a sharp gaze over the room.

"I second Councillor Abiodun's proposal," he said calmly. "Should we discuss this further, or shall we let it pass by acclamation?"

James waited, allowing a silent discussion of gazes and moral suasion to be carried out across the table.

"Then it stands," Sanada said as the silence lasted. "Vice Admiral Tecumseh, this provisional sector council supports your operation. Let us and our subordinates know what resources are needed."

He shrugged massively.

"Most of the true resources will come from Dakota by necessity, but I believe we can each commit our governments to carry our share of those costs," he told the others. "The fate of our sector hangs in the balance, after all."

34

Dakota System
19:00 November 24, 2737 ESMDT

THE MEETING BROKE up shortly afterward, but James found himself expertly corralled by the Dakotan staff and allowed himself to be guided to Chapulin's office.

The First Chief managed to make it there before him and was in the process of hanging up the complex harness of her regalia as he entered.

"Admiral," she greeted him.

"First Chief," he replied. "Thank you for your support earlier. I'm not sure they would have come onside without your urging."

"You'd be surprised," Chapulin said. "Spitz has legitimate reasons to be concerned, but Abiodun will carry water for you until the heat death of the universe." She grimaced. "I suspect she is still calculating the odds on you ending up as our military dictator."

"The thought makes my skin crawl," James said. "Civil and military authority need to be kept separate. Running a fleet is bad enough —I'm already responsible for fifty thousand lives in this system alone.

With the Security Protocol active, there's at least another fifty thousand in the rest of the sector I've taken command of."

"I know," the First Chief told him. "If I *didn't* know that with the certainty I do, I wouldn't trust you as far as I do, Admiral. In this case, I agree with your arguments anyway, though. This isn't entirely on trust."

"It should never be entirely on trust," James said. "Trust should only ever open the door for discussion; it should not bypass it unless secrecy is absolutely necessary."

The ex-Marine chuckled.

"Has anyone ever told you you have a stick up your ass?" she asked.

"James Walkingstick," James said bluntly. "At least, that was certainly the most *memorable* occasion I've been told that."

"There's a name I'm not looking forward to hearing an update on," Chapulin murmured. "He dragged us into the war that dumped us into this mess."

"To give him some credit, I don't think anyone anticipated the kind of Hail Mary sucker punch the Alliance threw at us," he admitted. "It wasn't my job to prevent, but I certainly didn't see it coming."

"Indeed." She shook her head. "So, it's war, is it, Admiral?"

"I *think* if we kick the Star Admiral's fleet hard enough and retake Persephone, Periklos will rethink whether our weakness is an opportunity for victory—or for avoiding defeat," James said. "I doubt, for example, that the Alliance is going to decline our peace negotiations as the League did.

"They took us out of the fight, but I doubt they got nearly as many of their ships back as they would have liked," he guessed. "Mission accomplished, but I wouldn't want to see their butcher's bill. What I know of ours…"

He shook his head.

"My senior fleet officers alone lost two siblings, four cousins and at least a dozen lifelong friends," James admitted. "I lost two friends in this mess and almost lost a valued colleague when Borgogni overran the Clockward Fleet."

Jessie Modesitt had commanded one of his ships when he'd been sent past the Alliance on the mission that had nearly ended his career. She'd come out of it looking better than he had, picking up her first star and a battleship command.

Of course, said battleship was one of the only two *Monarch*-class ships still in existence. Like James, she'd given her parole not to fight against the Alliance of Free Stars. So, she'd been given the crappiest battleship the Navy had and sent to join the Clockward Fleet.

"That's…part of why I wanted to talk to you," Chapulin said with a sigh.

"The Clockward Fleet?" James asked.

"Yeah. Can you get me a status update on Colonel Frederick Vega?" she said. "My…ex-husband. My daughter's father."

He nodded, running the name into his implant, and then sighed as the data came back.

"Commanding officer of the Marine contingent of the *Volcano*-class carrier *Pelée*," he murmured. "*Pelée* was in their Task Force Three, Quetzalli. They got jumped inside lance range by the entire League strike fleet.

"Colonel Vega likely never even knew his ship was under attack."

"That's what I was afraid of," Chapulin said softly. "Thank you."

At first blush, the age gap between a woman who'd retired as a Colonel twenty years earlier and a man who was *currently* a Colonel looked odd—until the record told James that Vega had been an enlisted man and had been mustanged to a commissioned rank around the same time that Quetzalli Chapulin had mustered out.

He was actually five years *older* than her—and had been one of the senior noncoms of her last unit.

"Were you still close?" he asked.

"No…and yes…and…" She sighed. "It's never simple, Admiral. Especially not with a kid involved. We…" She sighed again, even more heavily.

"We were in blatant violation of more regs than I can count," she admitted. "Sleeping with my headquarters company's senior noncom? He was directly in charge of the Marines responsible for my safety.

"But…somehow we managed to keep it under wraps until he got

mustanged to Lieutenant and I retired. We figured that surviving *that* meant we'd survive anything and got married straight away. I…"

She chuckled bitterly.

"We'd never seriously talked about kids and I made a huge assumption," she concluded. "I did want kids and got pregnant on his first leave after the wedding. At which point I discovered that he really, really, *really* didn't want kids."

"That's a hell of a communications blip, Chief," James said softly. As much to say *anything*—this wasn't a conversation they needed to have for their working relationship, but he also understood that she likely didn't *have* that many people who'd understand the military part of it.

"His dad died on deployment when he was very young," she said. "I didn't know that until the wedding. Should have been a clue about how much we'd missed, sneaking around to avoid getting caught out.

"In the end, we were divorced before Tlalli was born. Not even married for a full year. He was always going to stay in the Corps; I was always going to come back to Dakota and get into politics."

She looked down at her hands.

"Freddie didn't want to be a father and was so angry at me for thinking he did, but he didn't flinch from it, either. Might have just been another duty to him, but he was there for our daughter all along. I don't think Tlalli even knows she was why we got divorced.

"And now he's gone."

"I'm sorry," James murmured.

"You want my advice, James?" Chapulin asked, her eyes glittering with unshed tears as she focused on him.

He made a small go-ahead gesture, not at all sure where this was going.

"You stay on Dakota tonight and you spend it with Abey," she told him. "Then, as you have time while you're on your grand quest, you get straight in your head where you're going with my aide, Admiral Tecumseh.

"And when you get back, you either let her down gently or take her on a real date. There's no sneaking around required with you two, and

I cannot recommend against it strongly enough. You understand me, James?"

"I do," he murmured, considering her point. "I truly do."

"She's still here," Chapulin told him. "She's working. Like the both of us, she doesn't really know where to stop on that part."

"From what she's said, originally *seducing me* was supposed to be work," James noted drily.

"She realized that wasn't necessary pretty damn quick," Dakota's elected ruler told him. "So did I—and no, I *didn't* put her up to that, though I knew what she was doing. She needs someone who understands her dedication to her duty. So do you, I think."

"I wouldn't know," he murmured. "Been married to the Navy for a very long time, Quetzalli."

"Then get the hell out of my office and talk to the woman," Chapulin told him. "I need to be alone, anyway. And work out how to get a message to Tlalli's university on Earth."

———

JAMES'S neural implant was easily able to both guide him to Abey's office and send the assorted messages he needed to send to set up his staying on the surface. He hadn't actually been planning on returning to *Krakatoa* that night, though he hadn't *necessarily* decided if he was going to try to spend it with Abey.

The redheaded Navajo woman looked up as he knocked on her door and smiled in surprise.

"James, I was expecting you to head back to your ship," she admitted.

"The First Chief corralled me to ask about a friend of hers with Clockward Fleet," he told her. "And I wasn't sure if I should be pressuring the Tááła'í'tsin shuttleport to handle more night flights than I have to."

"I see," she said. "I'm pleased to see you. Will you…"

"My shuttle flight is scheduled for oh six hundred standard, which is about nine AM local time, as I understand it," he told her. "I could certainly go find a hotel room without much difficulty, but your boss suggested that I check with you first."

Abey laughed and blatantly undid the top three buttons on her shirt.

"I definitely have an alternative suggestion for where you can stay," she conceded. "If you're willing to take the step of sleeping at my apartment, anyway."

"Abey, I haven't done *any* of this since I was twenty-four years old," James warned her. "I have *no* idea what constitutes 'a step' as opposed to a continuation of where we're at. I *do* know that I'm about to go off to war, and that comes with all kinds of…weight, I guess."

She sighed and waved her console to sleep.

"It does," she admitted. "And I'm not going to pretend I'm going to get any work done with an attractive older man I've already slept with sitting in my office. My place is walking distance from here."

"I'm guessing you have Marines that will keep us company?"

"Discreetly," James promised. "I hope, anyway."

She laughed.

"And are they already scouting my place for security vantages?"

He winced.

"Almost certainly," he conceded. "The advantage of Táála'í'tsin is that there are always trees for them to hide in."

"Discreet. Right." She stepped around the desk and kissed him. "We'll make do, I suppose."

"They can't help but see, but they can keep their mouths shut," James promised. "*That* I can be very certain of."

She wrapped an arm around his waist and leaned against his shoulder.

"Then let's take a walk, shall we?"

35

Dakota System
10:00 November 26, 2737 ESMDT

"ALL SHIPS REPORT READY TO MANEUVER."

Commodore Voclain's plain report reverberated through the flag deck on *Krakatoa* like a portent of dooms to come.

It had been almost a year since James Tecumseh had last taken any warships into action. Six months since he'd arrived in Dakota, under a cloud of unofficial disapproval, for what had been intended as a quiet posting where he couldn't cause trouble.

Now seven warships of the Terran Commonwealth Navy and over forty thousand human beings awaited his order.

"Signal all ships: we will proceed on the planned course," he said crisply.

It was probably his imagination that *Krakatoa* seemed to leap into movement around him, an eager warhorse looking forward to her first true battle. The other ships in Sector Fleet Dakota had the scars and repairs to show of older battles, but *Krakatoa* was too new. She'd been commissioned during a period where the Commonwealth had focused its efforts on two real wars and never made it to the front of either conflict.

And that was about to change.

"All ships are at two hundred gravities' acceleration and holding," Voclain reported.

The verbal reports were redundant, duplicating data that was available to James both in his implants and in the massive hologram tank that centered the flag deck. Seven capital ships of the TCN. Two battleships, a battlecruiser, two strike cruisers and two carriers.

Only one of those ships was new, the rapid pace of recent A-S drive developments having left the *economized* ships of the *Assassins*' and *Oceans*' generation dangerously obsolete. The TCN had learned from its mistakes, but not before building almost three hundred capital ships that couldn't truly stand up to their contemporaries.

"ETA to warped space?" he asked aloud.

"Just under two hours. We expect to arrive in Meridian on December seventh, around twenty-one hundred hours," she concluded.

Eleven days. Eleven days in which James and his fleet would be completely incommunicado.

"Let's get final status reports from all of the fighter stations in Dakota orbit," he ordered quietly. He'd already received them from the ones at Base Łá'ts'áadah. Each of those platforms had about two thousand people aboard, half of them currently reporting through the starfighter corps.

That reminded James of something he needed to take care of.

"Once we have those reports, have Colonel Yamamoto report to my office," he ordered. "The CAG and I need to go over the starfighter wings' statuses."

———

JAMES MADE one small stop in a nearby quartermaster shop before Yamamoto made it to his new office, collecting a small box he put on his desk as he researched how the particulars of the situation lined up with the rules.

Or didn't, as the case turned out, since no one had ever *written* rules for this situation.

"Yamamoto, reporting," the Scottish-Japanese officer said crisply as he entered the office. He looked around the decorations Todacheeney's team had sourced for the room, and a smile threatened his stern-officer visage.

"I see that Dakota is busily claiming you as their own," he said.

"The situation with my family, my nation and Dakota is...not quite that straightforward," James admitted. "But all of this is from my people. About half of all acknowledged members of the Shawnee nation are here."

Most of the rest were still on Earth, though James knew there was a settlement group of about half a million souls in, of all places, the Castle Federation. While he didn't know for certain, there was a decent chance there'd been at least one Shawnee among the enemies he'd faced under Walkingstick's command.

"Home is where, when you show up, they have to take you in," Yamamoto said drily. "Nice to feel valued."

"It is," James replied. "Though the Sector's leadership understands where my loyalties lie. I serve the Commonwealth.

"But speaking of 'valued,' I owe you an apology, Colonel Yamamoto."

"Sir?" The Scotsman sounded confused. He also hadn't sat down yet, a habit that James was learning to tolerate—he, for one, wasn't going to be intimidated by someone standing while he was seated.

"When I initially activated Security Protocol Twenty-Six, I was the *acting* commander of Sector Fleet Dakota," James explained. "As such, I didn't feel it was appropriate for me to be handing out even brevet promotions.

"Which meant that you ended up responsible for two thousand starfighters and twenty thousand–ish people across six star systems with a reasonable argument of whether you even had the rank and authority to give some of those people orders."

"No one gave me any grief, sir, but I was wondering on that point," Yamamoto said levelly.

James smiled.

"The *apology*, Colonel, is because I didn't change that when I was promoted and confirmed as Sector Fleet Commander," he told the younger man, sliding the jeweler's box across the table.

"Congratulations, *Wing Colonel*," he continued as Yamamoto opened the box holding the single star of a Commonwealth O-7—a Navy Commodore or a Starfighter Corps Wing Colonel. "It's a more-appropriate rank for a full Fleet CAG, anyway, though we both know what it means for you flying the CAP yourself."

"I probably shouldn't?" Yamamoto suggested drily.

"You probably shouldn't even as *Krakatoa's* CAG, let alone as Fleet CAG, *let alone* as a junior flag officer," James pointed out. It was a common-enough failing on the part of fighter pilots that he hadn't bothered to yank the man up short, but the CAG really had no business flying in anything less than full-group maneuvers.

"This shouldn't change anything for you, but I wanted to get it handled before we went FTL," James continued. "All the other ships will be advised before we jump, but I recommend you have a conference with at least your senior officers before we warp space.

"You have forty-five minutes," he concluded with a grin.

"Then I need to be about it, don't I?" Yamamoto brogued, his accent clearly intentionally thickened. "Thank you, sir."

"You're welcome. Prove me right by doing the job."

"Yes, sir."

36

Deep Space
22:00 November 26, 2737 ESMDT

FIGHTER PILOTS BEING FIGHTER PILOTS, it was no surprise to Anthony Yamamoto that his announcement of his promotion to Wing Colonel had turned into an impromptu celebratory party. There wasn't that much for the fighter crews to *do* while a carrier was in FTL—simulations could help keep the edge from rusting off, but they weren't the same as real-space exercises.

So, a certain degree of...*impropriety* on the part of the fighter crews and their support personnel was ignored while in warped space. That willful blindness, Anthony knew, was also extended to the rest of the carrier's personnel.

Warped space was *weird*. There was no real physical aspect to it, unless you were one of the individuals who would find the external observation decks or turn off the simulated starfield projected to any of the virtual windows throughout the ship. Then you could see the twisted and warped reality of the light and energy fields wrapped around the starship, and *that* could be disconcerting.

For most people, though, it was a mental and emotional thing—and *Krakatoa*'s crew was discovering that a lack of communication while under A-S drive aggravated the sensation tenfold.

So, ten hours after they went FTL, Anthony was standing at the side of the pilot's lounge, watching two of the flight engineers wrestle *another* keg of Dakota-brewed beer up onto the table. It was, he reflected, probably time for the Fleet CAG to disappear.

"You know, boss, the party is supposed to be in your honor."

He looked away from the keg to find Şenol Badem standing beside him. The cyborg engineer gave him a small smile as they settled themselves onto the wall next to him.

"I was in the middle earlier," Anthony pointed out. "Now, though, I suspect that this party is in the process of becoming wilder than the Wing Colonel can admit to knowing about."

"Not nearly as stiff as you pretend, I see," Badem murmured.

"Practical, Badem. Practical," Anthony repeated, wondering what was on Badem's mind.

"And tradition says we turn a blind eye to a lot in FTL," they said, echoing his earlier thoughts. "One finds themselves wondering just *how* blind."

Anthony stayed silent, recognizing suddenly that Badem was wearing makeup. It wasn't much, just a few subtle touches of color that drew attention away from their visible cybernetics to their full lips and jade-green eyes.

He swallowed an audible sigh as he realized what the engineer was after—unfortunately, in the same moment that Badem mustered their courage.

"I was wondering if you wanted company as you wander away from the party," they ventured. "I...understand you're broader-minded than some."

Badem was artificially intersex—even Anthony had no ability to find out what their birth-assigned gender was or even the exact nature of their particular version of that artificial sex.

The transhuman movement, the people who believed that

humanity should go further than the ubiquitous neural implants and omnipresent subtle genetic and cybernetic upgrades common in twenty-eighth-century humanity, commonly embraced the concept of being AIS as part of that journey.

And while the Commonwealth would never consciously permit anything resembling prejudice to hold them back, they were unusual enough that he suspected they had difficulties finding relationships.

Of course, making a pass at not only the commanding officer of the entire fleet fighter group but the pilot of *your starfighter* was a terrible idea. Anthony's...flexible sexuality wasn't exactly common knowledge among his subordinates, either, so he wondered how Badem had learned about that without learning about the *other* problem with their idea.

"Lieutenant Badem, I am flattered," he told them gently. "But even with the blind eye we turn in FTL, some regs exist for a reason. It would not be healthy for us to go into a combat scenario with you actively furious at your pilot and commanding officer.

"And given the way my brain is wired, I suspect that is a near-inevitable end result," he said. "I believe the best thing to happen now, Lieutenant, is for me to retire to my usual intentional ignorance of the rowdy party...and forget this conversation ever happened."

Using his rank to shut them down was probably harsher than he needed to be, but Anthony figured Badem would be hurt less this way. Better to tear the bandage off now, *before* anyone discovered the hard way that some people were literally incapable of romantic interest.

"I'm...sorry, sir," they said, clearly struggling to remain calm.

"I am flattered," he repeated. "But I think we are both best served by letting this go, understand?"

———

WHEN THE LIGHTS in Anthony's bedroom refused to turn on, he didn't even bother to curse. His sidearm was in a closet with his day-uniform jacket. All he was currently wearing was the shipsuit base layer, the one that underlay every uniform since it could act as an emergency spacesuit.

"Reynolds?" he asked the darkness.

There was a moment of silence, then the lights in the room rose up to *dim*, allowing him to spot the CISS agent sitting cross-legged on his bed.

"Wing Colonel," she greeted him. "Congratulations."

"Thanks," he muttered at the petite blonde assassin. "Why are you *on my bed?*"

"Needed to talk to you," she told him. Like him, she was wearing the shipsuit underlayer. It was in the right colors and cut to pass a first glance anywhere on a Commonwealth warship. Anyone looking twice would realize that she wasn't wearing insignia and question her, but he doubted she'd let anyone take that second look.

"And if I'd been bringing someone back to my quarters to celebrate my promotion?" he asked drily. If someone he didn't need to watch his back in combat had made Badem's offer—and he had been sure they understood that sex was *all* they were getting—he would have considered it.

"Oh, I'd have been delighted to join in," Reynolds told him with a wicked smile. "It's been a while since I had a good railing."

He raised a silent eyebrow at that and she laughed.

"Your psych profile says you're a bisexual aromantic," she told him. "Which I'd have figured anyway. Takes one to know one." She shook her head. "If I thought it would help keep you onside, you'd have been inside me ages ago. Instead, it gets to be all business all the time."

Or, at least, most of the time. That particular admission was probably being too honest, to Anthony's mind, and he glared half-seriously at the woman.

"What do you *want?*" he asked. "I think it's pretty clear now that Tecumseh has the Commonwealth's best interests at heart. Isn't your mission just about done?"

"My *mission*, Wing Colonel, is to preserve the Commonwealth," Reynolds said sharply. "And, like the Vice Admiral, I have a broad remit and very little communication with my superiors.

"As a matter of fact, I *do* agree with your assessment of Tecumseh," she admitted. "Not enough to let even *you* know my cover identity, but enough to think that he's a better choice for all of our sakes than any other option on the table.

"Which actually brings me to one of the questions I wanted to ask you. If something awful happens to Tecumseh, Voclain takes over, right?"

"Right," Anthony confirmed. "She's the senior Commodore, followed by Commodores Volkov and Bardakçı."

"Fu-un," Reynolds replied. "Of those three, I'm pretty sure Volkov is okay and I'm pretty sure Voclain is watching for an angle. Banks was in my files, after all."

Anthony blinked.

"Vice Admiral Banks was in...*which* files?" he asked carefully.

"Do you really think CISS *doesn't* have a list of flag officers we expect to be problems in a situation like this?" Reynolds asked bluntly. "*Especially* Sector Fleet commanders who've had time to get all cozy with appropriate factions and organizations around them?

"Banks was on our list of 'most likely to turn warlord.' Tecumseh was, after his assorted stunts over in the Rimward Marches, on our list of 'we have no idea what this idiot will do.'" She sighed. "Now I have a decent idea of what Tecumseh will do, and off we go to the edge of the damn Commonwealth."

"Where's Washington on your list?" Anthony asked, curious.

"Reliable as granite," she said calmly. "Earthborn, older sister is Congressperson for Terra itself. Not a Unification fanatic, but he'll die for the Commonwealth. More reliable than Tecumseh, and I'd put the Admiral up there at this point.

"*Rutherford*, on the other hand, I don't have as detailed a file on, because he wasn't a Sector Fleet Admiral," she said grimly. "What I *do* have, however, suggests that he hitched his star to Marshal Amandine a long time ago and has risen on her coattails. They were lovers, have been for at least five or six years, but CISS's impression is that the *attachment* is strictly one way."

"Takes one to know one?" Anthony echoed back to her.

"If the Commonwealth's counterintelligence and counterinsurgency agency can't recognize when someone is being used, we aren't doing our jobs," she pointed out. "So long as the Commonwealth was the best game in town and Amandine's career was a boost to his, his loyalty to both our nation and his girlfriend was assured.

"Now… Well, there may be an update to his psych profile that I wasn't given," she admitted. "But I'm tagging along at this point, Anthony, to watch Admiral Tecumseh's back. The only knives I want in his back are those *I* approve."

"Why does that not make me feel any better?" Anthony asked.

"Because you know I value the principles of the Commonwealth over human life," Reynolds said sweetly. "And for most sane people, that's disconcerting."

"Which ones?" he replied. "I've seen a lot of freedom, justice and democracy sacrificed on the altar of unity, after all."

"Haven't we all?" she agreed. "But it's one of four to my mind, though I am *also* sworn to uphold the Commonwealth itself."

She smiled. She had a very cute smile for a human-shaped predator.

"I believe you swore basically the same oath."

"I did," Anthony agreed. "And that's why you picked me to use as your eyes and ears."

He shrugged.

"I'm guessing you want me to keep sending you meeting notes?"

"Yes," she confirmed. "I have a cover identity aboard *Krakatoa*. The drop box you have will still get to me. If you think there's an active threat to Tecumseh, or an emergency, drop a message to the box with the subject *Horny Redheads Play Ball*."

For a deadly killing machine in the form of a shapely woman of a hundred and sixty–odd centimeters, Reynolds had a very clear, dirty sense of humor.

"What exactly are we calling an emergency here?" he asked drily.

"Preferably 'someone is trying to stab me,' not 'I need to get laid,'" she said, with a crisp precision undermined by her choice of scenarios.

"I will keep that in mind," Anthony told her. "Now may I actually get some sleep?"

The disappointed pout she threw him was probably theatrical. *Probably.*

37

Sol System
12:00 December 4, 2737 ESMDT

IT HAD NEVER BEEN MEANT to come to this.

The Star Chamber of the Interstellar Congress was deathly silent as Marshal Fleet Admiral James Calvin Walkingstick made his way down the main aisle. Around him, what had once been the buoyancy tank of Earth's first space elevator—and still was, in truth, despite the massive redesign—gleamed with the wealth and power of the Commonwealth.

Over seven hundred politicians sat in that room, lit by a mix of carefully installed modern lighting and natural light from floor-to-ceiling windows onto the Atlantic Ocean. Banners for each of the Commonwealth's hundred-plus star systems lined the walls, and the big Cherokee Admiral wondered which of those star systems had already broken faith with Earth.

Every politician in the room had a rifle trained on them. The Star Chamber Lictors, the armed security responsible for the protection of the Senators and Congresspeople in the room, were huddled in a corner under the guns of another company of Walkingstick's Marines.

Those politicians' eyes were on the Marshal as he strode, intentionally slowly, toward the central stage. His Marine commander, General Krizman, walked two steps behind his left hand, with his senior task force commander, Vice Admiral Tasker, two steps behind his right. Four Marines followed them, and the footfalls of those seven souls were the only sound carrying through the chamber.

There were only two people on the central stage when Walkingstick arrived: a broad-shouldered, white-haired Black man and a frail-looking woman with pale skin and hair. They were Michael Burns, Senator for Alpha Centauri and head of the Committee on Unification, and Janet Lane, the Speaker of the Congress and second-most powerful person in the Commonwealth.

The *most* powerful person, of course, was the man in charge of the conquest of the human race. The President was a nonentity, but Michael Burns had been the Commonwealth's sword and strong hand for over a decade.

And James Walkingstick's friend—but all of Burns's power hadn't been enough to prevent the orders that had been sent to bring James Calvin Walkingstick back to be executed as a scapegoat for the Commonwealth's failures.

"When I warned you, I expected you to run," Burns told Walkingstick, ignoring the surprised looks and sounds from the rest of the chamber. No space in the universe had acoustics as well designed as the Star Chamber. Even his soft words were carried through the entire space.

"Bringing your fleet was treason, a Rubicon of unparalleled proportions."

Walkingstick winced, but anger burned under it. The Chamber hadn't even tried to talk to him. The moment his fleet had emerged from warped space, they'd ordered Home Fleet into battle. With Terra Fortress Command in tatters, those officers had declined to commit suicide.

He now commanded the hundred starships in the Sol System. What was left of Central Command—run by Fleet Admiral Oliver, a woman who'd been a Fortress Command *Vice Admiral* three months earlier—had conceded his command. That meant he commanded the entire Commonwealth Navy, at least in theory.

"If you were prepared to execute me, you were prepared to destroy the Navy out of paranoia," Walkingstick finally replied to Burns, his tone equally soft. Everyone would hear him anyway.

"You left me few choices."

"So, you chose treason?" Speaker Lane snapped.

"I chose my oath," he replied, his tone sharp. "To protect and serve the *Commonwealth*. Not the Congress. Not the Committee. Not the Senate or the Assembly. The Commonwealth.

"With the network gone, we must hold together our nation with duct tape and blood until we have restored it. This is not the time to turn on each other! But you turned on me."

He hadn't planned this. Part of him had wanted it, he couldn't deny that, but his oaths *meant* something to him. It was the anger of his people, his admirals and his generals, that had hurled him onto this path.

Inevitable as it had become, part of him wasn't sure any of it had truly been *his* choice.

The silence was deafening until Michael Burns stepped forward, ignoring the Marines and leaving Lane definitively behind him.

"You know how this ends now, James," he said firmly, the iron inevitability of his tone sending strange shivers down Walkingstick's spine. "From the moment you left Niagara with a *fleet*, you knew how this had to end.

"You set your feet upon an ancient path that can only end here. Can only end in one way. If you would save the Commonwealth, then do it," Burns ordered.

"You leave us only one choice."

Burns knelt, his words booming out across the Star Chamber with unexpected force.

"*Ave, Imperator Terrae!*"

38

Deep Space
20:00 December 7, 2737 ESMDT

THE LACK of communications in warped space was grating on James Tecumseh. The loss of the q-com network had defined his last two months, but he'd spent all of that time in the Dakota System. His interstellar communications had been gone, but he'd been able to talk to people on the planet and the other ships of his command.

For the entirety of the eleven-day journey from Dakota to Meridian, the only people he'd been able to communicate with had been aboard *Krakatoa*. A dozen complex scanning algorithms managed to detect the other Alcubierre bubbles and confirm that the rest of the fleet was still with him, but that was it.

"We are exactly one hour from emergence," Voclain announced on the flag deck. She glanced back at James. "Has anyone found this a lovely preview of hell?"

"Truthfully, I would hope that even hell would have more than seven thousand people in it," he said drily. "And to be fair, whose hell?"

What remained of the Shawnee traditional belief system had been run through a brutal winnowing in the late second millennium and was left heavily Christianized. James wasn't much of a believer in *anything*, but he suspected that the underworld he'd been taught about growing up didn't line up neatly with Christian hell.

"I don't know, but I'm assuming *someone*'s hell involves being out of contact with the people you care about," Voclain replied. "No offense to the other people on this ship, but it's been a *lovely* reminder that everyone I want to talk to outside of work is a few dozen light-years away."

"Our whole universe got yanked away from us two months ago," James agreed. "But yeah. Being trapped in just an Alcubierre bubble was worse than I anticipated."

He ran through the latest reports on *Krakatoa*'s readiness. The big carrier was operating at as high a level as she could. The simulations for Yamamoto's fighters were all looking good, and the training exercises for the rest of the crew were at the highest rankings.

All of that was simulations, though. There was only so much they could do in FTL, and without real-space maneuvers, James worried about his fleet getting rusty. Especially since none of his ships had seen action with their current crews.

Many of his officers—like Yamamoto, for example—had seen combat against the Alliance or the League or one of the single-system states the Commonwealth semi-regularly absorbed. None had done so as part of their current organizations, and James was all too aware of how much the rules had changed.

So much of their doctrine was built around instant communications. They'd practiced theories and plans to account for that, but the only way to prove out those plans and theories was in blood.

"Does anyone want to take the bet that Periklos has changed his mind, withdrawn from Persephone and sued for peace?" he asked.

"Unlikely," Bevan replied, the intelligence officer taking his comment more seriously than James meant it. "Periklos isn't one to give up when he's ahead. The Clockward Fleet has been hanging over his head for a year, and Star Admiral Borgogni just blew it away.

"We should probably be taking bets on whether *Meridian* is in League control," he said grimly.

"We have a contingency plan for that," James told the intel officer. That plan was based around the assumption that the SLN couldn't have taken out Sector Fleet Meridian, the survivors of the Clockward Fleet *and* Meridian's orbital defenses without getting hammered.

Hopefully badly enough that Sector Fleet Dakota could retake Meridian relatively easily. Because if James didn't think he could retake the system without major losses, he was going to have to withdraw—and if he withdrew, they were writing off an entire sector.

He wasn't sure the Commonwealth would survive that—but he couldn't sacrifice Dakota Sector's only defenders to avoid that possibility.

"Let's hope we don't need that plan," Voclain replied. "We'll know soon enough."

———

NORMALLY, James wouldn't stress much about arriving in a friendly system.

Of course, normally, they'd be receiving live telemetry from the system's traffic-control centers, with detailed directions of where to emerge, locations and vectors of possible debris, and be *scheduled* with the locals.

Arriving in Meridian, they had none of that. Admiral Rutherford presumably knew Sector Fleet Dakota was coming—or, at least, *hoped* Sector Fleet Dakota was coming—but even he would have no timeline.

Without knowing what else was going on in Meridian, they were emerging significantly farther out than usual, in a section of the system well away from any known stations or travel routes.

The system's lack of traditional asteroid belts reduced the number of routes crisscrossing it. Most of Meridian's raw resources came from the three gas giants and their trojan clusters. The Sector Fleet's logistics base was anchored on a rare hot gas giant, a smaller gaseous planet orbiting at barely three light-minutes from the star.

Greenwich, the main habitable planet, was a small and dense world with minimal liquid water but extensive plant life and massive peaks full of valuable minerals. The records James had on the planet made it a stark contrast to Dakota's planetwide nature sanctuary.

Meridian's central planet was a world of mines and factories, fueled by water taken from the trojan clusters. Even three billion souls couldn't fill a planet, though, and they'd focused their industry on the mountainous plateaus to the north and south. The equatorial regions were untouched vast arid plains, prairies the size of entire Terran continents and home to massive herds of imported buffalo and cattle.

"Emergence in sixty seconds," Voclain reported. "Last chance to change your mind about all of this, Admiral."

James snorted.

"Unless you've magically worked out how to communicate with the rest of the Sector Fleet while under A-S drive *without* having entangled particles, Commodore, the last chance to change my mind was almost two weeks ago.

"Carry on."

He leaned back in his seat, studying the hologram of the system and waiting for *Krakatoa*'s sensors to update it with current information.

"Emergence."

One moment, every piece of information James was seeing about the universe around him was a projection. The next, *Krakatoa* was once more in the real world, her sensors drinking deep of the light and radiation around her.

The first thing they had definitive data on was their sibling ships. All seven ships of Sector Fleet Dakota were present and accounted for in the first few moments, though James knew that Sumiko Mac Cléirich and her people would already be reaching out for updates on the fleet's status.

New icons filled in across the star system as Voclain's analysis staff dug in to the information they were picking up. *Krakatoa* was thirteen light-minutes from Meridian itself and four light-minutes from Greenwich.

Everything they were seeing was out of date, but four minutes wasn't enough to change its value for their current purposes. James concealed a sigh of relief as the icons of the Meridian Defense Command fortresses solidified. Their files gave them the numbers and orbits of those stations as of October tenth, but no one had bothered to send updates in the handful of mail exchanges since.

In-system clippers were all over the star system, the smaller sublight ships hurtling between planets with the critical cargos for even one star system's infrastructure. Those icons were mostly unimportant to James, though their presence—plus the fortresses—told him that the system was still in Commonwealth hands.

"Multiple large contacts above Greenwich," Voclain reported. "I am confirming...sixteen A-S starships. Thirteen appear to be warships."

"That should be Clockward-Two and Sector Fleet Meridian," James replied. "The others?"

"*Troubadour*-type freighters," the Commodore said. "From their position, they've been commandeered as fleet support."

James grimaced at that. He'd considered that before he'd brought Sector Fleet Dakota to Meridian, but his ships had an impressive organic logistics capability. Given the size and expense of even a civilian Alcubierre-Stetson starship, warships generally had to operate out of their onboard resources anyway.

They could build new missiles from raw iron, for example, but many of the parts involved had to be brought along. Given time, a capital ship could probably set up an exotic-matter plant, but that was more than regular logistics required.

If Rutherford and Washington were planning a counteroffensive, the support of those freighters could be absolutely critical. On the other hand, they might only end up fighting a single battle to retake Persephone, in which case James didn't see the point.

It hadn't been his call, though.

"Mac Cléirich, can you get me a recorded transmission to the Admirals?" he asked.

She was busy organizing the updates from the rest of the fleet, but he felt her acknowledgement in the network—and the delegation of the task to one of her subordinates, shortly followed by the arrival of a new icon on his implant display.

They might not have exchanged verbal words, but he had what he needed, and he'd been kept in the loop the whole way.

"Vice Admiral Rutherford, Vice Admiral Washington," James greeted the camera. "This is Vice Admiral James Tecumseh, commanding Sector Fleet Dakota. Admiral Rutherford requested assistance in standing off a League offensive from Admiral Banks.

"Unfortunately, Admiral Banks is no longer in command of Sector Fleet Dakota. I am, as confirmed by Central Command on Earth." He paused. "Unfortunately, there is a limit to how long I can keep this fleet away from the Dakota Sector in the current circumstances. We will need to plan to make the best use of the time I have available.

"I look forward to discussing our options with you both. Tecumseh out."

39

IN THE GRAND scheme of things, everything that needed to happen with Sector Fleet Dakota's visit to the Meridian Sector was going to be done in a rush. James's mental deadline to be back in Dakota was January tenth, which meant he had to leave Meridian by the twenty-ninth.

But physics was still an unrelenting mistress, and it would take three hours and twenty minutes for his fleet to reach Greenwich orbit. That meant there was no point in rushing the communications back and forth, and James's people had a full set of orbital slots worked out with Greenwich orbital control before James heard from his fellow Admirals.

And if something about the conversations he'd overheard between Mac Cléirich and the locals felt off to him, he was prepared to write that off as paranoia.

"You have an incoming transmission from...Marshal Rutherford?"

Mac Cléirich told him, her audible pause justified if that was the title Rutherford was using.

"Understood," James said, considering things for a moment. "I'll take it in my office," he decided. Something was odd, and he wanted to get a handle on the situation in private before he looped his people in.

"Yes, sir."

His office was attached to the bridge, making it a matter of moments for him to take a seat in the hand-carved chair and activate the security and privacy measures. He took strength from the art around him and its link to his ancestors.

Whatever was going on, he had his people's backing and he spoke for the Commonwealth. They'd deal.

He started the recording, recognizing the muscular officer who appeared in front of him from the message sent from Persephone.

"Vice Admiral Tecumseh, you have no idea how grateful I am to see your fleet," Rutherford told him. "This message is encrypted with L-C-Seven-Nine-H-D-Six-Four-L-O-Three-One."

There was a small pause as the computers activated the key and decrypted the rest of the message, only noticeable because James was looking for it.

"Gabriel Banks and I go back a long way," Rutherford's hologram said. "I appreciate you coming regardless, Admiral Tecumseh, but I hope you have an update on Gabriel's condition?"

He shook himself.

"Unfortunately, I understand all too well how this situation has resulted in strange inheritances," he told James. "Shortly after I detached *Ajax* with the message for your fleet, we received confirmation—'gloating about' might be a more accurate descriptor—of Marshal Amandine's death.

"Per the protocols on record for the Clockward Fleet, I inherited both the survivors of the Fleet and her Marshal's mace as commander of the Clockward Marches."

James had to admit that he didn't actually *know* how a Marshal's mace was supposed to be transferred, but he was under the impression that it could only be given by explicit act of Congress.

"And sadly, Greenwich is seeing an upsurge in anti-Common-wealth terrorist attacks," Rutherford said grimly. "While Brigadier Barbados has mostly managed to get matters under control, Vice Admiral Washington was killed in a bomb attack on his planetside home a week ago."

That reeked to high heaven to James, and he was glad this wasn't a live connection. His expression might have betrayed his thoughts with a bit more honesty than he suspected he could bring to this relationship.

"We'll want to discuss fleet organization in person when you arrive in Greenwich orbit," the Marshal said. "I'm not certain that we'll be able to return you to the Dakota Sector as quickly as you might like. Dealing with the League incursion must be our absolute highest priority."

"Like *fuck* I'm letting you tell me that," James muttered aloud. That had been his fear with Rutherford claiming the title of Marshal. When they were both Vice Admirals, with their respective areas of responsibility, there was no question that James was independent of Rutherford and operating Sector Fleet Dakota under his own cognizance.

If Rutherford was claiming Amandine's Marshal authority, then he theoretically *did* have the authority to commandeer James's ships and personnel. And there was no chance that James was going to let him do that.

"I request that you report aboard *Hancock* for a briefing and strategic discussion as soon as you reach Greenwich," Rutherford continued, thankfully wise enough not to make that an order. "I'll have my staff touch base with yours about any logistical needs your ships have.

"We have a lot of work to do, Admiral Tecumseh, and the loss of Admiral Washington leaves it all on you and me. I look forward to meeting you in person. Marshal Rutherford, out."

The message ended and James swallowed his curse. Regardless of what he thought of Rutherford taking the Marshal title, there was a reason he'd brought Sector Fleet Dakota there—and that reason was a Stellar League invasion fleet.

Still. There had been a name in Rutherford's message that he needed to double-check. There was, he was sure, more than one Brigadier Barbados in the Terran Commonwealth Marine Corps.

His implant and *Krakatoa*'s network confirmed that. There were, in fact, seven Brigadiers in the TCMC with that last name—but the one in command of the TCMC brigade assigned to support the Greenwich Planetary Army was Brigadier *Alric* Barbados, the Marine who'd backed James Tecumseh's decision to ally with the Castle Federation to take down the pirates who'd betrayed him.

With Commodore Jessie Modesitt in command of *King George V*, Meridian was home to several old friends. Old friends James was going to need to talk to.

First, though…

"Voclain, Yamamoto, Volkov," he said aloud, triggering his implant to connect him to all three of those officers. He was waking up at least one of them, he suspected, but that was the military life.

"I need you in my office *now*."

―――――

VOLKOV WAS the last of the three officers to arrive, though Chief Leeuwenhoek was still setting out drinks for everyone when *Krakatoa*'s commanding officer stepped in. The dark-skinned Korean-Russian officer's coloring helped conceal her fatigue, but James was grimly sure he'd woken her up.

"If you need anything other than the waters, let the Chief know," he instructed. "I'll be activating full privacy protocols once she's done."

"Tea, please, Chief," Volkov told Leeuwenhoek.

"Water is fine," Voclain said calmly, the chief of staff holding the glass in her hand as she studied James.

Yamamoto didn't even say anything. He was busy finding a section of wall to prop up that wasn't occupied by one of James's hangings.

A minute or two later, Leeuwenhoek delivered Volkov's green tea and then slipped out of the room. James activated the room's security systems again and leveled a grim look on his subordinates.

"So, I have now exchanged messages with Admiral Rutherford," he told them. "He and I will be meeting once we're in Greenwich orbit to discuss our next steps, but there are already some factors in play that I want us to keep a careful eye on."

"With the League, sir?" Voclain asked.

"With Admiral Rutherford," James admitted. "First of all, Admiral Washington is dead. Someone, believed to be a local secessionist movement, blew his planetside house up with him in it."

"How bad is the situation if the secessionists are bombing *Admirals*?" Yamamoto demanded.

"Unclear," James said. "I'm hoping to connect with the local Marine garrison commander. Brigadier Barbados was at Quebecois Bien with me."

Quebecois Bien had been the main base of the pirate that had betrayed James—and James had in turn liberated Quebecois Bien with the help of the Alliance of Free Stars. The officers and spacers and marines who'd served at that battle would always have a special place for James.

"If the situation was bad enough that Admiral Washington was at risk, he either shouldn't have been on the surface or his security should have been increased enough to make getting to his house almost impossible," Volkov said. "That stinks, Admiral."

"I agree." James sighed. "Especially as it appears that Rutherford has claimed Amandine's Marshal authority. I've checked the protocols, and while chain of command would see him assume control of the Clockward Fleet..."

"Amandine's mace is linked to her DNA," Voclain noted quietly. "You can't be a Marshal without the mace, and he doesn't have one, does he?"

"Not that I know of. Congress certainly hasn't had time to send him one." James took a sip of his coffee to gather his thoughts. "I know that one of the options the Governance Conference in Dakota considered was voluntarily declaring me Marshal over the systems, but that would have been a weird half-state until confirmed by Sol.

"It seems unlikely that Rutherford has been acclaimed by the Meridian Sector, which means he has taken it upon himself to basically declare himself military governor of the sector."

There was a long silence in his office.

"Given that the Meridian Sector is under direct threat from the League and a major effort will be required to retake Persephone and secure the rest of the systems, is that a bad thing?" Voclain asked slowly. "So long as he's loyal to the Commonwealth..."

"I don't approve and it's not the decision I would have made, but..." James sighed. "You're right, Madona. So long as Rutherford follows instructions from Terra and lays down the mace when the time comes, he'll go down in history as a modern Cincinnatus. A hero who saved the Meridian Sector from the League invasion."

"Which is why we're talking about things to keep an eye on," Yamamoto noted from his spot on the wall. "Star Admiral Borgogni is our primary concern, but the Marshal bears watching."

"Exactly," James agreed. "I also have some concerns about Marshal Rutherford attempting to keep some of our ships, which we can't permit. Madona—I'll want you to sit down with our staff lawyers. I want to make sure we have an ironclad legal case for refusing orders to detach ships to his command.

"We are here to assist in the defense of the Commonwealth, but Sector Fleet Dakota is assigned to Dakota, and we can't risk the sector more than our presence here already does."

He looked around his three senior officers. All three looked thoughtful, but they seemed on board.

"I'll also remind you all that Rutherford is *not* cleared for any of the information on Project Hustle," he told them. "You three are the mostly likely officers who know about the shipyards to end up talking to him. He does not know and should not learn about the shipyards.

"He has no need to know."

It was likely that some of the ships from Base Łá'ts'áadah might end up being sent to join Rutherford's anti-League fleet if peace wasn't negotiated in the next year. But that was a problem for when there were actual ships to crew and deploy.

"Understood, sir," Voclain said instantly. "I'll sit down with our JAG team. I'm...pretty sure there are regs we can lean on to keep the Sector Fleet together."

"So am I," James agreed. "Right now, this is just an itch on the back of my neck, people. I don't *like* how it appears Marshal Rutherford has set up his position here, but that doesn't make him wrong or an enemy of the Commonwealth.

"It just makes me uncomfortable." He shook his head. "I have a few friends here I want to talk to. I'm going to try to get a better feel for the situation on the ground and in the Clockward Fleet before I let my paranoia get the better of me."

"Given the circumstances, I feel it necessary to point out that even paranoids can have real enemies," Yamamoto said. "I suggest we *all* watch our backs. If the Marshal is planning...ugliness, securing support and weakening Admiral Tecumseh will be on his mind."

That sent a new chill down James's spine...not least because that was a much-twistier set of thoughts than he expected to hear from his Fleet CAG.

40

Meridian System
05:00 December 8, 2737 ESMDT

"SECTOR FLEET DAKOTA, ARRIVING!"

A traditional bosun's whistle echoed across *Hancock*'s flight deck as James stepped out onto the *Lexington*-class carrier's main landing zone. There was no sign anywhere that it was still early in the morning by ship's time, as a perfectly turned-out Marine honor guard escorted him across the metal decking.

Katanas and Longbows were visible in their hangar bays along the side of the flight deck. Every bay was full, which suggested that Rutherford had taken fighters and flight crews from the local defense forces—*Hancock*, after all, had been at Persephone, and her fighters had flown against the strike that had devastated Rutherford's task force.

The more immediate presence was of the massively muscular admiral himself. James Tecumseh wasn't a small man, but Rutherford towered over him by ten centimeters and was at least that much broader in the shoulders.

"Welcome aboard *Hancock*, Admiral Tecumseh," Rutherford said, offering his hand rather than a salute—a recognition, James suspected, of their theoretically equal rank.

James shook the proffered hand and inclined his head.

"She seems a fine ship," he murmured. "Though I understand you've had some rough days. *Ajax* is…Well, I've seen worse, but not by much."

His last command had been reduced to just the cruiser *Chariot*, and *Chariot* had been an A-S drive held together by duct tape and a few scraps of hull by the end. It was only by the grace of the Castle Federation that *Chariot* had made it back to the Commonwealth at all.

"They build the *Hercules*-class ships well," Rutherford agreed. "*Hancock* didn't take any fire in Persephone, though we did lose too many of our fighters. Sector Fleet Meridian only had the one carrier, an old *Paramount*, too.

"We had to strip the locals of their entire complement of Katanas to get back up to strength, and we're still short of bombers," he admitted. "I am *delighted* to see your carriers and strike cruisers, I have to admit."

"We have a hundred and twenty bombers aboard," James confirmed. "And I will be delighted to use them to remind Star Admiral Borgogni why he should be afraid of the Commonwealth Navy."

"We all will," Rutherford agreed. "My people have been working on a plan to make just that point to the Star Admiral. Shall we proceed to the briefing room?"

"She's your ship, Marshal Rutherford. Lead on."

———

NINETY PERCENT of the briefing room was entirely standard-issue. The Commonwealth flag was hung on poles in each corner, and the commissioning seal of *Hancock*—a gold etching of the namesake's signature in a circle—was emblazoned along one wall.

The unusual factor was a ragged American flag sealed inside an archival case on the wall facing the ship's seal. The ID tag in the case informed him that it was from a company of the United States Army

Seventy-Seventh Division that had been cut off in the First World War Battle of the Argonne.

"My ancestor was part of the color squad guarding that flag," Rutherford said quietly as he saw James looking at it. "Shelled by friend and foe alike, the flag was still mostly intact when they were relieved—but every member of the color squad was dead except my ancestor."

He chuckled.

"He probably shouldn't have *kept* the flag after that, but apparently, no one argued with him."

A steward popped into the room with a tray of coffees. James gratefully took one and looked around to see who else would be joining them. As the steward disappeared, he realized it was just him and Rutherford.

"We're going to need to keep a lot of details under wraps until we're in FTL or near enough," the other flag officer told James as he took his seat. "Meridian is close enough to the border with the League that there are League q-com systems around.

"That's been of use to us—but if I can talk to freighter captains and buy their information, the League's agents on Greenwich can report in on anything we say and do.

"From what I've seen so far, this system leaks like a sieve, to either secessionists or Periklos's people."

"I see," James said slowly. "I would hope we can trust our staff."

"Almost certainly," Rutherford agreed. "But the fewer brains that know everything, well…the fewer lips that can accidentally flap."

"Has it been that bad?" James asked.

"*Someone* sold out Mary," the Marshal said grimly. He sighed. "Marshal Amandine, that is. She and I go a long way back. Somebody told the League about our fleet dispersal. I don't think they needed anything beyond her willingness to try negotiating to trap *her*, unfortunately."

The point of spreading the fleet out, as James understood it, had been to make it impossible to know where the Clockward Fleet's task forces had been. He could think of three or four ways he could have circumvented that himself—but, as Rutherford was saying, he would have needed to know that the fleet *was* dispersed.

"You think you have a traitor in your staff?" James asked. "I *know* I can trust mine."

"I know I can trust mine," Rutherford agreed. "And yet I know someone sold out the Clockward Fleet. Not that many people had access to League q-coms *and* the full deployment plan. My staff did."

"I see."

"For that matter, Gabriel had concerns about some of his staff," the Marshal warned. "Voclain tried to seduce him into an affair before she really understood his relationship with his wife."

That was news to James. News he, admittedly, didn't wholly *believe* —but he couldn't exactly tell Rutherford that.

"She's been nothing but an exemplary chief of staff while we've worked together," he murmured. "But I appreciate the warning, Admiral. Regardless of our paranoias—and I won't blame you for yours if you don't blame me for mine—I believe we have work to do?"

"Paranoia's an occupational hazard in our work," Rutherford agreed. "I imagine you are as concerned over Admiral Washington's fate as I am over Admiral Banks's."

James chuckled.

"Touché," he conceded. "I'll admit it seems odd to me—but I can't imagine how Admiral Banks's medical retirement looks from the outside."

"Much the same, I expect," the other man said. "I know Gabriel; I know his devotion to his wife. I can see it...but I imagine many people who don't know him can't."

"And it's not like we can share the details with people," James noted. "I'm surprised you know that much."

Rutherford waved that off.

"Is he okay?" he asked instead.

"He's confined and under twenty-four-seven suicide watch in Táátá'í'tsin's finest hospital," James admitted. "The doctors tell me they can help him get past this, but it takes time, and his grief is a powerful weapon against his own psyche."

"His greatest strength and support turned against him," Rutherford said. "He was devoted to that woman, Admiral Tecumseh. Without her…I don't know how much of Gabriel Banks is left."

"Neither does he," James said softly. "That's the problem, I think."

The *other* problem, the one his counterpart had just waved off, was that there was no way in hell that Hans Rutherford should have known enough about Banks's condition to link it to Mrs. Banks's death. The Marshal had clearly either accessed the secure medical files on *Adamant* or talked Dr. Piccoli into betraying his professional discretion.

Having *met* Tihomir Piccoli, James was unfortunately sure he knew which of those two things Rutherford had done. If the Marshal could access secured files on a TCN battleship without anyone knowing about it, he either had some of the best hackers James had ever heard of—or he really *did* have the access codes and overrides from Amandine's Marshal's mace.

Both men exhaled long sighs in the same moment, and Rutherford snorted a soft chuckle.

"To absent friends, James Tecumseh," he said, raising his coffee mug in a toast.

"To absent friends," James agreed.

Rutherford slammed back the rest of his coffee and laid the cup aside. With a gesture, he brought up a geographic map of the region.

"Meridian Sector," he said unnecessarily. "Six star systems. Meridian, Cancer, Delta Zulu, Hachette, Lulu and Persephone.

"Regardless of my original tasking, the stark truth of the matter is that the communications loop means that control of these six systems is all I can truly exert. The other sectors exposed to the League are in real danger, but I have to hope that Borgogni represents their main deployable force."

"If we remove his fleet as a factor, we at least demonstrate that attacking Commonwealth space is unacceptable, even now," James said. "Do we have any more information on Persephone since you withdrew?"

Rutherford nodded and zoomed the display in on the star system in question.

It was just under twelve light-years from Meridian to Persephone,

James noted absently. Seven days each way, with a few hours' wiggle room.

"Persephone, like Meridian, is primarily valuable on a strategic level for its gas giants," Rutherford noted. "Two habitable planets, Dionysus and Zagreus, have made it a major target for colonization. The gas giants and their refineries made it a useful anchor point for the Clockward Fleet.

"Given how quickly we were pushed out of the system, very few of those resources were properly neutralized," he said grimly. "While the defenses were trashed along with the fleet, the League inherited the better part of a thousand spare starfighters and bombers, and thirty or so thousand missiles of assorted types."

"Plus the general logistics supplies and the refineries themselves," James concluded. "Persephone is a prize for the League, probably the best one in the Sector after Meridian itself. Even considering the political ramifications."

"So, we need to kick Borgogni the hell out," Rutherford said. "The good news is that the same thing that makes us vulnerable to *League* intelligence creates opportunities for us. We have assorted League q-coms and are talking to various shippers and so forth inside the League.

"We don't have any immediate information on Persephone itself, unfortunately," he continued. "But we do know quite a bit about Borgogni's fleet."

A set of images appeared next to the system. Twenty-six ships, ranging from two likely-brand-new carriers of the *Alberto da Giussano* class to eight ships with blinking highlights marking them as unknowns.

"Borgogni had to send well over half his ships back into the League for repairs," Rutherford noted, moving fourteen of the remaining ships of the League officer's command aside—including one of the carriers but none of the unknowns.

"So, we have an estimated twelve ships left, but we only know the types of four of them," the Marshal said. "The carrier *Alberto da Giussano*, name-ship of her class. The battlecruiser *Cyprus*. Two *Athens*-class battleships—last-generation forty-million-cubic-meter ships."

"And eight unknowns."

"Unfortunately, yes," Rutherford agreed, studying the icons of the twelve ships still in Persephone. "My information out of the League says that *Cyprus* and *Alberto* are the only modern ships they didn't pull back, but there were no sub-forty-million ships in their attack force at all.

"So, while we only IDed *Corinth* and *Thebes*, the other eight ships are likely of a similar age and size. *Athens*-class battleships, *Zara*-class battlecruisers and *Socrates*-class carriers."

James nodded thoughtfully.

"They would have had a slight edge over your forces," he said. "The new fighters and ships from Meridian might have been enough, especially since our flight crews are often better."

"I might have taken the risk, except..." Rutherford waved a hand and four new icons appeared. Smaller than the modern ships, larger than the older generation, none of the four were the same. "La Onorevole Compagnia di Guerra Violenta."

The Honorable Company of Violent War.

"Condottieri," James assumed aloud. Only a League mercenary fleet would name themselves something like that.

"Condottieri. Four cruisers under Admiral Pawnteep Metharom," Rutherford confirmed. "Nine twelve-fighter squadrons apiece, plus twelve heavy lances and twelve missile launchers. Built at various points over the last thirty years, but rebuilt where necessary to keep up with modern A-S drives.

"The League has generally preferred to keep the condottieri out of their fight with us, but that rule appears to have changed now they're attacking us instead of turning New Edmonton into a meat grinder. Admiral Metharom was sent out five days after the battle to back up Admiral Borgogni.

"So, they had sixteen ships to my thirteen, with a higher average cubage," the Marshal said. "There was no winning that fight."

"And now we have twenty ships to their sixteen and something far closer to individual parity," James noted. "They have no fixed defenses, and most of our warship and fighter crews are just as veteran, just as experienced as theirs—and our people are fighting for our home."

"The moral is to the physical as three is to one," Rutherford said. "A soldier fighting to defend or liberate will fight harder than one fighting to conquer.

"I won't dismiss that, but I'd rather rely on hulls and guns. And with your arrival, we now have them."

James smiled.

"I agree. You said you had a plan?"

"We do," the Marshal told him. "We don't want to jump in completely blind, but we have no way of getting FTL information from the system. We're intending to send one of our cruisers out twelve hours early.

"They'll get within a few light-hours of the system, get fresh scans of where everyone is, and then rendezvous with the rest of the fleet several light-days short of the Persephone System."

"We download the data, update the plans for any unexpected changes and then go straight in?" James asked.

"Exactly." Rutherford tapped one of the planets in the display. "If they're deploying anything like we did, their heaviest force will be at Persephone Three, between Dionysus and Zagreus. Without forts and needing to maintain orbital support, they will have to have *some* ships at each planet.

"Once we know where they're positioned, we'll adjust things. The basic plan is to repeat the stunt they threw at us," he said. "Zagreus is the most distant, so we jump in close to there, hit their Zagreus force with a heavy missile bombardment, then warp space to try to ambush their force at Dionysus."

"We keep our force together, we minimize our risk and take advantage of a weakness they almost *have* to have," James observed. "I like it."

It was clever but not complicated. The worst-case scenario was that Borgogni *hadn't* split his forces—which was unlikely, since the League officer *did* have two planets to conquer and defend.

"I'll run as much of this as you'll let me past my team," he told the other man. "It's straightforward enough, though."

"We don't need to take risks and we need to preserve our forces," Rutherford agreed. "For the next few months, at least, these twenty ships are the only thing between the League and twelve star systems."

"Not to mention the entire Commonwealth behind us," James said.

"Of course," the other man said. "Trying to keep my focus on what I can deal with, Tecumseh. Twelve systems and thirty billion souls is enough to start with, isn't it?"

41

"ADMIRAL TECUMSEH, it's good to see you alive and kicking," Jessie Modesitt told James. "How are the limbs?"

James shook his head at his former subordinate. The entire time he'd been on Modesitt's ship, he'd had three emergency cybernetic limbs. The replacements were *much* harder to see, but they were still there.

"Metal, plastic and silicon," he observed. "But they carry me around and they get the job done. How's your new ship?"

"I miss having a fighter wing, but there's something to be said for positron lances that can actually *hit* people," Modesitt replied. Her last command had been a strike cruiser, a ship type that didn't have a modern iteration due to being jacks of all trades and masters of none.

James wasn't convinced that discarding the entire type based on the flaws of the *Ocean* class was entirely justified, but no one was asking his opinion yet. The *Ocean* class's main positron lances were only six hundred kilotons per second, versus the *megaton* per second of the *Monarch*-class battleship.

That meant longer effective ranges and significantly greater overall killing power.

"And hey, they sent you to the easier war," James said. "Everyone told me that the League was going to be a pushover and Periklos was going to fall down the moment a TCN fleet showed up."

Modesitt made a rude gesture and he laughed. The joke was stupid and they both knew it, but it helped lift some of the last tension between the now-twice-promoted flag officer and the woman who'd followed him into hell.

"Suffice to say *that* didn't happen," she told him. *"King George* and I spent two months in New Edmonton before Amandine wrote it off as the bad deal most of the Clockward Fleet figured it was in the first ten hours. How many battles over a single star system have *you* seen last long enough to have reinforcements sent in at all, let alone *six months*?"

"A few on the reinforcements front," James said. "I wasn't *there* when Roberts ran circles around us at Huī Xing, but I was running logistical support."

In that case, the reinforcements had been from the rest of the Alliance of Free Stars, allowing then-Captain Kyle Roberts to deal yet another defeat to the Commonwealth. Having *met* Kyle Roberts, James suspected the man had been involved somewhere in the plan that had shattered the Commonwealth's communications.

That kind of "for the throat" operation was very much the other man's style.

"Yeah, well, I think Periklos was paying attention to that mess in particular," Modesitt told him. "Because his Admiral on the scene was playing the same kind of game with gravity wells. Luring us into them, keeping his fleets safe from us in them… for *six months*, Admiral."

She shook his head.

"If I were to meet her, I'm not sure if I'd shake her hand or punch her," Modesitt admitted.

"'Her'?" James asked. "I thought that was Borgogni."

"*A* Borgogni," the battleship captain told him. "Peppi Borgogni is still in operational command around this mess. His *sister*, Star Admiral Samantha Borgogni, went back to New Athens for a celebration with Dictator Periklos that apparently ended up including a ring and, if rumor has it right, a baby bump."

"I don't think that intelligence update made it deeper into the Commonwealth before we lost coms," he admitted. "But my impression is that Meridian has better links to the League still than most of us."

"That's true," Modesitt said sharply. Something in her gaze and clipped tone told James not to pursue that. Something...wasn't right there.

"So, you might not have heard that the Dictator proposed to his right-hand woman when she went back after kicking our asses all over the New Edmonton System. Don't know who had to argue who into it, but what rumors we're still getting say she's three months pregnant with the League's next ruler."

"And her brother is keeping up the family name by kicking us out of Persephone," James said. "We should have that sorted in a few days, though."

"That's the plan," Modesitt said. She sounded almost stilted.

"Jessie?" he asked softly. "You okay?"

"Yeah, I'm fine," she said with a sharp exhalation, shaking her head. "It's nothing. We're just not getting a lot of details of the plan filtered down. Rutherford is...careful with data."

"He's nervous about OPSEC. Seems fair enough, given the circumstances," James allowed. "I think we've got a day or two before we kick off. Think you can make time for a beer with me and Barbados, if I can pin him down?"

She swallowed and blinked.

"I don't think so," she said slowly. "I'm a warship captain, Tecumseh. You know how little time we have." She looked over her shoulder. "In fact, I believe duty calls. I'll talk to you another time, all right?"

"All right," James agreed. "I'll be in touch, Captain."

The channel ended and Vice Admiral James Tecumseh leaned back in his chair, drumming his fingers on the arm. If he hadn't known better, he'd have thought that Modesitt thought they were being overheard.

But that made no sense, did it?

Except that Rutherford had *also* been in the secure medical files on *Adamant*, and *Adamant* wasn't even a warship under his command. If he had the codes and people to do that inside a few hours, what could he have set up in the ships he'd had access to for weeks?

He tapped a command.

"Voclain, I need you to do me a semi-personal favor," he told his chief of staff. "I want to get down onto the surface and have a beer with Brigadier Barbados. Can you see what you can make happen?"

"Of course, sir."

————

JAMES SPENT the next hour going over the thousand and one reports and requests that consumed a fleet commander's time. Sector Fleet Dakota had left Dakota fully stocked on everything, so all they really needed from Meridian was food and fuel, both commodities the system had in plentiful supply.

He was surprised to see Voclain step into his office without knocking at the end of that hour, a concerned expression on her face.

"Commodore," he greeted her.

"Turn on your office security systems," she told him sharply.

"Commodore?" James repeated, concerned now.

"Just trust me."

Sighing, James did so. The security systems on the Admiral's office were among the most impenetrable on any warship—and, like most flag officers, James had picked up a few regulation-gray-area additional layers of software and hardware to increase that security.

"What's going on?" he asked.

"Tried to organize that beer for you and hit a blockade," Voclain said grimly. "I can't get in touch with anybody from the Six-Oh-One Independent."

The 601st Independent Brigade was Alric Barbados's command, responsible for supporting the planetary government on Meridian.

Roughly eight thousand Marines strong, it included everything from tanks to Piranha air/space fighters.

It also had a command element with almost four hundred people. Voclain should have been able to reach *someone*.

"That's...not good," James murmured.

"I poked around and pinned Mac Cléirich to a wall with some questions," his chief of staff told him. "She wasn't willing to commit to saying *anything* concrete, but from what she said, our communications are compromised."

"Define 'compromised,' Commodore," James said. He knew the low tone he was dropping into was dangerous—this situation was dangerous. There were only a handful of sources of potential intrusions into his flagship's communications systems—and most of them shouldn't have the capability.

"We're only able to talk to specific people outside Sector Fleet Dakota," Voclain told him. "Contact with the planet only appears to work when someone in Clockward Fleet knew about the contact in advance."

"How is that even *possible*, Commodore?" he asked. That was a nightmare—a nightmare that suggested only one possible culprit.

"I'm not sure," she admitted. "But if our communications are that compromised, I don't trust our internal surveillance systems, either."

James checked a report from his office systems.

"So far, they're at least listening to my orders to shut down," he told her. "But...I'm still trying to wrap my mind around just what's been done here."

"I suspect Mac Cléirich has a better idea of what's going on than she was prepared to admit in the corridor outside her office," Voclain said. "But summoning her to your office may draw attention, if things are that compromised."

"Of course. A full senior staff meeting, then," James decided. "If someone is playing that dangerous a game, it's time to start playing *back*."

42

Meridian System
17:00 December 8, 2737 ESMDT

James would normally have delegated double-checking the expansion of his office security systems around the breakout meeting room. Today, though, he did it himself, using a double-check program he'd picked up at the recommendation of the senior NCO on his first starship command to confirm that everything was working and clean.

Sallie Leeuwenhoek laid out glasses and drinks while carrying a bug-scanner wand. Neither of them thought that there would actually *be* bugs in the meeting room, but James was willing to be excessively paranoid today.

Finally, he took his seat at the head of the table and waited as his senior staff entered. He wasn't even sure that the level of system penetration Voclain had discovered would be *possible* without the complicity of one of his senior officers.

But he also was reasonably sure he could trust these people. There were only seven of them in the room, including him, and they'd made it through this entire crisis so far.

"This room is now sealed under the highest levels of security we have," he told them all softly as Yamamoto took up his usual stance of leaning against a chair. "Your implant radios are blocked, internal surveillance is turned off and a few other tricks even *I* don't fully understand are in play.

"Nobody on or off *Krakatoa* will ever know what happens in this meeting unless one of us betrays it."

He looked around the room, meeting each of his officers' gazes levelly until he reached Yamamoto. The dark-eyed Scottish-Japanese officer returned his inspection calmly—and then took a seat in the chair he was leaning on.

Everyone understood the level of seriousness James was implying.

"Earlier this afternoon, Commodore Voclain attempted to arrange a meeting between myself and an old subordinate for beer," James told them. "Simple, innocent enough. Except that Madona was unable to contact anyone in the Six-Oh-One Independent and began an investigation into our communications."

He turned his gaze to Sumiko Mac Cléirich, who closed her eyes and bowed her head as he spoke.

"Captain Mac Cléirich, we were under the impression that you felt you couldn't safely speak to Commodore Voclain," he told her calmly. "I hope that a fully secured conference room, under an Admiral's seal with every security measure I can think of, is enough for you to feel safe."

"If it isn't, we're all fucked anyway," she said. He'd never heard the woman slip into a full Irish lilt before. Most TCN officers learned to reduce their natural accents toward a semi-standard American English, but he'd met many who reverted under stress.

"What's going on, Sumiko?" James asked gently.

"You understand, sir, that *Krakatoa* is running approximately fourteen hundred artificial intelligences at any point in time?" she asked.

"Discounting the starfighters' and shuttlecrafts' onboard intelligences, that sounds about right," James agreed. None of those AIs had any true self-awareness. They were built to do specific tasks and to learn how to do them better over time, but they weren't designed to have personalities or become *people*.

"We're now host to at least one—probably multiple—*new* artificial intelligences," Mac Cléirich told him, her accent still audibly thick. "They appeared in our systems shortly after we entered orbit, and I have *no* record of receiving them.

"Thankfully, general security protocols limit the systems they can interact with, but they have near-complete control over our communications suite and are using that to eavesdrop on our internal surveillance."

She shivered.

"I believe the only reason they haven't piggybacked into anything else is that they're only intended to take control of those two items," she admitted. "Given the sophistication involved and the authorization codes these intelligences are using, I believe that most of our non-critical systems are vulnerable."

"What *isn't* vulnerable?" Voclain demanded.

"Engines, weapons, power, sensors," Mac Cléirich reeled off. "Those operate on separate systems with heavily secured interfaces to the main networks. I *believe* those interfaces should be enough, even against Marshal-level security codes."

Marshal-level security codes. James had expected that, but it still struck like a hammer.

"Only one person in this system has those codes," Bevan objected, the intelligence officer looking agitated. "Marshal Rutherford."

"Yes, sir," Mac Cléirich agreed. "But there is no question. I *believe* I have managed to keep the worms from realizing I've been tracking them, but they are definitely inside our surveillance systems."

She finally lifted her head and looked at James.

"Marshal Rutherford has complete control of our communications and internal surveillance, sir," she said flatly. "I *think* the Sector Fleet internal coms protocols are untouched, but that may be a *choice* on the part of the worm's controllers."

"Can we remove these worms from our systems?" James asked. "I don't care *what* the source is; we cannot have anyone controlling who we talk to." He turned to Bevan. "That's your area, Commodore Bevan."

"I..." The intelligence officer swallowed thoughtfully. "I would need to examine the information that Captain Mac Cléirich has collected," he admitted. "I've never had to consider engaging in cyberwarfare against an opponent equipped with top-level overrides against our own systems.

"My people are good, but that level of access is difficult to maneuver against."

"Work it out," James ordered. "Secure compartments only, Commodore. I *hope* that our intelligence team has as much ability to keep these worms from listening in as I do."

"I believe so," Began said levelly. "We will find a way, sir."

"Why would the Marshal do this?" Voclain asked. "I can see what's going on, but *why*?"

"I'm not sure," James admitted. "Though I have a question for you, Madona."

"Sir?"

"I apologize for bringing this up in public, but I think it's relevant," he warned. "According to Marshal Rutherford, you apparently attempted to seduce Admiral Banks into an affair to advance your career. What happened?"

There was a long pause, and his chief of staff flushed. From the uncomfortable looks scattered around the table, at least Bevan and Mac Cléirich knew what James was asking about.

"A comedy of errors, alcohol and mistaken intentions, sir," Voclain finally admitted. "The Admiral is—was, I guess, who knows?—the type of man who flirts and compliments as easily as other people breathe.

"*I*, when first posted to Sector Fleet Dakota, was a freshly divorced fool," she continued. "I misread all of that and, at a social event where I had too much to drink, made a very specific and blatant invitation."

Still flushing, she shook her head.

"The Admiral set me in my place relatively gently," she said. "But it wasn't a fun experience for anyone involved. I wouldn't have expected him to characterize it that way to his friends, but..."

She spread her hands helplessly.

"But Rutherford was trying to use a kernel of truth I could validate with others to undermine you with me," James said coldly. "This whole situation *stinks*."

He pointed a finger at Bevan.

"Commodore Bevan, I want you to find and kill those worms," he told the intel officer. "Rutherford can't admit to sending it into our systems, so he can't complain when we wipe it out. We have to assume it's on every ship in the fleet, so you'll need to neutralize it across all of our ships.

"I also want as many of Rutherford's Marshal codes identified and *deactivated* in our ships' systems as possible," he said grimly. "I cannot trust that man with that level of access to Sector Fleet Dakota."

He turned to Mac Cléirich.

"Mac Cléirich, as Bevan is working on the worm, I want you to think about how to get me a secure link to either or both of Commodore Modesitt and Brigadier Barbados. I want to talk to them in a way that we can all be certain isn't being eavesdropped on."

To James's surprise, Yamamoto coughed and cleared his throat in response to that.

"Wing Colonel?"

"I...may be able to help with that," the starfighter pilot said slowly. "I need to talk to someone first, though."

"Yamamoto...I am *very* sick of games," James warned.

"I know, sir, but I gave my word," Yamamoto said calmly. "I will see what I can do."

43

Meridian System
19:00 December 8, 2737 ESMDT

SOMEHOW, Anthony wasn't surprised when the lights in his office suddenly failed. He sighed, closed the report he was working on and waited.

Much of the reports he received and sent on to the Admiral was automatically generated by assorted AIs, but there was still a necessary level of human analysis that no one had learned how to replace. *Augment,* yes, with silent AIs that lived in people's neural implants, but never replace.

"Are you allergic to being seen entering a room?" he asked the darkness.

Reynolds chuckled, and the lights came back up to show her dropping into the chair across from him. She pulled herself up into the seat, sitting cross-legged with her feet away from the ground.

"It helps keep an air of mystery to create the proper mood," she

GLYNN STEWART

told him. "Plus, it amuses me, which is not without value. You sent an emergency code. What's going on?"

"You don't know?" he asked, pausing to check the security status on his office. The security software completely blanked on him, and he grimaced.

"I also hope that the security-status issue I'm getting is your fault," he noted.

"I wouldn't want these conversations reported to the Admiral," she replied. "Though I wonder why you're checking *this* time and not the last couple of times I was in here."

"Like I said, I figured you would have some idea," Anthony pointed out. "You did say you were watching the Admiral's back."

"And Sallie Leeuwenhoek is my new best friend," Reynolds said. "I wasn't expecting you to have dropped the emergency call to get laid, but my quiet watch on everyone's back hasn't pinged any immediate physical threat to anyone on the ship."

"That's a surprising set of blinkers for a spy," Anthony said.

"I'm *not* a spy," she warned him. "I'm an assassin, and you knew that from the moment I first showed up in your office. I have a lot of the tools of a spy, but my *job* is removing threats. I can do that in a defensive or offensive manner, depending on my orders, but I'll accept that criticism.

"What do you need a spy for?" she concluded.

He sighed.

"Rutherford has bugged *Krakatoa* and taken control of her communications," he said bluntly.

There was a long silence.

"Part of me really was hoping you wanted to fuck," Reynolds said crudely. "Because that would be a far more pleasant conversation than this one. The Admiral did *what*?"

"The *Marshal*," Anthony corrected carefully, "has used a combination of sophisticated attack AI and what I'm *guessing* are Amandine's Marshal override codes to take control of our external communications and make it look like most of the system was giving us the cold shoulder.

"He also, I'm told, has control of our internal surveillance network.

Admiral Tecumseh has his intelligence team working on breaking that, but it's still a big, ugly warning sign."

"It is," she agreed. "*Fuck*. So what do you want *me* to do?"

"You're CISS," he pointed out. "Compared to a Marshal, how do your security override codes stack up? I mean, you have complete control of my office right now."

Reynolds looked around and grimaced.

"It depends," she admitted. "I'm not entirely sure myself. Truthfully, I don't *have* override codes in the way a Marshal does. I have access to backdoors that circumvent the entire security infrastructure. I can get around his codes, but he can shut me out completely with a bit of know-how."

"Can you put the Admiral in touch with his former subordinates in a way Rutherford can't intercept or overhear?"

She pulled her legs tighter into herself as she considered.

"Maybe," she admitted. "But I'd need physical hardware pieces on both sides, Anthony. So, first, the Admiral would need to let me into his office—at which point any excuse I have of a cover is *completely* blown—and second, I'd need to get tablets to Modesitt and Barbados."

At least she knew which subordinates Tecumseh was going to need to talk to.

"Can you do it?" Anthony asked. "You're onside with us and don't think Tecumseh is a threat. Working *with* him is the best way to make sure this *isn't* a threat to the Commonwealth."

"Even if I agreed to blow my cover with Admiral Tecumseh, I'm not sure how I'd get tablets into the hands of two of the senior military officers in the star system, past their security, without *someone* noticing and at least scanning the things.

"At which point, assuming Rutherford has the same penetration on his own ships that you're telling me he has on *ours*, the gig is up."

"So, you're saying that one of CISS's chosen assassins can't get past the AI worms of one overly ambitious admiral who wants to be king?"

"You, Wing Colonel Yamamoto, are trying to manipulate a spy and assassin," she pointed out. "How do you think that's going to go for you?"

"I'm trying to convince you to do what you already want to do," he said with a chuckle. "We need your help. You're a wild card, something Rutherford doesn't know is in play. If anyone can get around his surveillance to let Tecumseh talk to his people, it's you."

"I…think I can," she told him. "But there's a price to be paid. If I'm blowing my cover, letting Tecumseh know I'm here and smuggling covert ops electronics to military officers, this is going well outside my orders and authority; you realize that?"

"Any support you need, any resources we can provide," Anthony promised. "I can make it happen."

"*That* was assumed," Reynolds said drily. "And now isn't really the time for anything but work. But when this is over, Wing Colonel Yamamoto, I am dragging you to a bed for several hours of enthusiastic no-strings-attached sex.

"Sound like a deal?"

He laughed.

"That's a price I think I can pay," he told her.

44

Meridian System
08:00 December 9, 2737 ESMDT

"WE WANT to get going as quickly as possible," Rutherford's image said, standing in front of James's desk. "Clockward Fleet is fully resupplied. Is there any holdup with Sector Fleet Dakota?"

James smiled thinly. He still wasn't sure what game Rutherford was playing, but the implied slight on his people was definitely part of it. For now, he'd let it slide—that had generally been his angle so far. If Rutherford thought that James was quietly going along with everything, he was probably going to end up with some rude surprises.

"*Adamant* and *Valiant* are finishing up refueling now," he told the other officer. "They expect to be completed within an hour, according to the crew of the tankers working with them. We are ready to go as soon as that is complete.

"Of course, I believe the plan called to send one of your *Assassins* ahead to scout the system?" he asked.

"True, true," Rutherford agreed with a wave of his hand. "We wouldn't want to deploy *Gavrilo Princip* until we were sure that the entire combined force was ready to sortie.

"If your ships are that ready to deploy, I will speak with Captain Dierickx and get her ship underway," he continued. "The rest of us will depart sixteen hours after she does, to give *Gavrilo* time to sweep the system and locate the enemy.

"Dropping out of FTL a few light-days short of the system will give us more than enough leeway to prepare the operation."

"Of course," James agreed. It was a clever plan, and it took into account their weaknesses as best as they could. He was now suspicious of it, but that was more because he now figured Rutherford could be trusted about as far as James could throw either of their flagships.

"I did want to raise one small concern," he continued after a moment. "I tried to get in touch with Brigadier Barbados yesterday. He and I served together against the Alliance, and I wanted to catch up with him over a beer, but my staff were unable to get ahold of him.

"Is something going on on Greenwich that I should be aware of?" he asked. "If there's a surface-side crisis, we can delay the operation by a day or two to keep a lid on things."

"We had a series of small issues yesterday," Rutherford told him with yet another casual wave of his hand. "Nothing too serious, but the Brigadier and his Marines were running from fire to fire all day. I'll make sure my staff on the surface know to pass on your regards, but time is getting rather tight at this point.

"Every day we delay is another day that three billion of our people are trapped under a League occupation. We have an obligation to see them freed."

"Of course," James agreed. "We'll kick the League out of Persephone unless your intelligence is out of date. My fleet won't be able to stay long after that, though," he warned. "We're already risking a lot, uncovering the Dakota Sector as long as we are."

"Our responsibility isn't for a single sector, Admiral Tecumseh," Rutherford told him. "We must defend as many people as we can."

"As you yourself said, Marshal, the communications loop is a problem," James said. "And my primary responsibility has to be the sector

I've been charged to defend. If something happened in Dakota today, I wouldn't hear about it until it was far too late to intervene."

Even at Dakota, some of the systems he was responsible for had a twenty-day response loop. From Meridian, that rose to almost thirty for some of the systems closest to Sol, like Arroyo. Shogun was *slightly* closer to Meridian than Dakota but still farther from Meridian than any of the systems in the Meridian Sector.

"We will need to consider the necessity of a shared defense when this is over," Rutherford said. "With word from Sol so distant...there are things we must do out here to maintain order and security."

"I'm here to fight the League, Marshal Rutherford," James replied. "Once Star Admiral Borgogni's fleet is driven off, my orders and responsibilities will require Sector Fleet Dakota to return to our Sector."

"With our communications shattered, we both know our responsibilities far outweigh our duties, Tecumseh," Rutherford warned. "We must be careful not to be blinded by what the world *was* as opposed to what the world has become."

"Perhaps. I need to check in on the fueling, and we'll want to get Captain Dierickx moving."

"Agreed," Rutherford said. "We'll speak again before we leave, but think on what I've said, Tecumseh. And where your responsibilities lie."

———

JAMES WAS STUDYING the careful knots of nettle in one of his woven hangings when the admission buzzer chimed. The plant would have been an inconvenience alive, a stinging nettle that could injure and distract. Dried out and woven into complex patterns, it was gorgeous and deep with meaning to any child of the Shawnee.

That meaning couldn't answer any of his current problems, however, and he silently ordered the door open. A moment later, his office's security system feed just...shut down.

"Sir, I have someone I need you to meet," Anthony Yamamoto told him as the door slid shut behind them. A short and slim blonde woman stood next to the Wing Colonel, looking around James's office with an intrigued glance.

"Wing Colonel, I just lost control of my office's security, so this better be good."

"That was me," the blonde woman told him. "Apologies, but I wanted to take a look through your security setup myself and see if we actually *were* going to surprise our so-called Marshal."

"And, Ms...."

"Agent," she replied crisply. "Agent Shannon Reynolds, Commonwealth Internal Security Service. I'm your assassin, Admiral."

James blinked.

"My *what*?" he asked.

"I'm the person tasked to assassinate you if you turned against the Commonwealth," she told him. "That we're having this conversation should tell you what *I* think the odds of that are, I hope?"

"I have no intention of betraying the Commonwealth or the principles it upholds," James told her.

"I know. That's why I'm here. You were a question mark, so someone was sent to keep an eye on you," Reynolds said quietly, taking one of the chairs without permission and perching on it.

Yamamoto, for his part, silently leaned on the back of the other chair—but his presence alone was an endorsement of this woman.

"And Rutherford?" James asked.

"Rutherford was already flagged as trouble, but so long as he was hitched to Amandine's star and the Commonwealth was the best game in town, he was controlled," Reynolds said bluntly. "CISS would have attempted to prevent him getting a Sector Fleet command—though we may not have succeeded."

"And now he's a Marshal."

Reynolds shook her head.

"No mace, no Marshal," she told him. "He's clearly had access to Amandine's mace and copied many of the access codes and overrides, but he doesn't have the mace itself—and even if he did, it's locked to her DNA.

"She had to give him access to it for him to be using as much of her codes as he's doing, but he doesn't have it. There's only one way to become a Marshal, Admiral Tecumseh, and he wasn't appointed by the Star Chamber on Sol."

"So, what is he, then?" James asked.

"At most, the military governor of the Meridian Sector, assuming that the planetary governments gave him that authority the way Dakota tried to give it to you," she told him. "He would then, arguably, be an acting Marshal until he received confirmation and a mace from Earth, but the systems of the sector could voluntarily act as if he had that authority."

"Or be required to, because he's the man with a fleet," Yamamoto pointed out.

"We have no evidence either way of that," James replied. That, he suspected, was because he hadn't managed to *talk* to the people who might give him that evidence.

"We have no evidence of anything," Reynolds said. "Except that Marshal Amandine gave Rutherford access to her mace that he shouldn't have had—and the psych profiles on that pair are very clear that she had been blind to him for a long time."

"In what way?" James asked. Surely…

"They'd been lovers for at least half a decade, and while I'm going off third-hand impressions, my understanding is that he had her wrapped around his finger." Reynolds shook her head. "I don't understand it myself, but that's hardly new."

"Okay. So, where does that leave us?" he asked.

"Wing Colonel Yamamoto here asked if I could establish a secure communication link with one or both of your former subordinates in Meridian," she said. "I started working on that about twelve hours ago. In the last twelve hours, I have learned of more 'accidental deaths' of CISS agents than I've heard of in the last twelve years."

"That bad?" James whispered.

"My files say I should have had CISS contacts on at least half of Clockward Fleet's ships," she admitted. "Contact protocols are vague at best, utterly anonymous dead drops at worst. So, all I can say for *certain* is that four contacts that should exist haven't responded to my contact requests.

"And that the operative on *Hancock* is dead."

James raised a questioning eye.

"I knew her," Reynolds said. "Old...playmate, let's say. We trained together. She was officially a mess attendant—but I'm not aware of many mess attendants who end up in position to have *airlock accidents.*"

"So, he IDed and killed his watcher," James said flatly. "I...suppose I can see the temptation."

"Don't get any ideas, Admiral," she retorted. "Bevan and his team are good. I'm better."

"So long as you're on my side, I don't care," he told her. "Can you get me those coms Yamamoto mentioned?"

"Good news is that a sector capital has a CISS office. A secured tablet will be delivered to Alric Barbados's office in"—she theatrically checked a nonexistent watch—"eleven minutes."

"And Modesitt?"

"I can give you a protocol that she can download and implement to give you a secure tunnel link," Reynolds said, laying a datastick on James's desk. "But I, frankly, doubt either of you has the tradecraft to have that conversation without triggering *every* alert that Rutherford has monitoring your conversations.

"So, that's something to use when you're ready to well and truly start bombing bridges from orbit. For now, in eleven minutes, you can have a secure conversation with Barbados—so long as *you* install the software from that stick on your office terminal."

She unfolded from the seat.

"For now, Admiral, that's as much as I can do," she admitted. "I'll keep my ear to the ground and try to find any weak spots Rutherford has left in place. Otherwise, I'm watching for immediate physical threats to *you.*

"Whatever has happened out here, I'm guessing I'm a better assassin than anyone Rutherford has found."

"Are you willing to bet your life on that?" James asked.

"I'm not, Admiral. I'm betting *your* life on that."

———

IN AN ERA where humanity's default skin tone was far closer to brown than white, Alric Barbados was among the palest people James Tecumseh had ever met. Tall and long-limbed, he'd been born and raised in the asteroid-mining colonies of Tau Ceti before becoming a Marine.

He and James had held their noses and aided pirates together—and, when those pirates had betrayed them, taken a full measure of revenge and justice together as well.

"It's good to see you, Brigadier," James said quietly as the Marine's image flickered into existence in his office.

"Tecumseh," Barbados replied, his face splitting into a wide grin. "I was wondering just *who* had snuck this little toy into my office."

"I honestly have no idea what you got or how," James told his friend. "Only that it's supposed to use some kind of encrypted tunneling protocol to make this conversation utterly secure—and that the hardware itself is providing a security jamming on your end."

There was a pause, and Barbados's smile faded into a grimly solid expression that James had seen before.

"So, the good *Marshal* isn't listening in," he observed, turning "Marshal" into a curse word.

"He isn't," James confirmed. "And the fact that that is a concern is why I needed to talk to you. I have the distinct feeling that everything I'm being told about Meridian is a lie, Barbados, and I need to know what's going on."

Barbados put his hands together and leaned his forehead into them.

"What has he told you?" he asked.

"That the secessionist group that killed Admiral Washington is waging a widespread terrorist campaign and that you, for example, have been busy running from fire to fire, pissing on them," James laid out.

"That was true for a bit," Barbados conceded. "Of course, Washington's death made Rutherford the unchallenged military authority in the Meridian Sector, so I think it stinks to high heaven.

"The Free Londoners are generally careful to avoid collateral damage, but I can't deny Pontius was a legitimate target," the Marine continued. "He was a good man, Tecumseh. His husband was local, too."

Barbados snorted.

"Fifty dollars says Lawrence was a Free London sympathizer but it was a *political* stance, not an active thing," he noted. "But Lawrence Stewart died in the same bombing that took out Admiral Washington. And that makes it stink even more than anything else."

"You think the secessionists would have regarded the Admiral's husband as worth protecting?" James asked.

"I think Stewart and Washington's sense of integrity had a decent chance of turning this whole mess in the secessionists' favor, depending on just what Earth did about it," Barbados admitted. "And...hell, Washington was on a very short list of Admirals I'd listen to if they ordered treason; you get me?"

What James *got*, with a shiver, was that the only reason Barbados was prepared to risk saying that much to him was because *he* was on Barbados's "very short list."

"So, you think Rutherford killed him," James concluded.

"I am *afraid* that Rutherford killed him," Barbados said carefully. "I have no evidence. Clockward Fleet subsumed Sector Fleet Meridian and provided their own investigation team to support the locals."

"And now?"

"The Six-Oh-First has been in barracks for eight days," the Marine said flatly. "Before that, we were playing fire brigade, but Rutherford was assembling a flying regiment out of the Clockward Fleet's Marines.

"*Officially*, we've been stood down to rest and recuperate while the CF's Marines take over and work with the locals," Barbados continued.

"And?" James prodded again.

"We've been put out of the way while Brevet Lieutenant General Ana Cantrell uses the excuse of the secessionists to take direct and complete control of the local army," the Marine said flatly. "The Marshal is using Protocol Twenty-Six to take full and complete control of all armed forces in the Sector."

Given that James had done that *himself* in the Dakota Sector, it wasn't as questionable as it sounded. And yet...

"I did that in Dakota," he pointed out, to see what Barbados said.

"Of course you did," the Marine agreed. "But I'm betting you didn't intentionally use specific local troops for frontal assaults on secessionist strongholds to undermine or kill specific officers, and take over the chain of command with people loyal to you, did you?"

"No," James murmured. "It's that bad?"

"I may be catastrophizing," Barbados admitted. "But we're using a hyper-secure channel provided by, I'm guessing, one of our intelligence agencies to make sure we have this conversation without him listening.

"Right now, everything is being done in the name of fighting the League and securing the Sector for the Commonwealth," the Marine continued. "But my entire brigade has been sidelined, and my understanding is that Marines from *Tsar Peter the Great* have taken over security for the Governor and planetary legislature.

"And rumor has it that at least half a dozen of the Gubernatorial Security Detail ended up *dead* as part of that process. Every system in the sector has been *ordered* to send representatives to meet with the Marshal by December thirty-first.

"Rutherford has laid the groundwork to declare himself the ruler of Meridian Sector, independent of the Commonwealth, and I think he's got the backing in his fleet to make it happen," Barbados concluded. "I've had one very quiet dinner with Jessie since they got back, and she told me that at least four Captains have had mysterious accidents after meetings with the Marshal."

"Damn. And you're sure *that* meeting wasn't overheard?" James said. "That could put Jessie in danger."

The Marine chuckled, a faint pink flush *very* visible on his coloring.

"That part of the conversation was, ah, pillow talk, sir," he admitted. "Unless there were some very oddly positioned listening devices, I don't think we were overheard."

"I see," James said, smiling. If Barbados and Modesitt were getting along *that* well, it was a tiny spark of good news in a giant mess of *bad* news.

"Thank you, Alric," he murmured. "That gives me an idea of what

I'm getting into. Now I need you to do me one favor, and it may be a...
bloody one, in the end."

"What do you need, sir?" the Marine said crisply.

"When we get back from Persephone, I need the Six-Oh-First to still
be here," James told him. "And if our worst-case assumptions are
right, Rutherford's people may try to arrest you, at the very least. I
need you to not let that happen."

It was a soft request, one that sounded simple and straightforward
—but James Tecumseh knew what he was asking. He was asking Alric
Barbados to order his Marines to fire on local army forces and likely
even other Commonwealth Marines.

"How did it come to this, sir?" Barbados asked. "This wasn't the
Alliance. I want to blame them for this, but..."

"They just hit us with a hammer, Alric," James said quietly. "The
fracture lines, the failures, the...conflicts that are coming from that?
Those are all ours.

"And perhaps they're a sign that we were never what we thought
we were."

"Perhaps," the Marine agreed. He squared his shoulders. "We'll be
here when you get back, James. Hopefully, that won't require more
than sitting on our asses."

"We can hope," James said.

Both of them knew that wasn't going to be the case.

45

"SIGNAL FROM *HANCOCK*," Mac Cléirich reported. "All ships are to move out."

"Pass it on," James replied. So far, at least, Rutherford was acknowledging that Sector Fleet Dakota was a separate formation, one he had limited authority over.

The Marshal wasn't *quite* treating James Tecumseh as a subordinate, but he was acknowledging some degree of separation.

"All ships underway at two hundred gravities," Voclain said a few moments later. "Scans confirm Clockward Fleet underway as well."

James looked over the twenty starships of the joint fleet and concealed a grimace. The combined force represented the entire annual economic output of a prosperous system—and probably somewhere around a fifteenth of the remaining starships of the Terran Commonwealth Navy.

For all that the Commonwealth had been winning both their wars, they had only just been beginning to reach the point of matching the starship production of their multiple enemies. Let alone building enough ships to replace their actual *losses*.

The war with the Alliance alone had seen around two hundred Commonwealth starships destroyed. Over a million Commonwealth officers, spacers and Marines lost in action. The fight with the League hadn't been quite as intense or dragged on as long yet, but it had inflicted losses of its own.

It was impossible for James to know the exact figures of ships lost in the knockout blow to the Commonwealth's communications, but given that *every* warship in the Sol System had been lost, he suspected that fully *half* of the six hundred starships the Commonwealth had mustered at the start of the war two years earlier had been destroyed.

Thirty-two new ones had been commissioned—newer and more-powerful ships, on average, than those lost, but many of the yards that had built those warships were gone now.

If the Commonwealth began to tear itself apart, those three hundred ships would be all that most of the new factions would have to hand. James had to wonder how many of them would survive the *next* two years.

And that thought inevitably drew his gaze to Greenwich behind them. Fourteen orbital platforms were supposed to base seven hundred starfighters, including seven squadrons of bombers.

But Clockward Fleet had stripped Greenwich's defenses to replace the fighters they'd lost at Persephone. There were no bombers and only two hundred starfighters left to protect Greenwich if something went wrong.

"Did you check into what I asked about?" he messaged Voclain via his implants. Now that they *knew* their internal surveillance was compromised, they were communicating by encrypted direct implant-to-implant coms.

"I did," she messaged back. "Can't speak to the rest of your friend's comments, but they were right on one thing: there are no Marines left on most of Clockward Fleet's ships."

Even in the most-secure communication form they could think of, they were still being circumspect about a lot of things. There were a dozen legitimate reasons why James would want to know the Marine strength available on Rutherford's ships.

None of them were why he'd asked Voclain to look into it, though, and for one glorious moment, he considered the possibility of unleashing *his* Marines on Clockward Fleet. He had just over four thousand of them across his seven ships, which was enough to storm half a dozen starships.

It wasn't enough to storm *eleven* simultaneously, though, and that was the only way they'd ever get away with it. And while the mountain of suspicious actions and circumstantial evidence was substantial, it was still *just* suspicions and circumstance.

Other than eavesdropping on James's ships, at least, and James could think of several ways *he* could have justified that to himself in Rutherford's position. Gabriel Banks had been a known quantity to Hans Rutherford, but James Tecumseh was not.

"That's one piece of the puzzle," he told Voclain. "Now if only I could assemble the whole thing."

"I think we both know what the whole picture looks like," she replied. "So, what do we do?"

James was silent and thoughtful for longer than he really liked.

"We have to stop the League," he finally told her. "So, we work with Rutherford until that's done. Then…we see what he does. But most likely, we do nothing."

Voclain's silence was almost as long as his own, and he saw the woman studying the display of the starships of their joint fleet.

"Even if he's declaring himself warlord of the Meridian Sector?" she asked.

"What's the difference between 'independent warlord' and 'military governor for the Commonwealth'?" James replied. "Because he can claim to be the latter right up until Sol sends him an order he doesn't like…and despite my moral problems with the latter, I have no authority to prevent it."

He kept his face impassive as he looked at the readiness metrics of the stations they were leaving behind.

"If I can, I'm going to *borrow* the Six-Oh-First when we go home, but I have to think of the Dakota Sector as well," he admitted. "Whatever happens, they are my first responsibility. If I see a way to protect both Dakota and Meridian, though…"

"Our duty is first to the Commonwealth, I suppose," Voclain agreed.

"And the citizens and principles thereof."

————

"CAPTAIN MODESITT, this message is encoded under a personal cipher you should know," James told the recorder. Barbados had provided the cipher, but even he wasn't sure it was actually secure.

He didn't have much choice, though.

"Included in the data packet is what I'm told is an undetectable, unbreakable, secure communication protocol," he continued. "My suspicion is that using it will draw attention from Marshal Rutherford, but I'll be watching for it once we arrive in Persephone.

"The situation here is…strange. I can't help but feel that there were things you could not discuss with me when we spoke before—and I have reason to suspect the Marshal's intentions."

He paused, gathering his thoughts as he faced the camera in his office. The recording was secure, but the transmission wouldn't be. There were ways he could minimize the risk, but all he could do was *minimize*, not remove.

"The borders of the Commonwealth must be secured," he finally continued. "We'll stand with the Marshal to drive back the League and protect the citizens and principles of our nation, but I fear I can't trust him.

"I look to you, my old right hand, to warn me if he plans to turn on us," James said. "I trust you. Duty calls us to this battle, and so long as we stand together, I will fight the League.

"I know what I'm asking of you," he admitted. He also knew that if his fears were correct, Hans Rutherford had already committed treason. "Thank you."

He ended the recording. There wasn't much more for him to say. A year earlier, Jessie Modesitt had followed him into joining with their enemies to defeat the pirate Coati. They'd saved a world from slavery together, and he had to hope that *she* trusted *him*.

The message transferred to a datastick, and then he wiped it from the system and walked out to the flag deck and over to Mac Cléirich's station.

"Sumiko," he said quietly as he placed the datastick on her console. "I need you to transmit this to *King George V*, Captain Modesitt's eyes only.

"Yes, sir," Mac Cléirich confirmed, an arched eyebrow wordlessly warning him about their concerns with the AI in their systems.

"You need to send it so it arrives just before *King George* warps space," he instructed. If they got the timing right, *Hancock* would already be in FTL by the time any sign of the lightspeed message reached Rutherford's flagship.

"I see, sir," she said slowly. "Of course, sir."

She gave him a firm nod and he stepped away back to his seat. In just a couple more hours, they'd be inviolate in warped space. It didn't matter what AIs and eavesdroppers Rutherford had in their systems once they were in an Alcubierre bubble.

And thanks to Commodore Bevan, James Tecumseh had plans for once they were in that inviolate space.

46

OVE BEVAN DIDN'T LOOK like he'd slept in two days. He and Thandeka Dubhain sat at the end of the table, and both of them looked like they'd been physically running since the fleet had entered Alcubierre-Stetson drive.

"Well, Commodore, Commander?" James asked the intelligence officers.

"We've cleaned the worm out of *Krakatoa*'s systems," Bevan said. "We had to segregate the entire network drive by drive and purge each one individually. The damn thing had spread further than we'd dared fear, but we've checked everywhere now."

"How bad *was* it?" Voclain asked.

"We found elements of its code in the computers running the main zero-point-energy cells," Dubhain said grimly. "It *shouldn't* have been able to bypass the security interfaces, but it was in guns, engines, power cores…everything."

James shivered as he considered the danger presented by a hostile computer virus in those systems.

"Fortunately, because we'd isolated the drives from each other, none of the individual sections of the virus knew that the other components had been neutralized," Bevan told them all. "The AI process wasn't smart enough to recognize the segregation as a direct threat to itself, so each time we went after it, it was easier as we learned its tricks."

"It still managed to self-delete before we could learn much about it the first, oh, twenty-six times," Dubhain said, but there was a cold satisfaction to her tone.

"How much did you learn in the end?" James asked.

"We have a full deactivated copy of its code and processes on a secured drive," Bevan told him. "That drive is in a Faraday cage, fully disconnected from *power*, let alone a network, and should be fully safe.

"But we learned a lot," the Commodore continued. "We have definitely disabled anyone attempting to use Marshal Amandine's mace and its overrides to affect *Krakatoa*'s systems."

Given the position of the Marshals and their authorities, that was probably against some regulation. On the other hand, the ship crews weren't even supposed to be able to *find* those override codes.

"Do I dare ask how?" he said.

"Well..." Bevan glanced at Dubhain and smiled sheepishly. "No *other* Marshal's override is going to work now, either. Or, uh, *any* override."

The intelligence officer had already held James's full attention. The Admiral raised a questioning eyebrow at the blond man, whose grin grew even more sheepish.

"Thanks to the virus, we managed to identify the part of the core operating system that contained the concealed overrides," Bevan said. "We deleted them. We couldn't verify which ones were which, so we deleted *all* of them.

"So, no Marshal has overrides for our systems. No senatorial representative. No one."

"Right now, I'm not sure that's a bad thing," Voclain noted. "Though I shudder to think how many regs we just broke."

"Fascinatingly, the regs only strongly discourage modifying the operating system code," Dubhain said quietly. "There is nothing in there about disabling any particular piece of code or undermining the software overrides given to Marshals and similar high-level authorities."

"Okay." James leaned forward on the table and leveled his best calm gaze on the intelligence officers. "It looks like the first thing you two are going to do is go *sleep*. After that, however, I have a job for your team."

"We are yours to command, sir," Bevan said. "Especially on that 'sleep' part. But what do you need from us?"

"I need you to take everything you've learned about that worm and build a counter-worm," James told them. "One that the AI won't realize has been delivered to a ship until it's been destroyed. I want to be able to send a code to our ships that they don't even need to intentionally activate.

"Marshal Rutherford has tried to get his ears and fingers into all of our ships. I want to cut those ears and fingers off. I'll fight alongside Rutherford, but I *won't* let him listen to my people, and I *won't* let him control who hears me.

"Can you do it?"

The two intelligence officers shared the long look of silent communication between people who'd been working together for two months now. Not even implant messaging, just the understanding of experienced colleagues.

"Yes," Bevan said quietly. "We can blind the bastard."

———

It was a relief for James to lean back in his chair and know that he didn't need to worry about being overheard by a potential enemy. It made him *slightly* more comfortable with the fact that he was sitting in a relatively small room with a woman whose job had explicitly been to kill *him*.

"I need you to help Bevan and Dubhain," he told Reynolds.

"I'm not a spy," she reminded him.

"I know that. But despite everything they've done, you still appear to have access to my ship that you shouldn't have," James pointed out. "Which means you may be able to help them find a hole to sneak into the rest of the fleet through."

"The difference between *my* access and a Marshal's access is that I'm not supposed to exist," the agent said. "Everything a Marshal does is supposed to be recorded and traceable afterward. Most Marshals have some kind of senatorial review when their role is completed, after all.

"CISS agents are supposed to be invisible, so there needs to be no record of what we do." She shrugged. "You'd need to code an entirely new operating system to close us out, I suspect."

"I'll keep that in mind," James said drily. "But that comes back to my point: I *need* those backdoors right now. What I'm telling *my* people is that I want Rutherford's access out of my ships."

Reynolds contorted somehow in the chair, remaining cross-legged but managing to lean forward and prop her chin on her fist.

"And what *do* you want, Admiral Tecumseh?" she asked.

"In five days, we're going to arrive in Persephone," James said. "There, we are supposed to collide with a hopefully inferior League force, under Rutherford's command. I half-expect him to attempt to use Sector Fleet Dakota as the shield to protect his ships—which, unfortunately, is *reasonable*, as Dakota has newer and heavier ships in the main.

"But it will also force us to take damage and losses that will leave us weaker when the dust settles. We will then be vulnerable once Persephone has been retaken—and he'll be in position to take advantage of that weakness."

Reynolds nodded slowly.

"I hate to talk down CISS's reputation of omniscience and omnipotence," she told him, "but I can't duplicate what he did to *Krakatoa* on his ships."

"I didn't think you could," he admitted. "I'm guessing most of your overrides are smaller-scale, designed to give you undetected access to places you aren't supposed to be?"

"Basically," she agreed.

"What I need to do, Agent Reynolds, is make sure that when I call out Hans Rutherford, the entire Clockward Fleet hears me," he told her. "Not just the people he knows won't care. Every Captain. Every officer. Every *maintenance tech* with a dirty sponge. Understand?"

"I don't know if fancy speeches are going to change many maintenance techs' minds," Reynolds replied, but she was nodding again as she spoke. "I think I can do it. It depends on how far Bevan's team makes it on their own—really, all I can do is make sure that their code isn't interrupted."

"That should be more than enough," James told her. "Come on. It's time to introduce the Commodore to his new best friend."

47

Deep Space
05:00 December 15, 2737 ESMDT

SHANNON REYNOLDS, as it turned out, had been exaggerating neither "several hours" nor "enthusiastic" when she'd set her price for helping Anthony out.

Anthony, for his part, had expected her to wait until they were back on Dakota to collect her "fee." Instead, on the second-to-last night of their trip to Persephone, he'd returned to his quarters to find the assassin waiting in his bedroom.

Given his particular wiring around sex, the vast majority of his dalliances had been with professionals. Reynolds was as attractive, enthusiastic and skilled as any of those—and while she was no more inclined to cuddling than he was, she'd fallen asleep in his bed afterward.

There hadn't been any blankets left on the bed by then, and she was still uncovered when he woke up, sprawled across the sheets in a manner he could only mentally describe as *lewd*.

She shifted slightly...in a way that managed to somehow expose more. Anthony chuckled.

"You're awake, aren't you?" he brogued softly.

"You've been ogling my bits for a good ten minutes that I noticed," she told him without opening her eyes. "Didn't see a reason not to enjoy it. You may have guessed that my job does *not* give me a lot of opportunities to get laid."

"I'm enjoying the view, but you did promise no strings," he warned.

She opened her eyes to slits and studied him. Anthony spent enough time exercising not to feel self-conscious about his own nakedness, and grinned back at her.

"I did and I'm holding you to that," she said firmly. "Neither of us has time for this to be more than sex, Anthony, even if either of us was wired for it." She stretched, then grinned wickedly as he felt himself involuntarily twitch.

"We're agreed on that, then," he told her. "I'll admit to being surprised by the timing."

She shrugged.

"If I thought I could find a way, I'd be transferring to *Hancock* as soon as we got to Persephone," she told him. "Admiral Tecumseh is concerned about *justice* and *circumstantial evidence* and making contingency plans."

"And you?"

"Freedom. Democracy. Justice. Unity," she reeled off sharply. "It's a principle of the Commonwealth, and I care about them all. But just as some of our colleagues will focus on one over all others, *I* have to devalue one beneath the others."

"Justice," Anthony said softly.

"Or at least the course of law." She shook her head. "We might be wrong. It might just be suspicion and some bad-faith assumptions... but I've killed people with a *lot* less evidence suggesting they're a threat than we have on Rutherford.

"Unfortunately, I haven't been able to find a way to get from Sector Fleet Dakota to Clockward Fleet since I decided that was the case," she admitted. "The good Marshal is paranoid enough to keep himself safe."

"You'd really just…go there and kill him?" Anthony asked.

"You'd really just strap on a starfighter, fly out into space and blow up five thousand people because it's your orders?" she replied.

He chuckled.

"You put it that way, I see your point," he admitted. "A bit less cold-blooded, but a lot more violence."

"I've killed forty-six people in my career," Reynolds said softly. "I know *exactly* how many. I know their names, careers, backgrounds… everything about them. Can you even say *how many* people you've killed?"

He shifted uncomfortably.

"Only in terms of estimates and statistical probabilities," he said, looking away from her. "But it's…a couple orders of magnitudes more than that."

"Exactly," she told him. "And tomorrow, you're going to jump into a starfighter and go do it again. While I sit back here and play body-guard and cyberwarrior, hoping that a few bits of code I only really half-understand are enough to turn the tide in favor of the cause I gave my life to."

"Fair," he allowed—and then audibly squeaked as her hand sneaked up on him and changed the subject.

"Now, it's still *well* before your shift, and you might well die tomor-row," she purred. "So, let's see what we can get *up* to in that time, shall we?"

48

Deep Space outside the Persephone System
20:00 December 16, 2737 ESMDT

GAVRILO PRINCIP WAS LATE.

The plan had called for the battlecruiser to be waiting when the fleet arrived at the rendezvous point outside Persephone. Instead, they'd emerged from warped space to find themselves completely alone in empty space.

"We're coordinating long-range sensor scans with the Clockward Fleet," Voclain told James. "We're not going to have nearly as detailed information as we were planning, but we should still be able to assemble a decent scan of the system."

"Everything will be several days old, but it's better than nothing," James said. "Carry on."

His attention was on their immediate surroundings—and on the thirteen warships of Clockward Fleet. The need for sensor data was seeing the two fleets spread out, but Sector Fleet Dakota had already had a measure of separation from their supposed comrades.

James didn't *want* to be regarding the Clockward Fleet as potential hostiles, but he wasn't seeing much choice. If he was being paranoid, it wouldn't change anything except maybe ruffling some feathers.

If he was *right*, he needed to make sure his ships were outside the effective range of Rutherford's capital ships' heavy beams. The need to get even slightly different angles of view on Persephone gave him an excuse, but he needed two hundred thousand kilometers of separation, *minimum*.

Most of the ships in both Terran fleets carried six-hundred-kiloton-per-second lances and refitted electromagnetic deflectors. Between those two systems, most of them could usefully range on each other at around a quarter-million kilometers.

The battleships in both fleets carried one-megaton-per-second guns, as did *Krakatoa*—and *Krakatoa*'s shields were more powerful than any of the non-modern ships. *Those* guns could range on anyone except *Krakatoa* at over four hundred thousand kilometers.

"Minimum separation is now fifty thousand kilometers between ships," Voclain reported. "That puts *Krakatoa* fifty thousand kilometers from *Hancock*."

And *Valiant*, the next nearest ship, was a hundred thousand kilometers from the Clockward Fleet carrier. A hundred and fifty thousand kilometers from *Black Sea*, Rutherford's single *Ocean*-class cruiser.

"Anything useful from the sensor coordination?" James asked.

"Nothing yet."

"Sir," Mac Cléirich interrupted nervously. "We just had a new iteration of the AI worm sent along with the data telemetry updates from *Hancock*."

"That better be handled, people," he said calmly.

"Tagged, redirected and isolated," Mac Cléirich confirmed. "Commodore Bevan has it locked down, but it seems that Rutherford realizes we found his electronic spy."

"Let him," James said. "Officially, we eliminated a League virus and are being quiet so we don't look bad for having caught it in the first place. Assuming he even asks."

They were now into the game of "I know you know, but do you

know that I know that you know?" James hated it, but he'd played the unsure and obedient ally enough to buy him some leeway.

He hoped.

"Voclain, Mac Cléirich. Orders to the fleet," he told them calmly. "All ships are to bring Class One manipulators to full readiness and stand by for immediate space warp. Fleet will stand by for my orders, but Captains are authorized to run for it on their own discretion."

His blunt description of what he was authorizing his people to do got him several concerned looks from the bridge crew.

"For ourselves, let's rig up a fleet course into the Persephone System," he continued. "Drop us in the orbit of Persephone V, close to Zagreus but outside everyone's gravity wells."

"That's a dangerous game, sir," Voclain warned. "Playing matador to *two* fleets— The hell?"

"Commodore?" James demanded.

"Our data is three days out of date, but half of Borgogni's fleet is missing," she told him. "I make it just the four condottieri cruisers above Zagreus and a three-ship group based around what I *think* is *Alberto da Giussano*. One sixty-million-cubic-meter carrier and a pair of older battlecruisers."

"Seven ships," James concluded. "Half what we were expecting— nothing that Rutherford couldn't have handled on his own."

Part of that might be bad information. Part of it might be timing. It could even be that the missing nine ships were on their way to Meridian right now, though James doubted any sane officer would have gone after Clockward Fleet *without Alberto da Giussano* if they had the chance.

Except he was looking at the battlecruisers in orbit of Dionysus and one was wrong. The *Zara*-class cruisers the League had brought to Persephone according to Rutherford were forty million cubic meters. The third ship in Dionysus orbit was under thirty million… It was, in fact, the right size to be *Gavrilo Princip*.

"Incoming tunnel link!" Mac Cléirich snapped. "One word, sir. *Coati*."

"Get every ship moving, maximum acceleration," James snapped.

"Deflectors to full; take us into warped space as fast as we can. The Persephone course."

The Clockward Fleet was already moving, the maneuver to spread out the scanners easily turning into ships opening their firing lanes and encircling Sector Fleet Dakota.

Three light-days from anywhere. Whatever happened, no one would ever know. Certainly, Dakota and Earth would never know—Sector Fleet Dakota could just disappear into the black.

Except that James was apparently paranoid *enough*.

"Stetson fields live," Voclain snapped. "*Arctic* and *Booth* have gone FTL. *Saratoga* has gone FTL."

"*Tsar Peter the Great* has fired!" That report was from *Krakatoa*'s bridge, but Volkov's tone was almost dismissive. "Range is too high, deflectors are fine—*we* are entering FTL."

Reality vanished into the simulated starfield and James breathed a sigh of relief.

"Can we confirm if anyone didn't make it?" he asked quietly.

"Only *Valiant* and *Mediterranean* were left," Voclain said after a few moments' analysis. "*Mediterranean* was out of effective range of any of their ships. *Valiant* was in range of *Tsar Peter the Great*, barely."

It was *possible* that the older battleship had managed to cycle their main beams for a full salvo at *Valiant* before James's ship jumped. On the other hand, James suspected that Captain Mašek's ship had only still been there to draw *exactly* that fire.

A *Resolute*-class battleship was still an eggshell armed with hammers, but it was a thicker eggshell than many. Almost half again the size of the *Monarch*-class *Tsar Peter the Great*, *Valiant* had a decent chance of deflecting most of the older ship's beams and weathering a couple of hits.

A far better chance, in fact, than the *economical Ocean*-class cruiser *Mediterranean*.

"Four hours, twenty minutes to emergence," Voclain said quietly. "What do we expect Rutherford to do, sir?"

"He's going to come to Persephone," James replied. "He was close enough to ID our vector when we jumped; he knows we're not heading to Meridian or Dakota. He very clearly has allies in Persephone, which means we misread the whole damn situation."

"Sir?" several people asked, sounding confused, but from the grim look Voclain gave him, his chief of staff saw the same thing he did.

"*Gavrilo Princip* is in Dionysus orbit," he told them. "That means she didn't scout the system at all. She went ahead to talk to the League, which she couldn't have done unless there was a prearranged truce.

"The plan was always to have two fleets gang up on one, people. But it appears that *we* were the ones Rutherford was planning to gang up on."

49

Deep Space outside the Persephone System
22:00 December 16, 2737 ESMDT

"THE WORD you're all looking for, people, is *treason*," Anthony Yamamoto told his collected flight crews. "That's the answer to the question of 'why am I awake in the middle of the ship's night,' the question of *'what the hell is going on,'* the question of *'why aren't we with Clockward Fleet anymore,'* and probably half a dozen other questions I haven't thought of yet."

The hubbub slowly died down as six hundred sets of eyes locked onto the Fleet CAG, and he smiled thinly.

"*Tsar Peter the Great* fired on *Krakatoa*, officers," he told them. "That was right around when we realized that our scouting cruiser was nestled up all cozy-like with the League flagship.

"Now, what you all don't know is that our intelligence team spent the whole flight out from Meridian purging one of the nastier cyberworms I've ever heard of out of *Krakatoa*'s systems—and we distributed a tool to purge it to the rest of the ships in the Sector Fleet when we dropped out of Alcubierre.

"So, *someone* was expecting to have all kinds of software tricks to play on us and didn't have them," Anthony concluded. "They played the game of spreading out to get wide sensor readings, but it was a trick to resend the virus, hoping they could pull those tricks anyway.

"But we were waiting for that, because the Admiral saw through Rutherford's *bullshit*."

He felt the ripple of emotion that ran through his teams. Six hundred pilots, gunners and flight engineers. He'd back *Krakatoa's* fighter group against their own numbers of anything in space—including people flying the same fighters and bombers they were.

"So, when things went sideways, Tecumseh got us out of there before anyone got hurt. But the mission hasn't changed: kick the League out of Commonwealth space. You get me?"

A chorus of positive responses came back and Anthony nodded firmly.

"But it's not going to be as simple as we thought," he warned them. "And depending on what Rutherford does, I may have to give an order I never wanted to give. An order I've been praying every night since the network collapse I wouldn't have to give."

In his heart of hearts, Anthony had known from the moment the q-com networks went down that this was coming. He'd also known that Admiral Tecumseh had made the same conclusion.

"If Marshal Rutherford comes after us, I will have no choice but lead you into combat against fellow spacers of the Commonwealth Navy," he told his people.

"But I can already tell that we won't be the ones to fire the first shots of the civil war that's starting here. Rutherford already did that. We will defend ourselves, and we will defend the citizens and princi-ples of the Terran Commonwealth.

"Today—well, tomorrow, according to the clocks." That got him a few forced chuckles. It wasn't much of a joke. "That is going to require that we fly and fight against our siblings-in-arms."

He paused, looking over the faces in front of him.

"I speak four languages, my friends," he told them. "*None* of those languages have the words for how sick this makes me feel. But I remind you and I beg you to remember: this is not *our* treason. And I *know*, in my bones and my blood, that Admiral Tecumseh will do all within his power to head off this battle before too much blood is shed.

"But…that requires a cooperative foe, and I do not believe that Rutherford has that in him. So, the Admiral will call for us to fight."

"And we will fight!" someone shouted.

Anthony wasn't even sure which of his officers had shouted, but his relief probably showed in his smile.

"I'll follow the old man to hell at this point," he told them. "I'll sure as hell follow him against a traitor. Who's with me?!"

"THERE'S no magic we can work here, sir," Chief Thales Brahms told Anthony.

The two men stood inside the hangar bay for Anthony's Katana, examining the starfighter. For the first time in his life, Anthony was looking for a weakness he could *use* on a Terran fighter.

He didn't like the feeling.

"Against the League's new Xenophons, you're a bit lighter and you can change your direction of acceleration a little bit faster," Brahms continued. "Ton for ton, the Katana eats the Xenophon's lunch—so they built the Xenophons a thousand tons bigger than the Katana. Makes up the difference and gives them a heavier lance to boot, but they can't pack quite as many of them into a ship or launch them quite as quickly.

"But against another Katana?" The deck chief shook his head. "Standardized and mass-produced, sir. Your engines are the same. Your guns are the same. Your *software* is the same."

"The last is what I'm worried about," Anthony admitted. "I don't fully understand what went down with the ship's systems, but I understand that we were *completely* compromised until the intel team tore it apart."

"We went through the fighter systems with them," Brahms told him. "*Every* fighter. There's no traces of the virus on any of them. You're clean on that front."

"But what stops them uploading the virus onto our ships in combat?" Anthony asked.

"Combat network won't allow executable download," the deck chief said instantly. "You literally *couldn't* install the virus during a fight if you wanted to. Hell, in combat, you won't even accept transmissions and telemetry except from…"

"…another Terran Commonwealth ship or fighter," Anthony concluded. "*Fuck.* How did we not even think of that?"

Brahms looked vaguely ill.

"We're used to having absolutely secure fighter-to-carrier coms through the q-com," he admitted. "And even without that, there's a lot of our software that never even enters *civilian* hands, let alone potential enemy hands.

"So, we don't plan for hostile access to our combat networks, though the combat networks themselves are extremely locked down by nature. We're not trained to think in terms of civil war, sir."

That wasn't *entirely* true, Anthony knew. The TCN and TCSF had been sent in to support counterinsurgency operations enough times that fighting their own hardware was a semi-common occurrence. But that was an entirely different set of protocols, thought processes, everything.

If there had been any insurgencies that had ended up in possession of TCN warships *at all*, let alone carriers, Anthony had never heard of them. The entire Starfighter Corps was less than fifty years old, after all, the Alliance of Free Stars having resurrected the concept in their first war against the Commonwealth.

"That means we need to rewrite our entire network protocol in the next three hours," Anthony said quietly. "At least enough to make sure that Rutherford's people can't listen in on us. How're you feeling, Chief?"

Brahms growled in the back of his throat.

"Get me some of Commodore Bevan's intelligence jocks down

here," he asked. "I'll make it happen either way, but they just spent a week tearing apart Rutherford's virus. I figure they learned something useful."

50

Persephone System
00:30 December 17, 2737 ESMDT

SECONDS TICKED DOWN TOWARD ZERO, and James realized he was holding his breath. There was no way Rutherford would have been able to position the Clockward Fleet or even get the League ships into position to intercept Sector Fleet Dakota, and he *knew* that all of his ships had made it out intact.

But it wasn't until *Krakatoa* burst back into reality in a flash of controlled Cherenkov radiation that all of that intellectual knowledge became certainty. Persephone V hung in the main viewscreen, a just-barely sub-Jovian gas giant, a hundred and twenty thousand kilometers across. Fourteen moons hung above the gas giant, playing gravitational anchors to the usual support industry of fuel refining.

Persephone V wasn't on James's mind today, though. The industry was intact, which made it part of why the system was of interest to the League, but at that moment, only ships that could move under their own power were relevant to what was about to happen.

"All ships report in," Mac Cléirich said crisply. "A couple of Captains are asking what the hell is going on."

"And what does Captain Mašek have to say?" James asked drily.

Instead of answering, Mac Cléirich flipped James access to the all-captains channel.

"Son of a bitch shot us," Mašek said flatly as the Admiral dropped in. "If we'd zigged instead of zagged at the last moment, *Valiant* would have been taken out by our decrepit older sibling."

"What the *hell* is going on?"

That was Captain Zubizarreta aboard *Adamant*, Banks's old flag captain.

"I'm still sorting out the exact details, Captain," James interrupted. The network would have told the Captains when the Admiral had joined the conversation. "But it appears that Admiral Rutherford has made some kind of agreement with the Stellar League.

"I am not yet certain of the consequences of that, but I *am* going to complete our mission in this system," he continued. "In the absence of intervention by Admiral Rutherford and Clockward Fleet, I intend to proceed to first Zagreus and then Dionysus and destroy the League forces in this system."

His Captains were silent for several seconds.

"He already shot at *Krakatoa* and *Valiant*," Volkov observed grimly. "This is all..."

"It's treason, Young," Zubizarreta said instantly. *Adamant*'s Captain might have been confused to start, but she was on the right page now. "He's coming after us. He has to."

"My suspicion is that he planned on using the virus he infiltrated into all of our systems, combined with the privacy of being three light-days from anywhere, to force our capitulation in secret," James told them. "In his worst-case scenario, he blew us away while the virus crippled our systems. No one in Persephone would be watching a particular piece of space for a battle they never knew took place—and no one else would ever be able to see anything.

"Dakota, Sol...the Commonwealth... None of them would ever have known what happened to us."

"And now, if nothing else, the civilians in Persephone are damn well going to know *something* went down," Bardakçı said flatly, James's old flag captain sounding very certain of herself. "*Saratoga* is with you, Admiral. What's the play?"

"*Adamant*'s crew is in."

"So is *Valiant*."

"I do believe we're *all* in," Captain Werner of *Mediterranean* noted. "And our crews. Lead on, Admiral Tecumseh. We will follow."

"The first step is to get ourselves moving toward Zagreus," James told them. "I *expect* Borgogni—or whoever is in charge of the League force—to concentrate their forces and try and meet us there.

"I'd rather take them separately, but until I know which way Rutherford jumps…we can't commit to an action just yet."

————

ADMIRAL PAWNTEEP METHAROM apparently needed restraining instead of prodding. She also clearly had q-probes somewhere in orbit of Persephone V, because after James took into account lightspeed lag, the four condottieri cruisers were underway within five minutes of his emergence into regular space.

It would take six hours for his force to reach Zagreus or for her force to reach Persephone V, but if they *both* started the trip, they'd pass each other somewhere in the middle near their highest velocities.

That would be a very short, very messy battle. The preamble between their fighter wings would take longer, but the actual clash of capital ships would be over in a couple of minutes.

Not least, James reflected, because he had five hundred fighters and bombers to her four hundred and thirty. And he had a *lot* more faith in his own pilots than he did in the most disposable class of League mercenaries.

"Looks like whoever is in charge just saw what Metharom did," Voclain told him. "She was charging toward us for seven minutes, then flipped to head toward Dionysus."

"Borgogni—or whoever is on *Alberto da Giussano*—figures they have a better chance with seven ships on seven ships and a fighter-strength *advantage* than they do with four ships on seven and handing us fighter superiority," James replied. "I suspect her charge was at least partially performative. She knew she was going to get called back.

"Any sign of Rutherford?"

The thirteen ships of Clockward Fleet were the question mark in the deck. If he hadn't been waiting for Rutherford, he'd take his ships back into Alcubierre drive and cut ten light-minutes off the distance between his ships and Metharom. That would prevent the SLN and condottieri forces from combining and allow him to take them on in isolation.

"None yet," Voclain told him. "You...you do realize we can't actually *take* the combined League fleet? They have us outgunned and our fighters outnumbered."

"Oh, I suspect we can make them change their mind on that perspective," James murmured. "But no, I'm not actually planning on fighting Borgogni's entire fleet today."

It was a reasonable assumption that it was still Peppi Borgogni on the enemy flagship. He might have had to send even more of his fleet back for repairs than anyone would have liked, but James doubted the League Admiral had abandoned the modern heavy carrier he operated from.

Plus, James suspected that Peppi Borgogni was seriously allergic to looking anything less than brave and capable to his new brother-in-law. His sister had proven her worth to Periklos, but he doubted that the younger Borgogni wanted to hide behind his sister's relationship with their dictator.

"Maintain a zero-zero course for Zagreus," he ordered. "Our opening gambit is on the board. So is Borgogni's.

"I want to see how Rutherford plans on playing this game before I start setting pieces on fire."

———

"CHERENKOV FLARES, NEW CONTACTS, NEW CONTACTS!"

The report echoed across *Krakatoa*'s flag deck, and James found himself stretching his fingers as he waited for the analysts across his fleet to resolve just what he was looking at.

"Contact is at the halfway point between Persephone V and Zagreus," Voclain told him after thirty seconds. "Twelve ships. IFF beacons disabled, but we are resolving mostly thirty million cubic meters and under.

"Probability that contact is Clockward Fleet approaches unity, sir."

"Understood," James told her. New icons appeared in the main tactical feed as the analysts broke the flares down into individual contacts. There wasn't enough information in play yet for them to identify specific ships, but the ships were too small to be first-line League units.

It was definitely Clockward Fleet. They weren't directly on his course to Zagreus, but they were in position to intercept him. One hundred million kilometers.

"One hundred eight minutes to lance range," Voclain told him. "For the *Resolutes* and *Monarchs*, anyway. Eighteen to main missile range."

"Understood," James allowed. "Get Yamamoto's people into space. They are to form up for a bomber strike but await my command."

They had fifty starfighters in space as a CAP, but it was time to put the real punch into play. Especially the bombers, whose torpedoes walked the line between the short-ranged, numerous fighter missiles and the longer-ranged but fewer capital-ship missiles.

"Fighter launches commencing."

None of his ships would take more than sixty seconds to get their full fighter capacity into space. The three *Paramount*-class carriers that hauled almost half of Rutherford's fighter strength would take two minutes, but the range was far too long for James to take advantage of that.

"Sir, we have an incoming transmission addressed to your eyes only," Mac Cléirich reported. "Flag-officer encryption codes."

"He wants to talk, does he?" James murmured. "I'll take it on my implant. Interrupt me if his fighters twitch toward us."

"His fleet is accelerating toward us. Two hundred gravities. Angles make net acceleration three hundred seventy-five," Voclain reported.

"Still seventeen minutes to missile range, correct?" James said. "We have time for me to view the good Marshal's e-mail."

It took only a few moments and a mental command to securely

receive the video message into his implants. An image of the muscular Marshal appeared in front of James, Rutherford clearly having adjusted his recorders so he was looking down at James.

"It shouldn't have come to this, should it, Admiral Tecumseh?" he asked softly. "Two Commonwealth fleets advancing on each other with hostile intent. But I guess that's where we are.

"There is still time to back down. I'm prepared to lay my cards on the table. Truth is, I didn't want *you* when I sent that message. I wanted *Gabriel*, my oldest and best friend, a man I knew I could trust at my right hand as we salvaged a new nation from the wreckage of the Commonwealth."

James had worked that part out. His showing up with Sector Fleet Dakota had thrown a wrench in all of Rutherford's plans—though the self-promoted Marshal had received enough warning to prepare for James's arrival.

"This would have been easier if you hadn't managed to short-circuit Harbinger," Rutherford continued. "Having this conversation while all of your ships were disabled by Amandine's codes would have made for a far-more-generous offer."

He grinned and shrugged.

"But here we are. I made a deal with the League: I let them take Persephone and we agreed to a nonaggression pact along the border between the League and Meridian.

"I wouldn't interfere with their operations against other sectors, and they would treat with me as an independent state. Dakota was... tentatively included in that deal, solidly enough that if you sign on, all of our worlds are safe.

"We hand a single system over to a government that can't afford to mistreat them and protect eleven systems. Three billion lives moderately inconvenienced to keep thirty billion safe from war. It seems a fair trade to me."

If Rutherford had actually been in the room, James would have interrupted—potentially with his fists. As it was, he couldn't even cut the man off except by missing the whole message.

"But we both decided to be clever and stubborn, so right now, we are waving fleets at each other and risking the lives of our people," Rutherford continued. "So, here's the offer, James."

That was the first time the Marshal had called James by his first name—and James recognized it for the tiny bit of manipulation it was meant as.

"I am military governor of the Meridian Sector. You bring the Dakota Sector in with me, and we operate in concert as a single entity. When the Commonwealth inevitably disintegrates, we hold our sectors together as a single nation, one that will rise from the ashes of the Star Chamber's folly as a strong and powerful successor state.

"Potentially even a nucleus around which we can forge a *new* Commonwealth. You can stand at my right hand as we build the next Roman Empire and provide the symbol and the unity our people need."

Rutherford shrugged.

"Or you can fight me, James. The odds aren't in your favor, and the League is on my side here. You won't win this. Are you prepared to get soldiers killed today and damn civilians to die tomorrow for your pride and arrogance?

"Work with me, James. We can save billions from the chaos that is about to overrun our nation. We cannot save the Commonwealth, but if we stand strong and stand *together*, we can save these two sectors, these eleven systems and thirty billion souls, from the fate that awaits the rest of our people.

"Please. Listen to me."

The message ended, and James tried to swallow down his anger. Rutherford did a good job of wrapping everything up in a neat message with pretty words, but James knew what the other man was suggesting was the *opposite* of what he was claiming.

"Sir?" Voclain asked.

"Rutherford wants to make himself warlord of Meridian and Dakota," James said calmly, summarizing the other man's words. "He traded Persephone for peace with the League and wanted to have Gabriel Banks as his right-hand man—not least to bring the industry and star systems of the Dakota Sector into his little empire."

There was a long silence.

"He already made himself military governor," the chief of staff observed thoughtfully. "He could spin that along for a long time with nominal allegiance to Terra, even as he actually did whatever he wanted to solidify his new empire."

"Exactly." James looked at the icons on the screen. Twelve ships to his seven. Seven hundred fighters to his five hundred. Three hundred and fifty million cubic meters to his two hundred and eighty.

As Rutherford had pointed out, the odds weren't in his favor. Except that James had at least one wild card he hadn't played yet.

"Fighters are in space?" he asked.

"Yes, sir," Voclain confirmed. "Yamamoto recommends holding ten Katana squadrons back as a CAP and using the rest to cover the bomber strike."

"He really thinks he can take Rutherford's birds at two-to-one?" James asked.

"He didn't really say, sir," Voclain replied.

Which meant that Yamamoto was planning a suicide play. He'd cover the bombers until they salvoed their torpedoes, then take his Katanas into the teeth of the enemy strike to reduce their fighter strength as much as possible.

The CAG wouldn't expect to get the three hundred or so fighters he took into that strike back, but he *was* expecting to take out more than his own numbers of Rutherford's birds. That would even the odds for whoever he left behind.

Which, of course, meant that Anthony Yamamoto wasn't planning on letting anyone else command the forward strike. James knew his Fleet CAG well enough to know he wouldn't order anyone else to fly a suicide mission he wasn't part of.

"Let's hold off on that particular option for a few more minutes," James said. "First up, I need to talk to Bevan. Then I need Mac Cléirich.

"The opening gambits are all in play. Now I have some calls to make."

51

Persephone System
01:00 December 17, 2737 ESMDT

"Greetings, Admiral Metharom."

It didn't hurt James in the slightest to be polite in his message to Admiral Pawnteep Metharom. The woman commanded the third-largest force in the system, if he regarded her mercenaries and the League forces as separate formations.

"I have a proposition for you, one that I hope you will find sufficiently remunerative to consider," he told her. "While I understand that you are under contract with the Stellar League to provide security for the Persephone System against Commonwealth attempts to retake it, I find that internal Commonwealth politics have complicated the matter from my end.

"I am prepared to guarantee a fourteen-day cease-fire against the League forces in Persephone to allow you to honor your original contract, and pay five times your standard daily combat rate in

Commonwealth dollars, if you deploy your ships and starfighters to assist mine.

"My lack of q-com communications will impact coordination, but we can certainly capture the forces answering to the traitor Marshal Rutherford between us."

He bowed slightly.

"I await your response."

The recording cut and he turned a calm smile on Mac Cléirich.

"Let's get that off to our condottieri friend ASAP," he told her.

"We have no encryption protocols for the League," she warned. "I have to send it in the clear."

"Funny, that," James said with a chuckle. "Make sure it's a wide-enough focus on the transmission that at least one of Rutherford's ships catches it too. Let's try to *look* like we're being sneaky and failing."

"Oh." Mac Cléirich paused for a long moment, then grinned evilly. "I'm pretty sure I can do that, sir."

"You don't expect Metharom to actually take your offer, do you?" Voclain asked.

"I would be *delighted* if she did," James admitted. "It would be a pain for my plans in some ways, since I would very much like to retake the Persephone System before this mess is over, but I will trade a fourteen-day cease-fire and a large amount of the Commonwealth's money to swing the balance of power against Rutherford."

"But she won't," Bevan said grimly. "The condottieri exist because the systems of the Stellar League *know*, beyond any reasonable doubt, that a condottieri ship or formation *will* keep their contracts. Even double-dipping like the Admiral is offering is frowned upon—and since Rutherford has a deal with the League, she'd probably be breaking her contract to move against him."

"And *she* has q-coms with Admiral Borgogni," James agreed. "If she's tempted, she'll ask permission from the immediate contract holder. Who will decline to give it because they have a deal with Rutherford."

He shrugged.

"But Rutherford, traitorous as he is, is a Commonwealth officer.

Even though we intellectually know that the condottieri's stock-in-trade is their reliability and trustworthiness, we're still not going to trust them. It will make him look over his shoulder."

"That won't change much," Voclain warned.

"Oh, I don't intend for it to change anything," James agreed. "It's just a free psychological attack, so I may as well take it.

"The *real* gambit here depends on whether Bevan got me what I needed." He turned to the Commodore. "So, Ove. Can you guarantee that everyone in the Clockward Fleet will see my message?"

"Can't do much more than that, unless they built no security against their own virus, but I can do that," the intelligence officer confirmed. "Your...friend was a great help. Thank you for finding her?"

"She found us, Commodore. Never think otherwise," James said. "But get your code ready. It's time to do what no admiral ever wants to do."

"What's that, sir?"

"Call on a fleet to mutiny."

———

"THIS MESSAGE IS *NOT* for Hans Rutherford," James said calmly, seated in his chair and leveling his calmest "wise elder" face at the recorder. "He will get it with the rest of you, but he already knows most of what I'm going to tell you.

"The key point to that is that Rutherford has committed treason against the Commonwealth. He has taken control of the Meridian Sector for his *own* aggrandization, not the service of the Commonwealth—as is easily seen in his placement of chosen followers in key positions to secure control of the Meridian System itself.

"He traded the system we are currently in to the Stellar League's dictator for a nonaggression pact that would allow him to solidify his hold on the systems he intends to make his future empire, and he has invited me to seize control of the Dakota Sector and join him."

James shook his head slowly.

"I imagine it is obvious from the breadth of recipients of this message that I have no intention of doing so. I am sworn to serve the citizens and principles of the Commonwealth: to provide her people with democracy, freedom, justice and unity.

"Imposing a military dictatorship over eleven star systems for my own power and advancement serves *none* of these principles for the thirty billion souls in those systems. So, I am *declining* Hans Rutherford's generous offer, which leaves us at an impasse."

He swallowed and spread his hands.

"As I record this message, ships of the Clockward Fleet and Sector Fleet Dakota are hurtling toward each other with lances charged and missiles armed. I do not know what story Hans Rutherford has told you about me, and I recognize that this is my word versus his.

"My people will attach key segments of his message to me to this recording, but I do not know how long it will take Rutherford's people to prevent you from seeing the remainder of my message.

"If you do nothing now, thousands of Commonwealth spacers are going to die," James said sadly. "Regardless of who wins the battle, all of us lose. The people of the Persephone System will remain under League occupation.

"That means I must ask you to do what I would rather never ask a spacer to do: recognize that your orders are illegal. Recognize that Hans Rutherford has committed treason and has neither moral nor legal authority to command you.

"There are few to no Marines aboard your ships, but I recognize that Rutherford will have taken precautions against resistance. I must ask you to resist regardless. There are sufficient Marines aboard *my* ships to secure your vessels if you permit them to board.

"I will regard any vessel that ceases acceleration as a non-combatant," he promised. "But I need *you* to stand against Rutherford's treason with me.

"Together, we can make this right. Together, we can retake the Persephone System and stop Hans Rutherford from making himself a warlord in the wreckage of the Commonwealth."

A mental command stopped the recording, and he looked over at Mac Cléirich.

"Add those segments of his message to me and bake it into Bevan's wrapper," he ordered. "Let's get that on its way before we're out of time."

"We're only thirteen minutes from missile range, sir," Voclain said quietly. "We will need to fire long before we really see their response to your message."

"I know," James said. "*Hancock* should stick out like a sore thumb; she's seven million cubics bigger than even the *Monarch*s. Pick out the bastard's flagship and hammer her with everything we've got."

"Understood."

"Sir!" a sensor tech exclaimed. "Their fighters have moved out. Estimate six hundred inbound."

Rutherford was holding back a hundred and fifty fighters as a reserve—but there was no way his bombers weren't in the strike formation.

"Release Yamamoto to operate at his discretion," James told his staff. "Primary target is *Hancock*. If we can kill Rutherford first, that might help head this mess off before it gets even worse!"

———

MISSILE RANGE at their current velocity was over five light-minutes, which meant that James was watching the final countdown toward range at the same time as he was watching for any sign of response to his message.

"Receipt was...now," someone on the flag deck muttered.

There was no visible change across the fleet heading toward them. James hadn't expected an instant reaction, but part of him was still disappointed. They were almost in missile range—and every ship that didn't open fire balanced the missile duel.

With *Gavrilo Princip* in Dionysus orbit, Clockward Fleet only had six more launchers than he did, anyway. If any of the non-carriers broke off...

"Status change," Voclain snapped. "I have *King George V*'s identity beacon—she's reversed her engines and is accelerating away from the rest of Clockward Fleet."

"*Black Sea* and *Caspian* have done the same," another analyst reported.

"That's three," James murmured. Two more than he'd expected, if he was being honest—he wasn't necessarily *surprised* that Modesitt had chosen to trust him over Rutherford, but he was definitely gratified.

"That's *six*," Voclain reported, a sharp glee in her tone. "The rest of Sector Fleet Meridian is falling back on *Caspian*. That's *Hollywood, Oswald,* and *Okhotsk.*"

"Damn," James said mildly. "That's...not what I was expecting."

A battleship, a carrier, *three* strike cruisers and a battlecruiser. The entirety of the fleet from Meridian and two of Rutherford's ships from the original Clockward Fleet had believed James's accusations enough to withdraw from the battle.

"That's just the ships whose command crews believed you, sir," Mac Cléirich pointed out. "That's not ships with mutinous crews. That's ships where the Captain ordered them to stand down."

"Thank you, Jessie," James muttered. "There's no way five capital-ship commanders I've only met in fleet-level briefings trusted me that much. They trusted Captain Modesitt—and she trusted me."

"Or they trusted Admiral Washington, and your accusations fit what they already feared," Commodore Bevan pointed out. "We still have a problem, sir."

"The starfighters," James realized aloud.

The entire six-hundred-starfighter strike was still coming toward them—and now it looked like they were adjusting course to allow the original Clockward Fleet CAP to catch up. Rutherford had clearly decided he needed fighters shooting at Sector Fleet Dakota more than he needed a CAP around his ships.

The capital-ship odds were now badly against Rutherford, but the fighter odds were still in Clockward Fleet's favor. None of the starfighters had turned back, even the ones belonging to Sector Fleet Meridian's carriers and strike cruisers.

"Not one fighter dropped out?" Mac Cléirich asked. "That seems...unlikely."

"Fighter squadrons are tight, loyal to the officers that fly on their wing," James admitted. "But that still feels...wrong."

"We rewrote our entire networking protocols to make certain there'd be no contamination or cross-communication with their fighters," Bevan said slowly. "They may have gone for a simpler solution and locked down all non-ship-to-fighter coms."

"And then locked all the coms to one ship, probably *Hancock*," James guessed. "They don't know why half their fleet just pulled out. They just know that their orders are to even the odds by taking down as many of our ships as they can."

"What do we do?" Voclain asked. "Missile range in twenty seconds."

He leaned back in his chair and spent five of those seconds assessing the situation.

"Update Yamamoto on what we suspect with their fighters," he ordered. "Much of this rests on his people now.

"Then target all of our missile launchers on *Hancock* and fire when ready."

52

Persephone System
01:20 December 17, 2737 ESMDT

THE CAPITAL-SHIP MISSILES would take a full hour to cross the divide between the fleets, carrying one-gigaton antimatter warheads and the most powerful semi-sentient electronic-warfare suites the Commonwealth had ever designed.

The Stormwind V used the fourth tier of acceleration efficiency in the interactions between mass manipulators and antimatter engines, accelerating at a thousand and fifty gravities. At that speed, they would use as much antimatter in that hour-long flight time as a starfighter would use in a full day.

And Anthony Yamamoto's fighters wouldn't reach *their* range of the enemy for eighty minutes. Their missiles were far-shorter-ranged and far less capable than the ones fired by the capital ships—inevitably, given that a Stormwind was roughly two thousand tons versus a Katana's fifty-five hundred.

His bombers would reach their weapon range of the enemy fleet—

and it still felt strange to refer to a formation made up of Terran warships as *the enemy*—ten minutes before his regular starfighters would. Then they'd salvo five hundred torpedoes, shorter-legged but just as smart as capital-ship missiles, at them.

Anthony's orders were to target the largest enemy carrier. That was overkill, but he saw the Admiral's point. His torpedo strike could probably take down all six of the warships still heading toward him, but if they could convince even *half* of those ships to flip sides once Rutherford was dead...that was fifteen thousand Commonwealth spacers Anthony didn't have to kill today.

"They can't have completely cut the fighters off from coms," Badem said as they reviewed the update from *Krakatoa*. "That's insane."

"If they didn't think they could recode the network protocols in time, it makes some sense," Anthony replied. "It's stupid, but it would protect them from us doing something clever. It also provides Rutherford more control, which almost certainly appeals to his ego."

"But you can't *run* a fighter formation like that. They have to talk to *someone*," Badem argued.

The engineer wasn't wrong. Anthony's fighter was currently linked, to one degree or another, with *every* one of the four hundred fighters and bombers flying with him. That was needed for everything from fire coordination to sensor collation.

"It gives us an edge, that's for sure," Anthony murmured. "But I'm guessing they're locked down to one-to-one coms, each fighter with their squadron leader, then each squadron leader up to the flight-group leader and so on..."

"Sir, you sounded disturbingly pleased with that concept by the end," Strøm noted drily.

"I am," he agreed. "Badem, start scanning for the radio chatter in their formation. If they've locked everyone down to one-to-one coms, we should be able to identify the formation leaders. Take them out, especially with the coms locked like that, and they lose any ability to fight as a unit."

Because the problem, when everything came down to it, was that the missile exchange between the *fighters* would take place six minutes before the bombers could launch torpedoes. And since he was flying the same ships as his enemies, there were very few games he could play to balance the field between four hundred fighters and seven hundred.

Unless, that was, the enemy's leadership had tied their pilots' hands behind their backs for him.

———

THE STORMWINDS WERE WELL AHEAD of the fighter wings now, the salvos from each fleet hurtling toward their own annihilation. The dropouts from Clockward Fleet had cut them down to barely a third of the launchers they should have had, sending merely forty capital-ship missiles toward Sector Fleet Dakota.

Dakota, in turn, had flung almost a hundred missiles at the Marshal's flagship.

"All ships, watch your safety margins on those cap-ship missiles," Anthony ordered. "And take any opportunity shots you find. It's not like lances run out of ammo!"

A positron lance was, at its core, a modification of a zero-point cell. Electrons came out one side of the cell and went into capacitors to help feed the starfighter's systems. Positrons came out the other side, to be focused into beams that would never touch regular matter until they hit their targets.

And so long as they didn't manage to somehow stay motionless compared to the entire universe, no zero-point cell *ever* ran out of energy.

"That's funny."

"Badem, please tell me that's actually a joke," Anthony said grimly. He was tracking missiles in his implants, coordinating four hundred starfighters and trying to line his own lance up with one of the incoming missiles.

"No jokes, sir," the engineer replied. There was still a chilly edge of formality to their mental tone since Anthony's refusal of their advances. They probably didn't even realize it was there, but implant-to-implant communication *always* carried emotional overtones.

"I'm working with the other engineers, and we're resolving their radio network, sir," Badem told him. "We're still identifying the formation leads, but we have a definite track on their link back to the fleet."

"Lieutenant Şenol Badem, I *will* come back there and beat what you've found out of you if I have to," Anthony snapped—and then twisted the entire five-thousand-ton-plus starfighter in a seventy-degree turn that lined his lance up with an incoming missile.

A blast of positrons later, and one fewer missile was heading for his bunk.

"Sorry, sir," Badem said. "It's just that we were trying to get an actual answer. We can't trace the link to which ship it *is* directed to, but it's definitely *not* directed to *Hancock*."

That was funny. The older fleet carrier was the largest and most capable ship in the Clockward Fleet, even if it traded missile launchers for a heavier fighter wing. It definitely had the best communications gear...and Anthony Yamamoto, for one, had thought it was Hans Rutherford's flagship.

"Get that fired back to the fleet," he ordered. "I don't know what to make of it...but that might just be above my pay grade anyway."

53

"League Force Bravo is coming out."

James nodded silently. It would take a few hours still before the two League forces rendezvoused, but their courses were clear. They were forming up to come up behind Rutherford's fleet—and it was anyone's guess, right now, whether they meant to support the rogue Marshal or crush him.

King George V and the other voluntary bystanders were accelerating away from that line now. They were out of the way of the oncoming League forces—but for all that they'd decided not to *follow* Rutherford, they also had declined to open fire on his ships.

That would have been a step too far for just about anyone, James figured. Modesitt's ship alone would have been able to obliterate every other starship in the Clockward Fleet before they could respond, but she hadn't known which ships would or wouldn't stand down.

"Keep an eye on our League friends," he ordered. "They're not involved just yet, but that can change."

The hour-long flight time of a capital-ship missile could be split up, after all. Thirty minutes of acceleration and an extended ballistic component would put League missiles into position to close with the Commonwealth fleet.

And, unlike James or Rutherford, the League had q-coms. *They* had a live view of what every force in the system was doing. Despite being almost a quarter-*billion* kilometers away, Admiral Borgogni knew more about Rutherford's and James's fleets than either Terran commander.

"Missile salvos at ten minutes," Voclain reported. "Our fighters took out twenty-five of their missiles. Their fighters took out forty-two of ours."

James made a mental note to discuss that ratio with Yamamoto later. The Clockward Fleet's fighters shouldn't have been *that* much more effective.

Though, he supposed, the enemy fighters had also had a lot more targets. There were only fifteen missiles heading toward Sector Fleet Dakota. There were still over sixty heading toward *Hancock*.

"Sir, we just received an update from Fleet CAG," Mac Cléirich said swiftly. "They're analyzing the enemy-fighter communication network and they've found something odd."

The fighter-missile exchange would start shortly before the capital-ship missiles hit. The first round of impacts in each engagement would actually occur around the same time—but there were another ten salvos of Stormwinds in space from Sector Fleet Meridian—and *twenty* from Clockward Fleet.

James couldn't spend all of his missiles on Rutherford, not with seven League capital ships occupying a Commonwealth system. Rutherford, on the other hand, clearly wasn't planning on retaking Persephone today.

The *Assassin*s that made up most of Rutherford's missile capacity only had thirty missiles per launcher. James's *Booth* was similarly supplied, as were his *Ocean*-class strike cruisers—and he was going to need those missiles for the SLN.

But still…

"What did Yamamoto's people find?" he asked.

"The network is locked down even more than we thought," Mac Cléirich said. "Each fighter is linked to their group commander, and all of the group commanders are linked back to a *single* ship in the main formation.

"They're not sure which ship that is, but Yamamoto is *certain* that it isn't *Hancock*."

James swallowed a curse and looked back at their analysis of the enemy formation. Three carriers, two battlecruisers and a battleship. Two of the carriers, *Champion* and *Goldwyn,* were old *Paramount*-class ships. There was no way Rutherford was using them as his flagship.

"What are the odds that he's letting someone *else* have their finger on the button?" he asked aloud.

"Low," Bevan said instantly, the intelligence officer looking at the same thing James was. "Everything we've seen so far said his flagship was *Hancock*. She's his biggest, most modern ship."

"Sir, we have less than sixty seconds to change targeting on the first missile salvo," Voclain warned. "One minute forty-eight seconds on the second salvo."

"I know," James replied.

He was thinking. He pulled the last communication from Rutherford into his implants and studied the background. It was...generic. It could have been any flag bridge in the fleet. In fact...

"Mac Cléirich," he snapped. "Rutherford's last message—is that background a generated fill?"

Precious seconds passed until his coms officer looked up and nodded.

"It is, sir. He's concealing which ship he's actually on."

"That paranoid ass—" Bevan cut off his own curse. "He's been playing a long game to convince us *Hancock* was his flagship all along. But then—"

"Retarget on *Tsar Peter the Great,*" James ordered. "All salvos. *Hancock* remains the secondary target for any missile that can't adjust, but hit the battleship."

Voclain's face instantly took on the glazed expression of someone sunk fully into her neural implants as she focused on passing the orders.

"Second-largest ship, most powerful battleship, arguably the most prestigious if you discount the carriers," Bevan listed off quickly. "It makes sense, sir. Officially, he was assigned to *Saint Raymond*, same ship as Marshal Amandine, but she used him as bench strength for subordinate commands."

"All of that's true," James agreed, "but it's not why I think he's on *Tsar Peter*."

"Sir?"

"Hans Rutherford seems to have a great deal of faith in his ability to rely on and control the women closest to him," the Admiral said calmly. "And the woman he put in charge of securing Meridian behind him was Lieutenant General Ana Cantrell—who was, until recently, *Colonel* Ana Cantrell, the CO of *Tsar Peter the Great*.

"For him to have had enough time to secure her loyalty, he needed to have been on *Tsar Peter* for at least a couple of weeks."

"I hope you're right, sir," Voclain said quietly. "Because the missiles are retargeted and we can't take it back. Fighters are already launching at each other, but losing that flagship link will disorient their command and control—and potentially render their torpedo strike ineffective."

"That part is Yamamoto's problem," James replied. "Missiles target *Peter the Great*, *Hancock*, and then the battlecruisers."

*Paramount*s might be poor excuses for warships, with no missiles and a pathetic lance armament, but they still carried decent numbers of starfighters.

Plus, their *commanders* also knew they were terrible warships. Hopefully, the Clockward Fleet would surrender before it got that far, but there was no way *Champion* and *Goldwyn* would try to continue the fight on their own.

54

Persephone System
02:15 December 17, 2737 ESMDT

"WE DON'T HAVE the group leaders nailed down," Badem warned. "One-in-three chance at best."

"That's still shooting at seventy fighters instead of seven hundred," Anthony replied. "Pass the targets."

Strøm was responsible for their fighter's missiles, though the gunner *also* helped handle the targeting for the entire fleet fighter group. Group-wide control was a semi-collaborative process, with every gunner and engineer on a squadron-leader-or-higher fighter contributing brain and computer power to the process.

Anthony understood that his old enemies in the Castle Federation had specific command fighters that traded munitions for dramatically expanded computer capacity. He figured that was only half the solution and that a proper "command starfighter" should have a fourth person aboard to help coordinate the fighter group.

No one had asked his opinion yet, though. He might have a chance to make some suggestions as Wing Colonel for the whole sector, but that required him to live through today.

"Targets laid in," Strøm reported. "I don't *think* they'll have been able to ID our command fighters."

"*We* are running a proper multi-faceted encrypted scramble network," Anthony replied drily. "Since *our* Admiral actually trusts us to make our own judgments and answer our own calls."

"Our Admiral isn't a traitor," Badem said. "That helps."

Anthony kept his peace on that. Despite everything that Reynolds had said about choosing him for his loyalty to the Commonwealth, he wasn't entirely convinced that he'd have resisted if Tecumseh had chosen Rutherford's path.

"Ten seconds to launch," Strøm told him.

"All ships, stand by for incoming fire," Anthony ordered over the all-fighters channel. A glance across the feeds showed him that his people were properly maneuvering, creating a seemingly chaotic twist of courses that still kept everyone's field of fire open.

It was a hell of a lot easier to do that if every fighter was talking to each other. He couldn't imagine how much load was being carried by the twenty-five or so crews who had passed Rutherford's standards for loyalty.

He also wished he'd made the chance to buy any of the Clockward Fleet's pilots drinks. The Admiral had talked half of the capital ships into standing down, but every single damn fighter was still coming.

"Range," he murmured, barely conscious that he'd been watching the distances plummet. He was still *fully* aware when they passed the invisible line where the two fighter wings were within six and a half million kilometers of each other.

Over twenty-two hundred missiles erupted from his fighters, four from each Katana and six from each Longbow, and for over twenty seconds, they seemed unanswered.

Then the light from the enemy launch arrived, and Anthony exhaled softly. Part of him really had hoped that some of the Clockward Fleet's fighters would find the moral courage of their Navy comrades—but there were over three thousand missiles heading toward his people.

"Second salvo launched," Strøm announced quietly. "Impact on target in one hundred twenty seconds."

"Lance range in one hundred thirty."

It took Anthony a full second to realize that report was *him* speaking.

————

FIVE THOUSAND MISSILES were joined by five thousand more. Thirty seconds after that, five thousand *more* missiles blazed into space.

Then it came down to the eternal game of cat and mouse, jammers and electronic-warfare programs versus counter-countermeasures as fifteen thousand of the dumbest weapons to qualify as "smart" in the twenty-eighth century hurtled toward each other and their targets.

A full twenty percent of Anthony's attention was still dedicated to commanding the fighter group, adjusting formations, preparing for the only clever trick he even had in his books for this point. The rest was focused on his own fighter, twisting the Katana through a series of maneuvers to augment Badem's electronic dance of confusion.

"All ships," he murmured at the hundred-and-twenty-second mark. "Stand by for Ripple-Two-Seventy."

Timing was everything for this trick. So was a vague, probably true, hope that the enemy fighters' attention to detail was hampered by their restricted communications.

Twenty-five seconds to impact.

Twenty.

Fifteen.

"Ripple-Two-Seventy, *now*," Anthony barked, suiting his own maneuvers to his actions.

Two-Seventy was an angle. Two hundred and seventy degrees to clockwise from a direct vertical above Anthony's cockpit—basically a ninety-degree angle to his left. Every fighter in his wing flipped their vector to run in that direction, changing the position of five hundred spacecraft by hundreds of kilometers from where the missiles would expect them.

On its own, that would do nothing. The mass movement might

cause some minor confusion, but the missiles were both intellectually and physically capable of following the maneuvers.

Except that every one of Anthony's fighters had just launched their most powerful electronic-warfare decoys in the opposite direction, programmed to create the illusion that his formation had carried out the same maneuver toward Anthony's *right*.

With q-probes in play, there would have been enough time—*just*—for the gunners on the enemy side to run scans and analysis and potentially pierce the illusion.

Even at the three light-seconds left of range, it was too much. At over ten percent of lightspeed closing speed, there was no time for the humans to engage, analyze and update their missiles inside the time frame.

Left to their own devices, half of the missiles would have missed—but a human on the other side made a call. They *guessed* which side of the formation was the real fighter wing.

They guessed wrong, and Anthony couldn't keep himself from whooping softly in his cockpit as three thousand missiles plunged down into empty space. Some of his fighters were inside the target zone, but the last-ditch lasers and lance deployment ripped the threatening missiles apart.

He'd faced over four missiles per fighter in his wing…and he'd lost five fighters and a bomber.

The Clockward Fleet wasn't so lucky. Almost every one of the seventy potential command fighters was gone. The complex web of hard-coded communication loops was gone, and with it any ability for the Clockward fighters to coordinate.

There was no time left for discussion. With the closing range, every missile salvo would strike home inside fifteen seconds, as did the lances.

"I have pod ejection!" Strøm snapped. "Multiple emergency pods ejecting across the enemy formation."

"Can't matter now," Anthony replied. "Hold the course. Ignore the pods; take down the fighters!"

He'd learn later how many of his former-and-hopefully-future comrades had chosen the "right" course. For now, he couldn't even ignore the fighters that had been abandoned.

In the seconds of the fly-through, all that was left was fire and maneuver.

———

"WE'RE CLEAR. WE'RE CLEAR," Strøm reported, exhaling heavily.

"Report in by squadron; bombers stand by," Anthony snapped. This was the moment of truth. It almost didn't even matter how many Katanas were left now—the Clockward Fleet had sent their CAP forward to join the strike after the mutiny, which meant there was nothing left between his bomber wings and the enemy capital ships.

Squadron reports echoed in, and he forced his face to stone. Ripple-Two-Seventy had rendered the first salvo ineffective, but there had been another six thousand missiles. Those had been mostly left to their own devices, but the decoys had been gone.

It could have been worse—it *should* have been worse—but that didn't make the scrolling list of losses as fifty squadrons reported in any better. He'd only lost twenty-two bombers, and he hated himself for being *glad* at that figure.

Especially since part of the reason for it was clearly that his fighters had covered the bombers, exactly as they were meant to. A hundred and ten fighters, a hundred and thirty-two missing spacecraft in total, was a slim price to pay for obliterating *seven hundred and fifty* enemy fighters and bombers.

But those four hundred names would join his list and nightmares.

"No enemy craft remain on the scopes," Badem reported. "All Clockward Fleet fighters were either destroyed or their crews have ejected. No fighters in play, no bombers in play. Clean sweep, sir."

"Understood."

"Two minutes to torpedo range," Strøm reported. "All capital contacts still on the board. *Tsar Peter the Great* has taken multiple hits but is continuing to maneuver with the formation."

Two capital-ship salvos had struck home. Sector Fleet Dakota was easily able to handle the leakers that had made it through the fighter wing, but Clockward Fleet's stalwarts were badly outgunned at this range.

That *Tsar Peter* had taken the hits she had and was still fighting was a testament to the survivability of the Commonwealth's battleships. Even most warships could only take one or two antimatter-warhead hits and keep fighting.

"One more salvo from the fleet before torpedo range," Strøm noted.

"Lay in the targets," Anthony ordered calmly. "Sixty bombers will target *Tsar Peter*. The rest will target *Hancock*. Bombers will break off immediately after launching. Katanas will close to lance range."

That was twenty-five thousand kilometers. The anti-fighter lances on the capital ships would range at five times that, but Anthony had faith in his people's ability to make it through that fire and close to knife range.

"There she blows!" Badem suddenly snapped. "*Tsar Peter* is hit again, at least three times. She is—"

They were still a light-minute away from the battleship when she went up, zero-point cells and antimatter capacitors alike clearly losing containment as the gigaton-range warheads vaporized massive chunks of the starship.

"Bombers targeting *Tsar Peter*, split between the two *Assassins*," Anthony ordered instantly. "Fire on ra—"

"*Hancock* has cut her engines and activated her beacon," Strøm interrupted.

"So have *Goldwyn* and— *Fuck!*"

The two old carriers had clearly been following the new ship in surrendering—except that one of the *Assassins* had just opened fire, her six-hundred-kiloton-a-second lances stabbing along the full length of *Hancock* in a brutal lightshow that could only end one way.

Anthony was too far away to do anything. Even the torpedoes his people were about to fire would take ten minutes to close the rest of the range. All he could do was sit and watch in horror as a forty-million-cubic-meter carrier with five thousand people aboard blew apart under the guns of a friend—and then swallow as *Simón Radowitzky* activated her IFF beacon.

No one had a chance to decipher what *Radowitzky*'s crew meant by that until she opened fire herself, delivering a summary and violent justice for *Hancock*'s crew on their fellow battlecruiser.

There was a long, pregnant pause on the fighter wing's communications network.

"All Clockward Fleet ships have cut acceleration and activated their identity beacons," Badem reported, their tone tired. "Orders, sir?"

"All bombers will maneuver to zero-velocity intercepts at one million kilometers," Anthony ordered. "All fighters will move into close escort formation of *Radowitzky*, *Goldwyn* and *Champion*. We will escort them to join the rest of Clockward Fleet and stand by for further orders from Admiral Tecumseh."

"And if any of them decide they want to do something different?" Strøm asked softly.

"We cut them to fucking pieces."

55

Persephone System
03:00 December 17, 2737 ESMDT

Sleep was a distant myth, a hope that James wasn't sure he would see anytime soon.

"Search-and-rescue shuttles are out, sweeping for emergency pods from all of the fighters," Captain Volkov reported. "Yamamoto's people looked to have the usual ejection rate, but almost a quarter of the Clockward fighters punched in the end."

"If we can convince them to sign on, they might be useful," James murmured. "That's good news. Word from the ship Captains?"

"They've all accepted Wing Colonel Yamamoto's plan to converge on *King George V* and wait for us," Voclain told him. "No one has definitely stated a stance on where things go from here. It's a mess."

"That is an understatement," James said quietly. "Technically, *all* of them are guilty of treason, but the argument for Modesitt and the others who stood aside is easy. It's a lot harder for the people on the ships that came out with Rutherford."

Sector Fleet Dakota had been lucky. They were down a hundred and thirty starfighters, but all seven of James's capital ships were still with him. *Valiant* had taken a single hit and was still assessing damage and casualties, but he still had a fleet.

Two of them, arguably, depending on how far he trusted the remaining Clockward Fleet ships.

"What's the League's status?" James asked, casting a wider glancing across the system.

"They'll complete the rendezvous of their forces in just over two and a half hours," Voclain reported. "At that point, they'll be roughly zero velocity compared to *King George V*'s current course and about twelve light-minutes away."

James nodded. At this point, he was using Modesitt's ship as an anchor to converge around. The Commonwealth had some internal issues to sort out before they dealt with the League.

Unfortunately, the Stellar League forces now had a *lot* more starfighters than he had left. He had them badly outgunned and outnumbered—*if* what was left of Clockward Fleet rejoined him—but those fighters could even the odds far too easily.

"And we'll rendezvous with *King George V* and Clockward Fleet about an hour before that," he noted aloud. "Doesn't give us a lot of time to sort through our own bullshit, does it?"

"No, sir," Voclain agreed. "It may be worth it to consider withdrawing from Persephone, sir."

"Worth it, yes," he agreed. "Whether it may be the *right* decision... I'm not sure yet."

He gestured to the screen.

"Right now, there are still seventeen Commonwealth ships in this system," he noted. "In theory, sixteen of them are going to rendezvous and assemble into a single formation in short order. We'll be able to rearm our starfighters and bombers, though it takes about twenty-four hours to unbox and assemble a spare fighter, so we can't reequip our dismounted flight crews.

"But if we can rely on those ships, we have over a hundred and seventy missile launchers and still field over three hundred and fifty fighters," James continued. "Combined with enough battlecruisers and battleships to make a lance-range engagement heavily in our favor."

He knew that several states—including, notably, both the Stellar League itself and the Alliance of Free Stars' key members like the Castle Federation—had basically stopped building battleships because lance-range engagements were so rare at this point.

But he still had three of them in his order of battle, and even with *Valiant* damaged, those three ships would rip the League fleet apart at close range.

"We will proceed to rendezvous with the rest of the Commonwealth ships in the system," he continued. "We have to assume *Princip* is lost to us and will join *Alberto da Giussano* in operations against us. But I will take seventeen ships, even without most of their starfighters, against seven."

Each of the fleets was headed by a modern carrier, and the League's older ships were bigger and tougher than James's older ships...but he'd take that risk over abandoning the system to Periklos's people again.

Assuming that Rutherford's people saw sense.

———

"WE DIDN'T KNOW EVERYTHING," Jessie Modesitt told James grimly. The recording was still over a minute old, the inexorable rush toward rendezvous continuing as engines flared across the star system.

"Some of us guessed that Rutherford had more in mind than just being Governor of Meridian, but what could we do? People who'd said too much had 'accidents.' We didn't realize how thoroughly he had infiltrated the ships until several *captains* were gone.

"Alric helped me see what we were in, but neither of us saw a way out. And then Rutherford told everyone he had evidence that you'd been bought by the League while you were in Meridian. That he was afraid that you'd faked Banks's disability to take command of the fleet, and that *you* were the traitor."

James had figured something along those lines. It was the only way he could see any of the fleet following Rutherford into combat against Sector Fleet Dakota.

"Alric and I knew the stick up your ass was too big for that," Modesitt told him with a smirk. "And I'd built some quiet channels with other captains. We were talking—but when it looked like everything was going to be resolved in an ambush with your ships trapped at point-blank range, we couldn't do *anything*.

"Then you managed to run, to rub everyone's faces in Rutherford's deceptions and betrayals," she concluded. "Turned out every single spacer in Sector Fleet Meridian blamed Rutherford for Admiral Washington's death. Given the *slightest* excuse to stab the 'Marshal' in the back, they took it."

She shrugged.

"And given my choice of treasons, I'd follow you over Rutherford any day. But the man is persuasive and convincing. I was surprised to see *Black Sea* break off with me." She shook her head. "I owe Rosheen Van der Stoep a drink. Probably more than one, given how she drinks."

"Of course, we also expected to be able to talk to our starfighters at that point," Modesitt noted. "That paranoid bastard. He's dead now, at least. Right? I will go out in a Katana and vaporize his flash-frozen body *myself* to be sure, if I have to."

There was no real way to be sure, James knew. Rutherford had been aboard *Tsar Peter the Great*, but it was theoretically possible he'd escaped before the battleship had been vaporized.

Separated from his fleet and power base, though, the man was far less of a threat.

"I am about ninety percent sure of everyone left," his old subordinate continued. "The only one, in fact, that I would actually *question* is Andrea Windsor on *Simón Radowitzky*, and well…"

Modesitt shrugged.

"Like Cantrell, I'm pretty sure Windsor was spending time in the Marshal's bed, and he appears to have a bloody *supernatural* effect on the women he's seduced," she admitted. "I don't necessarily see the appeal, but even *I* found him convincing.

"That said, Windsor put sixty megatons or so worth of positrons into *Giovanni Brusca* after they blew up *Hancock*, so I figure that bought her at least a little credit."

The Commodore sighed.

"Whatever happens, Admiral, I'm your woman. I can't say I want to take flight and leave the system to the League, but... Well, you know the odds as well as I do, and I can't promise you that this lot is in any shape to fight a real battle."

The recording ended and James stared grimly at the wall hangings behind where Modesitt's hologram had stood.

It was bad enough that two Commonwealth fleets had opened fire on each other. That the Stellar League Navy had enjoyed a front-row seat to the mess was a headache James didn't need.

If nothing else, he was quite certain that Borgogni could *also* match seventeen warships against seven in his head. It was only the lack of starfighters on the Commonwealth side that left the prospective battle remotely in question.

Even without the starfighters, the odds were in their favor. Except that the League commander would, rightly, figure that morale in the combined Commonwealth fleet was trash. A fleet that had recently been at war with itself wasn't going to be the finely honed war machine that could rip over seven hundred fighters apart without losses of their own.

James could run through every logical argument of resources and weight of metal and practicality, but his soul and his oath tore at the thought of abandoning three billion civilians.

The answer, though, didn't lie in *his* soul. It lay in the souls of the officers and spacers who had served Marshal Hans Rutherford.

56

"Sir, we have an incoming transmission for you," Sumiko Mac Cléirich told James. "It's…live, sir."

"Live?" James asked, then realized that there was only one way and one person who could be initiating a live conversation right now. "Where's the probe?"

"They dropped her stealth at two hundred thousand kilometers," the coms officer replied, highlighting the League q-probe hovering around his fleet. "I'm not sure we even had a ghost there before."

"We didn't," Voclain said grimly. "The League's q-probes are stealthier than we expected. We're only getting ghosts when they're within a hundred thousand.

"Believe me, sir, whoever is calling can read our hull numbers."

"Good to know." James grimaced and glanced around his flag deck. There wasn't anything visible that would betray anything about his fleet to the League officer.

"I'll take it here. Connect him," James ordered. With his flag-deck crew watching, he knew that whatever he said would be relayed to every member of *Krakatoa*'s crew within moments—to the rest of Sector Fleet Dakota within minutes.

The tanned and hook-nosed Greek man who appeared in front of James's command chair was instantly recognizable. Star Admiral Peppi Borgogni had a *long* file with Commonwealth intelligence, only exceeded by his sister and his new brother-in-law, Dictator Periklos.

"Admiral James Tecumseh," Borgogni greeted him with a slight bow. "Your reputation precedes you, but it appears Marshal Rutherford wasn't listening." He paused. "Or should that be Marshal Tecumseh now? I'm unclear on how that authority passes around at this point."

"*Vice Admiral* is more than sufficient, Star Admiral Borgogni," James said calmly. "I must, I find, inform you that Persephone is a member system of the Terran Commonwealth. Per the charter rights of any member system, I am called upon to defend her skies and her sovereignty with all necessary force.

"You will withdraw from Persephone or I will engage and destroy your fleet."

Borgogni smirked at him.

"I don't suppose the deal you offered Metharom is still on the table?" he observed calmly. "I will provide you full information on everything we discussed with Hans Rutherford and even return *Gavrilo Princip* to you in exchange for that two-week cease-fire."

For all of Borgogni's smirking, it was a good offer. James's fleet was far from ready to go toe-to-toe with any enemy. That two-week time frame was exactly what he'd need to fall back to Meridian, reequip and return.

Of course, as Borgogni well knew, there were basically no fighters left in Meridian for James to load onto his carriers. Two weeks might help James resolve the morale issue in his fleet, but it wouldn't solve his real issues.

By the time they returned to Meridian, they'd have unboxed and assembled all the spare fighters they carried—but Clockward Fleet had already *done* that on their first retreat from the system. They only had the ten percent allotment for Sector Fleet Meridian.

Thirty-eight fighters and twelve bombers. Given weeks in Meridian, they could manufacture starfighters with the carrier's onboard workshops, but they'd be notably inferior to proper versions in a dozen significant ways.

If James Tecumseh withdrew, no matter what terms it was officially on, he was conceding the Persephone System for at least two months. Probably more.

"It is against the principles and the honor of the Terran Commonwealth Navy to abandon a star system to conquest by a rogue mercenary turned dictator," James said softly. "I do not know or care what deals Hans Rutherford agreed to. I do not know or care what failures of honor that man embraced.

"*I* am an officer of the Navy of the homeworld of all humanity. The people of Persephone accepted Commonwealth sovereignty in exchange for the promise of protection, freedom, democracy and justice. I will deliver none of these things if I leave.

"So, *my* offer, Star Admiral, is this: withdraw from Persephone now and return this system to the control of its citizens, and I will offer the League that cease-fire. I will, indeed, commit to not prosecute offensive operations against the League until such time as the senate delegation sent to negotiate with Dictator Periklos returns their conclusions to Earth."

He smiled thinly.

"One does hope that their mission will pass more traditionally than Marshal Amandine's peace delegation."

The Star Admiral was still smirking and he shook his head.

"I'm afraid my orders from my Dictator are clear," he said. "Persephone is now League territory and will be incorporated as a modern system-state under that structure. Any attempt to forcefully reintegrate Persephone into the Commonwealth will be met with equal force.

"I am afraid, Admiral Tecumseh, that I must ask you to withdraw from this system. Commonwealth politics have become too complex for us to wait for their resolution to this matter."

Borgogni's unceasing smirk was starting to grate on James's nerves, but he gave the Star Admiral his most level and calmest look.

"Then we are at an impasse, Admiral," he told the League officer. "If the League does not withdraw, you will be destroyed.

"My oath is to protect the citizens and principles of the Commonwealth. I will serve neither if I allow your seizure of this system to stand."

With a mental command, he cut the channel and looked around at his flag deck. The whole room was still as a tomb, every ear and eye focused on their Admiral as he verbally sparred with the League officer.

James gave them all a soft smile.

"We *all* swore that oath," he reminded them. "I would no more ask the soldiers and spacers of the Commonwealth Navy to forsake that oath than I would cut off the one fleshy leg I have left.

"Look to your duties. We have a star system to liberate!"

57

Persephone System
04:40 December 17, 2737 ESMDT

"Range is eleven thousand kilometers to *King George V*," Mac Cléirich reported. "She's the closest non–Sector Fleet Dakota unit. Farthest unit is *Simón Radowitzky* at forty-two thousand kilometers."

She paused.

"All ships are close enough for standard virtual conferencing, Admiral."

"Understood." James considered taking this call in public on the flag deck as well—but that was probably going to be a step *too* far. The odds were that he was going to need people to admit to mutiny and treason and potentially throw themselves on metaphorical swords.

Private was better for that.

"Set up an all-Captains conference and include Commodore Voclain," he ordered. "I'll take it in my office, and we'll sort this mess out."

He knew he was projecting an overly optimistic face. There was *no way* he could sort this mess out in a manner that would allow him to take the fleet into battle, but what could he do? The League forces would rendezvous into a single formation in under an hour. A zero-velocity/zero-range intercept course after that would bring the two fleets to each other four hours and seven minutes after that.

James couldn't do that. His best chance was to form his ships into a massive hammer, protected against incoming fighters and missiles by their own fighter wing, and smash it into Borgogni's force. At missile range or lance range, the Commonwealth would carry this battle.

It was only if it came down to a fighter duel that James would lose.

That thought carried him into his office and his chair. A steaming green tea was waiting for him, though he barely caught a glance of Chief Leeuwenhoek vanishing through the side door.

The smell wasn't enough to replace the sleep he'd lost, but it still calmed his nerves. He took a sip of the hot drink and linked in to the conference.

The faces looking back at him looked as exhausted as he felt, but they met his gaze surprisingly levelly as he looked around at them.

"Captains. Commodore Voclain." Seventeen spacers, all O-6 or O-7. They hadn't risen to their ranks without a "command mentality." And yet...most of the people on this call had screwed up royally, to one degree or another.

"I think it is self-evident, at this point, the nature of Hans Ruther-ford's treason," James said softly. "But for those of you who didn't keep up: he traded Persephone to the Stellar League's Dictator in exchange for a nonaggression pact that he intended to use to make himself the warlord of the Meridian and Dakota Sectors."

He let that hang in the air, a bloody sword of Damocles that had already broken several of the people in the conference.

"Every one of the Meridian and Clockward Fleet officers in this call followed Hans Rutherford in at least part of his treason," he continued. "If nothing else, all of you contributed Marines to the occupying force currently securing control of Meridian's government for Rutherford.

"I could ask what you were all thinking, but I know," he said quietly. "In the pursuit of the protection of the people we swore to serve, we are often inclined to accept expediency. Military governance in times of crisis has a long and storied history.

"One that rarely ends well," he noted. "And yet. And yet."

He sighed.

"For all that I disagreed with Hans Rutherford's methods, I did not see treason in them," he told them. "There were questionable acts— using a computer virus to eavesdrop on *my* ships certainly did not help his case with me!—but until he actually attempted to disable my ships and take control of Sector Fleet Dakota, he had publicly done nothing I could say was treason."

James spread his hands.

"You, I'm sure, saw more questionable acts than I did," he noted. "But the point stands: so long as Hans Rutherford claimed to be acting in the service of the Commonwealth, none of us had grounds to challenge him.

"It was only when he ordered you into battle against a Commonwealth fleet that you truly had reason to question."

Again, James paused, letting his words hang in the air.

"And then Sector Fleet Meridian made their own choice," he observed softly. "Captain Modesitt knew me of old and made her own choice. Captain Van der Stoep, as I understand, trusted Captain Modesitt.

"But three of the people in this call—and three other Captains who are no longer alive—chose to follow their commanding officer into battle. Faced with the choice between the word of *their* Admiral and the word of another Admiral, you chose your own."

He waited to see if any of them would defend themselves further.

"Seventeen thousand, eight hundred and ninety-six officers and spacers of the Terran Commonwealth Navy and the Terran Commonwealth Starfighter Corps are now dead because of that choice," he finally said into the silence.

"We can't change that," he concluded flatly. "And I cannot argue that I would have necessarily done any differently in your place. Demanding that you defend your actions, that you surrender your commands, that you pay penalties for having done what appeared to be your duty… There is a logic to all of this. The Navy will inevitably hold a Board of Inquiry at the very least around what happened here today.

"But this conference call is not that Board," James told them. "We have a higher purpose here than to argue over the crimes and failures of the past."

A model of the system appeared in the middle of the virtual table.

"One point nine billion Commonwealth citizens on Zagreus," he reminded them all. "Another eight hundred million on Dionysus. Add in asteroid-mining colonies, orbitals around the gas giants, et cetera, et cetera, it rounds roughly to three billion people."

This close to the border, there were probably at least a few dozen million people who weren't Commonwealth citizens and likely hadn't been counted in any census.

"If we allow what Hans Rutherford did to divide us, to destroy the morale and integrity of the officers and spacers under our command, we fail," James told them. "Let that man bear the weight of his sins.

"Let us bear the weight of our duty—and our *duty*, Captains, is to those three billion people."

———

"FORMATION IS RENO-SIX," James told Voclain after the conference wrapped up. "Let's get Yamamoto's people back aboard and rearming."

"On it," the chief of staff replied. "Mac Cléirich, with me."

The two women linked into a closed network and began the rapid mental communication of sending out messages to the entire fleet.

James, meanwhile, was running the numbers on his enemy. If everyone was being cooperative and trying to rendezvous, it would take them over four hours. At a head-on collision course, both fleets accelerating at standard thrust of two hundred gravities, he would bring them into lance range of his battleship's positron lances in just under three.

For this purpose, at least, *Krakatoa* counted as a battleship. Vastly bigger than the *Monarch* and *Resolute*-class battlewagons, she carried the same megaton-a-second beams they did. More of them, in fact, than the older *Monarch*-class ships.

The problem was that the League fleet was, in many ways, more advanced than James's second-tier ships. The condottieri cruisers shared a similar shield power to most of his ships, but *Alberto da Giussano*'s electromagnetic deflectors were almost as powerful as *Krakatoa*'s —and every ship in the League fleet except the "borrowed" *Gavrilo Princip* had megaton-a-second lances.

Even assuming he made it through the League's fighters without taking critical lances, there'd be several seconds in which only the heaviest lances would count. James had an edge in those, but he had a far-larger edge once he could bring the six-hundred-kiloton lances of the rest of his fleet to bear.

"Fleet is forming up," Voclain reported. "Long-range scans suggest that the League fleet is moving toward us. Your orders, sir?"

"Once the fleet has formed up, we will move out at two hundred gravities," James ordered. "We will maintain course for a close-range lance engagement, opening with missiles at maximum range.

"We'll give Yamamoto's people a break," he continued. "Fighters will remain aboard until oh six hundred hours. Then they will deploy in defensive formation to protect us from enemy missiles and fighters."

"That will leave us vulnerable to bomber strikes," Voclain noted. She wasn't objecting, just pointing out.

"It will," James agreed. "The Longbows will join the Katanas in using their Javelins in missile-defense mode. We will maintain formation integrity throughout, cycling the Longbows and Katanas if possible to replenish their missiles."

Both fleets were now in open space. There was nowhere to hide and few clever maneuvers left. James had formed his fleet into a giant hammer, and he was going to treat the Stellar League Navy as a particularly stubborn eggshell.

If he was very lucky, he'd have a fleet left afterward.

58

Persephone System
06:00 December 17, 2737 ESMDT

THE KEEP-AWAKE FUNCTIONS of a twenty-eighth-century neural implant were a far cry from the amphetamines of an earlier age, but they used many of the same chemical channels.

And unlike amphetamines, the designers of the endurance functions of military implants had been well aware of the addictive potential. In some ways, Anthony Yamamoto knew, the systems keeping him awake into hour twenty-two were *intentionally* unpleasant to use.

Not in ways that were distracting. Never in ways that would degrade efficiency—that was, after all, the entire point of them—but a carefully, *carefully* calibrated list of non-disabling discomforts.

The missiles were already in space as his fighter was slammed back into the void, and a practiced eye watched the first wave of over a hundred and fifty smart munitions blaze off carefully.

It would be a few minutes still before they saw the enemy missiles, though there was one thing already missing from the display that Anthony was watching.

"Any sign of their starfighters?" he asked aloud.

"Not yet," Strøm replied. "That's weird, right?"

"I would have expected their fighter strike to launch shortly after they began maneuvering," Anthony admitted. "What is Borgogni playing at?"

"I don't know, but I wish the Admiral was planning on a missile duel," Strøm admitted. "We have almost two hundred long-range launchers to their hundred. We could stretch this out for a while."

"Except they have more actual *missiles* left than we do," Anthony pointed out. "And that's ignoring their fighters. The more we make this a capital-ship duel, the more we win. If we try to fight a missile duel, they'll send their fighter wings in."

"Where *are* their fighters?" the gunner replied.

"I don't know," Anthony admitted. "I hate it when the other side tries to be clever!"

He couldn't think of any particular reason why the League would be holding their fighters back. On the other hand, he wasn't going to complain. The bomber-and-fighter strike he was waiting for was going to gut what was left of the fighters under his command.

Too many officers and spacers he knew had already died today. He wasn't looking forward to leading more of them to their deaths.

———

"FIGHTERS IDED ALONGSIDE THE MISSILE LAUNCH," Strøm reported several minutes later, as the light from the first League missiles finally arrived. That had taken almost ten minutes—minutes in which the Commonwealth fleet had been firing a missile salvo every forty seconds.

Anthony was grimly aware that their older capital ships were about to run out of munitions. He didn't know what the plan was, but he suspected it was to shoot every ship in the fleet dry. There was no point in holding on to anything.

"How many birds are we looking at?" he asked.

"Eighty-six missiles, as expected…"

"Strøm," Anthony prodded as his gunner trailed off.

"I only have three hundred and forty fighters," Strøm reported. "It doesn't look like the condottieri ships have launched any fighters."

The League force still had a first-rate carrier and two battlecruisers, but if the mercenaries were playing games…that would explain the delay in fighter launches.

"They're assuming a similar formation to ours," Strøm concluded. "Bombers and fighters in an antimissile defensive perimeter."

Anthony wanted to take advantage of the apparent weakness and fling his fighters down the League's throat. Of course, it wasn't that simple. Even at full thrust, his fighters were still over an hour's flight away. Whatever was going on would be resolved before he could bring his people into range.

"Keep an eye on them," he murmured. "If they bring their bombers out with only a couple of hundred escorts, we'll meet them halfway."

Those weren't his orders—but he was Fleet CAG. Some decisions *had* to be his, and where exactly to intercept the enemy bombers was definitely one of them!

"Enemy missiles are expected in approximately forty-eight minutes," Badem noted, the engineer focused on their current mission. "Any change to formations?"

"Not yet," Anthony replied. "We're spread out between the fleet and the missiles. There's nowhere else for us to be yet."

Though from what he could see, he would have *loved* to be a fly on the wall in Admiral Metharom's flag deck!

59

Persephone System
06:30 December 17, 2737 ESMDT

"WHAT GAMES ARE THEY ALL PLAYING?" James asked softly.

"I think there's only one game being played," Bevan told him, the intelligence officer flipping through files on a heads-up-display no one else could see. "And it's a condottieri pushing the limits of her contract."

"The whole *point* of the condottieri is that they keep their contracts," James countered. That was what Bevan himself had been saying earlier. They'd never counted on Metharom to actually cause problems for anyone.

For that matter, James had neither expected nor received any *response* from his original message to Metharom. Borgogni had referenced it, so she'd clearly told her employer about it—which was what he'd expected from a proper League condottieri.

"Yes, but they're still *mercenaries*," Bevan said. "Borgogni is throwing the dice here. He might win, he might lose. His career is made if he wins, and it's wrecked if he withdraws. If he loses and lives, fighting covers his ass with his brother-in-law."

"And if he dies, he dies gloriously for the League?" James asked. "Honor and duty can lead us into some damn-fool decisions."

He didn't necessarily exclude his own maneuvers from that list. Persephone's people were arguably only his responsibility in the most distant and theoretical sense—except that he was there.

"And honor and duty mean very different things to a condottieri," his intelligence officer told him. "The *last* thing Metharom wants to be involved in is a defeat or a pyrrhic victory. If she loses her fleet, she doesn't even have the leverage to get the League to replace it.

"And her contract almost certainly allows her to refuse a battle she doesn't believe they can win."

"Interesting." James turned to look at the display. His first missiles were halfway to their targets—by flight time, at least, though not distance.

"Voclain," he called the chief of staff over. "Get the tactical officers on a network. We're targeting *Alberto da Giussano* with all the missiles, correct?"

"Yes, sir," she confirmed.

"We need to change that," he told her. "Pick one of the condottieri cruisers—it doesn't matter which one—and hammer her."

"Sir? We *can* ID the enemy flagship, so…"

"We might kill Borgogni, but if we kill Borgogni, his people will continue the fight," James said quietly. "But if we spook Metharom, she may just pull *four* ships out of the line. Everyone is in open space. Any of us can go FTL inside five minutes.

"There's no reason to make this a fight to the death except duty and honor. Admiral Pawnteep Metharom's main duty is to her crews and pilots. She isn't going to die for the League's expansion."

———

JAMES HELD his breath as the missiles came hurtling in. He had a full fleet with him this time, but there were over twice as many missiles coming in. This was where any failure in coordination, any drop in morale or attentiveness from the recent internal conflict would show up.

Where the consequences of his decision to push the battle would come home to roost.

"Missiles in outer defensive perimeter," Wardell Carey half-reported, half-chanted. The operations officer was lost in a gestalt of sixteen starships' tactical officers, coordinating defensive fire.

Their own offensive fire was beyond their control now. They'd fired off thousands of missiles and emptied the magazines of everything except the battleships and *Krakatoa* herself. Those four warships still had ten missiles left per launcher…just in case.

"Starfighters have engaged," Carey continued. "Estimate thirty-six contacts destroyed. Forty-five-plus inbound. Missiles in middle defensive perimeter. ECM online, positron lances engaging."

The whole flag deck was silent except for Carey's calm pronouncement.

"Estimate twelve missiles have entered the inner perimeter. Lasers engaging. Target is *Valiant*."

Pause.

"Missiles destroyed. No hits, repeat, no hits."

James breathed a sigh of relief, but he knew how short-lived it would be. There were still three minutes left before they saw the results of their own first salvo—three minutes in which four more League salvos would strike home.

Without instructions, Yamamoto's fighters were maneuvering, spreading out their formation toward the enemy fire to allow them to buy critical fractions of a second for lance engagement. Their missiles were critical to this defensive role, but there wasn't going to be time to rearm the fighters before the fourth salvo came in.

Two more salvos ran into fighter missiles and, combined with the inner defenses, were wiped out. Then the fighters were dry and all they had were positron lances.

That cut their effectiveness in the antimissile role by at least half, and James watched that reality take shape.

"Missiles in the inner perimeter," Cardell said grimly. "Detonating, missiles detonating."

There was a long silence.

"*Valiant* has taken surface damage, no direct hits," Mac Cléirich relayed. "Her sensors are fried, though. We're setting up a telemetry relay."

Valiant was a *Resolute*-class battleship. She might have been a decade old and riding the edge of obsolescence in the current era of technological advancement, but she was a tough, powerful warship.

But without q-probes to give her eyes, she was restricted to the sensors on her outer hull, systems critically vulnerable to exactly that kind of near-miss. Dozens of missiles off the fifth salvo, the last before James would see the results of his own fire, died on their way in.

Others missed completely, lured away by ECM and decoys. Three near-misses lashed both *Valiant* and *Adamant*.

And one missile made it past everything James's unnamed fleet could throw at it and slammed directly into the battleship's flank as Captain Mašek desperately tried to evade.

When the flash faded, *Valiant* was clearly in serious trouble. Her engines had cut out completely and her electromagnetic deflectors were flickering badly...but the battleship was still there.

"Readjust the formation," James snapped. "Paladin-Four; wrap *Valiant* up."

Paladin-Four was a standard formation, but any given group of ships had to practice it to make sure the right ships went into the right places to guard the crippled vessel. Even giving the order, James was expecting it to be a disaster—he was just hoping it was going to be a disaster that happened in *front* of *Valiant*.

Instead, there were about seven seconds of hesitation as the navigators ran through the vectors on their shared network and then his ships moved as one. It should have been faster, could have been smoother... but fifteen seconds after James gave the order, *Valiant* was behind a solid phalanx of undamaged warships.

And that was ten seconds before they *needed* to cover her. The next salvo was still focused on the wounded battleship, but those missiles had to pass a gauntlet of the missile defenses of every other ship in the fleet.

Not a single missile made it through—and then, finally, James had time to see the results of the missiles he'd flung at the League.

"We got at least one hit, sir," Voclain told him as she registered his attention. "Maybe two. One of the condottieri cruisers is falling out of formation, leaking atmosphe—"

"Cherenkov flare!" Cardell interrupted. "Multiple Cherenkov flares. The condottieri cruisers just warped space, sir."

James kept his spine rigid, but he *felt* every muscle in his body sag around his bones in relief.

The moral is to the physical as three is to one. Identify the enemy's morals and attack them there.

Admiral Pawnteep Metharom's first duty was to protect her crews, not fight a messed-up battle that could only result in a pyrrhic victory at best. Borgogni had pushed the contract to the edge of what he could demand—and when Metharom started losing people, she'd chosen them over her contract.

"More flares," Voclain said after a moment. "Borgogni has followed her out. Missiles are now without control."

"Let's still not play any games," James ordered. "Flip our vector, extend their flight times and send Yamamoto out to deal with them."

Mac Cléirich coughed.

"I also think we might have the Wing Colonel send a message, sir," she suggested. "Unless I'm misreading Commodore Voclain's data, Borgogni just...left his fighters behind."

James looked at the data and swore under his breath.

"Well, let's see if Persephone is prepared to offer sanctuary in exchange for service in their defense force," he suggested. "Because I suspect those flight crews just decided they *hate* the League Navy."

Leaning back in his chair and studying the display, he concealed a sigh of relief.

It was over. He'd still have to land Marines and deal with whatever troops the League had left behind, but it was over—and his ragtag assemblage of fleets certainly hadn't *performed* like they'd been shooting at each other earlier that morning!

60

Persephone System
12:00 December 18, 2737 ESMDT

TWENTY-FOUR HOURS OF, at least, *less* insanity than the preceding twelve brought a modicum of peace to the Persephone System.

It also brought *Krakatoa* into Zagreus orbit and James to a city of black basalt and intentionally—he hoped—red-tinged lighting named Asphodel. Tucked into the slopes of a mountain as dark-stoned as the city, Asphodel was the capital of Zagreus and the Persephone System's seat of government.

And its original architects had had a *very* specific sense of humor, James concluded as a convoy of armored vehicles delivered him to Pomegranate Hall. The central edifice of Persephone's democracy was a simple, if impressive, dome of black basalt suspended ten meters in the air by pillars carved with stories from the Greek mythology that inspired the planet's names.

All of the pillars except for two were of the same black basalt as the dome and the rest of the city. The carvings and sculptures were marked out in stark contrast with a bright-white mortar of local cement, drawing the eye to the artwork—and then, inevitably, to the two stark-white pillars at the entrance to Pomegranate Hall.

There were no stories carved into those pillars. They were simply single pieces of carefully designed structural stone…carved from Greek marble on Earth and shipped across dozens of light-years to mark Persephone's connection to its home world and islands.

Files of Marines in full combat armor lined the path from where the armored personnel carrier came to a halt up to those pillars. But at the pillars, the Marines passed over responsibility for James's security to locals.

From what James understood, there were only about forty members of the Cerberus Guard *left*, but the crimson-uniformed security officers with their three-headed-dog shoulder flashes still formed a solid line between the pillars and the entry to the actual parliamentary assembly building at the center of the dome.

The Parliament of Persephone was doing their best to put a good foot forward, with everyone in their regular suits and in the regular velvet-lined seats amidst the black stone fixtures of the Hall. They couldn't hide the fact that the system parliament was supposed to be two hundred and fifty politicians…and there were only a hundred and four in the room.

Thirty-six MPs had formed a rump parliament to run the planet for Borgogni. They were all alive but jailed and awaiting review of their actions by their peers in this room.

The other hundred and ten members of the system parliament were dead. Star Admiral Borgogni had literally decimated the Parliament when he'd arrived, selecting one-tenth of the MPs at random and having them publicly shot.

The rest had either been in the wrong place at the wrong time or been too openly resistant to Borgogni's attempts to pacify the system. The Star League admiral had only really had one approach to dealing with resistance—and without orbital support, most of the League garrisons had either been destroyed or had been *desperate* to surrender to Commonwealth Marines when James's ships had entered orbit.

Even with a hundred-plus politicians in it, James could hear his boots clomp on the polished stone floor as he walked down to the center stage. A surprisingly young-looking Black man stood on the stage, waiting for him.

As James stepped up onto the stage, he realized one of the more *theatrical* bits of Borgogni's brutality. When the League had decimated Persephone's Parliament, they'd done it *there*. The locals had done a lot of cleaning up, but he suspected the bullet holes along the back wall had been left intentionally visible.

Impulse struck him and he gave the man waiting for him a firm nod as he walked to the back of the room and gave those bullet holes, marking where twenty-five people had been murdered for the sin of trying to serve their people, a slow, perfect salute.

Then he turned back to the MPs and the man they'd picked to represent them and bowed.

"Mr. Kai De Laurentis?" he asked.

"I am," the young man replied. "Member of Parliament for Asphodel-Center." He swallowed. "Minister for Youth and Recreation. Uh... eleventh in the line of succession for Prime Minister, I guess."

"And confirmed by vote two hours ago," James noted, remembering the note. "Your people move quickly."

"We have had little choice," De Laurentis replied, his voice steadying. He'd almost certainly been the youngest member of the Cabinet before the League had arrived. "Parliament wished to directly express our thanks for your actions here, Admiral Tecumseh.

"It is our understanding that the battle you chose to fight was an extremely risky one for your fleet. While the League appears to have conceded our system in the end, we will always appreciate the stand you took for Persephone and her people."

James bowed his head.

"I am an officer of the Terran Commonwealth Navy," he told them all. "The protection of the citizens of the Commonwealth is and will always be my highest priority."

"So, what happens to us now?" someone called down.

James looked up but couldn't pick out the speaker.

"What do you want to happen?" he asked quietly. "I am not, technically, responsible for even the military security of the Meridian

Sector. Due to the events that led to my standing here, I am *effectively* responsible for it and will see to the safety of this system, but *you* are the duly elected government of Persephone."

The room was quiet for a long breath, then De Laurentis seemed to straighten.

"Our first obligation, of course, is to begin organizing a new election," he declared loudly. "We must also make efforts to restore communication with the rest of the Sector and the Commonwealth!"

"I cannot speak to your elections," James noted. "That is a matter of civilian authority. I *can* provide assistance in establishing communications with the rest of the Sector.

"I need to return my own core force to the Dakota Sector as quickly as I can," he continued. "I also feel obligated to undo the worst of the damage inflicted by Marshal Rutherford's treason, which will require me to detour via Meridian.

"I would be delighted to provide transport for a delegation from this Parliament to Meridian."

"You plan to leave Persephone defenseless?" another MP shouted.

"No," James replied. "You agreed to provide asylum to the flight crews of the starfighters Borgogni left behind. While the League did not have any basing facilities here, my team has calculated that the carriers *Goldwyn* and *Champion* should suffice to provide basing for those fighters."

It would be cramped, since those ships were designed to hold a hundred starfighters each *and* the League fighters were bigger than their Terran counterparts, but it was all James could justify leaving behind.

"Those ships will remain under the authority of Sector Fleet Meridian," he continued. "But they will provide a first line of defense against the League until the Commonwealth is in position to deal more permanently with Dictator Periklos."

James had no idea when that would be. He *hoped* that it wouldn't take more than a year for the Commonwealth to get sufficiently back on their feet to convince the League that peace was a better option.

"We will consult," De Laurentis said. "Those ships will be more than welcome, Admiral. When will your fleet be leaving?"

"Oh eight hundred hours Earth standard," James replied. "We have done all we can here, and I worry about the damage Rutherford left behind."

That sent a ripple of dismay through the MPs, but De Laurentis seemed unsurprised.

"We will have our delegation assembled well before then," he promised. "I know the rest of our sector would not have Persephone stand alone—and we would not leave *them* to stand alone, either!"

The young man might seem intimidated by the task before him, but James judged that Kai De Laurentis was going to do *just fine* by his star system.

61

Persephone System
23:00 December 18, 2737 ESMDT

"COME IN, JESSIE," James instructed. "Chief, bring the Commodore a drink."

Modesitt nodded to Leeuwenhoek as she was handed a glass of iced water and took a seat across from James.

"Nice digs," she said. "The art is Shawnee, isn't it? Your people?"

"Shawnee artisans on Dakota," James agreed. "The First Chief organized it as a gift after I ended up in command of the Sector Fleet." He shook his head. "I don't know if she thought of it as a bribe or just a reminder of where I come from. Could be both."

"We all need to remember where we come from, some days," Modesitt agreed. "And what we're fighting for."

"To the Commonwealth," James said, offering his own water glass in a toast and salute.

"The Commonwealth," Modesitt agreed. She sighed. "The one that gives us people like Hans Rutherford."

James shivered.

"I'd like to claim that Rutherford isn't the Commonwealth's fault, but it *also* gave us Captain Richardson and a few other mass murderers I can think of without trying," he admitted. "And yet…it's the people and principles of the Commonwealth we swore to serve."

"How does the old saying go?" Modesitt murmured. "'My country, right or wrong; if right, to be kept right; and if wrong, to be set right.'"

"Exactly," James agreed. "But first, of course, we have to protect those people. Hans Rutherford wasn't…very convincing in his commitment to do that."

"Hans Rutherford was disturbingly convincing when he opened his mouth in person," she admitted. "Even I felt it. I don't know if it came across coms links and video as much as it did in person."

She shook her head.

"Even guessing that he'd sold out Persephone didn't feel like enough to doubt the man the Marshal had put in command. We needed proof, and then it was too late."

"It wasn't, though," James replied. "When push came to shove, yes, it would have made life a lot easier if you'd vaporized *Tsar Peter the Great* instead of just standing aside—but that's a hell of a line to cross."

Officially, Admiral James Tecumseh knew absolutely nothing about Captain Andrea Windsor's counseling sessions. Unofficially, he'd had Bevan and Reynolds digging *deep* into what his new captains were up to.

Windsor had blown apart a comrade's ship in response to *them* murdering another ship, but it was still going to haunt her for a long time. James had his sympathies. He had his own nightmares about the day the Alliance of Free Stars had tracked Captain Richardson—a man who had literally *killed a world*—to bay and blown apart the man's battleship in front of James.

"You didn't have me fly over to your ship just to shoot the breeze, though," Modesitt told him. "What did you want?"

"An answer to a question, initially," James replied. "*Saratoga* or *Adamant*?"

"Sir?" she asked in confusion.

"I'm taking *King George V* and *Simón Radowitzky* back to Dakota with me," he told her. "Which do you want in trade for Sector Fleet Meridian: *Saratoga* or *Adamant*?"

Modesitt paused.

"If you're taking *King George V*, that leaves Sector Fleet Meridian with no battleships," she noted. "But they also only have one *Paramount*-class, with two of them staying here. Honestly, I'd say *Saratoga* if the decision was mine."

"The decision *is* yours."

James slid a velvet jeweler's box across the desk. The stars inside looked more worn than their age deserved, but they'd been through a lot with him.

"These are your Rear Admiral's stars," Modesitt said softly.

"No, Rear Admiral Modesitt, they're yours now," James told her. "So is Sector Fleet Meridian. I need to fall back to Dakota and look after my responsibilities there, but I can't leave the Meridian Sector hanging in the breeze.

"I figure it'll mostly come down to Alric Barbados to deal with most of Rutherford's garbage," he continued, "and I was under the impression that you and the soon-to-be-General work well together."

Modesitt managed to actually *blush* at that, and he grinned wickedly.

"It's going to be a hell of a lot of work," he warned. "And while the nature of your promotion means I will wear anything you do along with you, I can't give you a lot of support or feedback. You're going to be on your own out here, with a bunch of older ships, at least until Central Command decides what they're going to do about the League."

"Crush Periklos like a bug, I hope," Modesitt said grimly, but she took the stars. "I'll take the job. Till I die or you find someone better, anyway."

"I don't expect either of those to happen, Admiral Modesitt," James told her. "And my impression is that Alric would be very disappointed with me if I let the first one occur."

"He probably would, yes," she admitted. "Thank you, sir."

62

Meridian System
12:00 December 26, 2737 ESMDT

JAMES LOOKED at the tactical display of the planet beneath him and tried not to sigh.

Meridian's orbital defenses had declined to commit suicide, but no one even seemed to be sure who was in charge on the planet and *able* to surrender.

"Commodore Folke Blythe," he greeted the blond officer on his other screen. "I feel like the commander of Greenwich's orbital fortresses should be able to tell me *who is in charge of the damn planet*."

"President Maisuradze is dead," Blythe said grimly. "I'm not certain who in the chain of succession *is* still alive. Lieutenant General Cantrell is the one that seems to be giving orders from the Presidential Palace, but Brigadier Barbados has declared *her* a traitor."

"And?" James asked.

Blythe shook their head.

"Cantrell tried to storm Barbados's position four days ago," they noted. "When that failed, she ordered *me* to have the fortresses bombard the garrison."

James eyed the tactical display and the blinking question marks showing where they *thought* the assorted positions of the two separate Marine forces and the local army were.

"I'm not seeing signs of orbital bombardment, so I'm guessing you decided to remain sane," he said acidly. "If still noncommittal, even though someone *murdered your president*."

"That was eleven days ago, sir," Blythe conceded. "No one knew what was going on, and the Vice President seemed to be working with Cantrell at first. Then Barbados got on the air and accused her of murdering the president—and when Cantrell put the VP on the air to challenge that claim, he instead confirmed it."

James winced.

"And the Vice President?" he asked.

"He hasn't been seen since he backed Barbados's accusation of murder," the Commodore admitted. "Admiral...I don't have Marines. I have about five hundred Meridian Army troops across the entire constellation—the *only* way I can intervene in a planetside conflict is by orbital bombardment, and Meridian is my *home*."

"That's fair, Commodore Blythe," James admitted. "Under Protocol Twenty-Six, you report to Rear Admiral Modesitt now." He smiled thinly. "I'll note, Commodore, that the person Cantrell tried to get you to nuke is your new boss's boyfriend.

"I suggest you be very, very polite."

"Sir!" Mac Cléirich suddenly barked. "We have the Brigadier!"

"Transfer Commodore Blythe to Modesitt on *Saratoga*," James ordered. "I'll talk to Barbados."

Blythe managed to nod his understanding before his image disappeared, replaced by the shockingly pale face of Brigadier Alric Barbados.

The Marine was still in combat armor, his helmet visible on a counter behind him.

"Admiral. Damn glad to see you, but you seem to be missing a few people," Barbados said grimly.

"Left two ships behind in Persephone to keep an eye on things,"

James told him. "Rest went down when Rutherford decided he'd rather commit open treason than break his deal with the League."

"Doesn't that explain a lot," the Marine said. "What do you need, sir?"

"I needed you to stay alive and stop Cantrell becoming unquestioned dictator of the planet," James said. "You did that. Congratulations, *Lieutenant General* Barbados."

"Thank you, sir," Barbados said slowly. "But what about Cantrell?"

"If you can tell me where to call her, we can deal with her," James replied. "Got any ideas?"

"If she isn't *in* the Presidential Palace, she's receiving calls sent there and holding briefings there," the newly minted General said. "Is...Modesitt..."

"Rear Admiral Modesitt is fine. I'm going to dump keeping this sector intact on the two of you, so I hope your working relationship is solid," James said drily. "Now, if you'll excuse me, General, I have one more call to make."

―――――――

IT TOOK ABOUT thirty minutes to get everything James needed in place, but then they sent a tightbeam transmission to the Presidential Palace.

Since part of what that time had given James was Hans Rutherford's standard identification codes, it wasn't really a surprise that he got connected to Cantrell immediately.

Ana Cantrell was a tall woman with short-cropped black hair. Unlike Barbados, she was wearing her full dress uniform with rank insignia, sitting in an office that James recognized as belonging to the President of Meridian.

"You are not Hans Rutherford," she said the moment the channel opened. "How did you get those codes?"

"Here and there," James told her. "Hans Rutherford is dead," he continued bluntly. "Killed in a space battle triggered by his acts of treason.

"The *only* legal cover you could ever have pretended to have for what you have done on Meridian was that you were operating under orders from Marshal Rutherford as military governor," he said. "Since Rutherford's actions eventually exceeded any possible claim of legitimate authority and he is now *dead*, your fig leaf has burned away."

He waved a dismissive hand, intentionally mirroring the gesture Rutherford had repeatedly used with him.

"Of course, you realize that the reason he had you do this while he was *gone* was so he could disavow you if things went wrong," James noted.

"You have no idea what my orders were," Cantrell said. "You have to be lying."

She seemed honestly upset at the thought that Rutherford was dead. The people she'd murdered clearly hadn't been a problem for the rogue Marine, but she seemed to have cared about her would-be warlord.

"Hans Rutherford attacked my fleet," James said quietly. "*Tsar Peter the Great* was destroyed in the ensuing action.

"While it is *possible* that he survived, I have no evidence of it. If I were to find him, I would be obligated to intern him as a traitor to the Commonwealth. With the situation as it is, I would likely request that the Persephone judiciary try him."

"That would be murder," Cantrell spat.

"I believe most people would call it justice, General," James told her. "Just as it would be justice if I turned you over to the civilian Meridian judiciary for trial and execution." He raised his hand before she could challenge him.

"I recognize that at least some portion of the Marines you have with you on the surface will fight on at your command, and I would *like* to bring an end to the bloodshed and suffering created by Hans Rutherford," he said.

"Order your people to lay down their arms and surrender, and I will guarantee your life," he promised. "You *will* be going to prison, General Cantrell. But if you surrender, it will be a comfortable moral rehabilitation center on Dakota...not the military penal colony in HR-Seven-Nine-Five-Five."

"Such mercy and moral superiority," she snarled. "I am fully aware of how fortified this building is, *Admiral*. Good luck taking it without bombarding the city from orbit. I think I hold rather more of the high ground here than you do!"

James paused as a message pinged into his implant. It was even more promising than he'd dared hope, and he smiled at Cantrell calmly.

"You, of all people, General, should not underestimate either the precision or the power of the arsenal available at my command," he told her. "But, since it turns out that Vice President Arie Downer is alive and willing to order the Meridian Army to support my people and General Barbados, I'm not sure I need you anymore.

"My mercy has limits and my offer is expiring. You lost the moment you murdered a planetary president for Hans Rutherford, General. Surrender."

"Go to he—"

Cantrell's head exploded, and James sighed as a figure in shifting holographic camouflage appeared through a side door. Shannon Reynolds was only barely visible, but she was followed by a bruised and exhausted-looking older man trying to properly place a kippah skullcap.

Downer stopped when he realized that his guide had just shot someone, and then looked like he was going to be sick.

"She hadn't quite managed to run out the timer, Reynolds," James told the woman in camouflage as the CISS agent removed Cantrell's body from the president's desk. "Do... Either clean up or find a different place to have the President broadcast from."

"President?" Downer asked. "Who are... Admiral Tecumseh?!"

"Rutherford is dead, Mr. Downer," James told the man. "That means civilian government will be restored on Meridian. With President Maisuradze dead, that means *you* are now the President.

"I look to you to calm your people and bring your army back in line," he continued. "*I* will see Cantrell's Marines dealt with."

63

Meridian System
14:00 December 27, 2737 ESMDT

ANOTHER WEEK. Another planet. Another armored procession.

The situation on Greenwich was calmer than it had been on Zagreus. The problem *here* had been Marines who'd thought they were following legitimate orders—and because they were shipboard Marines and not one of the much-rumored, much-reviled Pacification Corps, they'd obeyed their orders with professionalism and dignity.

There were still far too many Marines in chains at the moment, but that was the price of peace. Over six hundred of the Marines Cantrell had brought to the surface would face Meridian's courts.

Cantrell wouldn't. James felt like he should hate that more...but the woman had been determined to get everyone around her killed as well.

And if his lack of bodyguards as he walked up the steps of the red-brick Greenwich Legislature was entirely illusory and there was a holographically disguised assassin within five meters of him at all times…well, Reynolds scared him as much as she scared the handful of other people who knew about her.

This was, at least, a less-formal meeting than the one on Zagreus. Black-suited Meridian Secret Service agents escorted him to the new president's office—*not* the one Cantrell had taken over and died in, thankfully—and he joined a small group of politicians from the Meridian Sector's six star systems.

"Admiral Tecumseh," President Downer greeted him.

The new President looked much better than he had the day before. He wore a clean suit and kippah, and his hair had been cut. He still was visibly bruised where his guards had beaten him, but that didn't seem to be impeding his ability to do his job.

"Thank you for inviting me, Mr. President," James said, glancing around the room. He recognized Chaza'el Papadimitriou, the swarthy man selected to speak for Persephone to the rest of the Meridian Sector, but the other four politicians were unknown to him.

His implant files confirmed that they were representatives for the Cancer, Delta Zulu, Hachette and Lulu Systems, though. He'd known Rutherford had ordered a similar gathering to the one James had suggested in the Dakota Sector, though he doubted the other man's intentions had been to create a sector-wide democracy.

"I feel a bit ambushed to find quite so much planetary-level authority in one room," James continued after a moment. "How may I help you all?"

Downer coughed delicately.

"In all honesty, Admiral, we were wondering how we were expected to help *you*," he admitted. "Marshal Rutherford was the military governor of the Meridian Sector, regardless of his other crimes, and you seem to have inherited his other roles.

"So, we look to you to advise what you expect from us."

That was not quite what James was expecting, and he swallowed a spike of harsh anger.

"I am not Hans Rutherford," he told them. "What Marshal Rutherford did does not—*cannot*—define what I will do.

"The principles of the Commonwealth: democracy, freedom, justice, unity… These things define our nation and what we all seek to protect and defend," he reminded them. "But while those principles pre-date our Commonwealth by ages, it is almost as ancient a principle that the military of a nation must be subject to the civilian governance of that nation.

"Any other ways lie coups and madness."

He swept the room with his gaze, meeting each of the system representatives' eyes in turn.

"Any gubernatorial authority I hold can only be transitional at best, until you establish a just democratic alternative," he told them. "In the Dakota Sector, for example, we organized a governance conference that has now created a transitional council of representatives from each system.

"They were in the process of negotiating a charter for the sector government with Congress when I left."

He shook his head.

"It is not my place to dictate how the people of the Meridian Sector will lead themselves," he said. "It is my place, due to the confluences of fate, to *guard* both the Meridian and Dakota Sectors."

The room was silent for a few moments, then Downer laughed bitterly.

"Many of my fellows in this room were *summoned* by Rutherford," he noted. "We here on Meridian already knew that he was intending to inform them that he had proclaimed the military governorship and would rule as Marshal of the Sector until the crisis had passed.

"Some suspected he didn't plan on yielding that authority, but the structure exists in our Constitution for a reason. Cincinnatus is a compelling myth, after all."

"But Cincinnatus was one man...and lesser men after him destroyed the Roman Republic," James noted. "If you would ask my *advice*, I would suggest that you send representatives to Dakota to learn from the governance conference there—to catch up for lost time by, well, copying their homework.

"But I will give you no orders. I have claimed full authority over all military force in this region, but I will claim no authority over your governments and civil affairs. *That* authority belongs to your people and the Commonwealth they gave it to."

"Taking the five of us and a representative from President Downer's people to Dakota makes sense," Papadimitriou said swiftly. "It would do us all good, I think, to see just what a sector with a *reasonable* military commander ended up looking like."

"As with Mr. Papadimitriou's trip here, I would be able and willing to provide transport to Dakota aboard *Krakatoa*," James offered. "The newly reorganized Sector Fleet Dakota must return to our Sector as quickly as possible.

"*Valiant* requires major repairs that we would rather complete in the sector we're responsible for, if nothing else."

"Of course, Admiral. When will you be on your way?" Downer asked.

James grinned as a feeling of déjà vu came over him.

"Oh eight hundred hours tomorrow, Mr. President," he warned. "It's time and past time I was back in Dakota. I promised I wouldn't be gone more than six weeks, and we are rapidly running up against that timeline."

64

Deep Space
0:10 January 1, 2737 ESMDT

GENERALLY, the use of even carefully designed safety candles was discouraged aboard warships. It wasn't forbidden, but there was a strong sense that it should be limited to special occasions and religious and personal rituals.

Six candles burned in a semicircle around Anthony Yamamoto as he knelt on a mat on the floor, the four traditional tools of Japanese calligraphy arranged around him, as he worked slowly through a series of kanji characters on the scroll in front of him.

Adapting non-Nihongo names into kanji wasn't the cleanest process, of course, and some of the people whose names he was carefully painting might even be offended to *have* their names so written.

But this scroll wasn't made for anyone else—and none of the names he was painting belonged to anyone who was still alive.

"I was wondering where you were," a voice said behind him.

Anthony closed his eyes. His office was supposed to be a secure location, and he'd *never* had anyone interrupt his semi-meditative New Year ritual before.

But, of course, Shannon Reynolds didn't seem to register that security was supposed to keep people out.

"What is all this?" she asked, her tone softening as she grew nearer.

"Kinenhi," he half-whispered, his brain very much locked in Japanese at the moment.

"The people who died under your command this year, I take it?"

Anthony was surprised that she understood the Japanese for *memorial*—and that she guessed what he was doing. What he had done every year since the first time a pilot under his command had died in a training accident.

This year had a lot of names. He'd started three hours before midnight, and he was hoping to finish before his shift began at oh nine hundred hours.

"Hai," he agreed, then coughed. "Yes."

"Huh." She was standing far enough back not to interfere with anything except by her presence, but right now, even *that* was disruptive.

"What do you want, Shannon?" Anthony asked.

"Badem was looking for you at the flight-crew party," Reynolds told him. "I think they were hoping for a midnight kiss."

Anthony shook his head. Badem wasn't handling rejection well. He was going to have to swap flight engineers with another fighter—and find a way to do it that *didn't* look like a punishment, as Badem was probably the best engineer he'd ever had!

"What were *you* doing at the flight crew party?" he asked Reynolds.

"Looking for you," Reynolds admitted. "I was *definitely* hoping for a midnight kiss."

The agent chuckled behind him.

"Don't worry; Badem and I had a meeting of needs that worked out quite fortuitously," she concluded. "Though I get the impression the good Lieutenant is a bit clingy for my tastes."

"Likely," Anthony said. "That's part of why I turned them down. Not to mention a little thing called *chain of command*."

"Which does not apply to me in the slightest," the CISS agent agreed.

"Since no one was looking for me for anything *urgent*, what do you actually want, Shannon?" he asked.

"Well, I *was* going to hand you my panties and ask if you wanted to fuck, but it sounds like you're really not in the mood," she admitted.

"I am not as smooth with my shodo as I should be," Anthony admitted. "And I have a lot of names to paint tonight. Another time, that plan would sound delightful. Right now...this feels...necessary."

"I understand," Reynolds told him—and he realized she'd moved from two meters away to right next to him without him noticing and without her disturbing a single piece of ritual setup. Delicate-looking but strong fingers gripped his chin and turned his face up to her, allowing Reynolds to kiss him fiercely.

Despite the enthusiasm and imagination they'd brought to their one-night stand, they'd never actually *kissed* before. It wasn't something either of them saw much point in.

"Do you?" he whispered softly when she released him.

"I now know everything there is to know about Ana Cantrell," Reynolds told him. "Like I do with every person I've assassinated.

"We bear different weights, the soldier and the assassin, but we bear those weights in our hearts. I understand, Anthony."

She rose and smiled down at him.

"And if you finish earlier than you think, I do believe I'm going to go nap in *your* quarters," she told him with a wink.

65

"THAT'S...CONCERNING," James said softly as the reports from Dakota started coming in. "Or good news. I'm not entirely sure after the last few months."

"We can hope for reinforcements, can't we?" Voclain asked.

The subject of their conversation was the new warship in the Dakota System, a ship that James hadn't heard anything about before leaving Meridian. A *Saint*-class heavy battleship, the sixty-four-million-cubic-meter warship was bigger than even *Krakatoa* and lacked any of her fighter capacity. If the fighters and bombers couldn't take her down, her twenty-four one-point-five-megaton-per-second positron lances could obliterate most of Sector Fleet Dakota in a single firing pass.

Given that James didn't even have a full fighter group aboard *Krakatoa* and his cruisers had left their surviving fighters behind to reinforce Modesitt's new Sector Fleet Meridian, he figured the odds were slightly better for the battleship than they normally would be.

They still *sucked*...except that the battleship was in orbit of Dakota, inside the defensive perimeter of the planet's orbital fortresses.

"Do we have an ID?" James finally asked.

"Yes, sir!" Mac Cléirich replied after a moment. "She's flying her beacon in the clear. *Saint Bartholomew*, Commodore Jessenia Knight, commanding." The coms officer paused. "She's also flying Star Chamber courier codes, sir."

"Well, whoever she's carrying is only flying around in a battleship to make a point," James said grimly. There weren't that many of the *Saints left* at this point. Twenty-five had been built, and the Alliance had accounted for most of them. If there were six of the modern battleships *left* in the TCN, James would be surprised.

"That's true, sir. What do we do?" Voclain asked.

"However nervous the last few months have made us, we still report to the Congress of the Terran Commonwealth via Central Command, Commodore Voclain," James pointed out. "She's an extremely heavily armed courier, which tells me someone has a point to make, but she's still a courier delivering mail from our government."

He hated that Rutherford's treachery had resulted in his people regarding the surprise presence of a Commonwealth warship as a threat. *Saint Bartholomew*'s presence should have been unquestionable good news, the powerful warship a welcome ally against the silence pressing in on the Dakota Sector.

Instead, because of Rutherford, her presence worried James—and even his own flag staff were treating her as a potential hostile.

And the worst part of all of it was that he couldn't *quite* convince himself that his people were wrong.

———

DESPITE THE WORRIES AND CONCERNS, *Saint Bartholomew* behaved exactly as a friendly ship would. She adjusted her orbit as requested by Dakota Control to make space for the Sector Fleet, and James saw the standard exchanges between a visiting ship and the local military command flicker back and forth between his staff and Commodore Knight's people.

"Sir, we have a direct private transmission for you," Mac Cléirich told him as *Krakatoa* settled into orbit. "Star Chamber codes."

"I see. I'll take it in my office," James replied.

He was going to need to check in on the status of the governance conference and the Provisional Transitional Dakota Sector Council before he did much of anything else. Conveniently, he could easily segue from that work call into a personal connection to Abey without even feeling guilty.

But Star Chamber codes—authorization codes provided by the Congress of the Terran Commonwealth—overrode a lot of things. His coordination with the local government would wait.

In his office, he took his seat and gestured the channel to life. A slimly built man in a sharply fashionable navy-blue business suit appeared in front of him and bowed as the connection completed.

"Vice Admiral Tecumseh, thank you for speaking with me," he said.

"A man who conjures with the authority of the Star Chamber is not something I'm inclined to ignore, Mister...?"

"It's Lictor, Admiral. Special Lictor Michael Hardison to the Imperator of the Star Chamber of Terra."

That was a mouthful...and included several titles that didn't fit the context. The Lictors were the security officers of the Congress, usually former Marines recruited and put through intensive VIP protection training.

The phrasing Hardison was using was closer to the original term, where the Lictors had been responsible for escorting—and carrying out the corporal punishments for—the magistrates with *imperium*.

But *that* was not part of the Commonwealth's legal structure...and neither was the title of *Imperator*.

"I'm afraid I'm not familiar with that title, Lictor Hardison," James finally said, carefully. "Or that of Imperator."

"There have been significant changes required of the Congress of the Terran Commonwealth as we deal with the current crisis,"

Hardison replied. He'd clearly expected the question. "Some of those changes are going to impact you quite directly, Admiral.

"The Imperator instructed that I speak with you in private to deliver his messages," Hardison continued. "I bear documentation and authorization to prove the integrity of both my commission and the Imperator's authority to issue your orders.

"May I come aboard your flagship to meet with you?"

The man was being perfectly polite and diplomatic—but he was also, from what James could see of his backdrop, sitting in the admiral's office aboard one of the Commonwealth's most powerful remaining battleships.

But the weight of the titles he'd given and called upon was heavy and worried James.

"Of course," he allowed. "I will have people standing by to meet you."

"No such formality is necessary, Admiral," Hardison told him. "I am far more used to quiet arrivals."

And that, James figured, completed the pieces. Whatever Hardison was *now*, he'd *been* CISS.

Who was the Imperator...and why was he sending *assassins* to deliver his mail?

———

AFTER EVEN THE short conversation James had had with Hardison, he felt like he needed a shower. Instead, he had Mac Cléirich connect him to Quetzalli Chapulin. Despite his hopes, he didn't even get a glimpse at Abey Todacheeney before he was linked into a call that had clearly been waiting for him.

"Admiral Tecumseh, welcome home," Chapulin told him as she and Sanada Chō both appeared in holograms in front of his desk. "Myself and the Provisional Chairman have been waiting to hear from you."

"And from others, but my expectations there are shrinking," Sanada noted grumpily. "It's good to see you, Tecumseh. Some of the updates we received from Meridian over the last month... I was concerned."

"Hans Rutherford did everything you were afraid I was going to do," James told them. "And then more. As Marshal and military governor, he betrayed not merely the Commonwealth but the people he was directly tasked to defend.

"Now he is dead. The Meridian Sector is secure, for the moment, against the League," James told them. "I have appointed an old subordinate I trust to run their defense. While I have no technical authority over Meridian, there were no flag officers available to put in charge."

And by promoting Modesitt the way he had, James had taken full responsibility for everything she did. It was a delicate balance and one that put him in charge of the security of two sectors.

"It sounds like you had quite the complicated trip," Chapulin told him. "We're glad to see most of Sector Fleet Dakota return. Was *Saratoga* lost?"

"No," James corrected. "She was left to act as Rear Admiral Modesitt's new flagship. While the Commonwealth's losses against the League and due to Admiral Rutherford were painful, Sector Fleet Dakota was spared the worst of them.

"We will need to construct and recruit new crews for replacement fighters," he continued. "But that was always expected as time continued. Fighters have...a very specific role in modern battle."

"So I am led to understand," Sanada rumbled. "While I understand that the PTC has limited authority to ask it of you, we would appreciate a report on the events in Meridian—as limited by classification and so forth as you see fit."

"I believe my staff may have prepared something already," James replied. "I have a favor to ask of the Provisional Council..." He paused, taking in the Shogun man's initialism. "The PTC?"

"*Provisional Transitional Council* makes for a logical and reasonable official name, but it's quite the mouthful when working on a day-to-day basis," Chapulin replied. "We are, of course, prepared to at least listen to any request you have, Admiral."

"Indeed," Sanada said. "The PTC has yet to go wrong by valuing your advice."

James was reasonably sure the PTC would eventually have existed without his intervention and encouragement, but he'd got the wheels moving sooner than they might have on their own. It seemed that was valued, at least.

"I have representatives aboard *Krakatoa* from the six system governments of the Meridian Sector," he told them. "I suggested that they may wish to review the proceedings of the governance conference and the structure of the PTC, to save themselves time in setting up their own new sector-governance structure."

"We would be delighted to have them," Sanada said instantly. "While I know it's late aboard your ship, Admiral, it's currently morning in the hotel complex we've been using for the continuing conference, and we will be convening a new session with the PTC and our support staff at oh five hundred standard time."

"That should work for them," James said. "I'll have them on a shuttle to the complex within a few minutes."

That would have them off the ship before Hardison boarded. Somehow, he had a feeling that would be wiser than not.

"Of course." Sanada bowed his head, then exchanged a long look with Chapulin.

It looked like Dakota's leader had been assigned the task of raising something with James, as she nodded and leaned forward. Taking a moment to straighten her regalia, she then took a breath.

"Admiral, have you heard anything from the crew of *Saint Bartholomew*?" she asked.

"We have exchanged the usual protocols between a visiting warship and the local fleet command," James said. "And I have spoken with Congress's representative."

"I see," the First Chief replied. There was a pause, long enough of one to make James nervous.

"We have heard nothing from the representative," she told him. "*Saint Bartholomew* arrived on December thirty-first, after a slightly longer-than-expected period of quiet from Sol. We have seen no ships from Sol since, but we've been seeing a ship about every week, so *that* isn't unusual.

"Prior to *Saint Bartholomew*'s arrival, though, we hadn't seen a ship in ten days. We haven't seen a single warship from Sol and never one flying Star Chamber codes," she continued.

"We thought, initially, that *Saint Bartholomew* may have been sent to deliver the terms of our Charter from Congress," Sanada noted. "Delivering that on a battleship might have been intended to be a reminder of the fact that we were receiving *delegated* authority and still ultimately answered to Sol.

"Instead…"

"Instead, we've heard nothing from Commodore Knight or her crew beyond the initial mail drop," Chapulin noted. "Not silence—they've had all the usual maintenance and operational communications—but no formal communication between the warship and even the Dakota government.

"They have been waiting for you."

"Was there anything unusual in the news from Sol they carried?" James asked, considering the title that Hardison had used. If there was an "Imperator of the Star Chamber," *that* should have made the news.

"Nothing significant," the First Chief said slowly. "Which is… strange enough in itself, in these times. There were no political updates —and our previous messages from Sol had acknowledged the receipt of our suggested Sector Charter.

"That ship is making my people nervous, Admiral. Something isn't right here."

"I have been told there have been some changes at the heart of the Commonwealth," James said. "I haven't been given more, but I will let you know whatever I feel I can after I meet with the Star Chamber's representative.

"I can't promise more."

"We appreciate that, Admiral," Sanada said swiftly. "All of us share the same loyalties, but the more games get played, the more nervous we get."

"I will do what I can to discourage games, then," James promised. "I'll get those Meridian representatives on their way to you. Then I will see what the news from Terra is."

66

Dakota System
04:00 January 9, 2738 ESMDT

HARDISON WAS polite and noncommittal the entire journey from the flight deck and his shuttle to James's office. He carried a small patterned briefcase that went perfectly with his high-fashion suit, and James suspected the whole ensemble was directly out of the latest tailors' magazines and fashion guides on Earth.

Wearing the TCN's working undress uniform of a semiformal jacket over a neck-to-toe shipsuit, James felt rather plain next to the well-dressed Special Lictor.

The two men were alone when they reached James's office, since Hardison had brought neither aides nor an escort with him from *Saint Bartholomew*. There was a TCN crew on the shuttle, but the Lictor clearly didn't feel he needed an escort.

That spoke to either faith in James...or faith in Hardison's own ability to handle most threats *Krakatoa* could throw at him—and James suspected he knew which one.

"Are you going native on us, Admiral?" Hardison asked, looking around the office. He then paused and gently slapped his own wrist.

"My apologies, Admiral Tecumseh," he followed up. "I recognize that is a poor turn of phrase to use around someone of your heritage. I will admit that I didn't expect to see so much local Dakotan artwork in your office."

"The artisans are from my own people," James replied. "Dakota is one of the two worlds with a major Shawnee population. I could have acquired the work on Earth, but I will admit the thought didn't occur to me.

"The local government arranged the decorations with my staff when I moved over to *Krakatoa*." James shook his head. "The cost was apparently well within the accepted budget for decorating a new office for a senior flag officer."

"I imagine the TCN takes good care of their top officers," Hardison replied. "Is this room secure?"

"It is the most secure space on this ship and probably in this star system, unless you have something *truly* unusual going on aboard *Saint Bartholomew*," James observed.

"I have access to a number of tools not generally available to the military yet," the Lictor said. "But it should do. My first duty is to be glorified mailman, Admiral, and deliver the Imperator's personal message.

"I then have a physical copy of the orders included in that message and have been thoroughly briefed to provide context and supporting information as required," he concluded. "Unfortunately, I won't have much time to do so. While I could not discharge my mission until you returned to Dakota, *Saint Bartholomew* and I need to be on our way as quickly as possible.

"The Imperator has a great deal of work to do and very few trusted voices to speak for him."

"I have to admit, I have never heard that title before today," James said.

"You are familiar, I presume, with the Marshal title as held by James Walkingstick on the Rimward Marches?" Hardison asked.

"I am," James said.

"By the acclamation of the Assembly and Senate of the Terran Commonwealth, in full joint Congress in the Star Chamber of the Commonwealth, James Walkingstick's Marshal authority has been extended over the entire Commonwealth for the duration of this crisis," Hardison said.

The words were level and formal, and they tore the ground out from underneath James.

"Given the scale of his new role and historical precedents, Congress felt that a new title was required to recognize quite so broad a sweep of Marshal-level authority. Imperator Walkingstick is tasked with no less a mission than the preservation of our Commonwealth at all costs."

Including at the cost of some of the key principles that *created* the Commonwealth, it seemed. There was a logic behind the motion, James knew, but his dismay that even the *Star Chamber* was prepared to lay aside the subjugation of the military to civil authority and proper democratic channels was real.

"I understand," he murmured finally. "You said you had a message for me."

"Two pieces," Hardison confirmed.

With the flourish of a stage magician, he laid the briefcase on James's desk and opened it. The interior was revealed to be a velvet case holding two objects, both an intentional mix of ancient tradition and modern artifice.

On the left was a palm-sized disk inscribed with the seal of the Commonwealth. Despite its appearance, James recognized it as a portable secure holoprojector. Whatever message was recorded on the disk would only be played for the correct recipient—it would be linked to his DNA, which Central Command would have on file.

The object on the *right* would also be linked to his DNA, sealed to prevent anyone else using the authority inherent in the symbol or the active security codes and overrides contained in its data-storage mechanisms.

It was the ceremonial mace of a Marshal of the Commonwealth.

———

JAMES KNEW that shock and hesitation were probably normal for anyone presented with a Marshal's mace who hadn't campaigned for it —but there weren't that many cases of a mace being handed out *without* the recipient campaigning for it.

Walkingstick himself had spent half a decade laying the political, logistical and strategic groundwork for his plan to take the war to the Alliance of Free Stars. Like all plans, it hadn't survived contact with the enemy, but Walkingstick had *wanted* that command and the war that came with it.

James had no idea *why* the Imperator had, but he had. And that had led them all to where they stood today, with Hardison on the other side of his desk, managing not to betray a single iota of the impatience he had to feel at the Admiral's hesitation.

"Sit down, Lictor," James finally ordered. As Hardison obeyed, James reached into the briefcase and removed the holoprojector disk. There was a small prick against his skin as the disk took a DNA sample, and it warmed in his hand as he placed it flat on the desktop.

Imperator James Calvin Walkingstick could have passed for cousins with James. It wasn't a fair comparison in truth, but they both had ended up with the same shade of tanned-looking skin and pitch-black hair. Both of them wore their hair in an Old Nations warrior-style braid, though Walkingstick's was much longer.

Walkingstick even wore the same undress uniform as James and sat behind a desk in a very similar office. Unless James misjudged, the Imperator was in his own office aboard the battleship *Saint Michael*.

Unlike James, however, Walkingstick's uniform no longer bore the stars of an Admiral. Instead, where the four stars of a Fleet Admiral should have been was a large golden eagle insignia, clearly patterned after the eagle of the Roman Legions.

"Admiral Tecumseh," Walkingstick's image greeted him. "I suspect I have a good idea how you feel about the entire concept of the Imperator title, and yet I find myself regarding you as one of the most trustworthy regional commanders the Commonwealth now has."

The older officer smiled wryly.

"While I'm sure the history books will record my actions with the derision they are likely due, we are where we are. The Star Chamber gave me no choice but to move against them after their own actions and weaknesses threatened the Commonwealth.

"I don't like where we have ended up, but the Commonwealth must survive," Walkingstick said levelly. "There are too many regional commanders we still haven't heard from. Of the sixteen Sector commands, two remain completely silent.

"Ships have been dispatched to investigate, but *Saint Bartholomew* left around the same time as those ships. It will be some time before even those of us in Sol know the fate of all of the Commonwealth."

Walkingstick paused, considering his next words.

"I know Fleet Admiral Oliver updated you on the status of our construction, but I'll give you the long and short of it," he told James. "We're fucked. Best guess is that fifty percent of the Navy is just...*gone*. There's about three hundred A-S warships in the Commonwealth right now. Sixty percent of our yard capacity is shredded debris in systems we thought were utterly secure.

"As I record this, I have not yet heard from the delegations sent to negotiate peace with either the Alliance or the League. Unfortunately, I *have* heard of the fate of Amandine's fleet. It will fall to you and the other second-layer sectors to backstop the frontier against the League while we convince Periklos to back off.

"We are unlikely to be able to defeat him," Walkingstick said flatly. "The Project Hustle shipyards represent eighteen building slips, Admiral Tecumseh. There are nine intact at the Proxima Centauri yards and, assuming nothing has happened that I *don't* know about, eleven in three other systems across the Commonwealth.

"That means you are now responsible for the security of a sixth of the remaining shipyards of the Terran Commonwealth," the Imperator said bluntly. "This is a charge that cannot fail...and a charge we cannot trust to an interim civilian government.

"I am aware of the request for a delegated Charter submitted by the leadership of the Dakota Sector. I recommend you use that structure to assist in the administration of the Sector, but the ultimate authority *must* be yours.

"The Commonwealth requires that Dakota dramatically expand those shipyards, an expense that cannot be borne by one system in regular times," Walkingstick continued. "You will need to levy drafts of equipment, resources and personnel to do so.

"An accelerated completion of the ships already under construction at Base Łá'ts'áadah will be necessary, as will the mass production of starfighters, starbombers and munitions of all kinds. As we attempt to rebuild the industry and military infrastructure of the systems the Alliance raided, I look to Dakota and several other systems to be the arsenal of the reborn Commonwealth.

"I look to Dakota first because I trust James Tecumseh to do the right thing," Walkingstick told him. "The mace gives you complete authority over the Dakota Sector. The Sector Fleet admirals will now become regional governors with direct control over their territories.

"I have three tasks for you to begin with: firstly, to secure direct and complete control of your star systems. Secondly, to begin a major project to expand the Virginia shipyards as rapidly and completely as possible.

"Thirdly, my understanding is that Hans Rutherford has taken control of the Meridian Sector." There was a pause. "If that situation has not been resolved by the time this message arrives, I ask that you work with Special Lictor Hardison to arrange deployment against Rutherford.

"I know Rutherford's nature. He is a snake that will betray us. If Hardison can assassinate the bastard without military conflict, I will regard that as an unquestioned win. If not, it will fall to you to remove Admiral Rutherford by virtue of your mace and your fleet.

"I will not see warlords tear apart our Commonwealth, James. I do not *want* the role fate has given me, but I will do it as best as I can.

"I will be our Cincinnatus, not our Caesar. I promise you that, James Tecumseh. And I want you at my side the whole way.

"Good luck...Marshal Tecumseh."

The recording ended and James looked down at the mace, his face still. He had not survived his rise in the Commonwealth Navy by being unable to conceal his emotions, which kept the turmoil—fear, anger, rage, hope and more anger—from his face.

"I have been briefed on your tasks and Project Hustle," Hardison told him crisply. "As I understand it, Admiral Rutherford is no longer a problem."

"Admiral Rutherford is currently contributing to the average background carbon count in the Persephone System," James said, playing for a moment to think. To try to understand what had just landed on him.

"Then I am clear to return to Sol with your report to the Imperator," Hardison told him. "I'm not sure there is more information I can provide beyond the Imperator's own message. There are, of course, further documents and information aboard *Saint Bartholomew* that will be transmitted.

"I believe, based on what I understand of your relationship with the local governments, that you would wish to update them on the new situation yourself," Hardison said. "So, Admiral Tecumseh, how may I assist you?"

James looked down at the mace and then sighed.

"Much of what the Imperator orders was already in motion, though at a more sedate pace," he noted. One that involved actually *paying* people for the value of their labor and resources.

"I took the liberty of drafting a few statements for general release for you," the Lictor told him. "They're included in the data packet *Bartholomew* will send over. I hope they are of some use."

"When will you and *Saint Bartholomew* be departing?" James asked.

"I'll have to speak to Captain Knight," Hardison said. "I believe we may still have some supplies and fuel to take on, but I'm no expert and have not kept up with the ship's status to that degree. I expect by about twenty hundred hours."

That, James suspected, was utter bullshit. He doubted that Hardison wasn't fully aware of everything going on aboard his battleship ride.

He also was grimly certain the man hadn't been *nearly* as quiet during his week in orbit of Dakota as the local government thought. If the Lictor hadn't been linking in to every CISS network on the planet—and probably building a few new ones—James would be surprised.

"Thank you, Lictor," he told Hardison. "I will be in touch if I need any more information from you, but I believe the Imperator has provided enough information to start with.

———

THE DOOR SLID shut behind Hardison, and James stared blankly at the wall...until the side door usually used by Chief Leeuwenhoek slid open. Someone tried to enter without being seen, but holographic camouflage wasn't *that* good and didn't stand up to moving in short range.

"You may as well just drop the camo, Reynolds," James said softly.

"Figured it was worth a shot." The personal stealth field came down, revealing the CISS agent in her usual vaguely uniform shipsuit.

"You do realize that security systems are not just meant for other people, yes?" he asked.

"You do realize that CISS likes recruiting people with difficulty forming attachments, yes?" she countered. "I'm aromantic and don't fall in love. They like me."

"And Hardison?" James couldn't keep himself from asking.

"He's a clinical psychopath and I wasn't sure he wasn't here to kill you."

"I almost wish he had been," James admitted before he realized what he'd just said. "Fuck. You heard it all, didn't you?"

"I did. I'm curious as to your take, though."

He swallowed his initial response when he remembered that Reynolds' original job had to been to kill *him* if he decided to betray the Commonwealth.

"I don't..." He exhaled. "James Walkingstick has overthrown our government at the point of a battle fleet. He wants me to turn the Dakota Sector into a military-industrial slave state, at least temporarily, to produce a new fleet for the Commonwealth as quickly as possible."

The CISS assassin took the same seat Hardison had just vacated, pulling one leg up under herself in a way he realized Hardison had also done.

Somehow, he'd been both more worried and less threatened by the man Walkingstick had sent than he was by the petite young woman he'd worked with for several weeks.

"If I follow his orders, I will turn part of our Commonwealth into a series of tributaries forced to provide soldiers, ships and supplies to fuel the defense and maintenance of the greater nation," he said quietly. "*That*, Agent Reynolds, would betray both the principles of the Commonwealth and the people I am sworn to serve.

"To my mind, the orders I have been given are treason."

That hung in the air.

"But to disobey those orders, given that the Star Chamber *has* granted Walkingstick the authority he claims—however voluntarily—is also treason."

Reynolds said nothing, sitting across the desk from him and clearly waiting for him to come to a conclusion.

"When I saw a ship from Sol ten hours ago, I did not expect to have to choose between betrayals, Agent Reynolds," he told her.

"And what do your honor and oath tell you, Admiral Tecumseh?" she asked softly.

He snorted.

"That your job is to kill me if I betray the Commonwealth," he told her. "And that means that the two of us are at a minor impasse."

"I have watched you for several months now, James Tecumseh," Reynolds replied. "The people and principles of the Commonwealth have been your guiding light in these trying times. As they have always been for me.

"And now we face orders from the Commonwealth that betray those people and those principles."

He met Reynolds' gaze across the desk and she shook her head.

"There is no impasse, Admiral Tecumseh," she told him. "But it appears that I may need a new job."

James saw the sincerity in her eyes. Saw that the *assassin* viewed the Commonwealth as the same thing as the Admiral did—and that, just maybe, one of the people who understood the decision he had to make best was the woman who had been supposed to kill him if he decided wrong.

"If you want a new job, I think I can find one for you," he told her. "It starts by making sure Hardison never leaves this ship. I'd *prefer* if we take him alive...but I understand what we're looking at."

67

Dakota System
05:30 January 9, 2738 ESMDT

THE DAKOTA SECTOR governance conference had been moved to what was, during other times of year, a ski resort. Since the region of the planet it was situated in was currently in late spring, the resort and hotel complex had apparently been completely empty.

And a hotel complex that was reachable by shuttle, aircraft or one road had probably sounded quite handy to the Dakota Assembly Watch personnel responsible for the conference's security.

Once James had returned, the Watch had been reinforced with a company of Marines. Now, as his shuttle touched down, those Marines were making themselves as scarce as physically possible. He could see confused-looking Watch guards stumbling out to take over posts from Marines and staring blankly after their TCMC counterparts as the Marines returned to their quarters on the south end of the complex.

Another shuttle was delivering Marines to reinforce the Watch checkpoint on the road. Appearances were key to the next few minutes, but reality was *also* a thing. The outer perimeter defenses of the conference were being reinforced, but in the core of the area, where James Tecumseh would speak to the leaders of two sectors, there wouldn't be a Marine to be seen.

He traded nods with his own escort and left the shuttle. Four Marines in full combat armor followed James off the spacecraft—and then very visibly and specifically grounded their weapons and settled down next to the shuttle.

James Tecumseh walked across the grass field toward the main conference center alone, carrying the weight of worlds in a small, overly fashionable briefcase.

Assembly Watch troopers flanked the doors to the low-slung stone and glass building. They were well trained, he noted, and only let half of their attention focus on him as he stepped up to the building and gave the four troopers a crisp salute.

"I need to speak to the conference," he said quietly. "It's important."

"He's not on the schedule today," one of the juniors said. "I mean, I know it's the Admiral, but—"

"Even *I* prefer that attitude," James told the Watch with a chuckle. "So, please, note that man's name down. But I do still need to talk to them. It really is important."

"It's fine, officers," Abey Todacheeney said as she emerged through the doors. James had hoped she'd make it, but he hadn't known if he'd be able to count on it.

Just seeing her was a relief—mixed with amusement as he realized her hair was no longer red. It was still long and lustrous, but it was now colored a cobalt blue so deep, it would pass for black in less-brilliant lighting.

"I'll take responsibility for this. Let him in."

"Of course, Madame Secretary," the senior Watch trooper said instantly, gesturing her troops aside to let James pass.

Todacheeney embraced James before he could say a word, squeezing him tightly enough to probably be inappropriate in front of the Watch, but he didn't care.

"Thank you," he whispered in her ear. "For trusting me."

He hadn't told her what he needed to speak to the Conference about. She was going on faith.

"I'm claiming time in your hot tub later as payment," she whispered back. "But I *do* trust you, James. So does everyone on the PTC. If you say it's important, it's important."

———

"REPRESENTATIVES of the Dakota Sector and guests from the Meridian Sector, I apologize for the interruption," Abey Todacheeney said a minute later as they stepped into the main auditorium.

Patience Abiodun had been speaking—something about standardizing trade regulations across the sector, as several worlds had stricter environmental and other regulations than the Commonwealth's usual rules.

Mostly Dakota, James knew.

"You are the master of ceremonies, Madame Secretary," Abiodun told Todacheeney. Her agate-like eyes settled on James as well, and the Arroyoan First Minister smiled thinly. "And I am more than willing to yield to Admiral Tecumseh, if that is required."

"The Admiral needs to speak to us all," Todacheeney confirmed. "He has told me it is important but has declined to even give *me* a warning of what's coming."

That got chuckles from across the room, and James realized that his and Abey's budding relationship wasn't even an open secret in this room. The *entire* governance conference knew the First Chief's Secretary was dating the Sector Fleet Admiral.

But that cut a tension that the room had held when he came in unannounced, so he embraced it and walked forward to the stage— and then stopped. There was a lectern on the raised dais where Abiodun had been speaking, but there was also a table just in front of the stage, in front of the larger audience.

Instead of the stage and podium, James walked over to the table and faced its occupants: both the Provisional Transitional Council of the Dakota Sector and the six high-level representatives of the Meridian Sector.

The room was silent as he laid Hardison's briefcase on the table and popped it open—and that silence turned to ice as James removed the marshal's mace and tossed the briefcase aside.

He held the mace—roughly thirty centimeters long, carved from black wood and inlaid with silver, concealing probably a quarter-kilogram of high-density electronics—in the air long enough for every single one of the representatives to see it.

Then James lowered the mace to his side and looked around the room.

"You all know what that mace means," he told them. "But the context behind it is absolutely critical."

He could hear the twelve politicians around the table *breathe*, the room had grown so quiet.

"James Calvin Walkingstick, Marshal of the Rimward Marches, has been declared Imperator of the Star Chamber," he told them all softly, relying on the acoustics of the room to project his words to every member of the Governance Conference.

"This gives him Marshal-level authority over the entire Commonwealth," James continued. "He was granted this authority with a battle fleet in Earth orbit that should never have left the Rimward Marches with him.

"*This* Marshal's mace comes from the Imperator, as part of the Star Chamber's authority that he has taken onto himself. He has charged me to become the regional governor of the Dakota Sector. To use the fleets and armies of the Commonwealth to keep this sector in line by any means necessary."

He met Chapulin's gaze and saw her face tighten—but she returned his regard and nodded levelly.

"This, perhaps, is a line I would cross," he admitted to them. "Behind the cover of this mace, I would have the authority to grant the Meridian and Dakota Sectors the mid-level governance authority needed to survive in these disjointed times.

"I *could* use this mace to allow us to proceed exactly as we intended...except that the orders I received from Imperator Walkingstick specifically forbid that course.

"I am tasked to turn the Dakota Sector into the arsenal of the

Commonwealth," he said flatly. "To expand the shipyards into a manufacturing complex akin to the yards we lost in Tau Ceti and Sol, to demand the other systems of the Dakota Sector provide resources and soldiers and technicians and all of the matériel of war.

"Our new Imperator would have me turn the Dakota Sector—and likely the Meridian Sector, once he realized I am effectively in control of your stars as well—into a series of tributary worlds, to fuel a new war machine born around the gas giant of Dakota."

James looked around the room one last time and met Abey Todacheeney's gaze. There was concern there...but he realized it was concern for *him*. She was not concerned, for one *moment*, that he would make himself the dictator she'd originally feared.

He nodded calmly to her—and then tossed the mace onto the table.

"I have *declined* to obey these orders," he told them all. "As we speak, Marines from the Dakota Fleet are storming *Saint Bartholomew*. Shortly, she will be under my control, bringing the total strength of the fleets under my command to seventeen warships.

"I place all of those ships, along with the ships under construction at Virginia, the officers and spacers under my command, and my own experience and skills at war, at the disposal of this conference."

He smiled thinly.

"If the representatives gathered here are prepared to accept the true fall of the Commonwealth and bow to Imperator Walkingstick, I will permit myself to be arrested and delivered to Sol in chains.

"But if you would stand free and proud, in defense of the citizens of these sectors and the principles that the Commonwealth was created to serve, then I will follow you on that path.

"And if this be treason...then let us make the most of it."

JOIN THE MAILING LIST

Love Glynn Stewart's books? Join the mailing list at

GLYNNSTEWART.COM/MAILING-LIST/

to know as soon as new books are released, special announcements, and a chance to win free paperbacks.

ABOUT THE AUTHOR

Glynn Stewart is the author of *Starship's Mage*, a bestselling science fiction and fantasy series where faster-than-light travel is possible–but only because of magic. His other works include science fiction series *Duchy of Terra, Castle Federation* and *Vigilante*, as well as the urban fantasy series *ONSET* and *Changeling Blood*.

Writing managed to liberate Glynn from a bleak future as an accountant. With his personality and hope for a high-tech future intact, he lives in Kitchener, Ontario with his partner, their cats, and an unstoppable writing habit.

VISIT GLYNNSTEWART.COM FOR NEW RELEASE UPDATES

CREDITS

The following people were involved in making this book:

Copyeditor: Richard Shealy
Proofreader: M Parker Editing
Cover art: Viko Menezes
Typo Hunter Team
Faolan's Pen Publishing team: Jack, Kate, Robin, and Leah.

facebook.com/glynnstewartauthor

OTHER BOOKS
BY GLYNN STEWART

For release announcements join the
mailing list or visit **GlynnStewart.com**

STARSHIP'S MAGE
Starship's Mage
Hand of Mars
Voice of Mars
Alien Arcana
Judgment of Mars
UnArcana Stars
Sword of Mars
Mountain of Mars
The Service of Mars
A Darker Magic
Mage-Commander
Beyond the Eyes of Mars (upcoming)

Starship's Mage: Red Falcon
Interstellar Mage
Mage-Provocateur
Agents of Mars

Pulsar Race: A Starship's Mage Universe Novella

DUCHY OF TERRA
The Terran Privateer
Duchess of Terra
Terra and Imperium
Darkness Beyond
Shield of Terra
Imperium Defiant
Relics of Eternity
Shadows of the Fall
Eyes of Tomorrow

SCATTERED STARS

Scattered Stars: Conviction

Conviction

Deception

Equilibrium

Fortitude

Huntress (upcoming)

Scattered Stars: Evasion

Evasion

Discretion (upcoming)

PEACEKEEPERS OF SOL

Raven's Peace

The Peacekeeper Initiative

Raven's Course

Drifter's Folly

Remnant Faction (upcoming)

EXILE

Exile

Refuge

Crusade

Ashen Stars: An Exile Novella

CASTLE FEDERATION

Space Carrier Avalon

Stellar Fox

Battle Group Avalon

Q-Ship Chameleon

Rimward Stars

Operation Medusa

A Question of Faith: A Castle Federation Novella

Dakotan Confederacy

Admiral's Oath

To Stand Defiant (upcoming)

STAND ALONE NOVELLAS
Excalibur Lost
Balefire

VIGILANTE
(WITH TERRY MIXON)
Heart of Vengeance
Oath of Vengeance

Bound By Stars: A Vigilante Series
(With Terry Mixon)
Bound By Law
Bound by Honor
Bound by Blood

TEER AND KARD
Wardtown
Blood Ward

CHANGELING BLOOD
Changeling's Fealty
Hunter's Oath
Noble's Honor
Fae, Flames & Fedoras: A Changeling Blood Novella

ONSET
ONSET: To Serve and Protect
ONSET: My Enemy's Enemy
ONSET: Blood of the Innocent
ONSET: Stay of Execution
Murder by Magic: An ONSET Novella

FANTASY STAND ALONE NOVELS
Children of Prophecy
City in the Sky

Made in United States
North Haven, CT
20 October 2022